CRUCIFIED

© Oraf

As devil's advocate, MICHAEL SLADE has acted in over one hundred murder cases, and has argued a dozen appeals in the highest court. His specialty is the law of criminal insanity. The thirteen Slade novels fuse the genres of police procedure, whodunit, suspense, horror, historical, war, and legal thriller. Visit Slade's website at: **www.specialx.net**.

CRUCIFIED

CRUCIFIED
MICHAEL
SLADE

severn House

This first world edition published 2008
in Great Britain and the USA by
SEVERN HOUSE PUBLISHERS LTD of
9–15 High Street, Sutton, Surrey, England, SM1 1DF,
by arrangement with Penguin Canada.

British Library Cataloguing in Publication Data

Slade, Michael
  Crucified
  1. Conspiracies - Fiction 2. Suspense fiction
  I. Title
  813.5'4[F]

  ISBN-13: 978-0-7278-6652-3   (cased)
  ISBN-13: 978-1-84751-080-8   (trade paperback)

All Severn House titles are printed on acid-free paper.

Printed and bound in Great Britain by
MPG Books Ltd., Bodmin, Cornwall.

Intravit autem Satanas in Iudam
qui cognominatur Scarioth unum
de duodecim.

And Satan entered into Judas,
who was surnamed Iscariot,
one of the twelve.

—LUKE 22:3

When the existence of the Church
is threatened, it is released from
the commandments of morality.
With unity as the end, the use of
every means is sanctified, even
deceit, treachery, violence, simony,
prison, death. For all order is for
the sake of the community, and the
individual must be sacrificed to the
common good.

—DIETRICH VON NIEHEIM,
BISHOP OF VERDEN,
DE SCHISMATE LIBRI III (1411)

GOLGOTHA

Clang . . . clang . . . clang . . .

Sunlight sparked off the hammer as the Roman nailed the wrist of the supine Jew to the crossbar that would surmount his execution post. The spike that pushed through the flesh was seven inches long, with a square head crowning a tapered shaft. As the legionary labored, insects buzzed around the Jew's wounds, birds of prey circled the crest of the hill, and a gathering mob taunted the doomed man. Nearby, soldiers boisterously cast lots for the Jew's robe, having stripped him of all but his loincloth. A woman—possibly his mother— sobbed as the spike passed through the nerve, causing the fingers to curl like claws.

Thud . . . thud . . . thud . . .

The nail sank deep into the rough-hewn wood.

Devised by the Persians and brought to the Mediterranean by Alexander the Great, crucifixion was raised to an art by the Romans. To communicate its unbearable pain, they coined the word *excruciatus*, meaning "out of the cross." By law, the citizens of Rome could not be crucified. It was a disgrace reserved for slaves, barbarians, and those who—like this "messiah"—preached heresy against Pax Romana.

This hammer-wielding Roman was a master at crucifixion. He drove the nail between the bones of the wrist because he knew the flesh of the palms wouldn't support the weight of the body. He was careful not to break the bones or pierce the arteries, for his aim was to kill the Jew as slowly and as agonizingly as possible. Having impaled the central nerve and several ligaments, the spike would shoot bolts of fiery pain up this arm until the wretch expired.

The heat of the midday sun drenched the Roman in sweat. He finished hammering the head of the nail down to the skin of the wrist and then crawled around to the other end of the *patibulum*. Aided by a cohort who tugged the Jew's free arm along the crossbar, he began to pound a spike into that wrist too.

Clang . . . clang . . . clang . . .

The man being crucified was already half-dead. Earlier, he'd been scourged with a whip called a *flagrum*, the lead-tipped leather thongs tearing his back to shreds. With a crown of thorns shoved down around his brow, he'd then been forced to carry this heavy crossbar from Jerusalem to Golgotha, the execution mound beyond the city's walls. Unable to bear the burden, he'd stumbled along the way, until a passerby was commandeered to help shoulder the weight. Up this rugged hill they'd come, with a Roman centurion leading the procession and a soldier carrying a sign announcing the Jew's name and his crime.

Clang . . . clang . . .

Done.

It took a gang of soldiers to hoist the crossbar up ladders to the top of one of the permanent uprights—the *stipes*—erected on the hill. Once the horizontal *patibulum* was fitted into its slot, completing the cross, the hammer man bent the Jew's legs at the knees and positioned one foot over top of the other. Then he nailed them through the arches to the vertical post. Finally, the sign—the *titulus* in Aramaic, Latin, and Greek—was pinned to the cross above the crucified Jew's head as a warning to others.

Iesus Nazarenus Rex Iudaeorum, the sign read.

Jesus of Nazareth, king of the Jews.

Taunts from the mob grew louder as the executioner stepped back to admire his handiwork. He'd ensured the death would be as slow as possible, with maximum suffering. Crucifixion killed in as little as three to four hours or as much as three to four days, depending on how much blood the victim lost during the lashing. So weakened was this Jew from the severity of his beating that the Roman was certain he would be dead by sunset.

Death would be by asphyxiation. Normally, breathing in is an active process, breathing out a passive one. Here, the weight of the Jew's body pulling down on his shoulders and outstretched arms would tug his chest muscles into a fixed state of inhalation. To exhale, he would have to push up on his impaled feet and flex his elbows, causing the pierced nerves to shoot pain through his body. His flayed back would scrape against the rough wood of the upright post, opening the wounds for greater loss of blood. Fight to breathe, fight to breathe. Every lift would make him weaker, and soon his gasps would be too shallow to support life.

Then he'd die.

"I thirst," the Jew murmured in a voice that could barely be heard. That, too, required exhaling.

One of the soldiers offered him wine vinegar from a sponge raised on a rod.

The Roman guards couldn't leave until this Jesus was dead, so the man who'd nailed him to the cross whiled away the time by watching the so-called king of the Jews pay for his heresy.

With the descent of the sun, the shadow of the cross crept over the execution mound until ominous clouds blotted out the blue sky with angry gray.

"That's the price," the Roman snarled, "of refusing to bow to us. Just as your shadow has vanished from the face of the earth, so you will be forgotten."

But the shadow of the cross continued to elongate until it reached through the centuries for almost two thousand years to the here and now.

NIGHT FIGHTER

✝

GERMANY, NOW

Clang! The sound of metal striking metal ground the bulldozer to a halt. Reversing the earthmover, the driver leaned out of the cab to peer around the dusty windshield. In front of the blade, there appeared to be an aluminum shark's fin jutting from the dirt.

"*Verdammt!*" the road builder cursed in German. How long would resurrecting the past stall his work?

It took them a day to unearth the plane, but finally they could read the nickname painted below the cockpit window of the long-lost Second World War bomber.

The *Ace of Clubs.*

———•◦•———

GERMANY, 1944

Whatever this secret mission, it must be something big.

Assassinate Adolf Hitler?

Is that it? wondered the pilot.

Is that why his orders—marked "For your eyes only"—commanded him to break away from the bomber stream and fly this solitary mission to an isolated village, to drop a bomb load on what appeared to be—from the target photo with his orders—a rural country estate?

Is it Hitler's hideaway?

A new weapon?

And why the secrecy?

If Flight Lieutenant Fletch "Wrath" Hannah died tonight, he'd like to know what he'd died for.

Through the cockpit window, the pilot watched the bomber stream—eight hundred Lancasters, Halifaxes, and Mosquitoes miles to the north—rain death by moonlight on Berlin. Tons of high explosives boiled like bubbles in a cauldron, blasting buildings to bits. The diamond white glare of the firebombs darkened to deep red once the flames took hold. It looked as though every factory, every house was burning. Berlin glowed like a huge hearth full of flickering embers. And even here—*Boom! Boom!*—driven by the wind, Wrath felt shock waves buffet his plane.

The pit of hell, he thought.

As the city belched fire and smoke, the hatred shot skyward in searchlights and flak. Sweeping back and forth in a slow frenzy, the blue beams were master lights that caught a wing or a tail so the slave beams could scale the ladders to "cone" the lit-up planes. Synchronized to the lights, anti-aircraft guns tore the sky apart, spewing tracers like sparks from a grinding wheel. Dazzling bursts and ragged smoke clustered near the planes, until the flak was so thick the pilots could almost land on it. Ninety-nine *whoomfs* could miss, but that hardly mattered if the hundredth ripped off a wing or riddled a crew with shrapnel.

There was only one way to counteract flak.

Our Father who art in heaven, thought Wrath dryly.

Each plane flew straight and level for the last leg of its run so the bomb-aimer could plant his crosshairs on the target. Wrath winced as one Lanc blew up in midair, the fuel tanks falling to the ground as balls of fire. A Halifax spun to earth in ever-tightening turns, twisting faster and faster until it disintegrated from centrifugal force. Engines flaming, controls shot away, crippled bombers were going down in every kind of distress. Exit hatches popped open so crews could bail out, their parachutes blossoming in the gunsights of Hun fighters.

There but for the grace of God, thought Wrath.

A moonlight monster gazed back at him from the glass. There was nothing human about his face. The seven crewmen wore the combat gear of RAF raiders. The pilot's head was sheathed in a leather flying helmet. Goggles protected his eyes from shrapnel. Headphone flaps covered both ears. Clamped over his nose, mouth, and chin, his oxygen mask dangled a tube like an elephant's trunk. Inside was a microphone he could use to communicate with his crew.

The TR9 intercom system was standard in British bombers. Each crew member connected to it by plugging in an electrical lead from the mike in his oxygen mask. The deep-throated engines made a lot of noise, so often the men were reduced to handing notes around or blinking the colored lights of the signal system. Rely on that in combat, though, and you wouldn't last long.

"Intercom check," Wrath announced as the glow of Berlin aflame retreated into the distance and the *Ace of Clubs* flew deeper into the lonely sky ahead.

"Rear gunner to pilot. What's up, Skipper? The war's back there. I see it behind us."

"Pilot to rear gunner. I don't know, Ack-Ack. Orders are to leave the stream and bomb a hinterland village."

"Their's not to reason why . . ."

Wrath didn't respond with "Their's but to do and die," to finish the quote from "The Charge of the Light Brigade." He didn't want to jinx them.

When someone switched on his mike, everybody knew it. The rest could hear the new arrival's breathing over the engines' roar. If he didn't talk, Wrath would ask who was on the mike. Because the system didn't identify the men's combat positions—all you heard was yakking on a common line—they had agreed to begin each exchange by saying who was speaking to whom.

"Pilot to mid-upper."

"Roger, Skipper?"

It was strange to hear a voice from the dorsal turret that wasn't De Count's. Monty Christie—thus De Count of Monty Christie—had been with the crew since training. Now branded with the cruel letters LMF—for "lack of moral fiber"—he'd been replaced by Trent Jones for this op.

"Interrupter gear up to snuff, Jonesy?"

"Aye, Skipper."

"You sound distorted."

"It's *cold* up here. Hope moisture from my breath isn't freezing in the mike."

Hours ago, as they'd approached the enemy coast, Wrath had given both gunners permission to test-fire their weapons over the sea. Deafening bangs and the smell of cordite had soon filled the fuselage. As arse-end Charlie of the *Ace*, Ack-Ack had the most dangerous position. Flying in the rear turret was like being dragged through the air backwards in a goldfish bowl. The average life expectancy of a tail gunner under attack was thirty seconds. That's because Nazi night fighters preferred to zoom in from astern and below. Without the rear gunner, the plane was a sitting duck.

"There's a balls-up, Skipper," Jonesy had reported. His turret sat halfway back on the dorsal spine of the plane. "The interrupter gear is giving me grief. I worry something broke during the test fire. The rear gunner should know. He's in my gunsights."

"Ack-Ack?"

"Here, Skipper."

"Get forward and help the mid-upper."

"Roger. Rear gunner going off intercom."

The plane's turrets were minor marvels of mechanical engineering. Each one was mounted on a pair of concentric rings. The inner ring, driven by a self-contained, electro-hydraulic power unit, swiveled around for high-speed tracking of Nazi night fighters. The interrupter gear kept the turret guns from firing when they aimed back at the *Ace*.

Wrath waited on tenterhooks.

He couldn't abort the mission.

It was dreadfully cold in the tail of the Halifax. Every bit of exposed skin was prone to frostbite. Because there was no heating, the gunners wore electric suits. Wrath could imagine Ack-Ack unhooking his main oxygen supply and intercom plug from his mask before attaching a portable oxygen bottle that resembled a small fire extinguisher. Climbing out of the rear turret, he would crawl up the murky fuselage in his heavy suit, then try to help fix whatever was wrong with the mid-upper's interrupter gear.

Those gunners were the bomber's only protection against attack. It unnerved Wrath to have either turret vacant. From the moment the *Ace* entered Nazi airspace until—hopefully—it landed safely back at base in Yorkshire, the gunners would be isolated in the plane's tail end, glued to hard seats for the duration of the run.

Tick-tock . . .

Time passed with agonizing slowness.

Then Wrath heard the familiar *puff-puff* in his earphones of a crewman checking his mike before speaking.

"Rear gunner to pilot. Problem solved, Skipper. Found the gremlin in the works."

"Pilot to Jonesy and Ack-Ack. We're counting on you. Don't want anything failing if the Huns attack."

"Aye," said the voice foreign to the crew.

"I'll stake my life on it," added Ack-Ack.

Wrath hoped *that* didn't jinx them either.

Now it was more than two hours later and the *Ace* was nearing its target.

"Pilot to both gunners. Keep your eyes peeled." Confident the two were swinging their turrets from side to side, constantly scanning the sky for night fighters, Wrath banked the plane like a teeter-totter so they could check blind spots under the wings for Huns moving into attack positions.

That took care of the rear three-quarters of the bomber—everything aft of the cockpit and the nose compartment.

"Pilot to engineer."

"Engineer okay, Skipper."

It was Hugh "Ox" Oxley's job to monitor the mechanical systems during flight—eye the instrument panel, maintain oil temperatures and pressures, cross-feed the petrol tanks when necessary. His station was the jump seat next to the pilot. At present, the flight engineer was checking the master fuel cocks.

"Pilot to wireless operator."

"Wireless operator strength nine, Skip."

The radioman, Earl "Sweaty" Swetman, shared the compartment below the cockpit with the navigator. They'd met an unexpected north wind, so he'd spent most of the flight receiving new meteorological info from HQ to help the navigator adjust wind speeds and directions. Now, for the final leg of the bombing run, he left his radio set to drop bundles of "window"—thin strips of metal foil that confused German radar images—down the flare chute.

"Pilot to navigator."

"Navigator loud and clear," replied Mick "Balls" Balsdon. His role was to guide the *Ace* to the target area, at which point the bomb-aimer would assume control for the final run to the actual target. With blackout curtains pulled tight around him, Balls worked with his compass and radar to guide them over the landscape. Unlike his counterparts in the planes pounding Berlin, he didn't have markers to follow or a helpful master bomber circling overhead. He was on his own with just the moonlight as an angel.

"Where are we, Balls?"

"ETA on target is five minutes, Skipper."

Jerks and rumbles shook the plane as the bomb doors opened with grim determination. Until now, they'd flown a gently weaving course to counter defenses. From here on, Wrath would trim the *Ace* straight and level.

"Pilot to bomb-aimer."

"They're in my sights, Skipper."

"It's all yours, Nelson."

"Left. Steady. Right a bit. Hold it there," the bomb-aimer said, correcting their flight path.

Down in the nose compartment, Russ Trafalgar—Nelson to his chums—hunched over his bombsight, zeroing in on the country estate that Bomber Command wished blown to hell and gone.

"Bombs going!" he announced, pressing the release button with his gloved thumb.

Relieved of its heavy cargo, the Halifax bomber seemed to rear up in the sky. As the rain of ruin fell on the ground below from fourteen thousand feet, the bomb-aimer snapped the photographic proof of their successful mission. Without it, the operation wouldn't count toward the thirty-ops total that would see them "screened" out of active duty. Every op completed was a flight out of danger.

Beneath the thundering noise of the four-engine bomber, the target area burst into flames. The scene of savage destruction took on a garish beauty; the rural estate was a patchwork of black smoke and livid red bonfires. As the bomb doors rumbled shut so the *Ace* could bank for home, streaks suddenly slashed through the darkness and the fuselage shuddered under a withering hail of close-range cannon fire. Staccato shock waves shook the back of Wrath's seat like the strokes of a jackhammer.

"Fighter! Fighter! Corkscrew starboard, Skipper!"

Nothing got hearts racing faster in the bomber than the sound of uncontrolled panic in someone's voice. Ack-Ack's warning was accompanied by a stuttering torrent of noise as German shells tore into the tail section. Out of nowhere, the Junkers Ju 88 appeared, closing in fast with its nose guns blazing. They weren't flashing "*Willkommen*" in Morse code.

Instinctively, Wrath thrust the control column forward, twisting the ailerons to put the plane into a violent dive. In the second it took to stand the *Ace* on its wing, the night fighter raked the bomber again at point-blank range. The plane shivered and rattled as it absorbed the punishment from that six-gun barrage, and the heavy vibration of a long burst fired from its own mid-upper turret shook the instrument panel in front of Wrath to a blur.

So steep was the dive to starboard that parachute packs, navigation instruments, and other loose gear flew about as if weightless. Wrath's legs felt light and the harness straps pressed hard into his shoulders. The Nazi night fighter overshot the cockpit, and Wrath saw the black crosses under its wings. The howls of the Junkers' engines jarred his teeth.

The freefall ended abruptly as Wrath wrenched the bomber up into a sharp climb. The standard tactic used to shake off a prowling fighter was called a corkscrew. Diving, climbing, turning, weaving, and using plenty of throttle, the pilot would constantly change the bomber's direction, speed, and altitude to hamper the gunsights of the Ju 88. Now, as the *Ace* cleaved the sky with its berserk twisting, the exertion left Wrath drenched in sweat.

"The bugger's at ten o'clock high, Skipper. Here he comes again!" warned Nelson.

From the corner of his eye, Wrath glimpsed the thin silhouette of the two-engine fighter against the moon. The blackness of the outline masked the swastika on its tail. Jutting from its nosecone was an array of chessboard-shaped antennae that fed airborne radars designed for hunting and killing the warriors of the night sent by Bomber Command.

Warriors like these seven.

Hosing streams of tracers before it like incandescent fastballs, the Ju 88 came at them full throttle. His heart in overdrive, Wrath felt as if the cannons were spitting in his face, with each shot aimed between his eyes. But in fact, the fighter again poured all it had into their arse end.

"Get him, gunners!" urged Ox.

But their weapons were of limited value against a night fighter at the best of times. And now, for some reason, neither turret opened up with a spray. Were both gunners dead? The rear gunner was certainly in the fighter's line of fire. Had the interrupter gear failed the mid-upper at the worst moment?

"Hang on!" Wrath yelled as the incoming Junkers gave the *Ace* a working-over, its machine guns chewing chunks out of tail fins, rudders, and elevators. Once more, he tried to corkscrew into a steep dive, but the control stick went sloppy in his hands, wagging loosely without response from the ailerons. When he pushed the rudders, the plane refused to yaw. Unable to bank or turn, the skipper wondered if the cables had snapped.

Strangely, the night fighter didn't close in for the kill. With adrenaline coursing through his bloodstream, Wrath watched it stop firing and break off its attack, the roar of the engines fading as it dashed out into the darkness. There, it circled while the crippled bomber fought a losing battle to fend off the clutch of gravity.

Down . . .

Down . . .

Down . . .

The bomber was losing altitude it couldn't afford to spare—five to seven hundred feet per minute, by Wrath's reckoning. Though he tugged on the wheel with all his strength, the plane wouldn't level up. When the altimeter read eight thousand feet, he was forced to decide. He had to leave enough time for the crew to pop the hatches and push themselves out into the slipstream. He couldn't let them fall too low for their parachutes to open.

"Pilot to crew. Bail out."

Whatever they had bombed, Wrath hoped it was worth it.

The *Ace of Clubs* was going to crash in Nazi Germany.

DESCENT FROM THE CROSS

✝

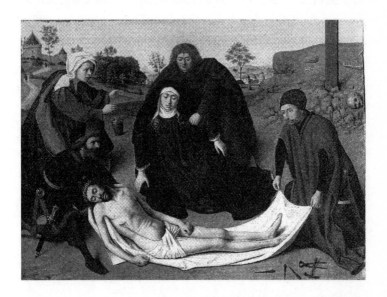

With his left hand overlapping the ring on his right, the Secret
Cardinal of the Roman Catholic Church stood in the painting
gallery of the Metropolitan Museum of Art and admired *The
Lamentation*, a ten-by-fourteen-inch masterpiece by Petrus
Christus of Bruges. Dressed in a single-breasted black clerical
suit, with a black Roman collar throated by the usual white
square and a simple pectoral cross hanging from a silver chain,

he looked like any parish priest serving Manhattan's faithful. His black hair and dark features complemented his clothes. In fact, the Spaniard had never worn the skullcap, three-ridged biretta, and blood-red choir dress—the color a symbol of his willingness to die for his faith—of his Vatican office. His faith—like that of most Catholics—embraced the Trinity of God, the divinity of Jesus, and salvation through living a good and unsinful life. Unlike the cardinal bishops, cardinal priests, and cardinal deacons who elect the pope, and whose names are published for the faithful to see, this man was a cardinal *in pectore*—Latin for "in the breast"—whose secret crusade was so fraught with peril that his identity was known only by the pope and God.

Hidden in *The Lamentation* was the reason why.

"Can you see the oval?" asked a voice with a hint of a German accent.

"No," replied the emissary from the Vatican. He turned to face the sickly man who'd joined him by the painting.

The Secret Cardinal exposed his ring.

"Eminence," the second man whispered. Bowing toward the proffered hand, he performed the *baciamano,* kissing the ring that bound the cardinal to the pope. The magnificent band stretched from the knuckle of the cardinal's third finger to its first joint. It depicted the crucifixion of Jesus, with the Virgin Mary and St. John at his side.

The cardinal covered his ring once more. "Interpret the oval," he said, returning his attention to the Christus painting.

That, too, was code.

Akin to a secret handshake.

Gaunt and pale, his body ravaged by leukemia, the Art Historian to the Secret Archives of the Vatican had selected *The Lamentation* as their meeting place because it effectively illustrated the threat to the Catholic Church. What he was about to explain would make the need for this secret meeting clear.

"The painting dates from about 1450," said the dying man. "None of the four gospels in the New Testament describes the removal of Jesus from the cross, or the grieving over his body once it was stretched out on the ground. For that, we have to go to medieval texts like *Meditations on the Life of Christ*. There, we learn that Joseph of Arimathea had trouble extracting the right-hand nail because it was long and so firmly attached to the wood. He passed it down to St. John as Nicodemus pulled out the left-hand nail. Finally, pincers withdrew the nail from Christ's feet."

There was no need to comment on the instruments of the Passion: the crown of thorns; the three nails, hammer, and pincers in the foreground; and the cross behind. Like the skull at the foot of the cross, all were common Catholic icons. The skull symbolized *where* Christ was crucified: Golgotha meant "place of the skull" in Aramaic, and Calvary was Latin for "skull." It also represented Adam—the first man to suffer death—and therefore reflected the belief that Jesus died on the spot where Adam was buried. Thus Christ's sacrifice completed the arc of human history that began when Adam fell from grace by eating the forbidden fruit in the Garden of Eden.

"John's is the only account of the Passion in which Nicodemus plays a part. He brought the herbs for embalming the body," said the Secret Cardinal.

The Art Historian nodded. "That's Nicodemus holding up the shroud at Christ's feet. St. John is catching the fainting Virgin Mary, with Mary Magdalene reaching out to help. And the bearded man supporting Christ's head is Joseph of Arimathea. The inspiration for this painting appears to be the Gospel of John, chapter 19, verses 33 to 41."

Though Joseph of Arimathea wasn't a disciple, he was authorized to take Jesus's body down from the cross, and he brought the shroud in which to wrap it. He had rights to an unused tomb near Golgotha, and that's where he laid the body of Christ to rest. The tomb was a cave hollowed out of rock, and Joseph had it sealed by rolling a boulder across the mouth. The morning after the Sabbath, the cave was found to be empty. Christ's burial shroud was left behind, and the faithful believe that shroud is the Shroud of Turin.

"The interlocking figures form the oval," explained the Art Historian, gesturing at the painting. "It begins with Nicodemus holding the foot of the shroud, dips with the limp Savior on the sheet, then rises as Joseph of Arimathea supports his head. Mary Magdalene frames the arch with her arms, and St. John tops it above. Note how the Virgin Mary's fainting emulates the pose of her lifeless son."

"*Compassio* and *co-redemptio*," the cardinal said.

"By giving them equal prominence in *The Lamentation*, Christus equates the Virgin's emotional torment with Christ's physical suffering. The Virgin Mary *is* the mother Church, so Mary's in the oval, at the center of the painting. Here, Christ's body rests not in her lap—as it normally does in the *Pietà*—but on the white shroud. That connects it to the sacrament of the Eucharist, which is performed at every church altar for Mass."

The Eucharist ritual dates back to the Last Supper. All four gospels describe Jesus taking some bread, blessing it, and breaking it into pieces. "Take, eat, this is my body," he says, distributing the morsels to his disciples. Then he blesses a cup of wine. "Drink from it, all of you, for this is my blood of the covenanting, which is poured out for many for the forgiveness of sin. Do this in remembrance of me."

The following day, he was crucified.

"Of all the dogmas of our Church, none is more difficult to grasp than Transubstantiation," said the Art Historian. "How does the Holy Spirit descend over the altar and change the wafer and wine of the Eucharist into the *actual* body and blood of Christ? *The Lamentation* probably once served as an altarpiece, to help church-goers connect the Host with the body of Christ. Just as the Host sits on the altar cloth, so Christ rests on the shroud in the Christus painting. Just as the priest raises the Host during Mass, so Joseph and Nicodemus prepare to lift Christ's body in the painting. And just as Transubstantiation turns the wafer into the body of Christ to redeem the faithful, so the raising of Christ's body in *The Lamentation* leads to his Resurrection."

Despite the Art Historian's illness, his eyes gleamed with hope.

The Secret Cardinal frowned. The longer he stared at the painting, the deeper he feared for his Church. It had suffered a blow to its primacy from the Great Schism of 1054, when Orthodox Christians broke away from the Roman Catholic Church. It had suffered a greater blow from the Protestant Reformation, that mass exodus of rebellious Christians away from control by the pope and the Vatican. It had suffered an even greater blow from Darwin's heresy, the theory that man was created by evolution, and not—as depicted by Michelangelo on the ceiling of the Sistine Chapel—by the hand of God. *This*, however, might be the greatest blow of all, the fatal nail in the Vatican's coffin. Every element of the possible threat from the Judas conspiracy was depicted in *The Lamentation*.

"What makes you suspect this British bomber is connected to Judas?" asked the Secret Cardinal.

"In March 1944, my father warned Judas to keep his discovery secret from the Nazis," said the Art Historian. "The rumor is that Judas conspired with Churchill to smuggle a package to Britain in the hands of a secret agent who'd been parachuted into the Reich. The *Ace of Clubs* was shot down in March 1944, on the *same* night that a Junkers 88 was given extraordinary orders to cripple an RAF Halifax on a solitary run in a way that would kill no crewmen except the rear gunner. Plus there's this." From inside his overcoat, the older man withdrew an article taken from the Internet. "This appeared in a British tabloid as you were flying across the Atlantic."

"Link to 'Judas' Traitor Discovered?" read the headline.

Below that was a photograph of Mick Balsdon, followed by an interview with the octogenarian survivor of a Second World War Halifax bomber recently uncovered in eastern Germany.

The cardinal read the interview. "The connection to Judas could be the fantasy of an old man, fueled by rumor," he concluded.

"Can we risk *not* investigating?" asked the Art Historian. "If the resurrected bomber yields a map to the Judas package, Christendom might be rocked to its two-thousand-year-old foundations."

Again, the Secret Cardinal eyed the painting. "You have a plan?" he asked.

"We need someone to investigate who—how shall I put it?—won't be afraid to cut the Gordian knot."

The cardinal stroked his chin.

"We need a crusader," the historian pressed.

The Secret Cardinal of the Inquisition fingered his ring. "The man I'll send is a legionary of Christ."

WYATT ROOK

You never know who you'll meet at a book signing. Even in a
bookshop like the Unknown Soldier.

Wyatt Rook knew the story about the obsessed fan who
plunked a copy of a horror writer's latest novel down on the signing table, handed the author a genuine quill pen, then slapped his
own arm down on the surface and slashed his wrist with a razor.

"Hey, man," said the ardent reader. "Sign it in blood."

Facing a nut with a bloody razor in his grasp, the scribe
wisely dipped the nib into the gash, smiled at his number-one
fan, and said, "To whom shall I autograph it, sir?"

But that was horror fiction.

That was to be expected.

Wyatt's line of work was much more staid.

Alas, no groupies.

At least not until the TV show came out.

Wyatt was a vagabond. He wandered the world in search of
his next subject, and when he found something worthy of his
attention, he stayed in that spot for as long as it took him to
research. He did, however, own the top floor of a brownstone
in New York: the loft in the Manhattan residence of his best

friend, Jack, and the unrequited love of Wyatt's life, his best friend's wife.

Love is the fart
Of every heart:
It pains a man when 'tis kept close,
And others doth offend, when 'tis let loose.

How true, poet Suckling, he thought.

The loft was an open library of floor-to-ceiling shelves, an archive of every book Wyatt'd owned since he was a boy. Study the titles and you'd have a road map of his mind. A hideaway bed pulled down from the wall for when he was in the Apple.

Home enough.

"So I'm sitting at the signing table," Jack had said one night when the three of them were having fondue in the brownstone, "and this meek, downcast woman fumbles her copy of my latest thriller when she's putting it down for me to autograph. As she grabs it, her sleeve pulls back to reveal scars on her wrist. She tugs it down quickly, but not quickly enough to hide the slashes from me."

"Attempted suicide?" asked Val. The way she arched her eyebrow broke her secret admirer's heart.

"Slashing," Jack replied. "Each cut's a cry for help. Slashers don't slit deep enough to kill themselves."

"It's a coping mechanism," Wyatt said, lifting his fork from the pot of bubbling oil. "The pain of self-mutilation dulls emotional distress."

"Thank you, Freud," said Jack. "Are you going to drink from the bottle, or will you share the wine?"

These two had been ribbing each other since they met at boarding school. Jack had attended because his parents were Ivy League, while Wyatt had scraped through on a trust fund because his parents were dead. Why his dad had vanished remained a national security secret. His mother's death the following day was said to be suicide.

Wyatt didn't believe it.

His mom had loved him too much.

As he refilled Val's glass from the bottle of Beaujolais, her phantom lover drank in her aura with his eyes.

Masochist, he thought.

"I glance up," Jack continued, "and take in her troubled face. As I sign the book to Greta—that, she said, was her name—I hear a muttered comment.

"'What was that?' I ask.

"'Nothing,' she replies.

"'I'm sure I heard you say, "Thanks for giving me back my life." What does that mean?'

"'Forget it.'

"'You can't leave me in suspense,' I argue. 'You must tell me, Greta.'

"'I hurt myself,' she mumbles.

"'So I see.'

"'I don't cut deep. But yesterday was different.'

"'Why?'

"'My mom was sick a long time and died at home. There were lots of pills near her bed. I was going to take them to end my pain. I was sitting on the sofa with the pills in my hand, about to wash them down with a quart of milk, and that's when I saw the ad by my feet. It said you'd be signing your new book here. You left your hero to die at the end of the last one. I didn't want to die myself without knowing if he did too, so I put off taking the pills until I read this novel. The truth is I feel much better today, so thanks for giving me back my life.'

"And with that, she clutched the book to her chest and shuffled out the door."

"Damn!" said Wyatt. "I don't get fans like that."

"You write history, buddy. We know how your books end. I'm in the adrenaline-rush biz."

"You just let her go?" asked Val.

Jack shook his curly thatch. "If I had, she might be topping herself even as we eat. I called her back to the table. 'Know what a blood pact is?' I asked. She shook her head. 'It's a promise you can't break, Greta, because it's sealed in blood. Well, I have a blood pact for you.' I encircled her scarred wrist with my thumb and index finger. 'That's the blood,' I said. 'The pact is this: If you promise me you won't try to kill yourself again, I swear I'll never stop writing books *for you*. Deal?'

"Greta thought about it. Finally, she said, 'Deal.'"

Jack turned to his wife and shrugged. "Sorry, Val. It seems I dealt our retirement away."

Overlapping her hands on her heart, Val batted her eyes. "My hero," she said with a falsetto voice. "You deserve something *special* for that."

They were still in bed when Wyatt left the following morning. He flew from JFK to Heathrow to promote the British edition of his latest book, and hopefully to clinch a deal for his TV show. That's why he was signing in the Unknown Soldier, a bookstore just off Charing Cross Road.

"Hello, Mr. Rook. My name's Liz Hannah."

Wyatt gazed up from the table to greet the next person in line, but instead of an armchair general smelling of pipe tobacco, he found himself face to face with an eyeful of cleavage. A knockout in her mid-twenties—about five years younger than he was—Liz was attractive enough to give Val a run for her money, and she'd spent the cash to purchase all three of his books.

White Sands.

Black Rain.

And his latest, *Dresden.*

"These look read."

"They are. Purchased weeks ago. After I saw the DVD of your TV show."

"You work in broadcasting?"

"Yes," she said.

"Liz with a zee? Or just my signature?"

Some people got his books signed with an eye to selling them to collectors. Others were after a dedication as proof they'd met the author.

"Mr. Rook," Liz said, "I have a proposition. Will you join me for tea once you finish here?"

———————

The teashop was just a hole in the wall, selected because it was three doors down from the Unknown Soldier and Wyatt had more publicity appearances to make.

"A Brit usually asks a Yank to coffee," he said, perusing the menu.

"You drink coffee in the morning and tea from noon on," Liz replied.

"Where did you learn that?"

"Here and there. The Internet. New York papers."

"Am I being stalked?"

"Yes, and now you're in my clutches. I know a lot about you, Mr. Rook."

"Like what?"

"You have both a law degree and a Ph.D. in history. Your doctoral thesis was on conspiracies. You parlayed that into two bestselling books. *White Sands* shows how the Pentagon whitewashed Wernher von Braun so he could arm America with nuclear missiles and later put a man on the moon. *Black Rain* reveals how President Truman set the Japanese up for atomic destruction so he could bend Stalin to his will in postwar Europe. Having put your boots to homegrown conspiracies, you're now going after Bomber Command for the firebombing of Dresden in the final months of the Second World War."

"That bothers you?"

"Not in the least. Damn the torpedoes. Full speed ahead. That's what I need."

"Tea?" asked the waitress, notepad in hand.

"Please." Liz ordered, shifting her attention. "And bring an Eccles cake for the gentleman."

"Is *that* on the Internet too?" Wyatt asked.

"It's in the *Post* photo. There's an Eccles cake on the table in front of you."

"You're observant."

"I like to know what I'm buying."

As she left the table, the waitress threw Wyatt a scowl reserved for gigolos.

"From what I gather, you're a bit of a ladies' man," Liz continued. "In every social photo, you have a different date. I suspect you go for intelligent females who won't tie you down."

"Is that your proposition?"

"Hardly, Mr. Rook."

"Then why undo two buttons on your blouse?"

"Fashion."

"Hardly, Ms. Hannah. For that, one would do. Two's because you want something from this 'ladies' man.'"

"Your attention."

"Well, you've got that."

"Mission accomplished," she said, buttoning up. "There, is that better?"

"No," he said.

"Damned if you do, and damned if you don't."

"You didn't need the honey trap."

"But setting it up was fun."

"Let's get down to business. Why was I lured here? What exactly *is* your proposition?"

"Have you read about the *Ace of Clubs*, the bomber resurrected in Germany? The pilot, Fletch Hannah, was my granddad. On my grandmother's behalf—to give her peace of mind before she dies—I want to retain you to find out why he disappeared."

———•———

"Why me?" Wyatt asked, sipping tea and munching the Eccles cake.

"How old were you when your father vanished?"

"Nine."

"You don't practice law?"

"No."

"So why the law degree?"

"I use it to access government files that officials want kept secret. It's a research tool."

"It's a powerful tool, judging from your work. When we screened your documentaries at the network, I was amazed by how many long-kept secrets you brought to light, and how little knee-jerk reverence you have for the sacred cows of your country."

"Four hundred thousand Americans died in the Second World War for *something*. It wasn't so a rocket man who climbed the ladder of Himmler's SS and was tied to the deaths of twenty thousand prisoners of war could be turned into an American icon. Two hundred thousand Japanese were fried in the bombing of Hiroshima, and it wasn't to save half a million Americans from dying while invading Japan. It galls me that my government still peddles those empty lies, so I explode them."

"Don Quixote."

"Tilting at dirty windmills."

"I think that's just the buildup. You're after much more. Once you have a reputation for getting to the truth, you'll go after the White House to find out what happened to your dad and why it's been covered up. Presidents consulted him on foreign crises. Then one day he vanished, and no one will tell you why. You want to crack that puzzle."

"Don't forget my mom. The lie is that she killed herself the following day, distraught over the loss of my dad. But no way would she abandon me to face life alone. Someone assassinated her, and someday—*believe me*—her killer will pay."

"I believe you." Liz took a sip of her tea. "So why write *Dresden*?"

"So critics can't accuse me of being a conspiracy theorist with an ax to grind with Washington. Dresden was Britain's Hiroshima. Here you have a city of minor industrial importance—after almost six years of war, it was one of the few unbombed cities in Germany—and it gets singled out for

razing by RAF firebombs in February 1945, at a time when
Dresden was crammed with refugees. No one knows how
many were incinerated, but it was anywhere from 35,000 to
135,000 people. These are the kinds of things that vex me."

"There you have all the reasons why I'm stalking you," said
Liz. "First, you know how to smoke out the secrets of Bomber
Command. Second, as an outsider, you won't pull your
punches. And third, you grasp why I—like you—need to know
the truth about my family."

"You've lost me."

"What does 'Judas' mean to you?"

"I assume you don't mean the disciple who betrayed Jesus?"

"No."

"'Judas' was the codename Hitler gave to a mystery man
who tried to betray him in 1944. El Alamein and Stalingrad
were turning points of the war. Those losses spawned a conspiracy within the German army to oust Hitler and negotiate peace
with the Allies. Allegedly, Judas made contact with Churchill
and offered him top-secret information about Hitler's atomic
bomb. He also planned to smuggle out recently found biblical
relics. Rumor is that Churchill told Bomber Command to
parachute in a German-speaking secret agent, who would then
smuggle the Judas package out by submarine. But the package
never reached Britain. The plot against Hitler failed. The traitors
were executed. And Judas's identity remains an unsolved mystery of the Second World War."

"Do you believe the rumor?"

"It's unsubstantiated. But isn't that how secrets escape?
A confidant lets a secret slip 'off the record,' and whisper
becomes rumor. With Judas, the rumor seems to come from
several sources."

"Did you see this?" Liz asked, handing him the tabloid interview with Mick Balsdon, the wartime navigator of the resurrected *Ace of Clubs*.

"No," said Wyatt.

"Read it."

So he did.

"Balsdon, my granddad's navigator, believes the secret agent was disguised as one of his fellow crew members. The flight plan he was given on the hush-hush never made sense to him. They were told to break away from the main bomber stream and fly a solitary run to an isolated target of no apparent value. That's how their plane got shot down by a lone wolf fighter, and why they had to bail out over Germany."

"It's not uncommon for vets to embellish their war records," Wyatt countered.

Liz shook her head. "Mick's put together an archive documenting his belief. It's taken him a lifetime. For years, he's kept in touch with his surviving mates and the relatives of those now gone. The discovery of the *Ace of Clubs* offers him a chance to prove he's right. Mick's confined to a wheelchair and is in failing health, so he can't make the trip, but he wants those who can to travel to Germany for the opening of the bomber. The plane's a time capsule from 1944. It might hold a clue to the Judas puzzle."

"You're going?"

"Yes."

"Where do I fit in?"

"If Mick's right, imagine the book and TV show you'll get out of this. Mick still lives in Yorkshire, the wartime base of the *Ace*. Will you at least go to see his archive?"

"Ms. Hannah—"

"Liz."

"I'm a busy man. I don't have time to—"

"Every man has his price."

"Yes, and mine's higher than two undone buttons."

Flick.

Flick.

Flick.

Liz undid three.

LEGION OF CHRIST

✝

Unbeknown to those around him—and even to himself—the Legionary of Christ was in subconscious combat with Satan for possession of his soul.

Here, in the heart of the Roman Catholic Church, the young priest sat reading in a secret locked room, encircled by wooden cabinets inlaid with symbolic designs and by frescoes depicting the trials of heretics during the Inquisition. So ancient were the books and documents burying his desk that their centuries-old dust grayed his plain black cassock. As he studied the blasphemies that were wrenched from heretics by torture, his fingers caressed the crucifix on his chest. The page before him bore an incantation that was said to conjure Satan up from hell, and as his mind absorbed the words the Church's cardinal inquisitor had recorded, the nail-hole scars through his palms began to throb.

The Crucifixion of St. Peter hung on the opposite wall. From it, the eyes of the upside-down apostle met his.

"Get thee behind me, Satan," quoted the priest.

The Secret Archives of the Vatican occupy thirty miles of shelving in rooms that border the Belvedere Courtyard, beyond St. Peter's Basilica and the Sistine Chapel. Founded by Pope Paul V in 1610, the archives were originally "secret" in the sense that the records were for the *private* use of the pope and his advisers. But since 1881, they have gradually been opened for outside research, and have proved to be a treasure-trove for historians. Some documents date back to the 700s, though most are from 1198 on. Recent revelations cover the years from 1922 to 1939, the era of Pope Pius XI, who some say was "Hitler's Pope."

The *real* secret archives of the Vatican were the dusty records in this room at the Palace of the Holy Office, or Sant'Uffizio, the home of the Inquisition. The building was tucked in the external crook of Bernini's colonnade, where the south arm arced in a semicircle around St. Peter's Square. For centuries—since 1542, when Pope Paul III set up the Universal Inquisition to defend the Church from heresy—confessions extracted under torture were filed here, building up history's largest library of satanism, witchcraft, and sorcery. Each means of torture was recorded in detail by a scribe and went into the heretic's file along with the evidence that had damned him.

Today, the Inquisition goes by another name: the Congregation for the Doctrine of the Faith. Before his election in 2005 as Pope Benedict XVI, Cardinal Joseph Ratzinger—called "the Enforcer"—ran this office for a quarter century, defending the Church against heresy and silencing those guilty of offending the faith. Outside of this room, around forty people— theologians, scripture scholars, and canon lawyers knowledgeable in the laws of the Church—labored in four sections: doctrine, discipline, matrimony, and punishment of priests. They examined writings and opinions for heresy, dissolved non-sacramental marriages, and investigated the sexual abuse of minors by clergy and "grave delicts" like abuse of the Eucharist.

To mark the third millennium of Christianity, Pope John Paul II decided to open "the archives of repression" to help the

Church come to terms with its history. Some secrets, however, must be kept forever. So that's why the Legionary was locked away with these books and papers, charged with deciding what should be moved to the *new* secret archives.

Through the windows of this room, the Legionary could see the Christian cross crowning the Egyptian obelisk at the center of St. Peter's Square. In ancient times, this marshy, hilly waste across the Tiber River to the west of Rome was called Vaticanus. Known for its malarial mosquitoes, snakes, and sour wine, Vaticanus is where the mad emperor Caligula decided to build his circus. At the center of the hub—the *spina*—around which chariots raced, he erected the obelisk plundered from Heliopolis. When Caligula was assassinated before the arena's completion, it fell to his nephew, the psychopath Nero, to finish the job. The Circus of Nero became that tyrant's favorite playground. He would personally take the reins of a chariot and drive it around in a frenzy to soak up the obligatory applause. When Rome burned for nine days in 64 A.D., Nero blamed the obscure sect of Christians for the disaster. Dragged to the circus for execution, those early Christians were torn to pieces by wild beasts, immersed in tar and set ablaze, or crucified. Among those crucified was the apostle Peter, who had come to Rome in Caligula's reign to spread the word of Christ. Because he felt unworthy to hang upright as Jesus did, Peter asked to be nailed *upside down* to his cross near the obelisk.

In *The Crucifixion of St. Peter*, the apostle is naked, except for a loincloth, and already pinned to the wood. Three Romans, their faces turned away, struggle to lift the cross with the martyr head down. Bearded and bald, with tufts of hair on his wrinkled brow, the old man suffers in pain and fear of death. His execution grim and humiliating, Christ's apostle glares at the nail affixed to his left palm.

"What in hell!" the priest exclaimed.

As the Legionary stared at the painting hung high on the palace wall, St. Peter vanished from the cross of his martyrdom, and what remained was the inverted cross of the black Mass.

Stranger yet, the scars on the Legionary's palms ceased to ache.

Conjuring Satan? the priest thought, recoiling from the blasphemy he had just read in the Inquisition record. He crossed to the windows that looked north to St. Peter's shrine.

After Peter's crucifixion, Christians secretly buried his body in the cemetery abutting the north wall of the circus. The next 250 years saw martyrs die by the thousands, forcing members of the persecuted sect to hide in the catacombs of Rome. There, they continued to practice the rites of their faith, and they passed on the secret that Peter was buried under a simple shrine known as the Trophy of Gaius. In the early fourth century, the Great Persecution reached its height. Christian writings were burned and homes destroyed, and those Christians not tortured or mutilated died as gladiators.

In 306 A.D., Constantine the Great, in Britain battling the Picts of Scotland, was proclaimed Roman emperor by his troops. By 312, he was in a struggle with Maxentius for the throne. As he led his army south through the Alps to face his rival outside Rome, Constantine saw a vision of a cross superimposed on the sun and heard the words "By this sign, you will conquer." Ordering his soldiers to mark their shields with the sign of Christ, he trounced Maxentius at the Battle of Milvian Bridge and became Rome's undisputed emperor.

Attributing his victory to the God of the Christians, Constantine the Great issued the Edict of Milan, granting Christians freedom of worship throughout his empire. The

Nicene Creed affirmed the divinity of Christ, deeming it heresy to denounce the son of God. Overnight, the Church of Christ was transformed from an underground sect to the official religion of Rome. To advance the banner of Christ, Constantine built the Church of the Holy Sepulcher above the tomb of Jesus in Jerusalem and St. Peter's Basilica here.

"You are Peter, and upon this rock I will build my church . . ."

So says Christ to the first pope of Rome in the Gospel of Matthew, back when Peter was the leader of his twelve disciples. Today, the words are inscribed in Latin around the dome of St. Peter's Basilica in the Vatican, and thanks to Constantine, Christ's biblical prophesy has *literal* meaning.

The Legionary of Christ's eyes slid down from the cross atop Michelangelo's magnificent dome to the church below. Hugging its flank was the Square of the First Christian Martyrs, at the center of which had stood Caligula's obelisk, close to the spot where St. Peter was crucified. The Arch of Bells between the church and the colonnade swept eastward into St. Peter's Square, which was dotted with worshippers splashing to Mass through gusting gray rain. The twin arms of the colonnade resembled shepherds' crooks. They ran parallel from the façade of the basilica, then bulged around the obelisk at the hub of the huge circle to give the plaza its keyhole shape.

"I will give you the keys to the kingdom of heaven . . ."

So Christ also says to Peter.

Across the square from the Holy Office, the papal apartments were dark. The pope was in St. Peter's Basilica for Mass. In his troubled mind, the priest imagined the rite. Directly beneath the cross surmounting the dome soared the twisted columns of Bernini's bronze canopy over the altar.

There, the pope raised the Host. The present-day basilica—begun by Pope Julius II in 1506, and completed 120 years later—stood on the footprint of Constantine's church, which was itself constructed over the cemetery and the Trophy of Gaius, preserving the grave of St. Peter. Between the pope at the altar and the bones of Christ's apostle in the shrine sixteen feet beneath his shoes ran a succession of 265 popes.

And from the beginning, centuries before the reign of Constantine, St. Peter's faithful had battled heretics.

"Get thee behind me, Satan . . ."

"You are Peter, and upon this rock I will build my church, and the gates of the netherworld shall not prevail against it."

Now, as he watched black clouds churn above the Vatican, the priest wondered how any believer could reject the Roman Catholic Church as the center of the Christian world. It was Peter who led the disciples after Christ ascended to heaven. He organized the election of Mathias as the twelfth disciple, in place of Judas, and turned all the disciples into apostles at the feast of Pentecost. He took the teachings of Christ to the capital city of their oppressors and passed them on through the Gospel of Mark, the record of his faithful companion. He "stretched out his hands" in crucifixion, just as Christ foretold, and became the "rock" upon which Constantine built the basilica. He was *first* among the apostles, and he passed that divine primacy down through the Vatican's popes so the rite of the Eucharist could provide the keys to heaven. The authority of the Roman Catholic Church was traceable from the current pope back without a break in the chain to Peter, and through him, to the son of God.

Amen.

Anyone who threatened that was a heretic.

Thus the Holy Office in which the Legionary worked.

A sudden flash of lightning took the priest by surprise. It must have cracked behind the building, out of sight, for all he saw was a burst of brilliant blue intensity. As the Vatican turned dark from a downpour of black rain, the Legionary glimpsed the netherworld on which it was built. The field of blood that once had soaked the Circus of Nero spread beneath the Palace of the Holy Office, and he could hear the wailing of Christian martyrs as they were burned, eaten alive, or nailed to wooden crosses. Below that, he gazed into the mouth of hell, a gobbling, fanged maw gorged with unredeemed sinners boiling in oil and broiling in flames.

Was the Last Judgment upon him?

Had time run out?

The priest could smell brimstone and the stench of burning human flesh.

Turning from the window, he found himself locked in battle with Satan, for instead of St. Peter, the demon riding the black Mass crucifix was the Devil himself. Never had a creature as foul as this plagued his imagination, for the monster seemed to be a great red dragon with seven horned heads. Its seven mouths flicked snake tongues from shark teeth surrounded by slimy black lips. Its filthy fingers were crooked claws and its feet were hoofs, and behind it lashed a cruddy tail forked with spikes.

Blasphemy . . .

Perversion . . .

Abomination! he thought.

The priest fumbled for the crucifix on his chest, his only defense against insanity.

But then he heard the snick of a key slipping into the lock, and the biblical vision of doomsday swiftly retreated into the subconscious pit of his mind. Gazing toward the door, the possessed priest was quite himself again, for there was the most influential person in his life, the churchman who'd recruited him into the Legion of Christ.

"How goes the work?" asked the Secret Cardinal.

"Slowly, Father."

"You've been secreted away in here how long?"

"Two years."

"That's too long to wallow in the muck of the antichrists' blackest heresies," said the older priest, twenty years his senior. "We have a crusade for you to undertake. This threat could be the worst in the history of our faith."

The Secret Cardinal held out the copy of the British newspaper given to him by the Art Historian to the Secret Archives of the Vatican yesterday in New York.

"What is your will, Father?" asked the Legionary of Christ, taking the paper in his hand. For his mentor to take him away from *this*, it must be for a reason of dire consequence.

The Secret Cardinal touched the photo of Sgt. Mick Balsdon. "Find this man and have him tell you what he knows."

"Forcefully?"

"If necessary. On *my* authority."

From the pocket of a suit that belied his status, the elder priest withdrew a ring and slipped it on his finger. Holding out his hand for the *baciamano*, he said, "This secret will remain between you, me, and God. Because the Inquisition no longer 'exists,' I'm the *Secret* Cardinal of the Inquisition. I hereby appoint you my Inquisitor, with all the holy power that entails."

Bowing, the Legionary kissed the ring depicting the crucifixion of Christ. Because the Devil was in him, hiding from sight, the band burned his lips.

WARRIORS OF THE NIGHT

"Is there someone here named Hannah?"

"That's me," replied one of the card players basking in the sun. "What do you want?"

"My name's Mick Balsdon. The notice board says we're crewed up."

"You lucky son of a bitch." The pilot slapped down a card before he stood up and shook hands. "Balsdon, huh? I'll call you Balls. That's what I want in a crew."

"Do I call you Skipper?"

"Call me Wrath. As in the wrath of God."

"Who dubbed you that?"

"No one yet. But the Nazis will."

"If I'm so lucky, how come you left your crew up to the luck of the draw?"

The sandy-haired pilot plunked his peaked cap down on his head at a rakish angle. He tapped the flying brevet sewn to the chest of his uniform. "Size me up," he challenged. "What do you think? Am I a good pilot?"

"Damned if I know."

"They say there's more to choosing a pilot than there is to choosing a wife. A bird-brained wife can still make you happy, but a bird-brained pilot is sure to get you killed. When we're in the thick of it over Germany and the first flak explodes in the black of night, can you tell from eyeing me what I'll do? Sure, I'll play the game every pilot's taught to play: change altitude, course, and speed to throw off the next burst. But will I stupidly balance the pattern with a symmetrical jog to the other side, so the Huns will be able to predict where we'll be and blast us out the sky? Or will I veer to a spot selected randomly, so you can watch the next shell explode where we would have been had I balanced it out? You don't know, do you?"

"Uh-uh," said Balsdon.

"Meet Ack-Ack DuBoulay, our arse-end Charlie." The pilot crooked his thumb at the player across the card table. "DuBoulay, like double A, as in 'ack-ack.' Get it?"

"Dick DuBoulay," the rear gunner said, offering Balsdon his hand. He was a lanky fellow, all sinew and bone, with tousled blond forelocks on his brow. "Welcome aboard."

Ack-Ack, the navigator thought.

Anti-aircraft gun.

"So again we're in the thick of it, pounding our first target, and in zooms a night fighter blasting at our tail. Can you tell by looking at him how Ack-Ack will react? Sure, he's got that gunner's wing on his chest, but you don't know his scores at gunnery school. In the face of a horrific hail of incoming cannon shells, with the odds against him, will he quash his fear and hurl back well-aimed fire? Or will he freeze and take us down with him?"

"Russian roulette."

"And what about you?" The pilot flicked his middle finger at the twelve-feather half-wing brevet on Balsdon's chest. "Are you skilled at analyzing navigational problems under fire?"

"What do you think?"

Hannah shrugged. "I won't know till we're shot full of holes. Nor would it help if I'd taken RAF Admin up on its offer to stroll around in a hangar and crew up like blind man's buff. 'I like your brand of smokes. Want to fly with me?' Or, 'You look like a boozer. I quaff, too.' The way I see it, chaps, life's a gamble. The odds are one in six against surviving a thirty-ops tour. They're one in forty against surviving two tours. If our number comes up, our number comes up. I'd rather gamble for money with the blokes fate assigns me. So pull up a chair, Balls. You may deal the cards. Once the rest seek us out, we'll find a pub and I'll buy the crew its first round."

"The ace of clubs," Balsdon said, holding up the card the pilot had slapped down. "Good name for a bomber."

DuBoulay grinned.

Hannah winked. "The *Ace of Clubs* it is."

What a weird way to fight a war.

From that operational training unit in Kinloss, Scotland, Wrath's crew—as they came to be called—were posted to a squadron down near York. Going to war had always meant shipping out or marching off to far-flung lands, not to return till the job was done. Rot in the trenches. That was war. But in Bomber Command, the men went to war for a few hours, returning at dawn to a near-normal life. A day at the pub, at the cinema, seeing family and friends, then these warriors of the night were outward bound again. What a clean, comfortable way to engage in battle, but the psychological stress accumulated with each op.

Bleak House—named for the Dickens novel—was their new home. It was a prefab Nissen hut on the squadron's airfield.

Sixteen feet wide by twenty-four feet long, the hut had a low ceiling and a concrete slab for a floor. All seven crewmen were sergeants, so they roomed together in double-deck bunks, snoring on lumpy mattresses stuffed with excelsior.

"I feel like the princess and the pea," grumbled Hugh "Ox" Oxley. The flight engineer was a ruddy-faced mechanic who could drink anyone into a coffin.

"Don't pee on me," said Russ "Nelson" Trafalgar, stretched out on the bunk beneath him. The bomb-aimer had been a professional athlete before the war.

"Want to switch beds?" Ack-Ack growled from the bunk farthest away from the small coal-burning stove. The stove radiated just enough heat to keep those within five feet of it warm. Crewmen relegated to the ends of the hut were forced to sleep under their overcoats and several blankets to survive the cold, damp nights. Coal was rationed and never lasted until dawn, so the airmen honed "midnight requisitioning"—illegal raids on the coal yard—to an art.

"Goodnight, ladies," groused Wrath. "If I don't get my sleep, I'll nod off in the cockpit."

Wrong thing to say to this motley crew.

"Good night, ladies," Ox's bass voice filled the dark.

"Good night, ladies," Nelson's baritone chimed in.

"Good night, ladies," Ack-Ack's tenor topped off the mix.

"We're going to leave you now." The barbershop chorus sang itself to sleep.

Come morning, the room reeked of body odor and stale cigarettes. The first man up stoked the stove, then put a record on the gramophone. Glenn Miller's "Don't Sit Under the Apple Tree (With Anyone Else But Me)." "Chattanooga Choo-Choo." The Mills Brothers' "I'll Be Around." Or one of the jazz discs that the crew had purchased from the personal effects of a squadron leader blown to bits over Nuremberg.

Bleak House was rendered a little less bleak by a poster on one wall. It showed an RAF pilot as handsome as Errol Flynn flying a combat mission over Hitler's Germany. Off to the side, a vampire in a Messerschmitt launched a cowardly attack on our hero, swooping down from the blazing ball of high noon. The poster warned, "Beware of the Hun in the Sun!"

Since Bomber Command no longer struck by day, one of the crew had added, "Und Be Vatching Also, Kinder, für das Goon in the Moon!"

"Torture time, lads," announced the early riser.

The latrines, showers, and washstands huddled together in a building at the center of several huts. From the yelps of those inside, it was clear there was no hot water today. The ordeal of breakfast was worse. In the mess hall, the men got powdered eggs and chalky milk and the ever-present mystery meat called Spam. "Ham that failed its physical," gagged Monty "De Count" Christie, the gunner who manned the dorsal turret atop the *Ace of Clubs*.

The best thing about going on a mission?

The preflight meal was eggs, sausage, beans, and fried bread.

Breakfast done, it was time to play roulette. Every morning at ten, the wing commander received a call from Group HQ, and every morning Wrath walked over to hear if there would be a war on that night.

"A *Yank*?" the pilot had moaned, back when they'd first crewed up. "How can that be? The Yanks still haven't figured out if Hitler's villain enough for them to join the war."

"I hear he volunteered to fly with the RCAF. Canada attached him to the RAF," said Balls.

"His name?"

"Swetman. Earl Swetman."

"He'll be Sweaty. What's his trade?"

"Wireless operator."

"He'll think he's a *radioman*."

"Give him a chance, Skipper. He doesn't have to be here. Surely, that's in his favor."

Wrath sucked on his pipe, then blew out a pair of perfectly round smoke rings.

"Mark my words, chaps. He'll be garrulous and pushy. He'll natter on about how everything's bigger in Texas. Nothing will please him. Our beer will be flat—not bubbly like Schlitz back home. His knickers will twist when he finds his bollocks don't have their own latrine. He'll have too much money, and he'll lord it over us. In the end, to keep our sanity, we'll have to shoot him ourselves and save the Nazis the trouble."

"Shall we bet?"

"A crown says he's a prat," declared Wrath.

Sweaty, however, had proved that pessimistic prophet wrong. The Yank was a freckle-faced carrot top who fit in from the start. So much so that you'd think the RAF grew up around him. Within a week of arriving in Yorkshire, he knew every pub and club for miles around Bleak House, and those who rationed the beer all knew—and *liked*—him. A pub crawl with Sweaty was a raucous affair. Publicans lost track of how many pints they served his group. He could spin a yarn that clung judiciously to the truth, or line-shoot the best duff gen around. Want to play cards? Sweaty could hold his own at friendly and cutthroat alike. Sit him at a piano and the place would jump to life. You'd think you were lost on Basin Street in New Orleans.

"They're overpaid, oversexed, and over here!"

Even when the Americans did enter the war, Sweaty was an asset. The Yanks had the most money, so they got the best-looking girls in the clubs. But Sweaty winked indiscriminately at every WAAF who came in the door, and since laughs reigned loudest at his table, the real fun-lovers were drawn to him.

"So?" said Wrath to Sweaty. "When do you transfer over?"

"Trying to get rid of me, Skipper?"

"Better money. Your countrymen. Seems logical."

"Nah," said Sweaty. "Can't break up the crew. If you guys got the chop, I'd think I jinxed you."

After that, the radioman was everybody's favorite.

Wrath's too.

———— ·•·• ————

YORKSHIRE, NOW
The next day

Fifty-five thousand crewmen killed and more than eight thousand planes destroyed. Now, as a crippled old man looking back on the war years of his youth, Balsdon knew the tally paid in blood by the crews of Bomber Command. Back then, the butcher's bill was something you could feel in your gut every time you came back in one piece from a hell-raising "shaky do." And if the wingco asked how it went, you said, invariably, "Piece of cake, sir."

But it *wasn't*.

It *wasn't* when you checked the operations board to see how many squadron planes hadn't come home. Every op incurred

losses, and some—like the February 19, 1944, raid on Leipzig—
cost the RAF about eighty bombers.

It *wasn't* when you waited anxiously for mates to return,
only to see their plane land with its rear turret shot away and
nothing but a gaping gash where the rear gunner had been.
It *wasn't* when you watched stretcher-bearers lower a legless
bomb-aimer from the nose cone followed by the blood-
drenched crewman who'd spent the trip home holding a tourniquet on the screaming man's thigh.

And it *wasn't* when you finally collapsed into bed, unable
to sleep because you could still hear the engines' roar in your
ears. You'd stare at the ceiling as your mind replayed in slow
motion every frantic moment of the past few hours, and then
you'd jitter with repressed fear.

The most unsettling incident involved the squadron dog.
Against all rules and regulations, one of the senior pilots took
his dog on operational flights. Just once, he didn't take it, and
that's the night he went missing. The dog went out to the runway to welcome its master home, and there it stayed for two
days in a terrible state, howling mournfully until they had to
put it down.

Thank God for Sweaty.

The Yank had a knack for hijinks that chased the blues
away. It must have been the "sparks" badges on the wireless
operator's sleeves that made him such a live wire. If the crew
squeaked through a nerve-shredder, he'd insist they gather at
the piano in the lounge, where he'd lead the barbershop chorus
through every dirty ditty in the RAF's repertoire. They'd drink,
drink, drink as things got out of hand.

One time, they cleared the furniture out of the center of the
room, then divided the drunkards into two teams. One by one,

the men leapt onto the backs of their mates, until finally one of the human pyramids collapsed.

Another time, they piled the furniture in the center of the room to act as a scaffold for Sweaty, who'd covered his bare feet in soot. Slowly, he was carried aloft until a trail of charred footprints staggered up from the fireplace, across the ceiling, and down the far wall to the door.

One night, Balsdon returned from leave to the sound of unbridled revelry in the lounge. Sweaty was leading a boisterous crowd of flyboys in a round of "Bang, Bang, Lulu." The men were naked except for black ties around their necks. Beer sloshed from pint glasses waved high as they trod on a carpet of clothes. One of the merrymakers spotted Balsdon at the door. "Get him!" he yelled, forcing the navigator to turn and run for his life, hotly pursued by a mob of birthday-suit hangmen jerking up their ties like gallows ropes.

Hurrah for Sweaty.

He got Wrath's men through the crushing stress.

All but one.

WITCH HUNT

✝

Her wrists tied behind her back, the suspected witch hung naked and shaved of all body hair from a ceiling beam in the dark York dungeon. He knew what they were searching for, these Dominican monks of the Catholic Church, as they meticulously examined her belly for the Devil's mark. He had read the unexpurgated version of *Malleus Maleficarum—The Hammer of Witches*—back in his locked room at the Vatican. Jakob Sprenger and Heinrich Kramer, also Dominican monks, wrote that theological encyclopedia in 1486 to tell witch hunters how to spot women guilty of copulating with the Devil, holding black "sabbats," thwarting the birth of babies, and instigating misfortunes like hailstorms, crop failures, illness, and insanity. The Dominicans in this dungeon were probing the heretic for her "witch's tit," a third nipple used to suckle demons. They might find it in a wart, a mole, or a birthmark. The test would be if the tit was insensitive to the jab of a "witch prickle" dagger.

Alone down here, with just the company of the waxwork figures, the Legionary was lost in the realm of the heretical books that had possessed his mind for the past two years. Because he was battling Satan for possession of his soul, he had no recollection of having hired a local burglar to bypass the after-hours alarm system of the Inquisition—a chamber of horrors that did good trade off the tourists who came to York for its bloody history. One moment the Legionary was the faithful servant of God and Christ, and the next moment he was in the diabolic clutches of the Devil.

"All witchcraft comes from carnal lust," he'd read in *The Hammer*, "which is in women insatiable."

He, of course, had never lain with a woman. Although so many other priests succumbed to sins with both sexes, the Legionary was forever reminded of his vow of celibacy by the nail-hole scars in his palms. As the beam of his flashlight ran up and down the voluptuous wax woman, he understood what St. Paul had meant when he said, "Now the works of the flesh are manifest: immorality, impurity, licentiousness, idolatry, witchcraft . . ."

Surely she had the witch's tit, this sexual playmate of Satan.

As did the wanton women he spied on the streets and in the media of modern times.

Was *this* what Christ had suffered and died for?

The Legionary's cross was to live in a decadent era drowning in a sea of sin.

Sodom and Gomorrah.

The stench of burning flesh assaulted his mind as he shifted his flashlight to the next exhibit. Here, the same woman was tied to an upright stake by a cord around her neck and a chain about her midriff. The cord passed through a hole in the post so the executioner, if desired, could strangle her. During the Inquisition, it was heresy *not* to believe in witches, and nothing eradicated allegiance to Satan better than fire. Perhaps a hundred thousand women had burned like this one. Cartloads of faggots—dry brushwood—were piled around the witch, and as he stared, the Legionary imagined the woman becoming engulfed by flames. Her arms flailed in a futile attempt to push the blaze away. Then she shrieked at the top of her lungs.

"Burn, witch! Burn!" cursed the crusader.

That curse, however, must have riled the Devil, for by the time his flashlight beam lit up the next exhibit, a vivid recreation of the Spanish Inquisition, the Legionary had once again lost control of himself. Satan was in the driver's seat, and the young priest was along for the ride.

A large crucifix was mounted high on a dungeon wall, and beneath it sat the cardinal inquisitor at a table. Flanked by candlesticks, he faced each broken heretic who was dragged over to confess. On one edge of the table, a scribe recorded what was said with a quill pen. Gibbers and screams punctuated their work as monks in the center of the dungeon cracked other transgressors. They cranked thumbscrews that squashed the ends of fingers. They held a writhing man's feet to the fire. The rack, the wheel, and the knee-splitter were being used. Arrayed on a bench along the wall were other devices, and that's where the possessed priest found what he required.

But that had been several hours ago, back in the city of York. Now, he was out in the countryside, at the top of a path wending down to a cottage. Strangely, a Christian cross guarded the way through the woods, and it burned his hand as he touched it, just as the ring of the Secret Cardinal had seared his lips.

The night was overcast, and the rural thicket was black. A window at the foot of the path was the beacon guiding him. Fallen leaves crackled under his feet like flames. He could hear the gurgle of a stream near the cottage. Careful not to be seen, he peeked in through the window, and there sat Sergeant Balsdon with his wartime archive.

Did those papers hold the key to the Judas relics?

Or was the key in the old man's mind?

Either way, the Legionary would get the answer.

He moved toward the door, carrying the Inquisition's means in his hand.

Could a chair be more aptly named than this?

The ultimate witch prickle.

TOP SECRET

1944

"There's a war on tonight," Wrath announced the morning of that fateful run. "Got bad news, chaps. De Count went LMF."

"LMF!"

"Jesus Christ!"

"What's the gen, Skipper?"

Gen—pronounced "jen"—was general information. It came in two forms: pukka gen, the real McCoy, as the Yanks would say, and duff gen, faulty word, which was spread by duff gen merchants.

"He went to the wing commander and said he'd had enough. The wingco told De Count to pull himself together. You volunteer in, but you can't volunteer out. De Count told the wingco to go to hell. He'll be sent to Uxbridge under arrest. He'll carry the 'lack of moral fiber' brand for the rest of his life."

"De Count a coward?" Nelson shook his head.

"I saw it coming," said the Ox. "He threw up after every op. He wept in his sleep."

"Will they jail him, Skipper?"

Wrath nodded. "A hundred and eighty days would be my bet."

"Who's the spare?" said Ack-Ack.

"A Welshman called Trent Jones. We'll take him up on the air test and check him out."

———•◦•———

Twelve was said to be the point you had to reach. Survive twelve ops and the odds got better that you'd survive all thirty, for that meant the crew functioned well together. The men of the *Ace* were far beyond twelve and could see the finish line. Each had a role to perform if all were to survive, and the role of both gunners was to protect the bomber from night fighters.

A new gunner skewed the odds.

He was odd man out.

Trent Jones was a sullen tailor with little meat on his bones. When new flight crews arrived in the mess, the old hands would bet on how long each man would last. The ones who enjoyed life, like Sweaty, were more likely to make it. But loners like Jones—blokes who sat off by themselves penning letters home—were destined to get the chop, the smart money said.

The Welshman's wife had left him and skipped with their child to Australia. Then he'd lost his original crew in a takeoff "prang" over the North Sea, when a pair of bombers laboring for height crashed into each other and plunged into the drink. He was the only one to escape. That was like a mark of Cain to other airmen.

By the time they completed the air test, the field was a beehive of action. Tankers drove around filling giant bombers with thousands of gallons of petrol. Trucks dropped off oxygen cylinders, and tractors towed ordnance trolleys to bomb-up the planes. Ack-Ack gave Jones a thumbs-up on how he handled the turrets and the guns. The other men left the gunners behind to polish the windows of their combat stations, and to strip and clean their guns as armorers fed long belts of ammunition into the rear of the plane.

Balsdon knew something big was up when they gathered later that afternoon outside the briefing room. The hut was surrounded by service police, and the men couldn't get in without showing ID and having Wrath vouch for them. Once inside, the men received a warning: "Tonight's mission is *top secret*. If word leaks out, the source of that leak will be summarily executed."

That grabbed their attention.

The crewmen sat on long wooden benches facing a large map of Europe that was shrouded from view by a blackout curtain. All rose to their feet when the cologne-soaked station and squadron commanders entered.

"Gentlemen, the target for tonight is Berlin."

With those crisp words, they drew back the drapes to reveal the map on which the men's flight path was marked with red tape. Known flak and searchlight batteries were emblazoned along the route.

After the briefing, the pilots obtained their maps from the station map stores. All but Wrath. He was taken aside by the wing-co for a hush-hush chat, and Balsdon saw the skipper get handed a for-your-eyes-only map. While the rest of the crew hurried off to collect their chutes and Mae West vests, Wrath—by now a flight lieutenant—ushered his navigator away for a cigarette.

With no one around, the two stood smoking behind the hut.

"What's up, Skipper?"

"I don't know, Balls. It's so deep cover, they won't say. But we're not going to Berlin with the stream."

"We're flying diversion? To throw off the Huns?"

Wrath shook his head. "That's what's strange. We're to break away from the others over Germany and make a solo bombing run on a town I've never heard of. The wingco says I can only tell *you*. Eight hundred bombers are striking Berlin to smokescreen our solitary mission."

———•—

They tried to give him parachute number 20812, but there was no way Balsdon would take it. Adding the digits together gave the number 13. He should have seen that as an omen.

The locker room was thick with stress. Despite the casual air of the *Ace*'s crew, superstitions, talismans, and rituals still ruled the day. Ox got dressed in the *exact* same order for every trip. If he made a mistake, he stripped down and began again. Collars were banned because they could shrink and strangle you in the water, so Nelson tied on a stocking from his latest conquest, having asked the dame to save its partner for his return. Ack-Ack flew with a silver cigarette case over his heart, in case a shard of shrapnel hit its mark. Wrath took a rabbit's foot *and* a St. Christopher's medal. The foot would keep him from getting shot down, he believed, and the medal would get him home to his family if he did.

Sweaty, of course, had the fun ritual. As he fastened his parachute harness, he pulled the crotch straps tight and let out the falsetto squeal of a Vatican castrato. Loosening them, he dropped his voice to a deep bass for a joke.

That day, it was a knock-knock joke.

"Knock-knock," said Sweaty.

"Who's there?" he answered himself.

"Gestapo.

"Gestapo who?

"Ve vill ask ze questions!"

The crew laughed *too* loudly, another sign of strain.

And another omen?

Wearing several layers of clothing—the gunners in their electro-thermal Taylorsuits were the chubbiest of all—the men walked stiffly from the locker room. They were taken to their plane on a rickety old bus, its headlamps covered with cardboard so the light was directed down to the ground, where it couldn't be seen from overhead. The bombers were dispersed around the perimeter of the airfield, as a precaution against enemy attack. Their ground crew was waiting.

For Balsdon, the few moments that Wrath spent checking the plane before they boarded were the most tense. So acute was the cumulative strain from all his previous missions that the muscles of his abdomen cinched his stomach back to his spine. His crewmates were gripped by the same turmoil. They chain-smoked cigarettes and couldn't stand still. A few pissed on the tail wheel for luck. To keep their minds occupied while Wrath signed a form for the ground crew corporal, they busied themselves with their personal contributions to Hitler's downfall: bricks and bottles they would toss out over Germany. Supposedly, the bottles made screaming noises as they fell, scaring the hell into the Huns below.

"Wizard, Chiefy," Wrath said, handing back the form. "I hope you scrawled appropriate messages to Hitler on the bombs."

"Aye," said the Scotsman, smirking.

They boarded the bomber through a door behind one wing. Inside, the fuselage smelled of gasoline mixed with cordite. The pilot, navigator, flight engineer, wireless operator, and bomb-aimer stooped their way up to the nose, while the gunners took their places in the turrets above the door and in the rear.

Outside, the ground crew hauled the battery starter into position under the port wing.

"Contact!"

The engines coughed, sputtered, and roared to life. Wrath did an intercom check to all positions. The wheel chocks were pulled away, and the pilot opened the throttles. The hulking bomber trundled and swayed onto the perimeter track, then taxied to the threshold of the runway. There, they waited for a green light to flash on the control van. Soon, they were lumbering faster and faster along the bumpy strip, holding the nose down to build up speed, until the skipper eased back the control column and the engine roar changed.

The Halifax left the runway at a little more than a hundred miles an hour and clawed its way into the night.

The *Ace of Clubs* was outward bound ...

It wouldn't be coming back.

———————

NOW

Tonight, sixty-odd years later, darkness cloaked the Yorkshire cottage where the crippled veteran was spending his old age. Confined to a wheelchair, Balsdon sat at a large oak table beneath rough-hewn ceiling beams and rearranged his massive Bomber Command archive. He'd spent his lifetime collecting every bit of information he could find about why the *Ace of Clubs* went down. The discovery of the long-lost bomber offered hope the mystery would be solved before he died, as did today's telephone call from Liz Hannah—Wrath's granddaughter—telling him that Wyatt Rook had the hook through his cheek.

"Can he come up and see you?"

"When?" asked Balsdon.

"Tonight or tomorrow. Depending on his promo tour and when he can catch a train."

"I'll be waiting."

Balsdon rolled back from the table with a yellowing photo in his hand. The 1944 shot of the *Ace of Clubs'* crew was snapped after the test flight that fateful day. The seven airmen stood under the plane's bomb bay.

The navigator flipped the photo and squinted at its back. There, he had recorded the names, nicknames, and combat positions of the doomed fliers:

F/Lt. Fletch "Wrath" Hannah	Pilot
Sgt. Mick "Balls" Balsdon	Navigator
Sgt. Hugh "Ox" Oxley	Flight engineer
Sgt. Russ "Nelson" Trafalgar	Bomb-aimer
Sgt. Earl "Sweaty" Swetman	Wireless operator
Sgt. Dick "Ack-Ack" DuBoulay	Rear gunner
Sgt. Trent "Jonesy" Jones	Mid-upper gunner

The old man's arthritic finger touched one of the names.

"Were you the traitor?" he asked.

The rhetorical question was interrupted by knocking on his door.

Rook? he wondered.

JUDAS CHAIR

✝

THE NEXT DAY

Clickety-clack . . .

Clickety-clack . . .

The pope and Wyatt Rook die on the same day and end up before St. Peter at the pearly gates. The keeper of the keys to heaven asks each man for his name and looks him up in a book. After passing out wings, halos, and harps, St. Peter says, "If you'll both come with me, I'll show you to your dwellings."

The three walk along the clouds until they come to an insignificant cottage. "Here's where you'll stay for the rest of eternity," St. Peter tells the pope.

From there, he leads Wyatt to his abode—a palatial mansion with a private swimming pool, a celestial garden, and a terrace overlooking the pearly gates.

"Enjoy your stay," St. Peter says, turning to go.

Taken aback, Wyatt blurts out, "There must be some mistake. You put the pope in a shack, and you put me here."

"No mistake," St. Peter says, shaking his head. "We have most of the two hundred or so popes in heaven. They're commonplace. But you . . . well, we've never had a lawyer."

Clickety-clack . . .

Clickety-clack . . .

Fat chance, Wyatt thought.

When he showed up at the pearly gates—assuming the Bible was right about the afterlife—he would probably be grabbed by the scruff of the neck and the seat of his pants by St. Peter's heavenly bouncer and given the bum's rush down to hell to join the other broiling lawyers. So many sins had Wyatt committed in his hedonistic life that he had begun to hope there really was nothing more. If not, he was damned.

Wyatt Rook is sitting in his loft one night when there is a sudden flash of light and smoke swirls out of the floor. The Devil steps from the twister to address the lawyer: "I understand you'll give anything to succeed in life. So I've come here to make you an offer. You'll expose every secret you go after, your books will all be bestsellers, and your documentaries will all win Oscars. In return, I'll take the souls of you, your parents, your grandparents, your wife, your children, and all your friends."

Wyatt thinks about it.

"So what's the catch?" he asks.

Clickety-clack . . .

Clickety-clack . . .

That's more likely, he thought.

However . . .

Had he been trundling north to York on this train *before* the book-signing at the Unknown Soldier, he'd almost certainly have been fantasizing about Val. "Thou shalt not covet thy best friend's wife," the Ten Commandments warn, so that would have been more for St. Peter to add to the hellish side of his scales. Yet here he was thinking about Liz Hannah and her wayward buttons instead, so perhaps even this sinner could be redeemed.

Unless, of course, his naughty thoughts were another sin.

A poor hand of poker.

He should have held out for her bra.

Wyatt didn't have the time to make this trip. He was in Britain to sell his books and flog his documentaries. Still, if there was a chance that Mick Balsdon held the key to solving the Judas puzzle, then Wyatt couldn't afford *not* to make this trip. But what had really convinced him was the thought of Liz's grandmother dying without knowing the fate of her husband. Wyatt's life was ruled by his need to learn what had happened to his parents, so he knew that walking away from the possibility of giving her mental peace was a sin that would haunt him for the rest of his life—and drop the hellish side of St. Peter's scales down with a *thunk*.

Clickety-clack . . .

Clickety-clack . . .

The train pulled into the station.

How could a historian not love York? Halfway up the British Isles between London and Edinburgh, this city was founded in 71 A.D. as Eboracum—"place of yew trees"—during the conquest of the north by Rome's Ninth Legion. Beside York Minster, where his troops proclaimed him emperor, stands a huge statue of Constantine the Great, Rome's first Christian leader. Then came the Vikings, in 866, and almost a century of the Kingdom of Jorvik. And no sooner had Eric Bloodaxe been expelled than the Norman Conquest came charging up. The Middle Ages brought reconstruction of York's walls, including Micklegate Bar, beside the train station. Traditionally, monarchs entered the city by way of that towering gate, and since 1389, they had touched the state sword on coming in. High up on its outer wall were hooks where the heads of traitors were left to rot.

Traitors like Henry "Hotspur" Percy, in 1403, and the Earl of Northumberland, in 1572. This was the home of Guy Fawkes, the Roman Catholic who tried to blow up Parliament with the Gunpowder Plot. And York was where the notorious highwayman Dick Turpin had danced on the end of a rope.

Remember, remember the fifth of November,
The Gunpowder Treason and Plot,
I see no reason why Gunpowder Treason
Should ever be forgot.
A penny loaf to feed the Pope.
A farthing o' cheese to choke him.
A pint of beer to rinse it down.
A faggot of sticks to burn him.
Burn him in a tub of tar.
Burn him like a blazing star.
Burn his body from his head.
Then we'll say ol' Pope is dead.

Ah yes, York.

Had Wyatt had time for a walk, he'd have crossed the River Ouse to amble through the Shambles. That street was like a time machine back to the Elizabethan era. The buildings leaned over the cobblestones until their roofs almost touched in the middle, and in places you could stretch your hands and brush the houses on both sides. The name came from *Fleshammels*— a Saxon word meaning "flesh shelves"—because butchers displayed meat for sale on the wide windowsills. Since livestock was slaughtered outside on the street, the pavement sloped to a channel where blood, guts, and offal were flushed away. The pandemonium and mess coined another term: a shambles.

In 1571, Margaret Clitherow married a butcher with a shop in the Shambles. She permitted her house to be used for Mass by Catholic priests, a capital crime in Elizabethan times, and so was executed at the tollbooth on the Ouse Bridge. Made to lie on her back with a sharp stone under her spine, she was stretched out in the form of a cross with her hands tied to posts. Then a door was placed on her and weighted down until she was crushed to death. In 1970, Pope Paul VI made her a saint, and her home in the Shambles is now a shrine.

But enough of blood and carnage; Wyatt was here to work. So the American rented a car and drove out of York, forsaking the wicked ways of the city for the countryside.

Out here, between the brooding moors to the northeast and the Pennine Hills to the west, lay the neglected airfields of Bomber Command. Today, most were little more than crumbling runways with rusty hangars that had long since lost the battle to weeds and grass. But in his imagination, Wyatt saw a time when the rumbling sky beckoned the warriors of the night, and the surrounding villages—a pub or two, an old Anglican church, and a hotel that served meals for the restricted price of five shillings— bustled with men who would never have meshed but for the anvil of war. The tough and the brainy, the pious and the heathen were all forged into seven-man groups that fought their lonely way across the dark landscape of Hitler's Reich and—hopefully— back home.

Wyatt wondered why Balsdon, who still lived here, couldn't leave it behind.

The Judas puzzle?

Mist and drizzle mixed to make the first half of the drive a somber journey. The windshield wipers flicked arches so Wyatt could follow the road through this broad expanse of rolling farmland dotted with ruined abbeys and castles. The legions of Rome had marched the route his tires were treading, and somewhere out there stood three monoliths called the Devil's Arrows. Dragged ten miles and raised for an unfathomable reason by prehistoric man, these standing stones were supposed to have come from a barrage shot by the Devil at local churches.

With weather like this, it's no wonder the local Brontë sisters dreamed up *Wuthering Heights* and *Jane Eyre*, and no wonder Captain Cook sailed off to the sunny South Seas. But as Wyatt neared Mick Balsdon's village, a break in the cloud cover let the sun shine through, and an iridescent rainbow arced over his destination. Just as all roads once led to Rome, these drystone walls converged on the tiny community at the center of their web. And on the outskirts of the snug stone village—basically, a cricket pitch doubling as a common, backed by an alehouse called the Cricketer's Arms—Wyatt located the lane that branched off to Balsdon's cottage, down near the old mill stream.

"Mill Cottage," read the sign at the top of a footpath descending through dripping trees.

Beside the sign stood a market cross from the plague years of the 1660s. The depression at its base used to be filled with vinegar, and customers would wash their coins in hopes that would save the miller from the Black Death.

"Kaah-kaah-kaah."

From somewhere above him in the limbs of the trees, Wyatt heard the cawing of his namesake (though he preferred to think he was named for the chess piece). Folklore holds that a rook can sense the nearness of death, and Wyatt could picture this scene in an Agatha Christie novel. He was Miss Marple in St. Mary Mead, off to see Colonel Mustard about the church raffle, unaware that the old boy had been done to death in the old mill cottage by a bonk on the noggin from a shepherd's crook. Wyatt imagined the bridge across the stream had a story, too. A local suitor would swim across to woo the miller's daughter, but her father refused to allow her to marry a ne'er-do-well. So the lad shipped off to the colonies to make his fortune in ivory tusks, and when he came back to marry the lass with the miller's blessing, he built the bridge across the water as a testimonial to undying love.

No wonder he was a writer.

It was in that overblown frame of mind that Wyatt knocked on the door.

The cottage was fashioned from dark gray millstone grit and had a red tiled roof. Ivy climbed the walls around the mullioned windows. Liz had phoned Balsdon yesterday to ask if Wyatt could see him last night or this morning, depending on how soon he could get free from his promo tour. The sergeant had replied that any time was fine by him. Confined to a wheel-chair, he was going nowhere, and his wartime archive on the *Ace of Clubs* was spread across the table, waiting for all to see.

So why didn't Balsdon answer?

Wyatt knocked again.

Louder.

And still no response.

Balsdon, Liz had informed him, lived alone. A housekeeper came by twice a week to bring him groceries and clean up. The elderly warrior was a fiercely independent man, and he had no intention of going quietly to his grave. No retirement home for him, he'd see out his life in solitude, with a link to the Internet to help him ferret out the secret behind the Judas puzzle.

Now, Wyatt wondered if his time had run out.

Had Balsdon died of old age in his cottage?

Or was he singing in the shower and couldn't hear the knock?

Wyatt tried the latch.

The door was unlocked.

Opening it a crack, he called out, "Sergeant Balsdon? May I come in? It's Wyatt Rook."

Nothing.

Then he saw it.

Blood streamed across the hardwood floor from around the corner to the left of the entrance hall. The hall was no more than a vestibule for shedding coats and footwear. Thinking that Balsdon had fallen and struck his head, Wyatt rushed to his aid—and found himself confronted by a murder scene far grislier than any in Agatha Christie.

Blood and carnage.

The room was dominated by a huge fireplace. The vaulted ceiling was spanned by heavy beams dangling farmland relics: sheep shears, a butter stamp, a pig-feeder, a bird-scarer, a flat iron, love spoons, and such. Naked, the old airman was slung by his hands and feet from one of the beams. He resembled a safari beast being carried on a pole. To muffle his screams, the killer had clad the suspended man in the leather flying helmet and oxygen mask of Bomber Command. The oxygen tube hanging from the poor guy's face made him look like a skinny elephant. A digital recorder at the end of the tube would have captured a permanent transcript of anything he confessed.

The ropes around his hands and feet were looped over the beam so Balsdon could be hoisted and lowered as slowly as the killer holding the makeshift pulleys desired.

Grease and gravity.

What an ugly way to die.

The wheelchair, flung aside, lay overturned in the corner. Beneath Balsdon's buttocks, another device took its place—a sturdy wooden stool with a metal triangle bolted on top. The pyramid-shaped chair, glistening with lubricant, had blood streaking down its legs from the pointed seat. Positioned so it aimed at Balsdon's anus, the thick spike had impaled its way through his abdomen, pushing his intestines out of their cavity as it jutted from his belly. His bowels hung down from the Judas chair like the elephant trunk from the face mask. Above the horror, from the hook of a discarded farm utensil, hung an upside-down Catholic crucifix.

Shocked, Wyatt reached for his cellphone to call the police.

———•—•———

Detective Inspector Ramsey, of Yorkshire CID, was a beefy man with a nose pushed off to one side, as if he'd run into a haymaker in the pub on Saturday night.

"So you don't know the victim?"

"No," Wyatt replied.

"Never met him?"

"No."

"Then why come here to see him?"

"To look at his archive."

"What archive?"

"One that focused on a bomber called the *Ace of Clubs*. He told a friend of mine that it was spread out on the table."

"The table's bare."

"It must have been stolen."

"Why?"

"For what's in it. Balsdon linked the bomber to a Nazi traitor who was never unmasked."

"Judas?"

"Yes."

Ramsey nodded. "I read the recent interview. So what does the victim's theory have to do with you?"

"I might write a book."

"About the *Ace of Clubs*?"

"Yes. To reveal why it was shot down."

"*Another* conspiracy?"

"Huh?"

"Aren't you the author of *Dresden*?"

"Yes."

"A muckraker?" asked the detective.

"I wouldn't put it like that."

"There's a lot of money in raking muck, is there, sir?"

"Where's this going?"

"Ran out of conspiracy theories on your side of the pond, did you? Is that why you came over here to milk some of ours for cash? Your reputation is that you stop at *nothing* to get what you want. Unmasking Judas would be a coup. How far would you go, Mr. Rook, to get your hands on the key to that puzzle?"

"Are you accusing me of murder, Inspector?"

"*Detective* Inspector."

"Are you?"

"Where were you last night?"

"In London."

"All night? Early and late?"

"Yes. Why?"

"The Judas chair that spiked the victim was stolen from a museum in York hours before Mr. Balsdon was killed."

"Then I have an alibi."

"Unless you have an accomplice."

"Do you think I'd go that far to muckrake, as you call it, Detective Inspector?"

"Why did you write *Dresden*?"

"I was intrigued by a quote. The more I thought about it, the more I had to know."

"What quote?"

"At the start of the RAF's bombing campaign, Sir Arthur Harris—'Bomber' Harris to the press, and 'Butcher' Harris within Bomber Command—said, 'The Nazis entered this war under the rather childish delusion that they were going to bomb everyone else, and nobody was going to bomb them. At Rotterdam, London, Warsaw, and half a hundred other places, they put their rather naïve theory into operation. They sowed the wind, and now they are going to reap the whirlwind.' Near the end of the war—February 1945—Harris had reached the point where he could state, 'I do not personally regard the whole of the remaining cities of Germany as worth the bones of one British grenadier.' That same month, his planes unleashed hell on Dresden."

"So you took him to task?"

"Wouldn't you?"

"My grandmother died in the Blitz, and my grandfather was killed in one of the Lancasters lost in that raid."

Uh-oh, Wyatt thought.

THIRTY PIECES OF SILVER

✝

"A Judas chair?" Liz said. "Why's it called that?"

She'd met Wyatt at King's Cross Station, after his long and eventful daytrip to York. Taking a cab to his hotel in the heart of the capital, they'd headed right to the bar on the revolving top floor, and here they sat sipping drinks—a single-malt Scotch for him and a gin and tonic for her—as the lights of London slowly swirled beneath their table.

"How well do you know the Bible?"

"Minimal," Liz replied. "Just what you pick up here and there. My mom was a second-wave feminist in the burn-your-bra years. She thinks the Bible's a sexist putdown of women."

"And you?"

"I never got into it."

"God is dead?" Wyatt asked.

"I wouldn't go that far. I've never seen a burning bush, I'm not Adam's rib, and She—by that I mean God—doesn't talk to me. Until I hear from Her, I'll remain a skeptic."

"What? You didn't slip me this in that teashop?" Wyatt joked. He touched the cartilage in his throat.

"I don't get it," Liz said, popping a peanut from the bowl on the table into her mouth.

"The tree of the knowledge of good and evil grew in the Garden of Eden. God forbade Adam to eat its fruit. But the serpent—Satan in disguise—persuaded Eve to eat from the tree and share the fruit with Adam. After he took a bite, Adam became aware of his nakedness. The end result was that God expelled them from Eden and cursed Eve by commanding Adam to rule over her. Thus was born original sin, us having to wear fig leaves, and"—he wagged his finger at Liz—"the need for you to keep your blouse buttoned up."

"I'm not wearing a blouse," she said, plucking her black pullover with her fingers.

"You were in the teashop."

"What do Adam and Eve and my undone blouse have to do with a Judas chair?"

Wyatt moved his Scotch aside and placed his laptop on the table. He found what he wanted on the Internet, then turned the screen around for Liz to read:

> *By his sin, Adam, as the first man, lost the original holiness and justice he had received from God, not only for himself but for all human beings.*
>
> *Adam and Eve transmitted on to their descendants a human nature polluted by their own first sin and hence deprived of God's original holiness and justice; this deprivation we call "original sin."*
>
> *As a result of original sin, human nature is weakened in its powers, subject to ignorance, suffering, and the domination of death, and inclined to sin.*

"And that," said Wyatt, "is why you mustn't tempt a weakling like me with undone buttons."

"Original sin?"

"No. Concupiscence. The passed-on pollution."

"Con-*what*?"

"Lustful desire," he replied.

"Peanut?" Liz asked, holding one out and throwing him the sexiest of pouts.

Wyatt grinned.

He *liked* this concupiscent game.

"So what about your cartilage?" Liz prodded, eating the forbidden peanut herself.

"The Bible doesn't identify the tree of knowledge. Mediterranean tradition says it was a fig tree, because Adam and Eve used fig leaves to cover their genitals. *Malum* is the Latin adjective for 'evil.' But used as a noun, *malum* means 'apple.' When the Bible was translated from Latin by northern Europeans, a mix-up occurred, and the forbidden fruit became an apple. The larynx in my throat is more prominent than yours because the apple Eve gave Adam stuck in his gullet when he swallowed. So men have 'Adam's apples.'"

"I still don't know what a Judas chair is."

"Want another drink?"

"No, I've got a pile of work to finish up tomorrow before I leave for Germany."

Wyatt motioned to the bartender for their check.

"Christianity is based on original sin. Without mankind's fall from paradise into ongoing sin and death, there would be nothing for Jesus to redeem us *from* with his crucifixion. Without original sin, he would be a messiah without a mission. And why was Christ crucified? Because of betrayal. And who betrayed him?"

"Judas," said Liz.

"Why?"

"Greed. Thirty pieces of silver."

"That's in the Gospel of Matthew. But what's the deeper reason given in the Gospels of Luke and John?"

"Give me a clue?"

Wyatt punched the keys of his laptop and showed her the result:

Luke 22:3

Intravit autem Satanas in Iudam qui cognominatur Scarioth unum de duodecim.

"Satan?" said Liz.

Another keypunch revealed the translation, and the similar passage from the Gospel of John:

And Satan entered into Judas, who was surnamed Iscariot, one of the twelve.

John 13:2

Et cena facta cum diabolus iam misisset in corde ut traderet eum Iudas Simonis Scariotis.

And when supper was done (the devil having now put into the heart of Judas Iscariot, the son of Simon, to betray him).

"Judas is the villain of the crucifixion of Christ, yet the Bible tells us little about him," Wyatt said. "Betraying his master to the temple priests earned him a paltry sum: those thirty pieces of silver. Jesus exposed him as his traitor at the Last Supper, then left Jerusalem with his eleven faithful disciples for the Garden of Gethsemane on the Mount of Olives. During the night, Jesus awoke and warned his followers, 'Look, my betrayer is at hand.'

Judas entered the garden with troops carrying torches, clubs, and swords. He told them, 'The man I shall kiss is the one. Arrest him.' Then he walked up to Jesus and said, 'Hail, Rabbi,' and kissed him. A scuffle ensued, during which a disciple—the later St. Peter—cut one ear off the high priest's slave with his sword. Jesus patched the man up and was led off to crucifixion."

"So where does the chair come into this?" asked Liz.

"You tease me with buttons, I respond with suspense."

"You devil."

The check arrived and Wyatt paid it.

"The Bible offers two versions of how Judas died. The Gospel of Matthew says he repented and confessed his sin, then tried to give his blood money back to the priests. They refused to take it, so Judas flung the money into the temple and went off to hang himself. The money was used to buy a potter's field as a burial place for foreigners. Matthew calls it the field of blood."

"*Still* no chair," said Liz.

"The Book of Acts, the second gospel of Luke, says cryptically that"—Wyatt fingered more keys and read off the screen—"Judas possessed a field of the reward of iniquity, and being hanged, burst asunder in the midst: and all his bowels gushed out. And it became known to all the inhabitants of Jerusalem: so that the same field was called in their tongue, *Haceldama*, that is to say, The field of blood."

"Weird," said Liz.

"See the connection? Satan entered into Judas, and Judas's bowels gushed out. So during the Inquisition, Catholic torturers built a Judas chair to disembowel the Devil's disciples. And now, for some reason, that device was used on Balsdon."

"It's a house of cards," said Liz.

"What is?"

"The Bible. It demands internal consistency from the beginning—Genesis—to the close of the New Testament if it's to withstand scrutiny."

"That's why Darwinism dealt the Bible such a severe blow. There went Adam and Eve and original sin."

"It reminds me of my mother and her feminist friends."

"How so?"

"Second-wave feminists engineered a social philosophy that was internally consistent to the nth degree. They tried to rewrite language and create a non-sexist male. Victoria Frankenstein—that's how I taunt her whenever we clash over my generation. My mom and her friends are dumbfounded by sexed-up girl power."

"You're not your mother's feminist?"

"Girls just wanna have fun."

"No one—not even God—can fight genetics," Wyatt replied.

As they left the bar and headed for the elevator, Liz said, "So will you come to Germany?"

"That's difficult."

"But not impossible?"

"I have meetings set up to market my documentaries."

"They can wait. This can't. Don't you want to be there when they open the plane?"

"Of course, but—"

"My grandmother's dying," Liz interrupted. "I desperately want to unravel the secret behind her husband's disappearance before she's gone. From your point of view, how can you *not* go? Unmasking Judas would give you one hell of a book and TV show. Who knows what Christian relics might be in the Judas package, but someone thinks they are valuable enough to steal Mick's archive and gut him on a Judas chair. If you don't go, you'll regret it for the rest of your life."

They reached his floor.

The door slid open.

Wyatt stepped out into the hall.

He turned to face her.

Liz kept her finger on the Open button.

"You drive a hard bargain," he complained.

"I'm a good poker player."

"So I see."

"Y'ain't seen nothin' yet."

"I'm poor at poker."

"Why do you say that?"

"Your buttons in the teashop. If I knew how to bluff, I'd have held out for your bra."

"What bra?" Liz said, grabbing her pullover by its waist and hiking it up to her chin like a partygoer at spring break.

In the time it took him to blink, she'd pulled it back down.

"How do you like them apples?" Liz asked, mimicking the voice of the possessed girl in *The Exorcist*, then flicking her tongue like a serpent in the Garden of Eden and hooking two fingers from her temples as devil's horns.

The lift door closed and she was gone.

Actually, Wyatt was an accomplished poker player.

Yep, he thought. I'm off to Germany.

THE GREAT ESCAPE

✝

At five o'clock in the morning, the windy, cold night began to give way to the dull gray light of a winter dawn. Skinny pines with naked trunks packed together around the prisoner-of-war camp, shutting out the world and increasing the sense of isolation. Earlier, yet another RAF raid on Berlin, a hundred miles to the northwest, had plunged Stalag Luft III into blackout. But with the all-clear, the lights had returned, and now, after an uneventful yawn of guard duty, the Nazi in the "goon box"—what the prisoners called the watchtowers around the camp—was cold, tired, and bored.

Glaring south like a stilt-legged Cyclops with a ray-beam eye, this goon box was the central tower on the north perimeter. From up here, the sentry shone the searchlight over a barbed-wire fence into the *Vorlager*, an oblong yard stretching the width of the camp from the guardroom and the gate in the northeast corner. Left to right, the yard held the hospital, "the cooler," and the coal shed. The cooler was the camp's solitary confinement block, a prison within a prison for *kriegies* who tried to escape.

Kriegie was short for *Kriegsgefangene*.

Prisoner of war.

Here, in the north compound of Stammlager der Luftwaffe No. 3—Stalag Luft III—the prisoners were officers who flew with Fighter and Bomber Command.

The searchlight roamed the *Vorlager* and crossed swords with the beams of other watchtowers. A pair of fences, nine feet high and five feet apart, confined the area where the POWs should be sleeping. Between the fences, coils of barbed wire bristled spikes. Beneath the fences, buried microphones listened for sounds of digging up to fifteen feet below. Beyond the fences, a German shepherd trained to leap for the throat prowled with his *Hundführer*. Inside the fences, fifteen wooden huts were raised above the snow-covered ground on piles, with only the concrete under the stove and the washroom touching the earth. In the middle of the front row was Hut 104. Briefly, the searchlight lingered on that one-story barracks, then it moved on.

The sentries didn't know it, but the *kriegies* weren't asleep. Tonight was the night of their great escape—the culmination of a year's labor on three tunnels dubbed Tom, Dick, and Harry. Harry, the only one they finished, was the work of 650 men. It burrowed horizontally for 336 feet at 30 feet below ground. For hours, the 200 airmen selected for the break had stood crammed together in the rooms and halls of Hut 104, each waiting for his turn to go.

Deceptive escape costumes disguised this motley crew—trilby hats and plus-fours and smart business suits; ratty coats and workers' trousers and moth-eaten berets. Two were even flaunting mock "goonskins," their German uniforms topped off with belts made of paper and pistols carved from wood. All carried forged papers and escape rations: a concoction of oatmeal, chocolate, and raisins touted to provide enough calories for two days.

"Next," called a voice from the escape room.

The next airman's number was in the seventies. Unforeseen snafus had slowed the pace of escape, and with dawn streaking the horizon, the man feared missing the cutoff. The hut was divided into eighteen rooms, each fifteen feet square, with bunk beds and a corner stove. The hole down to Harry was hidden beneath the stove so the shaft could descend through the concrete block under the hut. To trick the "ferrets"—the guards with the job of detecting escapes—the men kept the stove burning night and day. Using wooden handles and a flexible pipe, the POWs could open and close the hole in twenty seconds.

"Go," said the topside controller, having inspected the airman for bulk that might jam the tunnel.

Wooden rungs guided him down the claustrophobic, thirty-foot shaft to the sand-dispersal chamber, the workshop, and the pump room. "Penguins"—named for the way they walked with bags slung inside their pants—had scattered the dug-out sand around the camp. The workshop had tooled bed boards into tunnel struts. The pumper rowed back and forth on a sliding seat to squeeze the canvas bellows that pushed fresh air along the tunnel through a pipeline of powdered milk cans.

"Lie flat on your belly," said the traffic controller at the mouth of Harry.

Holding his suitcase in front of him, the would-be fugitive stretched out on a flatbed trolley and gave the rope a tug to let the man at the other end know he was ready to be pulled. During the digging, this shuttle had carted boxes of sand, but now it was transporting men. Strips of blanket had been nailed over the first fifty feet of wooden track so the wheels would make no noise. A sensation of speed thrilled the POW as he rumbled along the hundred-foot haul with his nose three inches from the earth. The tunnel was lit by stolen wiring the men had tapped into the camp's electrical circuit. The air-raid blackout had slowed the escape to a crawl, but now the POW could see the lights of Piccadilly Circus—the name of the first of two transfer points on this underground railway—closing fast.

"Move it!" the sweating hauler snarled in the cramped bulge of the tunnel. The POW scrambled across blankets that had been laid down to keep his escape clothes clean and pulled back the trolley from halfway house number two. Another tug and he was on the move again, flying through the earth toward Leicester Square, where a second changeover launched him to the end of the line. The final fifty feet of track were also muffled with strips of blanket.

Hanging blankets deadened noise and screened light from the tunnel. Worming through, the POW reached the bottom of the exit shaft. Gazing up, he saw stars framed by the opening twenty feet above. Climbing the ladder to a rope tied to the top rung, he yanked and waited for the tug that meant all was clear. When it came, he clambered out onto the frozen snow.

Now for the tricky part: the open-air crawl from the escape hole to the woods. The Germans had cut the forest back so tunnelers would have no cover unless they extended their digging a hundred feet beyond the wire. That was the plan for Harry, but a miscalculation meant that when the last few feet of the exit shaft were dug away, the POWs found the hole *wasn't* in the woods.

Oh shit!

Plan B called for the POW to follow the signal rope to a heap of brushwood just inside the trees. The controller who kept track of the guards patrolling outside the compound would direct him from there to the meeting point in the forest, and then he and those he was traveling with would head for freedom.

Crunch . . .

Crunch . . .

Crunch . . .

More trouble!

The goon box in the center of the northernmost fence was just forty-five feet to the south, on the other side of the road to the camp's gate. With his back to the escape hole, the sentry pointed his searchlight south at the barracks. The hole was in the open, but darkness was its protector as long as the sentries pacing back and forth outside the fence didn't veer across the road to walk the edge of the woods.

Crunch . . .

Crunch . . .

Like now!

A thick column of steam rose out of the open hole. Wind whistled through the dim line of trees. The sentry had yet to adjust from the fence lamps and searchlight beams to this gloom. Was the detour just a change to cope with boredom, or was he looking for a spot to urinate? His boots crunched methodically across the snow, and the silent shadow came toward the POW lying prone beside the hole.

Twenty feet . . .

Ten feet . . .

Five feet away . . .

The sentry wore a greatcoat with belts crossing his chest. His rifle stuck up behind his square helmet. He missed the hole by inches, but his boot grazed the POW's elbow. That stopped him in his tracks, and he looked around, finally spotting the broad, black trail of slush left by the seventy-six POWs who were on the run.

Shrugging the rifle off his shoulder, the sentry raised it to his face, about to fire.

A POW behind the brushwood knew the jig was up, so he jumped from hiding and called out, *"Nicht schiessen, Posten! Nicht schiessen!"* Don't shoot, Sentry!

Bam!

The shot went wild.

Whipping out his flashlight, the sentry shone it down the hole and saw the next escaper on the ladder. Fishing out his whistle, he gave it a shrill blow.

Now the guard in the goon box was on the phone, and that drew a rush of soldiers with machine guns. On reaching the exit from the tunnel, they fanned out into the woods.

———•———

In the guardroom by the gate, the red-faced commandant screamed at the *kriegies* his men had caught near the hole. Meanwhile, his underlings were frantically placing telephone calls. When the chief of the criminal police in Breslau heard how many POWs had escaped, he ordered a *Grossfahndung*. The highest level of search in Germany, it raised the hunt nationwide.

So much smoke billowed through Hut 104 that the barracks seemed as if they were on fire. Forging papers was a serious offense, but phony IDs were the only option for "hard-arses," those unable to bluff by speaking German. With the escape blown, they burned their fake documents as fast as the stove would take them. Others crushed makeshift compasses and tore civilian buttons off their disguised uniforms, or gobbled escape rations to store away enough nourishment to survive on weeks of bread and water in the cooler.

Bam! Periodic shots cracked outside as thwarted fugitives tried to dash back to their huts through the groping fingers of the searchlights.

"Ferrets!" warned the "stooges" at the windows of Hut 104.

The first to burst in was the *Hundführer* with his Alsatian. The dog sniffed about the stove that hid the shaft to Harry. Then troops in full riot gear marched into the compound to shutter the windows of every hut and aim machine guns at the doors. *"Raus! Raus!"* the ferrets shouted as they hauled the POWs out one by one and made them strip in the lightly falling snow. "Cooler!" ordered the commandant for every POW whose clothes had been modified to look like civilian wear. Even he used the English slang for the *Vorlager* prison. Eventually, so many were jailed that the cooler ran out of room.

Outside the camp, the search for the fugitives broadened by the minute. As German radio broadcast the national alert, the SS, the armed forces, the Hitler Youth, the home guard, and all police units were called out. Old men and young boys for miles around rushed from their homes to watch over fields and lanes. Factories emptied. The Gestapo swarmed airports, set up roadblocks, and worked through moving trains, checking papers. Hotels and farms were searched. In ports like Stettin and Danzig, the Kriegsmarine watched for stowaways trying to slip across to neutral Sweden. Czech, Swiss, Danish, and French borders were secured. Before long, five million Germans were involved in the greatest manhunt of the war.

Against that maelstrom of activity, a deadlier threat to the Reich drove up the road toward Stalag Luft III. The guards in the front of the car were glued to the radio, itching to drop off their prisoner and join the search. They wanted to be sure that those loose in the countryside couldn't escape to the Allies and attack in bombers again. But the real peril to the Nazis was actually in the back seat. Their prisoner would hold the key to the outcome of the war.

"Roadblock," said the driver.

"How does that make sense?" the guard beside him asked. "We're heading *to* the camp, not away from it."

The terror-flier in back understood every word they spoke, for though he appeared to be English, his mother—long dead—had been German. His proficiency in her language was one of the reasons Bomber Command had chosen him to smuggle the Judas package back to Britain.

The roadblock was just a single car. It was parked on the shoulder, not across the road. As the vehicle carrying the RAF airman braked, the person manning the feeble roadblock hurried over to the driver's window.

"We're coming to you," the driver said, obviously recognizing the uniformed man, who looked more like a paper-pushing bureaucrat than a soldier.

"I came to intercept you. Seconds count. The Gestapo needs every available man at Sagan train station. Transfer the prisoner to my car and join the hunt."

So far, the Judas agent had followed his plan to the letter. After bailing out of the *Ace of Clubs*, he'd parachuted down to a moonlit field, where he'd shucked and buried his flying suit and his sergeant's uniform to switch identities like a chameleon. Sporting the uniform and carrying the papers of an RAF officer, he'd quickly surrendered to the local Gestapo. Now, days later, he was on his way to Stalag Luft III, the chief camp for shot-down Allied air force officers. Judas would know where to find him when the time was right to smuggle the traitor's package out of Germany.

So what was this?

A snafu?

Situation normal: all fucked up.

Eager for action, the guards hauled him out of one car and shoved him into the other. Having passed his papers and the key to his shackles to the bureaucrat, they sped off through the smudge of dawn and left him at the roadblock.

"Do you like Beethoven?" the new man asked in German.

The Judas agent tensed.

That was the code that would introduce him to his contact from the anti-Hitler conspirators.

"The *Moonlight* Sonata?" the German asked. "You bring death by moonlight."

"I prefer the *Pastoral* Symphony," the airman replied in German. "It's—how should I put it?—"

"What we all long to return to," said the bureaucrat, finishing the code Judas had provided.

Instead of driving up the road toward the camp, the German pulled the car off into the woods. Undoing the shackles, he told the Judas agent to strip to his skin and don the Nazi uniform he fetched from the trunk.

"It will fit you. I know your size. These papers will pass scrutiny by anyone who stops us. The focus will be on the escapers, not on those hunting them. From here on, you're German. Hide everything English in this satchel. We'll throw it off the first bridge we cross. This wasn't how we planned it, I know, but there's been a huge escape from Stalag Luft III. I keep the records from the gate. Instead of signing you in and sneaking you out later, I will be able to erase your very existence in the flurry of tonight's escape documents."

"Where do you hide a tree? In a forest," said the airman.

"Yes. And I'm the woodsman."

"Where are we going?"

"To hide you somewhere safe."

"And after that?"

His handler told him.

A deathtrap, if ever there was one.

CRUSADERS

✝

The smell of smoke was in the autumn air, and for a second, as he gazed through binoculars at the two people having breakfast across the street from this hotel room, the Legionary had a vision of this medieval town back in the Inquisition. Nowhere had the witch hunt been as zealous as it was in Germany. Here, there were no limits on the use of torture, and denunciations spread like wildfire. "Are you now, or have you ever been, a member of a witches' coven?" In some districts of the Rhineland, no woman over forty remained alive. Inquisitors ran so short of wood that it became necessary to burn witches in groups. In this town, it was said, so many charred stakes stood in the central square that it looked like the Black Forest after a fire.

The vision faded, but the phantom flames did not.

The Legionary watched them lick around the image magnified by the binoculars.

The man in the ring of fire was Wyatt Rook. The young priest recognized him from tabloid photos as the New York historian who'd stumbled on Balsdon's body. Tall, lean, and smartly dressed, Rook had been asked to investigate the fate of the *Ace of Clubs*. Would he be a help or a hindrance to the Legionary's crusade?

The woman encircled by hellfire was Liz Hannah. The priest paid close attention to her. Unlike a pious female, who would pull herself in so as not to offend the religiosity of holy men, this wanton wore her hair in streaked abandon, and painted her face like a whore, and fingered a button of her blouse to toy with Rook, and dressed to show off instead of hide her shame.

Was there any doubt?

The Legionary of Christ shook his head.

Beneath that godless exterior, she had a witch's tit.

———•—•———

"Why history? A good-looking bloke like you—why not the thrill of the courtroom?" Liz pressed Wyatt over a hearty breakfast the morning after they arrived in Germany.

This town sat on foundations from the Stone Age. The castle at its heart dated back a thousand years. The higgledy-piggledy buildings were mostly brown stone, with small windows and red tiled roofs. The skyline boasted fairy-tale towers, steeples, and weathervanes. Down through the years, there'd been sieges and a battle with Napoleon. A sign by the door of their quaint, renovated hotel advised that Bach and Wagn r had both slept there.

"What did you say to lure me here?"

"Many things."

"One thing in particular as you pulled up your top."

Liz rolled her eyes. "Men," she scolded. "It's *so* easy to pull your puppet strings."

"Marionette," he corrected. "That's the proper term. A puppet is a glove-like figure manipulated by hand. A marionette is a puppet-like dummy manipulated from above by strings attached to its jointed limbs."

Wyatt winked.

"That's why I study history," he added.

"To be a smarty-pants?"

"No, to solve puzzles. Everything we say or do has a history. The best cops and lawyers are historians. The history of the killer and the victim leads to murder. The best doctors are historians. The history of a patient leads to illness. The best politicians are historians. The mess in Iraq dates back centuries. I could see it coming. The politician who didn't earn a C in history at Yale."

"'How do you like them apples?' I think that was the come-on that lured you here."

"Yes," said Wyatt. "So what does that mean? You chose an idiom with a history."

Liz smirked. "Tell me."

"In the First World War, a Stokes gun fired a trench mortar that looked like an apple on a stick. Troops called the mortar rounds toffee apples. If they took out an enemy tank, the men in the trenches would shout, 'How do you like them apples?'"

"Now I grasp why you don't have a girlfriend, Mr. Rook. Dating a walking encyclopedia would drive me nuts."

"You chose me."

"Okay, here's a question: Supposedly, Bomber Command used the *Ace of Clubs* to insert a double agent into Hitler's Reich. I can see why our side kept that information from the history books. But after the Nazis lost the war, why was the German side not exposed?"

"What are you willing to bet me for the answer?"

"You are a wicked man."

"Strip poker was your idea."

"I'll bet my shoe."

"I'm not a foot fetishist."

"Let's put the shoe on the other foot, then. If you can't think up a valid answer to my question, you'll take me out to dinner dressed in drag."

"What!"

"You heard me, smarty-pants. Let's up the ante. Losing this hand will put you in touch with your feminine side."

"No wonder we got expelled from Eden."

"I'll even do your makeup."

"I have a reputation to maintain," said Wyatt.

"I'm not afraid to take my clothes off in public, but you're afraid to put them on?"

"My fear is that you'll snap a picture and put it on the Internet."

"Then you'd better not lose."

"I don't suppose you'd settle for my pants instead?"

"Nice try."

"Some like it hot, huh?"

"That's what my mother and her second-wave feminists don't grasp. *This* is what they spawned."

"I like the second wave. Puzzle out the internal consistency, then you know how to win at their game."

"I much prefer wild card poker."

"So I see."

"Playing with smart men who won't tie me down."

"Touché."

"Well? Are you chicken?"

Liz was playing him like a fish. Not for nothing was she employed as a researcher for a TV network. In playing out the line, she let him run free, peppering her conversation with Americanisms picked up from lots of movies and life in a global village. To deliver the punch lines, she'd assume an American accent. To jerk on the line, she'd drop in something homegrown like "bloke," to let him know she knew exactly who she was. And while she was teasing him verbally, she used body language to keep him on her hook.

Sex it up.

That was her third-wave game.

"In for a penny, in for a pound," he said, throwing back his best rendition of a British accent.

Liz dug in her bag and withdrew a tube of lipstick. She set it up in a phallic manner between them on the table.

"You got a purty mouth," she drawled, as if the line was strummed on a dueling banjo.

"Trying to psych me out?"

"Go on, sport. Play the ace of clubs."

"Say I'm a strategist with Bomber Command. Churchill orders me to insert a secret agent into Germany in such a way that those plotting to overthrow Hitler can find him. Why use a bomber? Because I can choose *where* to insert him. Why use the *Ace of Clubs*? Because my secret agent is among its crewmen. If an RAF officer bails out where we know the *Ace* went down, he'll almost certainly end up a POW in Stalag Luft III."

"My granddad was the only officer aboard. The rest of the airmen were sergeants."

"If I'm a strategist with Bomber Command, I can create any cover story I want. That's how secret agents stay secret. I issue him a false ID and an officer's uniform to wear under his own. Once the traitors sneak him out of Stalag Luft III, they give him a German identity. The fake ID from me is shed like a snake's skin and can't be traced by Nazi spies in Britain to a real person."

"How was he sprung from the camp?"

"Say I'm a strategist with the Judas traitors. Those opposing Hitler were in the German military. With almost ten thousand POWs from Bomber Command alone, how difficult would it be for a well-placed mole to lose track of a prisoner? Burn a piece of paper and—*poof!*—he's gone. He could vanish during a purge, when prisoners were being moved from one camp to another. Or he could vanish as a ghost, a POW who fakes an escape and hides in the camp, then escapes for real when the guards are off hunting for him."

"Is that your theory?"

Wyatt shook his head. "My bet is they used the Great Escape. Shortly after the *Ace* went down, seventy-six POWs broke out of Stalag Luft III. Hitler was enraged and ordered all be shot. The head of the Luftwaffe thought that would be a mistake. It would look like murder, and there could be reprisals against German POWs. Hitler compromised, and fifty were shot. All but three of the escapees were caught. And the man who decided who should live and who should die was Artur Nebe.

"Nebe put each man's name and personal details on an index card. He shuffled through them and said, 'This one is very young. He can stay alive.' Or, 'This man has no children. He'll be one of them.' Those culled for death were shot in small groups in the woods along the roads back to the camp.

"It turned out that Nebe was among the traitors plotting against Hitler. When the assassination failed, he and five thousand others were arrested. Though tortured for two months, he betrayed no one. He and the other leaders of the conspiracy were hanged by piano-wire nooses strung from meat hooks. The slow strangulations were filmed for Hitler to view later."

"So you think Nebe let the Judas agent slip away?"

Wyatt shrugged. "I'm saying there are many ways the agent could disappear. And if Judas and those advancing his plot got caught up in the executions . . ."

"That would explain why the German side wasn't exposed after the war. Judas and his ilk were dead."

Wyatt cocked his finger at Liz. "I win," he said. "*You* guessed the answer, so it must be logical."

The tube of lipstick returned to her bag.

"The next time we bet," Wyatt said, "let's go back to wagering for your clothes."

"Want to up the ante again?" Liz asked.

"How?"

"Let's go for broke."

She pretended to push her entire stash of poker chips to the center of the table.

"Since you seem to work to incentive," she said, "I'll make you an all-or-nothing deal. If you can solve the puzzle of where my granddad is now, I'll *fuck* the socks off you, Mr. Rook."

Well, there you have it.

The thinking man's conundrum.

A choice between divergent views of the world.

On the one hand, there was original sin. Adam and Eve, the apple and the snake, in the Garden of Eden. Here was a modern Eve, tempting him with her apples, while he, thanks to concupiscence, was teetering on the brink. He knew he should wag his finger at her, refuse to be made a sex object (her mother would like that), and demand that their clergy get together to work out sinless Marquis of Queensberry rules before any rumpy-pumpy.

The high road.

On the other hand, there was human evolution. My, how Darwin had tossed a monkey wrench into righteousness. Ninety-nine percent of his genes were the same as those of a chimp. Most of his body language came from the R-complex—the old reptile brain—at the top of his spinal cord. Like a snake flicking its tongue. This sexy stuff originated in the limbic system—the irrational mammalian brain—lurking at the center of his noggin. Home of the four Fs: feeding, fighting, fleeing, and fucking. And the game-playing? That came from his cerebral cortex—the rational brain—the new kid on the block. All that was happening here was survival of the species, and what if he took the high road and then got hit by a bus?

He'd never get to taste the apple.

Tsk-tsk ...

"Fuck the socks off me, huh?" he said.

"Don't tell me you know the origin of that idiom, too?"

"I believe the expression is '*knock* the socks off you.' It dates back to fisticuff days in the nineteenth century. That's boxing hyperbole for a knockdown fistfight so savage that the loser got knocked out of his socks as well as his shoes.

"But, hey, let's not quibble. I much prefer a carrot to a stick."

Wyatt held out his hand.

"You're *on*, Ms. Hannah," he said.

The hotel room across the street was the Art Historian's. Growing weaker by the day, he was on a crusade as important as any undertaken by Christian knights to the Holy Land. If he didn't find his Holy Grail soon, leukemia would end his life. So while the Legionary spied on Liz and Wyatt, the dying man sat in the shadow of the priest, listening to Balsdon's screams and reading the sergeant's archive.

"Jesus Christ!" the German exclaimed, tearing the headphones off his ears when he could no longer take the confession his agent had extracted with the Judas chair.

The Legionary turned.

"Don't swear," he said, glowering at the cringing man.

"I can't hear what he's saying through the shrieks. Why's there an echo in the recording?"

"I held the recorder at the end of a tube from an oxygen mask on his face."

"Did he reveal anything new?"

"No, just what's in his archive. He repeated the name of the Judas agent several times."

"That's merely his suspicion. These papers contain no proof. Nor does the archive"—the Art Historian flicked a dismissive hand at the other papers stolen by the Legionary—"of the crewman he suspected of betraying the *Ace of Clubs*."

"Let's pray there's a clue in the bomber itself," said the young priest.

"And use this fellow Rook."

"Do you know him?"

"No, but I just finished reading his books. He's a digger, and he's got an inquiring mind. In his search for Hitler's Judas, he might stumble across our Holy Grail."

"Who was Hitler's Judas?" the Legionary asked.

"I'll give you three clues, and you can puzzle it out. Play detective on the Internet.

"Clue one: Cyrenaica.

"Clue two: Blue Max.

"Clue three: *Wüstenfuchs*."

GRAVEDIGGERS

✝

War of the Worlds.

Alien.

The Thing.

Standing on the rim of the pit above the *Ace of Clubs*, Wyatt felt as if he had wandered onto the set of one of those science fiction films in which a crashed UFO has cratered the ground. He hoped aliens would emerge from the wreckage.

Nope.

What impressed him first was the *size* of the unearthed bomber. Its wingspan was a hundred feet, its length seventy feet, and its height twenty feet or more. He'd once seen a photo of squadron crews fronting a similar plane. Wingtip to wingtip, it took more than thirty men to span a Halifax.

Surprisingly, the aircraft was still intact. The *Ace* had belly-landed in a valley, skidding along this hollow flanked by trees. The force of the crash had destabilized one slope, causing a landslide to crumble down and bury the plane. With bombs dropping night and day, churned-up dirt was the rule, not the exception. If a plane falls in a forest and there's no one around to see it, does that imprint a memory?

Evidently not.

So here the *Ace* had languished for sixty-odd years, camouflaged by the neglect of East Germany, a Communist country virtually frozen in time at the end of Hitler's war. Only the fall of the Berlin Wall had lured development east, and now autobahns were reunifying its medieval cities with the west.

Highways like this one.

With the biggest pothole in the world.

"This reminds me of *Gulliver's Travels*," said Sgt. Earl Swetman. With the recent death of Mick Balsdon on the Judas chair, Sweaty—that's how he'd introduced himself at the hotel—was the sole survivor of the *Ace*'s crew. Once a redhead with a freckled face, he now sported white hair and liver spots.

With a little imagination, this could have been Lilliput. The gigantic plane did resemble a staked-down man—his head the cockpit, his crucified arms the wings, his belly button the mid-upper turret, his feet the double-finned tail. An anthill of little people swarmed around the castaway. By squinting his eyes, Wyatt could turn the salvage scene into Gulliver lashed to the beach in Jonathan Swift's novel.

"I don't like that," said Sweaty.

"What?" Wyatt asked.

"The rear turret. The guns point back."

"Shouldn't they?"

"Not for bailing out. The quickest way for Ack-Ack to escape would have been to swivel his turret to point like that, open the doors behind his seat to grab his chute from just inside the fuselage of the plane, then rotate the turret to one side. With the guns pointing left or right, he could backflip out the opening and drop from the other side."

"So if Ack-Ack did that, the guns should still be pointing sideways?"

"Yeah, not to the rear. The way they're pointing means the turret doors open *into* the plane."

"Could he escape that way?" asked Liz.

"Sure. But he didn't. Before I bailed, I glanced along the fuselage tunnel. I saw the mid-upper gunner descend from his turret. I didn't see the rear gunner crawl forward."

"He didn't get out?" said Wyatt.

"That's my fear."

Under a sodden gray sky threatening rain, these four who had met up in Germany circled the unearthed plane. The trek was slow, as Sweaty struggled with a gimpy leg. "I hurt it when I landed after bailing out," he explained. "By the time you reach my age, your chickens come home to roost. I'm booked for a hip replacement once I return to the States. But I couldn't miss this. I owe these guys. And I've got to know *why* we went down that night."

Like Sweaty, their fourth member—about thirty, well dressed and obsessively groomed—was also from the States. He'd told the others at the meet-and-greet this morning at the hotel that he was Lenny Jones, Trent Jones's grandson.

Trent Jones had been the mid-upper gunner.

"Liz Hannah," Liz had said, offering her hand. "Granddaughter of Fletch Hannah, the *Ace of Clubs*' pilot."

"Wyatt Rook."

"I've heard of you," Lenny said, shaking his hand. "The historian, right?"

Wyatt nodded.

"So," asked Lenny, "how do you fit in?"

"I hired him," Liz responded. "My family wants to know why my granddad disappeared."

"We have that in common."

"Yes," Liz said, agreeing. "Our grandfathers and Ack-Ack were the three crewmen who vanished that night."

———·•·———

The four of them had driven here in Wyatt's rental car. A rural road ran parallel to the graded bed of the new autobahn. The routes split up at the mouth of the valley cradling the *Ace*. The old road arced around to leave the hollow as it was, while the highway under construction plowed through the virgin meadow. Just as the plane had done when it crashed in 1944.

Luckily for Sweaty, given the state of his leg, dump trucks hauling earth away had rutted a makeshift path. Armed with an official pass to the site, Wyatt had bumped them along the track until the VW reached the pothole.

The manmade pit was more than a hundred feet across.

Big enough for the *Ace*.

Not to be thwarted by the inconvenience of salvaging the plane, road construction continued on up the valley. Once the *Ace* had been trundled off to a British museum—at the end of the war, the RAF had scrapped every Halifax not lost in combat—the road crew would fill in the pit and run the autobahn over top.

That, thought Wyatt, is why German trains run on time.

Halfway around the rim of the pit, Lenny pointed to the mid-upper turret and asked, "Why did my grandfather crew with you that night?"

"Our regular gunner—we called him De Count—was pulled from ops and branded LMF."

"What's LMF?"

"Lack of moral fiber," Sweaty explained.

"What does that mean?"

"He cracked under the strain. There were many ways a guy could get the chop. Get killed. Planes could crash on takeoff or in flight. Planes above could drop their bombs in error on our heads. Planes beside could wander into our space. Enemy fighters or flak could shoot us down or set us afire, and we'd be gone. Ditch in the sea, and we'd drown or freeze to death. If oxygen failed, hello anoxia. Frostbite and icing could weigh us down. Stripped to basics, the *Ace* was a flying bomb loaded with gas and ammunition. A bullet, a spark, a leak—any one could blow us sky-high long before we got to club the target."

"Heavy duty," Lenny said.

"Literally. The stress from each op accumulates. Operational twitch. Loss of nerve. Mental exhaustion. Shellshock. Signs were everywhere. The RAF had a single word to cover all those conditions: cowardice. LMF was the euphemism."

"Sounds draconian."

"It was. They thought LMF was contagious. The 'infected man' was swiftly marched away to quarantine, then humiliated, vilified, and drummed out of Bomber Command. Demoted, he was sent to the army, the navy, or down the mines. 'LMF' was stamped on his file to plague him the rest of his life. His flying badge got forfeited. In the case of De Count, that was ironic."

"Why?" asked Lenny.

"The air gunner's brevet had the letters 'AG' to the left of a single wing with twelve feathers. Originally, there were thirteen, but that could bring bad luck. To quell superstition, the brass clipped a feather off with nail scissors."

"But the jinx got De Count anyway?"

"Bingo," Sweaty said.

"Why such harsh treatment?"

"As a deterrent. The strain affected all of us to varying degrees. If there'd been a way to leave ops with honor, a lot of men would've bailed out. Instead, they kept on flying until their number came up. God knows how many planes went down because men who were afraid of the LMF stigma continued to fly when they shouldn't have."

"Do you know what broke De Count?"

"Probably. Another crew in the squadron came home from a shaky do. The Achilles heel of a British bomber was its underbelly. A Halifax had no ventral turret. Not only did flak batteries blast up from below, but Nazi night fighters were armed with upward-slanting cannons to give us a kick in the gut.

"The plane that ran into trouble took a double hit. A night fighter blew the balls off its mid-upper gunner. The castrated man dropped from his turret with both hands between his legs. He ran around, jumping up and down, screaming, 'I've been hit!' Then flak tore a leg off the bomb-aimer. The wireless operator spent the next two hours lying in a pool of blood in the frigid nose cone, trying to keep a tourniquet cinched around the injured man's stump. The bombardier was thrashing about in pain and had to be subdued, so the radioman kept knocking him out with punches from his fist.

"When the stricken bomber landed, we were out at the pan. Every man knew that could be him—castrated or legless—on the next op. De Count was shaking. His face blanched white."

"Stress with a capital S!" said Lenny.

Sweaty winced. "I should have seen it coming. One day, about a week before De Count cracked, they lined us up in the crew room for important news. Her Majesty was on her way to pay us a visit. We were told in no uncertain terms how to behave. When she offered us her hand, we were to say nothing more than 'How do you do, ma'am.' Hours later, the queen arrived at the air station. When she offered De Count her hand, he was overcome. Grasping her palm in both of his, he wouldn't let go. He kept saying, 'I'm so pleased to meet Your Majesty . . . So pleased . . . So pleased . . . So pleased . . .' That breached every rule in the book, but the queen was gracious. All she did was put her other hand on top of his and say, 'No more pleased than I am to meet you, Sergeant, I assure you.'

"I thought De Count was going to cry.

"Shortly after, he went to the wingco and refused to fly."

"LMF," said Lenny.

Sweaty nodded. "The poor bastard. What a dirty label. How many guys found ways to avoid risking their lives for their country? Cowards who spent the war behind a desk? De Count stepped up to the plate and took it for as long as he could. The guy *volunteered* for dangerous duty, then suffered disgrace."

"So you got my granddad?"

"Trent was an 'odd bod,' a spare gunner attached to no particular crew. Having lost his own plane in a crash over the North Sea—he bailed out through the rear hatch just in time— he tagged onto any crew short of a gunner."

"What was he like?"

"As a marksman? We took him up for an air test before that fatal flight. Ack-Ack gave him a thumbs-up on how he handled the turrets and the guns. Jonesy exemplified the air gunner's unofficial motto: 'We aim *not* to please.'"

The three listeners laughed.

"What was he like as a man?" Lenny asked.

"Quiet. Withdrawn. Skinny. Eaten up inside. He said his wife had left him and taken their child. She was in Australia, if memory serves me right."

"It does. That child was my mom. She married an American. That's where I was born."

"Where do you call home?"

"Now? I recently moved to Wales. My mom leased a house in my granddad's hometown and we took back her maiden name. We hope to stay there for a year and dig into our ancestors' Welsh history. That's why I'm here on this odyssey. To learn how my granddad died."

"De Count?" said Wyatt. "What became of him?"

"He blamed himself for jinxing the crew after the *Ace* went down in Germany. I spent the rest of the war in a Stalag Luft camp. Only when I got home did I hear what had happened to him. The day De Count was told the *Ace* went missing, he took the opportunity to hang himself."

SKELETON CREW

As Wyatt walked the length of the resurrected bomber, he took in details of the fuselage. Dark green and brown camouflage colors mottled the top of the Halifax, with matte black along the sides and below. A playing card—the ace of clubs—and that nickname, chosen by the crew, were painted under the pilot's window at the nose of the plane. The rows of clubs beneath that represented the bombing ops completed by the *Ace*. Both wings bore the bull's-eye insignia of the RAF, as did the fuselage back near the entry door. For having survived a crash and landslide burial, the bomber was in surprisingly good shape. Cannon-shell damage was solely to the tail.

Twin fins and rudders book-ending high-mounted mini-wings formed the tail assembly. Where the alloy skin was shot away, the historian could see the spars of the metal skeleton. Peppered with holes, both fins were chunked as if they'd been chewed by sharks. No wonder the *Ace* had gone down.

"Amazing," Sweaty marveled. "That's what I call luck. The night fighter ripped the tail to rat shit on *both* sides of the gunner, but the turret wasn't smashed."

"Anyone see a bullet hole?" Wyatt asked.

The others shook their heads.

"So gunners who live in glass houses *can* throw stones," declared Liz.

"If Ack-Ack didn't bail out and he wasn't shot, what happened to him?" Lenny asked.

"I didn't say he wasn't shot," Sweaty replied. "Even if the turret is undamaged, the night fighter could have drilled him through the hole in the bubble."

"What hole?" inquired Liz.

Sweaty pointed. "See the missing panel? Off the assembly line, a Boulton Paul turret offered the illusory protection of a totally enclosed Perspex cupola. But miles up in the night skies over the Reich, the temperature outside the unheated turret sank to minus sixty degrees Fahrenheit. That's numbingly cold. Just as a car windshield does in the winter, the glass surrounding Ack-Ack would mist over and then freeze up."

"So he removed the panel?" asked Liz.

"Lots of gunners did. Without a rear turret, a plane was a sitting duck, so night fighters blasted in from behind and below. Too many bombers lurched home with a shattered rear turret and a dead gunner inside. I could tell you stories of wounded guys with half a turret who kept on firing as long as they had a functioning gun. Once that ran out of ammunition, they sat defenseless in the teeth of Nazi cannons, advising their skippers on evasion maneuvers until they were dead."

The four were standing at the tail of the *Ace*, sighting up the fuselage as if it were a bowling alley and the turret a ball about to rumble down its lane. From this spot on the far edge of the pit, Wyatt saw why the rear gunner huddled in the loneliest outpost in the sky.

"An arse-end Charlie," Sweaty said, "had a hairy job. Crouched in total darkness, Ack-Ack searched the night for telltale shadows that might solidify into oncoming fighters. Up, across, down, and back again, he moved his turret quarter by quarter behind the *Ace*, convinced that every speck on the glass was a Junkers 88. Of all his weaponry, our rear gunner's best defense was his 'Eyeball, Mark I'"—Sweaty poked a finger at his own eye—"so that's why he removed the panel from in front of his turret seat."

"To see better," Liz said.

"Yeah. For *clear* vision. So if the Junkers that got us shot through that gap, he sure as shootin' hit Ack-Ack."

"One way to find out," Wyatt said, and he reached into his pocket for his gravedigger's pass.

At times like this it paid to have a translated history of Dresden riding high on German bestseller lists, as well as powerful contacts within the ranks of military historians.

Contacts like Rutger, who had arranged the pass.

You reached the bottom of the pit through a cluster of ladders, the top rungs of which were controlled by no-nonsense security guards. Waving his pass, Wyatt descended from Lilliput to the topsy-turvy realm of Brobdingnag. Wyatt was a miniature Gulliver dwarfed by the humongous plane.

The *Ace* lay on its belly in the cradle of earth, its wings supported by platforms of dirt. Astern of the port wing was the entry door. By luck, the historian approached just as the hatch was being forced open by the Jaws of Life.

Wyatt peered inside.

A time capsule, he thought.

Rutger, Germany's foremost historian on the Second World War, turned out to be a magic key, he was held in such high esteem. One look at the pass he'd procured and the men of the entry team were inviting Wyatt along on the first foray into the bomber since 1944.

By way of welcome, they gave him a flashlight.

The Wyatt who entered the fuselage had three eyes in his head—the two flanking his nose and the one in his mind. His mind's eye didn't live in the twenty-first century. Instead, it pictured the *Ace* as it was the moment before the Junkers 88 raked the tail.

He was back in Hitler's war.

Along the deep, oval-ribbed tunnel to his left, Wyatt pictured the phantom lower body of the mid-upper gunner in the dorsal turret. The head, shoulders, and arms of the ghost would be in the bubble. Up front, past the deafening roar of the four radial engines, he imagined the over-under quintet who flew the Halifax. Side by side in the cockpit were the pilot, Wrath Hannah, and Ox Oxley, his flight engineer. Below, the wireless operator, Sweaty Swetman, fronted the curtained-off cubicle of Balls Balsdon, the navigator. Beyond, in the extreme nose, hunched the bomb-aimer, Nelson Trafalgar.

A walkway ran the length of the fuselage, past Wyatt's position to the rear turret. As he swept the flashlight beam toward the tail, he saw the *Ace* for what it was: a flying bomb more dangerous to its crew than to the enemy.

Two thousand gallons of gas sloshed in the fuel tanks. Gun turrets, flaps, and flying controls fed off miles of pipeline filled with flammable hydraulic oil. In the bomb bay lurked tons of high explosives and firebombs. Oxygen lines, electrical wires, and intercom cables could—with a single spark—blow the *Ace* to bits without help from Nazi flak guns or night fighters. Ten thousand rounds of ammunition were belt-fed back along the port side by four ammo tracks linking the forward magazines to the rear turret. Set them off like firecrackers and the plane would turn into a shooting gallery.

No wonder Sir Arthur Harris, the man who sent the death-traps out night after night, was nicknamed "Butch" by those at the "sharp end" of Bomber Command.

"Butch" for "the Butcher."

With his spine to the cockpit, Wyatt closed the distance to the rear turret. The hoops overhead and the stretched metal skin reminded him of the flatbed of a covered wagon. Shut, the turret's concave doors bulged toward him. Caught in the beam of the flashlight just outside the doors, the gunner's parachute offered a strong clue that instead of bailing out, Ack-Ack had gone down with the *Ace*.

Straining, Wyatt opened the sliding doors.

Unlike the ghosts his mind had seen manning the forward combat positions, the sole remaining warrior of a *real-life* skeleton crew occupied the rear turret. So claustrophobic was the cage-like turret that it reminded Wyatt of a Tower of London torture chamber known as the Little Ease. The dimensions of that room were such that no matter how a prisoner contorted himself, he couldn't stretch out in any direction. Before long, the cramped quarters snapped his mind.

The same was true of the little ease of this rear turret. In life, the tail gunner had crouched almost immobile within his goldfish bowl for the six, eight, or ten hours of a bombing run, unable to stretch and relieve the kinks in his back, legs, and arms. Surrounded by metal and Perspex, he sat on the hard, backless bench with supports under his arms. His hands gripped the operating stick jutting through a diamond-shaped hole in the control table. Moving the stick left and right swiveled the turret. Pulling and pushing the stick raised and lowered the guns. The four Browning .303s were mounted in pairs on both sides of the control stick, and were linked to the reflector sight in front of the gunner's eyes. Aiming with that gunsight, he saw an illuminated dot in the center of a glowing circle. The guns were fired by triggers on the control stick. Each spat out 1,150 rounds per minute. In effect, like a turtle, the man and his shell were one. That's why there was no room inside for his parachute.

Ever the historian, Wyatt knew his subject.

For a moment more, his mind lingered in 1944. Cut off from the rest of the *Ace*'s crew by half the length of the plane, with only the crackling of muted voices in his earphones to assure him that other humans were flying this op too, Ack-Ack braved the freezing air let in by the missing Perspex panel. The only sounds were the soft hiss of oxygen in his mask and the creaks and groans of the turret reacting to high altitude. Six-inch icicles hung from the rubber of his face mask. With his goggles pushed up on his brow so he could see, he blinked repeatedly to keep his eyelashes from freezing. His eyes watered, his nose ran, and cold seeped into his multi-layered battledress. With the chill came a lethargy that undermined his efforts to stay alert.

Then he saw it!

Through the missing panel!

The outline of an incoming Junkers 88!

Rat-a-tat-tat!

Bullets tore through his chest.

Down came the *Ace*.

Followed by the landslide.

And here the plane lay buried for sixty-odd years, as time reduced the rear gunner to this skeleton.

The desiccated remains were still on the turret seat, the torso sprawled forward on the control table between the guns. Through the hole created by the missing panel, Wyatt could see Liz, Sweaty, and Lenny watching from the rim of the pit. The rotting flesh within had reduced the Michelin Man to a shroud draping bones. Daylight struggled to filter through the dirty bubble, so Wyatt enhanced it with the flashlight's beam. He shone the pool on the back of the corpse to illuminate three holes near the spine, seemingly made when night-fighter bullets blew out exit wounds.

That's when the historian spotted something protruding from one of the holes.

Strange, he thought, extracting it.

What Wyatt held in his hand forced him to rethink the puzzle he'd believed the crash of the *Ace* had posed.

The puzzle wasn't why Ack-Ack hadn't bailed out.

The puzzle was *how* he had died.

INQUISITION

THE VATICAN

How many people did God kill when the act of original sin filled Him with disgust?

Answer: Every living creature on earth, except the few Noah saved with his ark. Genesis 6:5–7.

How many sinners did God kill in Sodom and Gomorrah because they'd engaged in perverted sex?

Answer: Every living thing. Genesis 19:24–25.

How many sinners did Moses kill under God's command because they turned against Him?

Answer: About 3,000. Exodus 32:27–28.

How many sinners did God kill for daring to look into the Ark of the Covenant, the chest holding the stone tablets with the Ten Commandments?

Answer: 50,070. 1 Samuel 6:19.

How many Israelites did God deliver into the hands of the men of Judah to slaughter?

Answer: Half a million. 2 Chronicles 13:14–18.

How many Ethiopians did God kill for His chosen people?

Answer: One million. 2 Chronicles 14:9–13.

How many Assyrians did God kill after their king and his servants made fun of Him?

Answer: 185,000. Isaiah 37:36.

How many sinners did God kill in one day for having sex outside of marriage?

Answer: 23,000. 1 Corinthians 10:8.

And when God eventually completes His killing spree, how many sinners will be dead?

Answer: Enough to cover the earth. Jeremiah 25:32–33.

So says the Bible. The Word of God. And either you believe it or you don't. If you *believe* it, you will have no doubt that God isn't into Wrath Lite. God demands worship, and sinners suffer His wrath, either in this world or in the next. And the Secret Cardinal also believed two more truths: that Christian devotion is *objective* and outside the realm of free thought, and that the most sacred duty of the Roman Catholic Church is to protect that original deposit of faith.

Thus the Inquisition.

To those who worked in the Palace of the Holy Office, the heart of the present-day Congregation for the Doctrine of the Faith, the word "inquisition" was a sacred one. Inquisition was a procedure developed by Roman law. It left the entire process of investigation, accusation, interrogation, trial, and punishment in the hands of a single official. Inquisition built the Roman Empire, and after that empire was Christianized by Constantine, inquisition guarded the Roman Catholic Church.

Inquisition was—and *is*—defense of the faith.

Who was the first inquisitor? God, of course. The first inquisition was God's handling of the Satan-inspired original sin of Adam and Eve in the Garden of Eden. "God became the first and greatest teacher of the Inquisitors of heretical depravity," wrote Luis de Pàramo, the canon of Leon and the inquisitor of

Sicily, "Himself providing them with the example of a just and legal punishment."

Jesus, John the Baptist, St. Peter, St. Paul, and the other apostles were inquisitors too, and from them, the Catholic popes inherited their inquisitorial powers. Before the sixteenth century, popes appointed individual priests as inquisitors. From then on, they empowered the Inquisition to stamp out heresy. Today—when public relations requires inquisitors to hide— modern popes are back to appointing individual priests.

Secret cardinals protecting the faith.

That sacred duty would never wane.

And to the mind of this inquisitor, the threat posed by the Judas relics was greater even than the heresy of 1517, when Martin Luther nailed his 97 Theses to the door of the Catholic Church in Wittenberg, Germany, touching off the Protestant Reformation.

Today, there are two billion Christians in the world.

Only half are Catholic.

It distressed the Secret Cardinal to think of all those souls lost to Christ and his Church because Satan had lured the blind away through Orthodox and Protestant heresy.

But never again.

Not on *his* Vatican watch.

So while it saddened him to read about the torturous death of Mick Balsdon in the tabloids spread across his desk, he couldn't help thinking that it wasn't a steep sacrifice in the larger scheme of things.

At least Balsdon got to equate his suffering with the love of God, as the Secret Cardinal had in the Philippines.

That—to the heart and soul of this inquisitor—was the greatest sin of the secular world.

It didn't *love* suffering.

Finished with the papers, the Secret Cardinal got up from his desk and crossed to the windows. As he gazed out from his sanctuary behind the Vatican walls, the inquisitor could hear billions of people wailing in despair, wondering why God allows brutality and injustice to overwhelm the earth. Has that not always been the vexing question of Christian life?

When Christ was crucified, who watched him suffer from the foot of the cross? His mother, the Virgin Mary. Imagine the torture! But what did she do? *The Lamentation*, that Christus painting, shows that she embraced his suffering as her own. "I am here, and I am suffering with you." Is that not what her presence said? All suffering is meant to be an expression of love, for true love takes on pain as its own.

The holy art of suffering isn't easy to learn. Christ didn't come to abolish the cross we bear. He came to lie down on the cross *for* us. Love is not only to suffer with but to suffer *for*. As he laid down his life for us, Christ was saying: "Come close to my heart that has bled *for* you; that has suffered *for* you; that was pierced by a lance *for* you." He suffered for us so the gates of heaven could reopen for us. That's the meaning of Christianity. To suffer isn't a tragedy. It's a test of faith. That's why the earth is soaked to its core with tears. So we can equate our suffering with the love of God.

The Secret Cardinal had grasped that in the Philippines, and he'd be damned if he was going to allow the Judas relics to destroy it.

The priest thought back . . .

It was Easter in the Philippines, so the faithful were cele-brating. *Semana Santa*. Holy week. In the village of San Pedro Cutud, a depressed little barrio on the outskirts of San Fernando City, forty-odd miles north of Manila, Lenten rites were under way. In the colonial era, Augustinian and Dominican friars had planted the faith, and the Philippines of today are predominantly Catholic. Nowhere in the Christian world—the Vatican included—do the faithful act out like this.

Tsssk! Tsssk! . . .

Tsssk! Tsssk! . . .

The Catholic priest and the boy with him acted like father and son. Surrounded by fresh green palms festooned with red ribbons, the two jostled for position to watch the parade. Along both sides of the crowded road, the residents of Cutud stood at the windows of their cinder-block houses gawking like the tourists, or they did a brisk business selling chips, fried fish balls, water, and San Miguel beer at refreshment stands out front. The morning sun had hours to go before it reached its zenith, but already stifling heat radiated off the dusty landscape.

Tsssk! Tsssk! . . .

Tsssk! Tsssk! . . .

The parade of barefoot, shirtless, faceless men—their heads veiled with black hoods held in place by crowns of thorns that were in fact leaves—streamed along both sides of the narrow, two-lane road. Judging by their wobbling, some had fortified themselves with *gin bulag*, the kind of alcohol that can make you blind. Flagellation was an all-male ritual, and boys as young as ten marched with the men to learn how penance could wash away their sins. The whips they used to scourge their backs were made of braided thongs tipped with bamboo sticks.

Tsssk! Tsssk! . . .

Tsssk! Tsssk! . . .

The sound of wood flaying raw flesh, splattering blood left and right.

The push of the crowd blocked retreat.

Girls squealed as blood drops spattered their clothes.

Occasionally, the men would pause so an assistant could pound on their backs with a wooden mallet embedded with glass. At other times, they would stop and lie face down on the road, offering onlookers a chance to deliver blows. Photographers would zoom in for money shots of shredded backs, then the procession would move on.

"That must hurt," said the boy.

"Yes," replied the priest.

"Why do they hurt themselves?"

"To live their faith. Self-mortification is how they get close to the suffering of Christ."

"Should I hurt myself?"

"No. There's no need. Jesus hurt himself for you and me. He died so we can be forgiven for our sins."

"I'm hot," said the boy.

"Take off your shirt. I'll rub this lotion on your skin so you won't burn."

As the broiling sun rose toward noon, the Filipino penitent playing the role of Christ was sentenced to death in the village's dusty basketball court. From there, he began the two-mile trek to Cutud's Golgotha, a rice field with a mound holding three black crosses. The way to Calvary was led by a Roman centurion riding a white stallion and carrying a long spear. Legionaries in red robes and glinting helmets marched beside the *Kristo* shouldering his cross. Crying Filipina women shuffled behind, playing the Virgin Mary and Mary Magdalene. As Jesus fell to his knees from the weight of the cross, they grabbed the hem of his garment and begged the Romans to free him.

"Can we see Judas, too?" asked the boy.

"If you wish," replied the priest.

In Minalin, also in the province of Pampanga, people would stuff a life-size effigy of Judas Iscariot with firecrackers, then blast him into bits and pieces with shouts like "You deserve it, traitor!"

How could the priest deny a boy as beautiful as this one?

Surrogate father and son.

Never had the missionary felt as parched, burnt, and hot as he did amid this sweaty mob surging toward Golgotha. The heat, the horde, the hawkers, the din. Was this what it was like when they crucified Christ? A circus? A Coca-Cola van inched its way toward the mound, and in his mind, the priest could hear the commercial: "The crucifixion of Jesus Christ is brought to you by Coke. Coca-Cola. It's the real thing!" Overhead, streamers advertised Tang. That would taste better than vinegar on a sponge, thought the priest. A stall at the side of the road was stocked with toys. Plastic guns and hand grenades. What more did the faithful need to celebrate Good Friday? For entrepreneurs, this was like Christmas. Some would earn a year's income in a single day.

Water, thought the priest.

"I thirst!"

That's what Jesus had cried from the cross.

Ahead, beyond the wide-brimmed hats and sun umbrellas, the hill was ringed with barbed wire. Authorities parted the press of people to let the *Kristo* through. As the two Marys knelt on the slope of Golgotha and began to wail, the executioner stripped Jesus down to his loincloth. This year, Jesus was a housepainter who had fallen several stories from a ladder and survived, and so was offering his thanks to God. The men who would flank him on the other crosses hoped God would cure a sick child or restore wavering faith.

As attendants positioned Jesus on the middle cross, setting his feet on a shelf to support his weight and strapping his wrists to the horizontal beam, the executioner held up a fistful of nails. The boy broke away from the priest and ran to see.

Was it the insufferable heat?

Was Satan tempting him?

The priest watched the boy run to Jesus, and as he ran, the shorts covering his buttocks seemed to vanish, as if his nakedness belonged in Eden . . .

With a jolt, the Secret Cardinal was back in the Vatican, grinding a thumbnail into the scar filling the hole through his other palm.

Among the thousands of files on priests under investigation by the Palace of the Holy Office, two hundred concerned "sexual abusers" in the Philippines.

There was no file on the Secret Cardinal.

He had been saved from sin by the scourge and the cross.

Out there, beyond the walls of the Vatican, the boy, now grown into the Legionary, advanced the crusade.

The Secret Cardinal prayed he wouldn't wake up tomorrow to the words "Vatican Hit Man Arrested!"

IMPOSSIBLE CRIME

GERMANY

It was Oktoberfest in Germany, and the beer hall was packed. Had this been the Munich Hofbräuhaus tent, there would have been ten thousand inebriants drowning in a sea of suds. True, this wasn't Bavaria, but the local brewmaster was capitalizing on Oktoberfest all the same. In the far corner played an oompah band, leading the drinkers in a rousing version of "Beer Barrel Polka." The Ratskeller trapped the aromas of bratwurst, *spätzle*, and sauerkraut. Brewmeisters in lederhosen tapped huge wooden kegs while strong Brunnhildes in dirndls hoisted trays of glass mugs. Their server was too buxom for the low-cut, tight confines of her lacy blouse and cross-stitched bodice, so when she bent over the table, she almost put out Lenny's eye.

Sweaty sighed.

"If only I were younger."

"I've heard stories about you and the WAAFs in the mess," teased Liz.

"Unfounded rumors."

"Not according to them."

"She likes you, Lenny," Sweaty said, nodding his head toward the retreating waitress.

"Lenny Jones!" Liz ragged. "I do believe you're *blushing*."

"She's not my type," he replied.

"Not your type! She's female, ain't she?" Sweaty said. "Youth really *is* wasted on the young."

They were almost shouting to be heard above the oom-pahing tuba and the arm-locked drunks singing at the top of their lungs. Thankfully, the band stopped to swill some hops, too, reducing the roar by a zillion decibels.

"Hear that sound?" Wyatt said, wiggling a finger in his ear as if to clear it of water. "That's me thinking."

Sweaty hoisted his beer mug. "To Ack-Ack!" he said.

They clinked glasses and downed gulps, leaving foamy mustaches on their upper lips.

"So who knows the tale of Sergeant Griffin?" Sweaty asked. He looked at each of his new friends in turn. "No one? Then I'll tell you. It was 1939, about two months into the war. Five Whitley bombers went off to shower propaganda leaflets on Germany. While flying home, one ran into a snowstorm. The cylinder head of one engine blew and burst into flames. The other engine faltered, so the plane lost altitude. At two thousand feet, the pilot trimmed the bomber for gradual descent, told the crew to bail, and jumped himself.

"Unfortunately, the rear gunner didn't hear the order. His intercom failed. So Griffin sat in the tail turret as the plane came down, hit with a belly flop, lurched, then bumped to a stop somewhere in France. Jarred by the landing, the gunner crawled up the fuselage tunnel to check on the rest of the crew. When he saw the cockpit was empty, he knew the plane had landed itself.

"Griffin stumbled, burned and battered, to a nearby village. To his surprise, he found his chums had met up after bailing out and were enjoying a drink in the local café."

Sweaty quaffed a gulp himself and wiped his lips with the back of his palm.

"Poor Ack-Ack," Liz said, shaking her head. "If only the *Ace* had landed itself."

"He should have bailed," said Lenny.

"That, too, could be dicey. Who's heard the tale of Flight Sergeant Smith?"

Wyatt laughed. "*Which* Smith, Sweaty?"

"Smith was the rear gunner in a Halifax. On the flight home from attacking a German coastal base, he climbed out of the turret to stretch his legs. Just then, something went awry with the camera that snapped damage to the target, and it blew a four-foot-wide hole in the bottom of the plane. As Smith ran back in the dark fuselage to get his parachute, he suddenly felt himself pitching downward. Just as suddenly, he found he was being slammed against the underside of the plane by the cold slipstream rushing past *outside* the fuselage. The hooks on his chute harness had caught on the jagged metal of the hole, and he was hanging upside down by a short length of webbing thousands of feet above the open sea."

Sweaty paused.

"So?" said Wyatt.

"So it'll cost you a beer if you want the rest of the story."

"Liz?"

"One's my limit."

"Lenny?"

"I'll pass." He'd only sipped the first one.

Sweaty shook his head. "What gives with you young squirts? You can't drink, won't fight, and don't chase dames like the old days. Where has the hell-raising gone?"

Wyatt held two fingers up to the waitress.

"Son, she's *German*," scolded Sweaty.

"Huh?" said Rook.

"You just gave her Churchill's V-is-for-victory sign."

"Sweaty," said Liz, "you left us—and poor Flight Sergeant Smith—hanging."

"No one knew Smith was dangling under the bomber," he resumed. "If the hooks gave way, he'd be kaput. If the crew bailed out, he'd get the chop. But as luck would have it, he hung on all the way back to England—that's two and a half hours—getting buffeted numb by the wind. As the plane descended to land, however, a new fear hit him. If he hung lower than the wheels, he realized, they'd be wiping him off the runway." Sweaty paused for effect. "Fortunately, he cleared the ground by inches. As they carted him off to the hospital, he slipped into a coma. His last words, through frostbitten lips, were for the pilot: 'Good show, Skip.'"

"Does that count as a bail-out?" Lenny asked.

"Incoming!" Sweaty warned. "Guard your eyes, buddy."

The waitress plunked down two more mugs, and foam frothed over the rims.

"Sergeant Sweaty," Liz said, "the WAAFs are right. You are an inveterate womanizer."

"If we had to rely on these two"—he nodded at Lenny and Wyatt—"the species would die out."

The old warrior chugged half a mug.

"The best tale of all is Flight Sergeant Nick Alkemade's," he continued.

"Tell us," said Liz.

"Nick Alkemade was the rear gunner in a Lanc. In 1944, his crew flew an op to Berlin. On the trip back, they fell prey to a Junkers 88. The night fighter's cannons tore open a wing. Fuel exploded, setting the fuselage ablaze. The skipper ordered his crew to bail out, so the gunner swiveled his turret to face aft and twisted around to open the back doors. His parachute was stowed in the fuselage tunnel of the bomber.

"Instantly, his face and wrists were scorched by flames. The mask over his mouth began to melt. Wind howling in through the wing holes drove the fire at him with blowtorch intensity. Nick's chute was blazing, so he pulled the doors shut. He faced a terrible choice: fry alive in gas and oil, or open his turret doors and freefall three miles to earth."

"Phew," said Liz. "That thought makes me shiver. Like that photo of the man falling from one of the towers on September 11."

"What would you do?"

"Jump, I guess," she said.

"That's what he did. Nick took the plunge. With only a parachute harness, he fell eighteen thousand feet through the dark sky and hit the ground."

"*Splat!*" said Lenny.

"Uh-uh." Sweaty shook his head. "Three hours later, Nick opened his eyes and saw stars."

"No way!" Liz exclaimed.

"How?" Wyatt asked. The historian knew the answer, but he played along.

"Alkemade found himself lying on his back in snow in a thicket of trees. Though cut, bruised, and burned, he was still in one piece. A fluke of fate had plunged him into the tops of some highly sprung pines. The trees had bounced him branch to branch, breaking his fall. Beyond the thicket, the earth was bare, but in the shadow of the pines, the ground had snow."

"Unbelievable," said Liz.

"That's what the Gestapo thought. Nick's leg was twisted, so there was no escape. The Nazis thought he'd hidden his chute somewhere. But the web lifts on his harness weren't extended, as they would have been if he'd pulled the ripcord. And when the wreck was found, lo and behold, there were the charred remains of his chute.

"By then, the gunner was a POW in a Stalag Luft camp. At a prisoner parade, the Gestapo presented Alkemade with signed proof that he had fallen from three miles up."

"Amazing," said Liz. "Life's roulette wheel. One gunner hobbled away from certain death, while poor Ack-Ack never got out of his turret."

"At least we know what happened," Sweaty replied. "The Junkers shot him through the chest."

"No," Wyatt said. "He wasn't shot. Ack-Ack was the victim of an impossible crime."

LOCKED ROOM

"I thought you said Ack-Ack had three holes punched through the back of his flying suit?"

"I did," Wyatt agreed.

Sweaty frowned. "So when that Junkers 88 shot our tail to shreds, three bullets entered through the gap in the turret and struck Ack-Ack in the chest?"

"No," Wyatt said.

"Why not?"

"If the Junkers got him, wouldn't there be three holes in the *front* of his suit too?"

"So Ack-Ack was shot in the back when he turned around to get his chute."

"No," said Wyatt. "Ack-Ack wasn't shot at all. He was stabbed in the back with a knife."

"Stabbed!" Sweaty exclaimed.

"Yes. Three times. The third stab was so hard that it snapped the blade off the knife."

"That's impossible."

Wyatt shrugged. "So it's an impossible crime."

He'd snapped a slew of digital photographs in the *Ace*, and now he used the camera to put on a slide show for Sweaty, Lenny, and Liz. Some of the shots showed the blade he'd withdrawn from the skeleton.

"It seems to me," Wyatt said, "that what we have here is proof that Judas was behind the last flight of the *Ace*. Let's assume the *Ace* was going to be the means by which to insert a secret agent into the Reich. What better way to do it than to shoot the plane down in a manner that allows the crew to bail out? If I were in charge of the operation, I would separate the *Ace* from the bomber stream."

"Why?" asked Liz.

"So other British planes wouldn't be around to open up with their guns when the *Ace* got attacked."

"That fits," Sweaty said. "Our secret mission. Splintering the *Ace* off to bomb the village."

"Why *that* target?" Lenny asked.

"No particular reason," Wyatt replied. "Any lonesome village would have done. The village wasn't the target. The target was the *Ace*."

"Christ!" cursed Sweaty. "You should have seen the brew-up. We hit it with incendiaries punctuated with bombs. All those civilians killed for *nothing*!"

"Not for nothing," Wyatt said. "They were sacrificed to down the *Ace*. That was sneaky. The operation was masked by the tactics of Bomber Command."

"I don't understand," said Lenny.

"The war over Germany was a cat-and-mouse game. The British swamped Nazi defenses by funneling as many aircraft as possible over each target in the shortest possible time. The Germans reacted with their night-fighter system. They allocated levels of artillery altitude above their cities to searchlights and flak guns. Above that, *Wilde Sau*—'wild boar'—fighters were free to roam at will. They used the lights to pick off bombers below. Even more lethal were the *Zahme*

Sau—'tame boar'—fighters. They infiltrated the bomber stream and tracked the RAF with onboard radars. But because Nazi controllers didn't have enough interceptors, they had to guess *which* cities would be targets that night, then dispatch enough planes to meet the threat."

"We were cunning," Sweaty said, taking over. "To trick the Huns, Group HQ launched 'spoof' raids at targets far away from the real ones, and ordered diversionary attacks of a size the Nazis couldn't ignore at secondary objectives. Meanwhile, the main bomber stream flew a complicated dog-leg course over Germany, only veering toward the primary target at the last minute. To maximize confusion, we wireless operators jammed their ground-to-air radios, then *our* German-speaking controllers issued phony countermands."

"What did you think you were doing that night, Sweaty?" Wyatt asked.

"Flying a top-secret mission."

"And the main bomber stream attacking Berlin?"

"We thought that was a big diversionary raid to mask us."

"Now, consider the *Ace* from the Nazis' point of view. After you were shot down, how would those *not* party to the Judas conspiracy see your op?"

"As a spoof raid for the main attack."

"And the Junkers?"

"It got lucky. The lone wolf fighter was on its way to save Berlin when it chanced upon us."

"So," said Wyatt, "if I controlled the British end of the conspiracy, I'd hide the secret agent among the crewmen of the *Ace*, send the plane on a solitary op over the Reich, and tell my German counterpart the name of the target village. And if I controlled the other end of the plot, I'd send a night fighter to shoot down the *Ace* without killing the agent. I'd have the Junkers 88 destroy the tail. The only crewman in harm's way would be the rear gunner, but he could ruin the whole plot if he fired back. The only surefire protection would be to have the secret agent stab Ack-Ack to death *before* the night fighter attacked. With the *Ace* crippled, the six forward crewmen would bail out through the front hatch. When he landed, the secret agent would surrender to the Gestapo. Imprisoned in a Stalag Luft camp, the airman would be where Judas could find him."

Sweaty shook his head. "Your theory doesn't fit the facts, Wyatt. Ack-Ack was alive when the Junkers attacked. *He* was the one who raised the alarm. We'd been mates since training. I *know* it was him."

"Couldn't the agent have stabbed him *after* that?" asked Lenny.

"Impossible. We were all in our battle stations every second of the way on our lonely run. Our only hope of survival was one hundred percent teamwork by every man. Our only defense against enemy fighters was coordination between Jonesy, our mid-upper gunner, and Ack-Ack, far back in the rear turret. Between them, they commanded a wide field of fire. Just as we relied on our navigator to guide us to the target, we relied on our gunners to warn us of incoming fighters and advise on the evasive maneuvers to take.

"From where I was stationed, I could see every combat position in the bomber. Wrath, the pilot, and Ox, the engineer, were above me in the cockpit. Balls, the navigator, was with me, and Nelson, the bomb-aimer, was up front in the nose. Jonesy, the mid-upper gunner, was in the dorsal turret. The lower half of his body was visible in the fuselage tunnel.

I could see the passage back to the tail, so I *know* none of us went back to the rear turret from the moment we strapped in for the bombing run until the moment we bailed out."

"You're sure?" pressed Lenny.

"Cross my heart. The moment Ack-Ack shouted 'Fighter! Fighter! Corkscrew starboard, Skipper!' through the intercom, every man reacted. A moment's delay invited disaster. A split second later, the night fighter raked our tail, Wrath plunged the *Ace* into an evasive dive, and our mid-upper guns returned fire. But the plane was crippled, and we were going down. There wasn't a minute to lose if we hoped to bail out. Glancing back along the tunnel, I saw the mid-upper gunner descending from the dorsal turret. He—like everyone except the rear gunner—would escape by the front hatch. There was no sign of Ack-Ack, and now we know why."

"That doesn't make sense," said Liz. "How was Ack-Ack stabbed three times in the back when he was *the only airman in the rear turret*?"

"What we have here," Wyatt declared, "is a 'locked room' puzzle. If we solve the *how*dunit, we'll solve the *who*dunit."

"We unmask the secret agent?"

"How *equals* who."

"But how do we solve it?" Lenny asked.

"We seek help."

"Help from whom?"

"From John Dickson Carr."

Some brains do crossword puzzles. Some play chess. Some calculate the odds of Texas hold 'em poker. It matters not what you do to exercise the 'little gray cells'—as Hercule

Poirot put it—as long as you do something to keep your mind from atrophying.

Wyatt solved mysteries.

Historical and detective puzzles.

"Carr?" said Lenny. "You mean the mystery writer?"

"Read him?"

"No, but I've heard of him. Before we moved to Wales, I worked as a librarian."

"Carr," Wyatt explained for the others, "was a grand master in the golden age of detective fiction. He's still the undisputed king of the locked-room puzzle. The setup in a locked-room puzzle is this: A body is found, *by itself*, in a room with no secret escape. The cause of death is such that seemingly the murderer must still be in the room. But he or she isn't, so how was the 'impossible crime' committed?"

"Poe?" said Sweaty. "'The Murders in the Rue Morgue'?"

"A telling example. Most consider it to be the first detective story ever written. Murder by razor in an apparently inaccessible fourth-floor room."

"An orangutan did it," said Sweaty.

"And then we have Sherlock Holmes. 'The Adventure of the Speckled Band.' Probably the most famous story. The victim is frightened to death in a locked room."

"A snake dunit," said Liz.

"Uh-huh. A swamp adder. Sir Arthur Conan Doyle explained how to solve such a puzzle. 'It is one of the elementary principles of practical reasoning,' he wrote, 'that when the impossible has been eliminated, the residuum, however improbable, must contain the truth.' Here's a sneaky example: The cops convict a killer of murder, but they can't send him to jail or execute him. Why?"

"Beats me," said Liz.

"Because he's inextricably joined to his Siamese twin. One half is guilty. The other half is innocent."

"Why turn to Carr?" asked Lenny.

"Because he wrote the book on solving locked-room puzzles. *The Three Coffins*, or *The Hollow Man*, as it was called in Britain. In it, Carr offers the seven ways to solve a locked-room puzzle. Explanation one: The crime isn't murder but a series of coincidences ending in an accident that looks like murder. For example, the victim's skull is cracked as if by a bludgeoning, but in fact, he fell from a book-shelf ladder and struck his head on the furniture, then crawled across the room before he died."

"Stabbed three times in the back," said Lenny. "That can't be what happened to Ack-Ack."

"I agree. Explanation two: It's murder committed by someone impelling the victim to kill himself or die in an accident. Here, the example is death by autosuggestion—a film with subliminal messages urges the fatal action. Years back, a test was done with split-second 'Buy Popcorn' ads spliced into a drive-in movie. The popcorn stand was mobbed by the audience in the intermission."

"Doesn't fit either," said Liz.

"I agree. Explanation three: It's actually death by suicide, made to look like murder."

"Example?" asked Lenny.

Wyatt grinned. "A man stabs himself with an icicle, which melts and evaporates."

"The rear gunner's seat," Sweaty said, "had no back support. So Ack-Ack couldn't have stabbed himself three times on a knife attached to the seat."

"Could the knife have been fixed to the doors?" asked Liz.

"No," said Wyatt. "I checked. Besides, someone removed the knife's handle from the turret after the blade snapped off."

"Why?" asked Lenny.

"I have no idea. Presumably so nobody would find it. But why would that matter once Ack-Ack was dead in the turret?"

"Explanation four?" asked Liz.

"It's murder complicated by illusion or impersonation. The victim lies dead in a watched room. With witnesses by his side, the killer shines a flashlight through the window. Inside, they see a shadowy figure move. But when they enter, all they find is the corpse. The witnesses didn't know it, but the killer had taped a small silhouette to the lens of the flashlight."

"Forget that," Sweaty said. "It doesn't fit here. Ack-Ack was alive when the Junkers attacked. I'll swear to that, and to the fact that no one went back to the turret between the time of the attack and our bail-out."

"Strike four," said Lenny. "What's next, Coach?"

"Explanation five: The victim is thought to be dead long before he actually dies. A drugged man passes out after locking himself in a room. When the door is broken down, the first person in stabs the victim while those who follow him are distracted."

"Strike five," said Lenny.

"Okay. Explanation six: It's murder committed by a killer outside the room, although it seems as if the killer was inside. For example, the victim is stabbed through the keyhole while peering out."

"No cigar," said Sweaty.

"You're down to your final means," said Liz. "What's explanation seven?"

"Murder by a mechanical device planted in the room."

"Example?"

"How do you hide a razor in plain view of everyone in a room?"

Liz shrugged.

"Attach it to the blade of a whirling fan."

"That's ingenious."

"The killers in Wilkie Collins's 'A Terribly Strange Bed' smother their sleeping victims by screwing down the canopy of a four-poster bed from the room above."

"Wicked."

"Locks and keys aren't essential for a locked-room puzzle. All that's needed is an isolated space. How do you cut a victim's throat and leave him sprawled in virgin snow with no footprints but his own? Hurl a knife-edged boomerang. Crack a bullwhip with a razor tied to the end. What could explain a body with fresh stab wounds found on a beach with no footprints in the sand? The victim's a hemophiliac whose blood didn't clot while the tide came in and ebbed."

"So where does that leave us?" Lenny asked.

"If explanation seven is the only one that fits, we must determine what kind of mechanical device stabbed Ack-Ack three times in the back in his turret, then vanished into thin air with the handle of the knife, leaving the blade wedged in his spine."

HAMMERHEAD

✝

It looked as though the Legionary was driving the second-hand Fiat, but actually, Satan was behind the wheel. The car passed in front of the hotel window through which the possessed priest had spied on Wyatt and Liz that morning. Tonight, they dined by candlelight at the same table, but each was so engrossed with the other that neither glanced out at the masked hearse. By the time the priest regained his mind, the car was snaking along a dark rural road that hugged the bank of a river. Not only could he not account for his memory gap, but the Legionary was unaware that Satan's latest harvest was hog-tied in the trunk.

Clang . . . clang . . . clang . . .

Stones clanged in the wheel wells of the Fiat, for this road was used as a detour to the end of the valley by trucks from the highway construction crew. The noise reminded the priest of Good Friday in the Philippines when he was a boy . . .

"Father?"

"Yes?" said the priest who would become the Secret Cardinal.

"Why does my father hate me?"

"He doesn't hate you. He's just a busy man. He must work hard as the ambassador, so he sends you to boarding school. My task is to teach you the lessons of the Bible."

"I'm not his."

"I beg your pardon?"

"That's what my mother yelled. I heard my parents arguing before she died. My father said my mother was screwing around, so she yelled that I wasn't his."

The priest sat down and cupped the boy's hand. "Remember what I taught you about the Garden of Eden?"

"Adam and Eve. The apple and the snake."

"Yes. Original sin. That's why parents fight and shout such things. Jesus died for our sins, so your mother is in heaven and your father loves you."

"My father loves the women he sleeps with at the embassy. I'm in the way. That's why I'm at boarding school. I wish *you* were my father."

"I am. In a sacred way."

"Why are you a priest? To stop original sin?"

"No, to keep from sinning."

"Did Jesus save you?"

"Yes, he did."

"When I grow up, I want to be a priest."

The missionary wrapped his arms around the boy and hugged him a mite too long.

"May I see it?"

"See what, my son?"

"How Jesus saved my mother. Tomorrow is Good Friday. Boys in my dorm say they crucify Jesus in San Pedro Cutud. Will you take me to see?"

And so they ventured north on that brutally hot day, the man and the boy who seemed to be father and son, to watch the crucifixions in the village's dusty rice field. The boy had to break away from the priest and push hard through a throng of sweaty onlookers to see.

Clang!

The sound of the hammer striking the head of the first nail sent a jolt of electricity up the boy's nerves. It felt as if the spike had pierced *his* hand.

Clang . . . clang . . .

The executioner gave the nail a double tap to sink it into the wood, then positioned another nail over the soft part of the *Kristo*'s other palm.

Clang!

Clang . . . clang . . .

Jesus stifled a cry and bit his lip. A pack of photojournalists called out for the Romans to clear the way so they could capture the grimace on his face for readers back home. With a heave and a haul, three attendants erected the cross, then the executioner pounded nails through the soft tissue between his toes. His feet were nailed individually, instead of overlapped, so the *Kristo* could support his body weight on the shelf of the cross.

Jesus seemed sublime as he whispered to himself.

Was he dreaming?

Was he praying to God?

The boy felt the hands of the priest on his shoulders, giving him a massage.

In less than fifteen minutes, they took Jesus down.

Clang . . . clang . . . clang . . .

The executioner nailed another *Kristo* to that cross.

Thirteen men were crucified before the Passion was done, and that burst of faith would stay with the boy for the rest of his life. Was being crucified not the ultimate affirmation of the sacred narrative at the heart of the Church?

And as he was to learn, Father felt just like he did.

The heat soared to a scorch the following day, and the blazing sun beat down like a hammer on a nail. To cool off, the priest took the boy to a swimming hole at a lonely mission outpost.

"Well?" said the priest. "Who are you? Tom Sawyer? Huckleberry Finn?"

The boy grinned. "My mom read me those books."

"Of course she did. All American boys read about Tom and Huck. Shall we swim?"

"I don't have trunks."

"No need for swimsuits. Tom and Huck skinny-dip. Is this not the Garden of Eden? No fig leaves here."

And so the boy shucked off his clothes and dashed for the inviting water, expecting the priest to follow. Instead, he found himself alone in the pool, and when he looked back to see why, there was the priest, on the edge of the pit, with tears streaming down his cheeks.

"What's wrong, Father?"

"Come here," summoned the priest.

From the look on his face as he gazed at his reflection in the pool, you'd think he was staring at himself burning in the depths of hell. As the boy emerged from the water, the priest averted his eyes.

"Get dressed," he said. "I have sinned. We *do* need fig leaves. The snake is loose in Eden. Satan is trying to possess me. He's after my soul, son. I need help to exorcise the demon."

"What can I do?"

"The *cross*," sobbed the priest.

It took the rest of the day to gather what they required. On the way to Cutud to purchase one of the whips sold to tourists as souvenirs, the missionary told the boy about the Jesuit priest who was martyred by Iroquois Indians in the 1600s. "What faith!" he said. "They stripped his flesh to the bones on his arms and legs. They blistered him with boiling water to mock our baptism. They roasted him in a belt of blazing bark soaked in pitch. They hung red-hot hatchets from a ring around his neck. They scalped him and pressed burning coals into his eyes, but still Father de Brébeuf kept praying to God. So they cut off his lips and tore out his heart. That, my son, is how a Catholic suffers for his faith."

Next, they drove to a hardware store for tools and beams of wood. On returning to the mission, the priest told the boy about mortification of the flesh—modern monks who whip themselves raw in monasteries; Opus Dei faithful who wear the cilice, a metal chain with spikes, locked around the thigh; and believers who bear stigmata, bleeding wounds that correspond to Christ's.

"'And they that are Christ's have crucified their flesh,'" quoted the priest. "That's St. Paul's letter to the Galatians. After Pope John Paul II was shot in St. Peter's Square, he wrote on our need to suffer. 'As the individual takes up his cross, spiritually uniting himself to the Cross of Christ,' he explained, 'the salvific meaning of suffering is revealed before him.'

"Are you strong?" he asked the boy.

"Yes," the boy replied.

Early Easter morning, the priest set things up. The boy helped him build a whipping post in the yard and watched him join the beams as a cross. The top of the crucifix angled up to rest on a stone wall.

"Here," he said, handing the boy the bamboo-tipped scourge. "Hit my back as hard as you can until it bleeds like the backs of the men you saw in Cutud."

Stripping off his shirt, the priest hugged the pole. "Do it!" he said.

So the boy skinned him alive.

"Take that, Satan!" the priest wailed again and again, his voice so raspy that it frightened birds out of the trees. The ground around him was red with blood when he finally groaned for the boy to stop.

Soaked with sweat, the boy panted from exertion.

Too weak to walk, the priest crawled to the cross on his hands and knees. The boy trailed him with the hammer and several nails. The flayed priest slowly climbed the slanted beam, then struggled to reverse himself. He gasped when his shredded back made contact with the wood.

"Ready?" asked the boy.

"Do it," said the priest, with less conviction than the first time.

The boy poked the tip of the nail into his quivering palm, just as the executioner had done on Friday, then he raised the hammer over his head, and—

"Save me!" cried the priest.

—brought it down.

Clang!

The boy had bounced from one boarding school to another as his father, the ambassador, took postings at various embassies around the world. In the end, his father's lust for women embroiled him in scandal, making him a pariah in Washington. Finished with school, the son announced that his life's work would be for the Church, and that caused his irate father to summon him home. There were money troubles that required new hands on the oars, a front man to puppet for the sinner.

The would-be priest got out of a cab and followed the path down through colorful autumn trees to the summer cottage above the ocean. It was no longer legal to build this close to the sea, but his father's hideaway had been grandfathered in as an exception to the law. The sinner didn't want a railing through his panoramic view, so there was nothing between the deck and the thirty-foot drop to the sea except a narrow strip of grass along the lip.

His father was sweeping leaves off the deck when he rounded one side of the cottage. His arrival made the sinner turn, and he slipped on a wet leaf, flying off the deck in a flail of arms and legs. With nothing to keep him from plummeting over the edge, he tumbled down the cliff face and struck the rocks in the foamy surf below.

The son approached the edge and looked down at his father.

The sinner was floating face down in the brine.

He was still alive.

The son felt nothing from all the neglect his father had heaped on him.

God would decide if the sinner should live or die.

The son waited . . .

And waited . . .

Until his father ceased moving.

Then he went into the cottage to call for help.

———

"Hello, Father."

"Hello, my son."

It was more than a decade since they'd last seen each other in the Philippines.

"You recognize me?"

"The eyes are the window to the soul. And you have such striking eyes. What brings you to the Vatican?"

"I wish to become a priest."

"So you said when you were a boy. Remember?"

"Yes."

"You kept my secret. About my crucifixion."

"I said I would."

"That means so little these days."

"Not to me, Father. Will you hear my confession?"

"In the confessional?"

"Here will do."

The would-be priest spread his arms to take in the vast expanse of St. Peter's Square. A rare snowfall had whitened the cobblestones around the larger-than-life figures in the Nativity scene next to the well-lit Christmas tree by the obelisk. Bundled up, nuns slipped by with umbrellas to protect their cowls. Except for the striking of clocks, sounds were few in Bernini's colonnade.

The penitent told the priest about his father's death.

"There's a difference between misfeasance and nonfeasance," said his confessor. "You didn't push your father off the cliff. Your sin is that you weren't the Good Samaritan."

"Father?"

"Yes?"

"I wish to join the Legion of Christ."

"Ah," said the priest. "The shock troops of the Church."

"To feel worthy, I must test my faith."

"Test it how?"

"As you did. Will you crucify me?"

———

Clang!

Never had he felt such agony! So excruciating was the pain from his skewered palm that his mind had to scrunch like his eyes to hold back the scream.

Clang . . . clang . . .

In slipped the nail like a razor.

Mine eyes have seen the glory of the coming of the Lord,
He is trampling out the vintage where the grapes of wrath are
stored,
He has loosed the fateful lightning of His terrible swift sword,
His truth is marching on.

The shadow of the hammer-wielding priest circled around the rock walls to the young man's other hand.

Let the Hero, born of woman, crush the serpent with his heel
Since God is marching on.
Glory! Glory! Hallelujah!
Glory! Glory! Hallelujah!
Glory! Glory—

Clang!
As the nail impaled his other palm, the penitent's eyes flew wide. He was suffering amid the foundations of Christianity, in the vault beneath the ruined church. Back then, believers had cowered in this catacomb, while martyrs were fed to the lions above. Now, through tears, he took in the flames of countless votive candles flickering around the altar that was *him*. And as he concentrated on the Christian marching hymn that his iPod earphones fed to his soul, the pain in his temples pounded the lights into the same fiery cross that had once converted Constantine.

In procession, that Christian battle hymn bled into another.

Onward, Christian soldiers, marching as to war,
With the cross of Jesus going on before—

Clang!
One foot was nailed to the cross.

At the sign of triumph Satan's host doth flee;
On then, Christian soldiers, on to victory!
Hell's foundations quiver at—

Clang!
His other foot was nailed to the cross.

Like a mighty army moves the church of God;
Brothers, we are treading where the saints have trod . . .

Suddenly, the pain was gone and all he felt was bliss. The cross blazed before him like a beacon in the darkness. The road behind him was the Way of the Cross, and he was now the vanguard of a long, *long* line of popes, and saints, and inquisitors, and crusaders, and martyrs, and apostles. Henceforth, the Legionary of Christ would march against all those who threatened *his* Church.

The crucifying priest signed him with the cross.

"Put you on the armor of God," he said, "that you may be able to stand against the deceits of the Devil."

Ephesians 6:11.

"Endure hardship, as a good soldier of Christ."

2 Timothy 2:3.

"It is *written*," he said.

———

Founded by Marcial Maciel in 1941, the Legion of Christ took its inspiration from the Cristero War of the 1920s. Waged by men known as Cristeros—soldiers of Christ—this was an uprising against anti-Catholic laws in the Mexican Constitution of 1917. "I envied the ones who went out to fight for Christ," Maciel once said. "I, too, wanted to give my life for him."

As the youngest founder of a religious congregation in the history of the Catholic Church, Nuestro Padre—Our Father—as Maciel came to be called, modeled his militant order on the Roman legions that spread Christianity throughout the empire after Constantine. There was no room for nonsense in the Legion of Christ. A legionary's crusade was to extend the Kingdom of Christ, and his life focused on the gospel, the Eucharist, and the cross.

That's what the Legionary wanted.

But Satan had other plans.

Who else could have perverted the devotion to Christ of the *Kristos* in the Philippines? In 1996, a Japanese non-Christian was crucified in Cutud so he could petition God to cure his sick brother. He turned out to be an actor in sadomasochistic porn. His crucifixion was filmed for video release in the sex shops of Japan.

Who else was polluting sinless souls with pop culture, with a false madonna mocking the Virgin Mary and Christ's crucifixion onstage, and with peddlers of heresy suggesting that Mary Magdalene had mothered Christ's child and begotten a line of royalty in Europe?

Who else was to blame for Nuestro Padre's fall from grace under allegations of sexual abuse?

And now, with darkness closing in on the Kingdom of Christ—and with infidels, heretics, atheists, pagans, skeptics, perverts, and heathens gathering for the Apocalypse—who was trying to unleash the satanic threat of the Judas relics on the foundations of the Roman Catholic Church?

Only the Legionary stood between the darkness and the light. But how could he hope to defend his Church in this all-or-nothing crusade when—having verbalized the blasphemies in those accursed Inquisition records—he had conjured the Devil and let Satan take possession of his mind?

Good Lord!

Was that, too, not *written* in the Bible?

Jesus asked him, saying: What is thy name? But he said: Legion. *Because many devils were entered into him.*
—*Luke 8:30.*

For he said unto him: Go out of the man, thou unclean spirit. And he asked him: What is thy name? And he saith to him: My name is Legion, *for we are many.*
—*Mark 5:8-9.*

With that in mind, the Legionary of Christ slipped away, and Satan once again took the wheel of the car. The Fiat abandoned the road for a bumpy path that ended in a dark pocket on the riverbank. Here, the possessed priest parked, got out, looked around, and walked to the back of the car.

The corpse of Lenny Jones lay hog-tied in the trunk. The killer hauled the remains out and lugged them down to the water. Then he went back to the trunk for a hammer. Swinging it repeatedly, he pulverized Lenny's face beyond recognition. After dumping the mangled mess into the stream and watching it float away, he cleaned himself up in the water and churned the bloody ground into mud.

As he embarked on the journey to his next kill, the clouds broke to reveal the hunter's moon.

HARD LANDING

THE NEXT DAY

"That looks tasty," Wyatt said. "What is it?"

"Hopple popple," Liz replied, isolating the casserole's ingredients with her fork. "Diced potato, bacon, onion, and scrambled eggs. You're late, and we couldn't wait."

"Sorry, but a colleague phoned with a promising lead. Speaking of which, where's Lenny?"

Yesterday, in the beer hall, they had agreed to meet for brunch in the hotel's restaurant so Lenny could show them the war archive kept by his grandfather, Trent Jones. In an email sent shortly after the bomber was found, Lenny had told Balsdon and Swetman that he'd bring the file to Germany.

"Missing in action," Sweaty said. "I rang his room, but he wasn't there."

"So what are *you* eating?"

"Apfelpfannkuchen."

"Gesundheit," Wyatt blessed him.

"Apple pancakes to you."

"But not to you?"

"I *did* spend a year in a Stalag Luft camp."

Wyatt caught the eye of the waitress across the restaurant and used sign language to place his order. He pointed to Liz's hopple popple, then to himself. The blonde with two braids smiled, nod-ded, scribbled on her notepad, and went to the kitchen.

Rook sat down.

Unlike the beer hall, this restaurant irked him. Those around him wore suits, ties, jeans, and designer labels. There wasn't a dirndl or any lederhosen in sight. Years ago, Wyatt had cleaned out a stash of his dad's youthful relics, includ-ing a grade three social studies text. Published in the mid-1950s, the book was a trip around the world, with Dutch kids in wooden shoes and Chinese kids in triangular hats. Wyatt wished it was still like that—not a global village of homog-enized beings produced by jet planes, franchises, and TV.

But then, of course, he'd be wearing a coonskin cap.

"Strange, Lenny being late," said Liz. "Can't imagine what would be more pressing than us."

"Maybe that barmaid who was . . ."

"Who was *what*?"

"*Zaftig*," Swetman suggested.

"Right," Wyatt agreed.

"You think Lenny's in bed with that buxom beer-hall babe?"

"She would be more pressing," the historian punned.

Liz rolled her eyes.

"While we're waiting," Wyatt said, turning to the radioman of the shot-down Halifax, "tell us what happened the night you bailed out over Nazi Germany."

———— + · —————

"'Pilot to crew. Bail out.' That's what Wrath said to the six of us through the plane's intercom," Swetman told his two brunch companions all these years later.

Listening to him, Wyatt and Liz could picture the frantic scramble in the *Ace of Clubs*. The guns of the Junkers 88 had obviously done real damage to the tail section. That was evident from the erratic way the crippled plane was flying. Swetman and Balsdon were in the compartment under the cockpit and behind the nose cone. Above them, Wrath struggled to keep the *Ace* as level as possible while the crew prepared to abandon the aircraft. Ox, the flight engineer, secured the skipper's parachute, then descended to the nose compartment, where Nelson, the bomb-aimer, was about to open the hatch in the floor. Having doused the reading lights within his blackout curtain, Balls, the naviga-tor, crawled forward to join the queue. All except the rear gunner would escape by the nose hatch.

"Ack-Ack, can you hear me?" Sweaty repeated several times into his mike.

No reply.

"Go!" Wrath ordered. "I'll be on your heels!"

The wireless operator disconnected his oxygen tube and pulled his intercom plug. Releasing the straps of his seat belt, he jumped up. It was so dark back in the fuselage that all Sweaty could see with his final glance was the outline of the mid-upper gunner descending from the dorsal turret, and he saw that only because moonlight stabbed down from the Perspex bubble. Wind whined into the fuselage through bullet holes, and metal plates shrieked like banshees from sprung rivets. Suddenly, Sweaty imagined the gunner beating him to the hatch and clog-ging it because he was too fat in his Taylorsuit to shove out.

That's when panic hit him.

Fire! Sweaty thought.

There were lots of ways to die on a bombing run. If the flak didn't get you, the night fighters could. If the fighters didn't get you, your own side could drop a bomb from above. Or you could succumb to extreme cold, oxygen starvation, battle fatigue, or mechanical failure. But of all the horrors that plagued an airman's mind, none was quite as terrifying as the nightmare of being trapped with fire inside your plane.

Driven by the worry that he was going down in a flying petrol can, the radioman clawed his way to the front of the *Ace*. There, he found a parachute and clipped it on. Tearing off his helmet so he wouldn't break his neck, Sweaty jumped out through the floor hatch into the rush of the slipstream.

Now he was tumbling head over heels. There was the plane; there was the ground; there was the plane again. The cold at this altitude was bone-cracking. Freefalling through the sky, the plunging airman counted slowly to ten, then pulled the D-ring hard to deploy his chute. The harness straps over his shoulders and around his legs jerked, and the "escape boot" developed by MI9 flew off his left foot. Above him, the silk canopy spread out like a mushroom cap. He grabbed the shroud lines and hung on for dear life, afraid he might not have hooked the parachute pack on right. Lose it and he would fall to earth like Icarus.

Out of the frying pan, into the fire?

Sweaty swiveled his head about, looking for danger in the moonlit sky. Beneath him floated three white chutes. Balls, Ox, and Nelson? Had to be. Those three had already jumped by the time Sweaty abandoned the plane. But where was the fourth chute to prove that Ack-Ack had escaped by the rear hatch? Nowhere that Sweaty could see. Above him billowed two more canopies. Jonesy and Wrath? Logically. And off to his right, going down without its crew, was the *Ace of Clubs*.

Oh no! thought Sweaty.

Not the goon in the moon.

As the wind from the north scattered the chutes across the sky, the Junkers 88 circled the six shot-down airmen like a shark in bloody water. If it banked and came at them with nose guns spitting, they'd be torn to tatters before they hit the ground.

Come on.

Get it over.

If that's what you plan to do.

But the Ju 88 seemed content to let the ground have them, as if that served its purpose *better* than death.

Why? Sweaty wondered.

Chivalry?

When the trees came up to meet him, he locked his knees together, fearful that a branch might literally rip his balls off.

Crack!

Swishhhh . . .

Into the trees . . .

"Cripes!" howled Swetman.

The pain was so acute that he was sure he'd broken his leg. Forced to shuck his chute in the trees and monkey down from their branches, he struggled with a leg that was numb from hip to foot. Sweating from the exertion it took to reach the ground, Sweaty wiped the back of one gauntlet across his face. Only now could he pause for a moment to collect his thoughts. Up there, as he was facing death, his survival instinct had kicked in.

Currently, however, all he needed was a cigarette.

So he lit one.

His first thought was about tomorrow night's date. Once a month, the air station bused in local women for a Saturday night dance. A pretty brunette had caught his eye, so he'd asked her out to see a movie this week. Now it appeared that he wouldn't be able to meet her in town as agreed, and he hoped she wasn't going to think that he'd stood her up.

Damn!

He knew he should gather up his parachute and poke it under a bush. However, he could barely stand—let alone climb—so he had no alternative but to leave it up in the trees. He might as well have been waving a white flag of surrender.

Stubbing out the cigarette, Sweaty turned his mind to escape and evasion.

For every five airmen killed in action, one got forced down over enemy territory. Nearly ten thousand would end up in the twenty-odd prisoner-of-war camps scattered across Germany and Poland. Some—no more than a thousand—would evade capture, thanks to the escape gadgets of MI9.

MI9.

British Military Intelligence Section 9.

Sweaty struggled out of his Mae West and flying suit. Beneath, he wore a blue-gray waist jacket and trousers, with his sergeant's stripes on the right sleeve and the word "Canada" on the shoulders. Attached to the left collar fastener was a whistle to attract his mates.

Should he blow it?

No, he decided.

The Brits and the Huns had been at it again since 1939, two years longer than the Yanks. Sweaty knew his mates would be in for a rougher time with the Gestapo, and he didn't want to draw them here with that chute flapping overhead.

No, he'd wait for one of them to whistle.

And if no one did?

Then he was down to MI9's gadgets.

Stuffed in his pocket was an escape box cleverly disguised as a water bottle. Removing the false side of the container, he withdrew an escape map; Horlicks tablets, chocolate, chewing gum, barley sugar, and a tube of condensed milk; water-purifying tablets and Benzedrine—"wakey-wakey" pills—to combat tiredness; and matches, a needle and thread, and fishing twine. The stopper unscrewed to reveal a tiny watch and compass.

Sewn into Sweaty's jacket lining were packets of real foreign currency—Dutch guilders, German marks, French and Belgian francs—and a waterproof map detailing the best escape routes and frontier crossings in Europe. And he had "pimpernel" pictures, in case he made contact with the Resistance.

Those were the mundane gadgets.

The others were sneakier.

Regretfully, Sweaty wished he'd taken evasion more seriously. Group Captain John Whitley had put together his own escape kit, which he carried in a haversack clipped to his parachute harness. In the sack was a civilian tie, the jacket of a lounge suit, and a peaked cap. He'd wear the trousers of the suit under his uniform pants, and a blue check shirt with collar attached beneath his battledress. In his pockets were a razor, a tube of brushless shaving cream, a toothbrush, toothpaste, and his nail file. Needless to say, Whitley was the butt of jokes among aircrews. But when he was shot down over Europe in 1943, his personal kit had helped him escape through France and Spain.

He who laughs last, laughs best.

If he was going to escape on foot, Sweaty had to be able to walk. Not only had he sprained his ankle—if he was lucky—but he'd lost his sock along with his escape boot. The remaining boot was a lace-up walking shoe with a sheepskin-lined upper section. Concealed in the lining was a knife that Sweaty could use to hack the flying boot down to civilian footwear. That would be less conspicuous, if only he had the pair.

Bad luck.

Unless he found another shoe, he was going nowhere. So Sweaty dragged his bum leg through the thicket of trees to the edge of a farmer's field. It was after midnight and the farmhouse was dark, but he could see it silhouetted by moonlight. Limping across the fallow earth, he knocked on the door and waited for the snick of a lock.

The woman who opened the door gasped in shock, and her hands flew to her mouth.

"Karl?" she murmured, breaking into tears.

Shock became dread when she realized that she'd mistaken the black outline for someone else. Her hands dropped to clutch her bathrobe over her nightgown.

"American," Sweaty said, raising his palms to prove he had no gun. He figured he was better off identifying himself as an American. Then, to show her why he'd knocked on her door in the dead of night, the downed airman pointed to his crippling bare foot.

The woman stepped aside, inviting Sweaty in, and as he struggled across the threshold, she supported him by the elbow on his injured side. A short hall led to a dark living room, where dying embers burnished the hearth. She sat him down in an overstuffed chair and handed him a photograph from the mantel. The picture was of a young German in a Luftwaffe uniform.

"Karl?" asked the airman.

The woman nodded. She was a heavyset farmer with a devastated face. Sweaty wondered if her son was dead, missing in action, or a POW in Britain.

"Earl," said the American, tapping his chest.

"Elke," the German replied, pointing to her heart.

A sniffle made the airman turn toward a staircase off the hall, and through the spindles of the banister, he could just make out a little girl with a rag doll locked in her arm.

"Heidi," said the woman.

A Heidi she certainly was, blonde braids and all. She was probably the blondest child Sweaty had ever seen, as she rubbed a sleepy eye with her fist and approached the edge of the room. The threadbare doll looked like a hand-me-down.

Before each bombing run, RAF crews were given sandwiches and flasks of coffee for the return flight, together with slabs of chocolate and barley-sugar sweets. Heidi no doubt knew chocolate, but had she tasted the traditional English hard candy made by melting and cooling sugar cane?

"Heidi," Sweaty said, flashing the girl a smile and holding out the sweets from his return meal. To confirm they were safe, he popped one into his mouth.

Hesitantly, the child drew nearer. Tentatively, she plucked a candy from his palm and put it in her mouth. Sweaty winked as he pretended to feed another to her doll, and the girl rewarded him with a playful grin.

The airman filled her hands with the sweets.

Convinced the stranger meant them no harm, the woman fetched a basin of warm water to bathe his injured foot. As she sponged him clean and shod him with a pair of boots, did she hope an English mother on the far side of the Channel would treat her son with similar compassion?

Finished, she gave him a walking stick and a meal to go of cheese, sausage, and bread. Then, ushering him to the door, she saw him off and wished him luck in German.

Outside, the moon beamed down on the silver landscape. Awed by the serenity of his surroundings, Sweaty felt pangs of guilt over the destruction wrought by the *Ace of Clubs* tonight. But then—could it be?—he heard an RAF whistle. Leaning heavily on the cane, the wireless operator hobbled as fast as he could along the rutted road toward the shrill call. Which mate, he wondered, would it be? The answer came when a shadow emerged from the roadside woods, followed by two black specters with Luger pistols in their fists.

The whistleblower wore a Gestapo uniform.

"For you, the war is over," he said in a thick German accent.

And that, Sweaty told Wyatt and Liz all these years later, is how I ended up in a Stalag Luft camp.

RELICS

"What are pimpernel pictures?" asked Liz, bringing the conversation back to the MI9 gadgets.

"Passport-size photos," Sweaty replied. Placing a metal box on the table, he opened the lid and withdrew a strip of headshots snapped from different angles, using various lighting effects.

"Who's that handsome fellow?"

"Me," he said.

"You were a hunk, Sweaty."

The old warrior winked. "I still am, baby. See how they made me look gaunt and undernourished in this one? That was in case our plane went down over Holland. The lighting in that one makes me look ruddy-faced and well fed. That was in case the *Ace* went down over France. Pimpernel pictures were a must for all operations. They could be used to produce forged identity papers if we made contact with the Resistance. *The Scarlet Pimpernel*. Have you read the book? He's a mysterious English lord who helps French aristocrats escape to Britain so they won't lose their heads to the guillotine during the Revolution."

Sweaty quoted: "'They seek him here, they seek him there. / Those Frenchmen seek him everywhere. / Is he in Heaven?—Is he in hell? / That damned annoying Pimpernel.'"

"I thought it was 'That damned *elusive* Pimpernel'?" said Liz.

"That's the movie version. It fits better, actually. The Scarlet Pimpernel is a master of disguise, and pimpernel pictures were supposed to help us evade capture."

"What else have you got in there?" she asked, pointing to the open box.

The old man passed her a tunic button.

"Unscrew it," he said.

Liz gave the button a hard twist.

"It won't budge."

"Not for you. And not for the Gestapo. You're actually screwing it tighter. That's because the threading is reversed. Give it a sharp twist the other way."

Liz did and the button popped open to reveal a miniature compass inside.

"These," said Sweaty, "are two buttons from my fly."

"Torn off when some *Fräulein* removed your pants in a brothel?" teased Liz.

"I wish."

The sergeant set one small, domed button down on the table. Its dome was surmounted by a tiny, sharp pin that spiked up vertically. The other button had two dots on one edge and one on the opposite edge. When the radioman placed the dotted button on top of the spiked one, the two dots immediately revolved around on the pin to line up with magnetic north.

"Cool," said Liz.

"See this pencil?" Sweaty asked, pulling it from his box of relics from the war. "Break it at the letter 'B' on the side and you'll find a compass within."

"That's a lot of compasses."

"With a compass, a map, and some pimpernel pictures, it was possible to sneak home."

"Who dreamed up this stuff?" asked Liz.

"MI9."

"Like in James Bond?"

"That's MI6, Britain's external security agency. MI9 aided the Resistance and recovered Allied troops from Nazi-controlled Europe. It's now defunct."

"Do we know who Q was?"

"Q was a composite of several inventors," Wyatt cut in. "A First World War pilot and movie PR man named Christopher Clayton Hutton designed most of the compasses and Sweaty's escape boot. He became so popular that he dug himself a secret underground bunker in the center of a field so he could work in peace."

"Thus the term 'mole'?" joked Liz.

"The Gestapo thought Colditz Castle was an escape-proof prison. They were mistaken. The first British officer to make it out was Airey Neave. He escaped through a trap door under the stage during a theatrical production. He made his way back to Britain by way of Switzerland, France, Spain, and Gibraltar, then was recruited as an evasion expert to help MI9. At one point in the war, MI9 was able to smuggle a complete floor plan of Colditz Castle to prisoners still inside."

"Hocus-pocus," said Liz.

"Those words best apply to Jasper Maskelyne. Three generations of Maskelynes were stage magicians. Jasper was a star in the 1930s. When the war broke out, he put his sleight-of-hand tricks into effect in North Africa, cobbling together a group of illusionists called the Magic Gang. To divert Nazi bombers from the port of Alexandria, he built a fake harbor in a nearby bay, complete with a dummy lighthouse and a dummy anti-aircraft battery that fired thunder flashes. To protect the Suez Canal, he outfitted searchlights with a revolving cone of mirrors that spun off a wheel of blinding beams nine miles wide."

"Smoke and mirrors," said Liz.

"Jasper's best deception was Operation Bertram, before the Battle of El Alamein. The Magic Gang hoped to convince the Desert Fox—Field Marshal Erwin Rommel—that Monty's attack would come from south of the German line, instead of north. To that end, they created two thousand fake tanks out of plywood and painted canvas where there was no army. They even found a way to make the fakes leave tracks. To bolster the illusion, they created a fake water pipeline under construction, complete with sound effects like workers riveting things together and swearing when they dropped their hammers on their toes. The Nazis tracked the progress from the air. Did they assume nothing would happen until the army got its water? For whatever reason, when that attack came, the Germans were caught off guard."

"So Jasper saved the day?"

"He thought so. And the next we hear of him, he's at work in MI9, designing hiding places for escape aids."

"Too bad you didn't get to use them, Sweaty," said Liz.

"But I did. The barley sugar in my escape box, remember? I gave it to the little girl in the farmhouse. You know, I often think of Heidi to this day."

"Want to meet her?" Wyatt asked.

———————

Lenny Jones never did show up with his grandfather's file, so they left without him.

With Wyatt driving the rental car and Sweaty seated beside him—"You take the front," Liz had said, "to see if the panorama matches what you recall"—the three foreigners forsook the picturesque medieval town for the countryside. The green of summer was giving way to the red-orange-yellow of autumn, and the last crops had ripened enough for harvesting. Already, the highlands off in the distance were whitened by snow.

"How did you find her?" Sweaty asked.

"Easy," Wyatt replied. "My friend Rutger—the fellow who set up the *Ace of Clubs* pass for me—knows the records the Nazis kept better than anyone. To my mind, he's the best historian of Hitler's Reich. With the date of the crash and the location of the unearthed plane, he was able to search Gestapo files. He found a record of your arrest and the statement given by the farmer living nearby. I phoned the farm this morning to confirm."

"Elke turned me in?"

"No. In fact, the Gestapo gave her a very rough time. What saved her from execution was your 'admission' that you had threatened her and her child."

"I was afraid for them."

"And rightly so," said Rook. "She could have been shot for helping the enemy to escape."

"What put the Gestapo on to me?"

"Your parachute caught in the tree. What's interesting is that earlier that night—*before* your plane was shot down— the Gestapo throughout this region got orders to take any downed RAF airmen alive, and to separate them from one another."

"Judas?"

"That's another piece that seems to fit our puzzle."

A lazy river with wooden bridges meandered through the hills and dales, fields and pastures. Man and horse worked the fields together as they had for centuries. With the help of German shepherds, farmers in funny-shaped hats and leather pants that never wore out herded cows for cheese and pigs for sausage. Apples shone red in the orchards. Soon, this world would be forced to give way to modern times, when the auto-bahn brought *Fahrvergnügen*—"the pleasure of driving"—to pollute its tranquility.

"That barn!" said Sweaty, pointing. "That I remember. Its beamed sides reminded me of Shakespeare country, and its roof drapes down like a nun's cowl."

"Check the map," Wyatt said to Liz in the back seat.

She laughed. "I assume the German cross you scrawled means X marks the spot?"

"Yes."

"Okay. We're here."

"And that's the farmhouse," Sweaty said, finger pointing again. "I hobbled across from that windbreak of trees, leaving my chute billowing in the branches."

Wyatt turned up the long driveway that led to the farmhouse door. They bumped about until they reached the end, where a woman was watching from the threshold. When they parked and got out, Sweaty smelled smoke in the air. It reminded him of childhood autumns back home in Wisconsin.

"Welcome," said the woman with gray streaks in her back-combed hair.

"Hello, Heidi. You've grown up," replied the old airman.

Holding out a metal box in one callused hand, the German raised its hinged lid and flashed him a smile. The same smile he'd seen when he'd fed candy to her doll.

"Have one," she offered. "I order them from London. You left me with a sweet tooth for barley sugar."

Selecting a candy, Sweaty placed it on his tongue. More than half a century had passed since he'd last sucked one, but the distinctive taste flew him back to the war. Never again had he felt such camaraderie. And after all the faceless Germans they had killed from the air, this woman's mother was the one he'd saved.

Down memory lane, he thought.

The parlor hadn't changed much since the war. There was even a blaze on the hearth to ward off autumn's chill. Heidi motioned Sweaty to the same overstuffed chair as Elke had, then served her guests coffee and a Bundt cake.

"Karl?" inquired the sergeant, eyeing the photo of the young man in the Luftwaffe uniform still displayed on the mantel. "Did he come back from the war?"

"*Ja,*" said Heidi. "From a prisoner camp. That's where he learned English, which he later taught to me."

"Your English is good."

"I watch English-language films." A TV and DVD player were the only updates to the room.

"And your mother? Elke?"

"She died in a farm accident when I was a teenager. After that, my brother and I worked the land."

"That's a lot of work."

Heidi nodded. "Now he's gone, so I plan to sell."

"It's *good* to see you."

"You, too," she said. "I've waited a lifetime to thank you for not betraying my mother. Did they beat you?"

"No, they were decent. But I didn't want the Gestapo hurting your mother for helping me."

"You were Karl."

"I know," Sweaty replied.

Heidi offered Liz a second piece of cake. "I hear your grandfather piloted the plane?"

"Yes," said the younger woman. "He vanished that night. I'm here in hopes of unearthing what happened to him. Wyatt found no trace in the Gestapo files."

"That's because the Gestapo didn't capture him."

Liz sat bolt upright. "You know his fate?"

"*Ja*," Heidi replied. "My childhood playmate grew up on a nearby farm. That night, he was awakened by the noise of a descending bomber. His father grabbed a pitchfork and ran off across their fields to intercept a parachute he spotted in the sky. The next morning, he gave his son new toys."

From beneath her chair, Heidi retrieved a rusting biscuit box. With both hands, she passed it to Liz.

"When I heard you were coming, I went to my friend. He wants to remain anonymous, but he gave me this to give to you. These are the 'toys' his father gave him that morning."

Liz took a deep breath and thumbed off the lid. Inside, she saw the insignia of a pilot's battledress, including the wings of RAF Bomber Command. One by one, she removed the trophies from the box, examining the gadgets designed for escape and evasion by the brains of MI9. Finally, she turned the box upside down, and into her palm fell a wedding ring.

"For Fletch, with love" was etched into the band.

"What happened?" Liz asked.

"Your grandfather landed where the farmer was waiting. He'd lost his parents when Nuremberg was bombed."

"Oh," said Liz.

"That's why we were always told," Sweaty interjected, "to give up to the military, and not to civilians."

"When the farmer heard that the Gestapo wanted to take the crewmen alive, he feared for his life. He swore his family to secrecy, and no one found out, except me. I said nothing, until now."

"Thank you for telling me."

"If Karl had been killed in England, I would have wanted to know. Not far from here is a magnificent tree. The pilot was secretly buried beneath its canopy. If you'd like to go for a walk in the country, I'll accompany you to his grave."

U-BOAT

✝

Entering the U-boat was like crawling through the neck of a bottle. With the hatch closed, you said farewell to the sun, the moon, the stars, the earth, and everyday life. Suddenly, your world shrank down to this oppressive, claustrophobic, constricted steel tube. The *Elektro* boat—a new weapon in the arsenal of the Reich—was half the size of the submarines that had begun the war. Less than ten feet wide, it wasn't designed for the comfort of its crew. The sub was a battle engine stuffed with machinery and torpedoes. It gave the men just enough room to vegetate and perform the chores essential to their mission. For weeks on end, the fourteen-member crew would stoop, step up, slip sideways, and bang their heads on pipes and hand-wheels as they moved along the central aisle. The Judas agent felt like Jonah inside the whale as this mechanical predator slipped silently beneath the sea toward its target.

His codename was Stürmer.

Daredevil, in English.

And daring indeed was this plan to smuggle Hitler's atomic secrets to Churchill in the *Black Devil*.

The tide had turned in the Battle of the Atlantic. In the early years of the war, wolf packs of U-boats had attacked convoys on the surface, then submerged to escape from destroyers. But by the end of 1943, sub losses were greater than the number of ships torpedoed. What tipped the scales against Germany were aircraft equipped with radar. Forced underwater, the wolf packs were deprived of surface mobility, and solitary hunters had little chance against an escorted convoy. Clearly, Germany required a new type of sub.

The Judas agent had been sequestered in a hideaway on the Baltic Sea for a crash course on the revolutionary Type XXIII *Elektroboot*. Diesel power, Stürmer learned, was obsolete. By replacing it with electric motors juiced by high-capacity batteries, the Germans had built a machine that could stay submerged for 194 nautical miles, so it couldn't be "starved out" by surface pursuers. The electric boat could maintain a lightning attack for over an hour, and it was almost immune to echo-detection by sonar-probing destroyers. With double the attack speed of other submarines, the Type XXIII had the option of silence over swiftness by switching to an auxiliary electric "creep" motor.

Run silent, run deep.

That was the *Black Devil*.

Sneaking Stürmer aboard the sub had not been difficult. By 1944, the mauling of the wolf packs had bled experienced crews dry. The Kriegsmarine had to take whatever manpower it could get. From the hideaway on the Baltic Sea, Stürmer was sent to the main torpedo-training school for officers at Mürwick. By then, his German was up to snuff and his papers were real. He was just an ex-Luftwaffe marksman going to sea. His studies focused on torpedoes and how to launch them. Practical lessons took place aboard a converted minesweeper, which had a pair of torpedo tubes mounted on the forecastle and a simulated U-boat control room below deck. So dire was the need to get subs and men into combat that Stürmer was sent directly to the *Black Devil* for the first *Elektroboot* test run in the North Sea.

When he first spied the sub in its Hamburg pen, he had marveled at its small size. Built in four separate sections, the boat could be shipped by rail and reconstructed for operations in the Mediterranean and Black Seas. The conning tower was large in proportion to the hull, as it housed the periscope, snorkel, and torpedo computer. That tower was his battle station in the sub.

He was the *erste wach offizier*, or the first watchkeeper.

The 1WO.

The second-in-command.

His primary responsibility was the sub's weapons system: the torpedoes and the computer used to aim and fire them.

His other task was to assume command if the CO died or fell ill.

The forward compartment of the *Black Devil* had two torpedo tubes. Called an *Aal*—an "eel"—by the crew, a torpedo was twenty-three and a half feet long. Instead of being inserted nose-first into the rear of the tubes like shells in a shotgun, the torpedoes were dropped in externally like the balls of an antique muzzleloader.

No reloading meant the sub had just two shots.

As 1WO, Stürmer had supervised the arming of the boat. First, the *Black Devil* was ballasted at the stern to raise the bow clear of the water. Then, using cranes and pulleys on a barge, the torpedo boys had hoisted the heavy, unwieldy, greased eels and slipped them into the tubes.

Tube caps sealed, the sub had gone to sea.

The trip up the coast of Britain had proved a piece of cake. All the way, the sub had lurked beneath the waves. Even when the diesel engine was used to recharge the batteries, nothing had broken the surface except the head of the snorkel. Extended high above the tower, it had sucked in fresh air and exhaled exhaust fumes. Stürmer could see why the Judas traitors were using the *Black Devil* to deliver their package. As disaffected members of the German military, they had selected the *safest* machine in their arsenal, and the route that offered the least suspicion to the Gestapo.

On setting sail, the sub had looked like a butcher shop. Sausages and smoked hams hung from ceiling pipes. Hammocks overflowed with loaves of hard, dark navy bread. With space at a premium, every nook and corner was crammed with edibles.

The Hanging Gardens of Babylon, Stürmer thought.

The bread turned moldy as the days went by, for humidity in the sub was intolerable. The crew called the mildewed loaves "white rabbits." Grabbing them by the "ears," they tore out the edible innards. Food produced by the tiny galley tasted like diesel oil.

Clammy clothes never dried, and draping them on machinery had little effect. Fresh water was strictly for cooking and drinking. The men cleaned themselves—if at all—with saltwater sponge baths and a cloying cologne that fouled the already reeking air. If the sub sank below eighty feet, the toilet in the overused head refused to flush. Woe betide the sailor who lost track of depth, for the outside water pressure reversed the flow.

Hygiene was a joke. Underwear was dyed black so it wouldn't look grubby. Whores' undies, they called it. Because denim withstood oil and grease from the machinery, that was their uniform. Bunks were built into both sides of the passage, aft of the torpedo tubes. A man coming off a shift would flop, fully clothed, into the bed just vacated by the man relieving him. Hopefully, neither man had crabs or head lice.

Day and night were the same in the *Black Devil*. With no skylights and no portholes, the sun and the moon were the perpetual glare of electric lights. Privacy didn't exist. Even the captain's quarters was simply a cubicle shielded from the central passage by a green curtain. Sleep was constantly torn to shreds by light, noise, and motion. The slightest transfer of weight—a single seaman moving forward or aft—could disturb the underwater balance and set the U-boat swaying.

Sometimes, Stürmer would lie on his back in the hot bunk, staring up at the curve of the pressure hull, and ponder the twist of fate that had put him here.

His father was English. His mother was German. And he was born in London just after the First World War. Through all his boyhood years, he'd kept his background secret, for Germans were hated by the British people. In every town around the isle, there was a common with a cenotaph listing the names of local men slaughtered by the Hun. Still, his mother taught him German and told him about the prewar history of his Teutonic ancestors.

He was descended from knights!

Imagine that.

In school, of course, he was taught about God, king, country, and the white man's burden. By then, the world was gearing up for another war, and to make sure they were primed for the fight, he and his classmates were taught the atrocities of German barbarism.

He remembered most the story of the crucifixion. According to his teacher, the incident had occurred in 1915, near the Belgian battlefield of Ypres, on the Western Front. A Canadian soldier had been crucified to a barn door with German bayonets. The outrage was depicted in the film *The Prussian Cur*, and a statue called *Canada's Golgotha* was displayed at a London exhibition of wartime art.

He had told his mother.

"That's a lie," she replied. "We call it propaganda. Do you know what that means?"

His mother's hatred of Hitler had peaked on Kristallnacht, when her stepfather, mistaken for a Jew, was beaten to a pulp by Nazi storm troopers. How thankful she'd been to see her son enlist in the RAF. His hatred of Hitler had climaxed during the Blitz, when a Luftwaffe bomb destroyed his childhood home, killing his father outright and crushing his mother beneath a beam, where she burned to death.

Put it all together, and that's why he was here.

"The wingco wants to see you."

That's how this had begun.

For instead of the wing commander, he was met that day by a mystery man from MI13, a branch of military intelligence so secret it didn't exist. MI13 knew everything there was to know about him, plus a thing or two he didn't know himself.

"How many men have you killed for your country?" the shadowy officer asked.

"Thousands, I guess."

"How far would you go *personally* to overthrow Hitler?"

"All the way."

"Would that include snuffing one of your own countrymen, if it was deemed necessary?"

"To stop Hitler?"

"To save millions. Millions of us. And millions of *good* Germans, like your mother."

He thought about it.

He nodded.

"Including that," he said.

So here he was in the *Black Devil*—a secret agent so secret that only a handful of people knew he existed—on the verge of delivering a package that would topple Hitler. If only his mum could see what he was doing *for her*.

He wondered if he would survive.

Maybe not.

But the odds were no worse than they were flying in the *Ace*.

Now that they were here.

Having churned its way up the "liquid triangle" of the North Sea, the *Black Devil* had entered the inland jut of the Firth of Forth, along the north shore of Edinburgh. Their mission was to test the sub, so this was a dry run of how it would be. Get in, sight the enemy through the periscope, and get out without detection. Combat was authorized only if sub hunters closed in on the U-boat.

Self-defense.

That was their rule of engagement.

The single propeller in the stern was being powered by the creep motor for low-noise, low-speed cruising into the heart of Scotland. The engine room was manned by machinists wearing gloves to protect their hands from the hot parts of the propulsion system. A confusion of pipes and cables wormed everywhere. The sub was constructed of two superimposed pressure hulls, the one up here for the crew, their equipment, and their battle stations, and the one underfoot for storage batteries and the fuel and dive tanks. No smoking was allowed in the sub because explosive gases were emitted when wet batteries were charged. The men wore felt shoes to muffle their footsteps on the floor plates, in case sub hunters were listening for telltale sounds, or it became necessary to play possum to deceive British destroyers.

A bulkhead divided the engine room from the control center. Here, amid a maze of valves, gauges, and wheels, technicians manipulated controls to stabilize the vessel, monitor its vital signs, and steer this sliver of steel deeper into the Firth of Forth.

This nerve center was also home to the radioman, the only crewman who had contact with the outside world. He used just one headphone over his ears so he could hear both incoming signals and orders within the sub. Since leaving port, he'd kept *stumm* because high-frequency direction finders—HF/DF, called huff-duff—could home in on radio transmissions between a U-boat and its headquarters.

Incommunicado.

That was his test-run order.

From the lower chamber, a ladder ran up to the conning tower that crowned the hull. This was where the captain—a lieutenant-commander called the Old Man—and his 1WO directed operations. At the moment, the snorkel was telescoped down and the periscope was up. The skipper wore casual clothes, except for his hat. To maintain authority, captains had to wear at least part of the uniform signifying their rank. With his eyes glued to the optical tube that used two prisms and a lens to offer him a scan of the surface world, the Old Man wore his cap shoved back from his brow.

Stürmer stood poised by the torpedo computer. The skipper assumed he was waiting to perform his primary task: feeding instructions from his boss into the computer to aim and—if necessary—fire the torpedoes. But actually the Judas agent in a sea wolf's clothing was preparing to take control from the captain.

"Alarm!"

The captain barked the dreaded word.

Stürmer tensed.

"Action stations! We've been spotted!"

Alarm signals blared and flashed.

"How many, Skipper?"

"One destroyer. Dead ahead."

"And with it?"

"Empty sea. Open tube caps. Flood tubes one and two."

JUDAS KISS

✝

The next day

In the dreamy haze between sleep and wakefulness, Wyatt remembered a *Punch* cartoon from long ago. Two French foreign legionnaires in those caps with the flaps down the back to protect their necks against the sun are chatting in the desert. One says to the other, "I joined the legion two or three weeks ago to try to forget a girl called Elsie or something." In his case, Wyatt could now adapt that to say, "I flew to Europe days ago to try to forget a girl called Val or something." For beside him lay the woman who'd spent the night paying off her gambling debt.

His socks were on the floor.

His feet were in the bed.

Hmm, he thought.

For a while, Wyatt lay with his head propped up by his palm and studied this beautiful sleeping creature. The way her messy hair fanned around her peaceful face. The way her breasts expanded with each shallow breath. The way the sheet hugged her hips, as if jealous of him. He decided that coming to Germany ranked at the top of his list of best decisions.

Up and at 'em, he thought.

Wyatt was in the bathroom when the phone rang, twice. This was her room, so Liz took the calls. The first was obviously from her mother. Women, in his experience, took on a special tone when dealing with the matriarchal tut-tutters of their lives. The next call came from Sweaty, so Wyatt stayed mum. Never compromise a lover's reputation.

"Problem?" he asked, emerging after Liz got off the phone.

"My grandmother's taken a turn for the worse. An ambulance took her to the hospital. If I want her to have the relics from my grandfather's uniform, I'd better catch the next flight home. Sweaty called to say he's leaving too. And there's still no sign of Lenny. I wonder if he went home. And if so, why no goodbye?"

"Hey," protested Wyatt, "what about me?"

"What about you?"

Raising a leg, he pointed to the sock on his foot.

"I thought we had a deal."

"Nice try," said Liz, and she threw back the sheet to rub salt in his wound.

"Yikes! What happened to you?" Wyatt asked when Liz came out of the elevator into the hotel lobby, dragging her suitcase on wheels. She was dressed like she was off to a shareholders' meeting at Virgin Atlantic.

"It's the real me. I'm off to see my mum."

"But"—he took in the corporate outfit—"you look so businesslike. What happened to the free spirit I've known up to now?"

"That trollop was for *you*."

"I liked her."

"I'm sure you did."

"You mean she's gone?"

"Uh-huh."

"I feel so *used*."

"You'll get over it," said Liz. "In a decade or two."

With the next landing of the elevator, out stepped Sweaty. He was sporting a blazer with the squadron crest.

"This was sudden. You okay?" Wyatt asked.

"When you reach my age, problems magnify. It's nothing serious, but I want to see a doc who's fluent in English. I've got one of those multi-day erections they warn you about on TV."

Liz laughed. "The dose is *one* pill, Sweaty."

"Now you tell me, sweet stuff."

Halfway to the airport, they hit the autobahn. Cars went zooming past them at a thousand miles an hour. By the time they'd parked at the terminal, Wyatt's nerves were shot. If that's what German drivers called the pleasure of driving, he was glad he lived in a country with speed limits and highway patrolmen lurking in trees with handheld radar.

"Good luck with the puzzle," Sweaty said on the terrorists' side of the security gate.

"Call if you hear from Lenny. I'll hunt for him here," said Wyatt. "I'll see you in York."

"It's not the meeting Balls proposed, but hopefully, his funeral can honor his crusade."

"And thanks for these," said Liz, holding up the relics from Wrath Hannah's uniform. "I know they'll give my grandmother comfort."

Liz kissed Wyatt on the cheek.

"Hey!" grumbled Sweaty in his best James Cagney voice. "That's *my* girl."

"Of course I am," said Liz, looping her arm through the sergeant's to guide him off to the security desk.

Let's settle out of court, Wyatt mused. Liz can be your moll and my maul, respectively.

———— ·•·—— ————

Having seen their plane off to London, Wyatt hung around the airport for the flight from Berlin. Before Liz and Sweaty altered their plans, he had arranged to greet an arrival today. The *Ace of Clubs* puzzle had grown so complex that Wyatt knew it was time to bring in his Big Bertha gun, Rutger.

The last time he saw his Teutonic buddy, Rutger was the size of a Wagnerian opera heroine. His weakness was food. Put him in a kitchen and out would come gourmet schnitzels and mugs of cool beer. Though he had many friends who qualified as bon vivants, Wyatt thought Rutger was the best host of all. So he was surprised when the man who came through the gate looked like Jack Sprat.

"What gives, Rutger? You are but a mere shadow of your former self."

"I have a new girlfriend who's threatening to break up. She says I crush her in bed."

We work to the same incentive, Wyatt thought.

As do most men.

"Thanks for coming."

"Yours was an offer I couldn't refuse."

"Is that them?" Wyatt asked, indicating Rutger's over-stuffed briefcase.

The German nodded. "A copy of every Kriegsmarine file describing a U-boat mission to Britain between the shooting down of the *Ace of Clubs* and the failure of the generals' July

Plot to assassinate Hitler. If—as you theorize—the secret agent parachuted in by the RAF bomber was to smuggle out the Judas package by submarine, he must have sailed to Britain in one of these U-boats."

"Gotta be. Wouldn't Judas want his peace offering in Churchill's hands for the surrender negotiations immediately after Hitler was eliminated from power?"

"That's logical."

"How does fifty-fifty sound? To split the royalties?"

"Overly generous."

"I could not have written *Dresden* without your help. Not a penny did you ask of me. Like most who speak the world's dominant tongue, I can't read yours."

"Surely you studied a language?"

"You'll laugh."

"Try me."

"I studied Latin."

Rutger laughed. "That's of use."

"I'll have you know that I have read *Winnie-the-Pooh* in Latin."

"Not many Americans can say that."

"Judging by what I hear on TV, few could read it in English either."

Rutger laughed again.

"It's getting so bad that publishers are sending books overseas for editing," Wyatt added.

"To England?"

"Hell no. They can't speak English either. The last vestiges of the language are in India."

"So what is Pooh in Latin?"

"Winnie-ille-Pu."

"Do you do readings?"

"*'Ior mi,' dixit sollemniter, 'egomet, Winnie-ille-Pu, caudam tuam reperiam.'*"

"Sounds grand. What does it mean?"

"'Eeyore,' he said solemnly, 'I, Winnie-the-Pooh, will find your tail for you.'"

Rutger laughed a third time. "Fifty-fifty? You mean it?"

"One, I need your research. Two, I need a translator. Three, I think we could jointly write a good book. Four, I owe you for *Dresden*. Five, I plan to work at your house over gourmet meals with fine wine. And last, you found the grave of Wrath Hannah for me. His granddaughter is most thankful."

Rutger gave him a meaningful look.

Wyatt grinned. "I couldn't possibly comment."

———•——

Rutger's arrival at the *Ace*'s resting place caused a stir. While he was off holding court amid lesser historians, Wyatt was intercepted by a hard-eyed detective with the Federal Criminal Police.

The Bundeskriminalamt.

It sounded worse in German.

"Herr Rook?"

"Yes."

The cop presented his ID. "Detective Inspector Horst Stritzel. May I ask you some questions?"

"About what?"

"Herr Jones. Do you know him?"

"Lenny Jones?"

"Yes."

"Yes, I know him. What about him?"

"When did you see him last?"

"The day before yesterday. We were to meet for breakfast the next morning, but he didn't show up."

"How long have you known him?"

"We just met. Why?"

"Herr Jones's body was fished from the river yesterday."

Wyatt scowled. So that's why Lenny had missed brunch.

"Has he been identified?"

"Is there some reason for doubt?"

Wyatt caught the narrowing of the eyes in the tight-skinned, bony face. He'd seen that same look of suspicion on the face of Detective Inspector Ramsey of Yorkshire CID when he was being questioned at the Balsdon murder scene.

Uh-oh. Déjà vu.

"Who identified the body?"

"Should that present a problem?"

"I got the impression no one here had met Lenny before."

"Interpol returned a match from Jones's fingerprints in America."

Wyatt shrugged. "So why ask whether I doubt your identification?"

"Herr Jones's face was bludgeoned beyond recognition."

"With what?"

"What do you think?"

"Are you trying to trap me?"

"I'm trying to discover the motive for Herr Jones's murder. His face was bashed in with a hammer. Why would someone do that?"

"Why indeed? We live in the era of DNA. You don't need teeth or fingerprints to identify someone any more."

"What brings *you* here, Herr Rook?"

"I'm researching a book."

"About the *Ace of Clubs*?" asked the BKA inspector.

"Yes."

"And the Judas agent?"

"I was asked to investigate by the granddaughter of the bomber's pilot."

"We know. I've been in contact with Detective Inspector Ramsey. Herr Jones was living in Wales."

Suddenly, the American's nerves were on high alert. "Have you reason to doubt that Lenny was who he said he was?" he asked. "A descendant of the gunner?"

"No, he was definitely the grandson," said Stritzel.

"How do you know?"

"DNA."

"That was quick."

Actually, Wyatt wasn't surprised by how quickly the test results had come in. These days, a lab could produce Lenny's DNA profile within hours.

"The geneticist who tested Herr Jones's DNA," explained the cop, "was also the forensic scientist who extracted DNA from the skeleton found in the bomber."

He indicated the turret of the plane in the pit.

"Those DNA profiles matched," Stritzel said, "proving that Herr Jones was the rear gunner's grandson."

The *rear* gunner? thought Rook.

HOLY GRAIL

London's airport was the crossroads of humanity. While the Legionary and the Art Historian waited at the gate, heads talking languages neither had heard before milled around them. There was a lingering smell of high-end Scotch from a duty-free purchase someone had dropped on the floor. A distressed young man rushed past them on his way to the toilet, muttering, "That will teach me not to eat the special in the Marrakech bazaar."

"You touched it?" asked the young priest, his voice low for this tête-à-tête between conspirators.

"Yes," replied the Art Historian. "The Holy Grail."

"When?"

"As a boy. In 1944."

"Where?"

"At home. In Germany."

"How did that come about?"

"I was dying when, by chance, Judas called on my father. My father was also Art Historian to the Vatican. He wasn't a member of the Nazi Party. He was a Catholic above all else. But because of his expertise as an art historian, he received a visitor one stormy night in 1944. I sat near death up in my room."

"From what?" the Legionary asked.

"Meningitis. Exacerbated by the effects of black-market penicillin."

"Penicillin?"

"Yes. It was a brand-new wonder drug, but I was allergic to it and had a terrible reaction. My father had to tie me to an armchair to keep me from clawing myself to shreds. The doctor told my father he'd return in the morning to sign what would undoubtedly be my death certificate."

"But you pulled through."

"Thanks to Judas. He knocked on the door an hour later to ask my father's opinion on relics he possessed."

"The Holy Grail?"

"Right. The Holy Grail isn't the chalice from the Last Supper. Nor is it the body of Mary Magdalene. Those are merely myths spun from the twelfth century on."

"The relics are authentic?"

"That's what my father deduced because of the map and the document the man also had. But the absolute proof occurred when he carried the relics up to my room."

So vivid was that childhood life-or-death experience that the Art Historian began to relive it as he described it to the Legionary.

Thunder rattled the windowpanes of the upper-floor room where the delirious boy sat lashed to the arms and legs of an antique chair. The walls of this room—like those of the rest of the rooms in the house—were decorated with artwork seized from galleries that were "Aryanized" by the Nazis or stolen from Jewish collectors who'd fled to freedom or gone to death camps. This was the clearinghouse for the best pieces. To those who bought and sold treasures on the black market, there was nothing better than authentication by his father. The loot would be integrated into museum collections or shipped to anonymous hoarders, never to see the light of day again.

Rembrandt, Van Gogh, Monet, Matisse, Picasso—all hung within these walls.

The artwork displayed in this room, however, had divine pedigree. To the Nazis, it was sacrilege that works of religious sanctity had found their way into grubby secular hands, so they'd given the Art Historian an opportunity to rectify that travesty. He assessed the sacred works that came into this house, picking the best for a secret gallery hidden behind the fortifications of the Vatican.

"Itchy and a burny and a sting!"

That's what the boy blubbered repeatedly in his delirium.

He was only five, but he sensed that he was dying. One minute he was burning with fever, and the next he shivered with chills. His head ached, one eye twitched, his neck felt stiff, and he recoiled from light and sound. As the storm filled the room with flashes of blue light, images in the paintings came to life.

Hell was a pit under crimson skies, where oceans of fire and billowing smoke broiled and choked tormented sinners. Grotesque monsters—half demon, half machine, with hunks of human anatomy—tortured those who'd been abandoned by the Church. Overseeing the horror was Satan, with horns on his head, a black goatee, flaming red skin, and a long tail tipped with a triangular barb. In his hand, he held the piercing tines of a dung-heap pitchfork.

Sinners got skinned alive.

The boy thought they were lucky.

He would have sold his soul to the Devil to be skinned alive, too.

Anything to stop the insects burrowing beneath his raw skin.

"Itchy and a burny and a sting!"

The boy threw up.

Then a crack of light appeared around the door, and he thought the angel of the Lord was coming to harvest him.

Instead, it was his father with the Holy Grail.

"Christ, cure my son," his father prayed, and he touched him with the relics.

"And by dawn the next day," the Art Historian told the Legionary, "I was better. The doctor said the penicillin must have won the struggle, but I knew it was a miracle worked by the Holy Grail. I'm *still* allergic to penicillin. Deathly so. Imagine what will happen if the Judas relics end up in secular hands. The healing power of Christ won't rest in his one true Church. How can we *not* use every means we have to obtain those relics for the Holy See?"

"Here he comes," interjected the Legionary.

Exiting from the arrivals gate, Sweaty stopped to scan the crowd for a familiar face. He spotted the men waiting for him and hauled his suitcase over.

"Why the secrecy, Lenny?" Sweaty asked the Legionary.

JUDAS GOAT

✝

Wyatt was inside the fuselage of the *Ace of Clubs*, counting the number of unexpended rounds in the ammo boxes and belts that fed shells to the rear turret, when Rutger heaved himself in from the pit outside.

"Interesting," mused the American.

"What is?" the German asked.

"The guns in the dorsal turret"—Wyatt pointed overhead—"were each fed six hundred rounds from boxes within the bubble. Almost all the rounds were expended when the mid-upper gunner opened fire on the Junkers 88."

"That makes sense."

"Right. What Sweaty—Earl Swetman, the wireless operator—told me was that as Ack-Ack—the rear gunner, Dick DuBoulay—shouted a warning through the intercom, the Junkers 88 strafed the plane. The pilot yanked the bomber into a dive, while Jonesy—the mid-upper gunner, Trent Jones— fired back. He made no mention of gunfire from the rear turret, which would have been drowned out, had it occurred, by the deafening din of the closer guns."

"Was the night fighter hit?"

"Probably not. It came at them again. But that time, neither turret shot back."

"Why?" wondered Rutger.

"Sweaty feared the rear gunner was dead. By then, the Junkers had torn the bomber's tail to shreds, and Ack-Ack's turret was smack-dab in the line of fire."

"And the other gunner?"

"Hours before, as the plane was nearing the coast of Europe, both gunners had tested their weapons over the open sea. The interrupter gear of the dorsal turret malfunctioned, so while the rest of the crew prepared to enter enemy airspace, both gunners got together to solve the problem. Later, as the Junkers attacked, Sweaty feared the gear problem wasn't fixed."

"So the dorsal guns ceased firing?"

"Possibly. *After* Jonesy had all but emptied his ammo boxes at the fighter in its first pass."

"What's so interesting about *these* boxes?" Rutger asked, nodding his head at the ammunition supply for the rear turret.

"Almost all the rounds are here. The number of expended shells is what I'd expect from the test fire alone."

"Meaning the rear gunner didn't fire a single shot during the night fighter's attack?"

"So it would seem."

"Perhaps the guns jammed?"

"All four at once? Unlikely."

"So?"

"So the rear gunner must have been killed *before* he could fire back. I could accept the logic of that if his body was riddled with bullet holes. But not when he got stabbed three times in the back."

Rutger frowned. "First, the Junkers attacked, strafing the tail with cannon fire but missing the rear turret. Then Ack-Ack yelled a warning to the crew by intercom. The pilot jerked the plane into a defensive corkscrew as the mid-upper gunner fired at the Junkers. But before the rear gunner could fire back, too, one of the crew knifed him to death."

"Impossible. According to Sweaty—and I believe him—all seven men were in their combat positions."

"So how do you explain it?"

"I thought Ack-Ack might have been killed by some sort of mechanical device hidden in his turret. A machine that could knife him several times, then vanish along with the blade's broken-off handle. But a thorough search of the bomber has failed to yield any evidence of that."

"Puzzling."

"The only possible explanation is that Ack-Ack was already dead inside the rear turret long before the Junkers appeared on the scene."

"So when was he killed?"

"Back when both gunners were together at work on the problem with the interrupter gear. While our victim was sitting in the rear turret, the traitor stabbed him three times in the back, then closed the doors, pocketed the snapped handle of the knife, and climbed up into the mid-upper turret for the bombing run. From that point on, the crewmen remained in their combat positions until they bailed out."

"So the killer was Trent Jones?"

"Consider the case against him: That was his first mission with the crew of the *Ace of Clubs*. Jonesy was the odd man out, and more important, he was stationed halfway back from the forward five crewmen, which meant that his comings and goings would be the least in view."

"But why kill the rear gunner?" Rutger asked.

"To keep him from shooting back. The Junkers 88 was sent by Judas to shoot down the *Ace* and insert the secret agent into Hitler's Reich. The British conspirators had to guarantee success, so they sacrificed the rear gunner and doomed the other five crewmen to captivity or death."

"Jones became a Judas goat: the decoy that lures other animals to the slaughter."

"It seems that way."

"You don't sound convinced."

"Two things trouble me. Why does the DNA of the skeleton found in the rear turret match that of the bludgeoned body pulled from the river? Was Lenny Jones really Ack-Ack DuBoulay's grandson? If so, why did he lie?"

"And the second worry?"

"Sweaty swears that Ack-Ack DuBoulay *himself* raised the alarm through the intercom. He's certain that Ack-Ack was alive when the Junkers attacked. They'd known each other since bomber training."

"But that can't be if Ack-Ack was knifed before the *Ace of Clubs* entered Nazi airspace."

"True," Wyatt agreed. "So either Jonesy impersonated Ack-Ack well enough to fool Sweaty, or Ack-Ack wasn't in the rear turret as everyone thought. The intercom didn't indicate where voices came from. It was simply an audio circuit that each crewman plugged into when he was manning one of the combat stations. Sweaty heard Ack-Ack because it was Ack-Ack's voice in the intercom, but it was coming from the mid-upper—not the rear—turret."

"The gunners had switched positions."

"The crucial defense station in a Halifax bomber was the rear turret, since night fighters usually attacked from behind and below. If the rear gunner was shot, the mid-upper gunner took over, because the plane wasn't out of danger until it landed in Britain. And sometimes—as we both know—not even then."

Rutger nodded. "The Luftwaffe lurked over English bases to shoot bombers coming home."

"According to Sweaty, Trent Jones joined the crew of the *Ace* after his own Halifax crashed in a takeoff accident. He'd survived by bailing out through the *rear* hatch, the escape route of the tail gunner. And before the *Ace* departed on its last mission, the crew took their new gunner up on a test flight so that Ack-Ack could check Jonesy out on the turrets and the guns. Turrets in the plural. He wanted to make sure Jonesy could defend them and the plane from either the dorsal or the rear turret."

"So the voice the other five heard through the intercom wasn't Jones's. It was Ack-Ack mimicking the voice of the new gunner."

"Ack-Ack stabbed Jonesy in the rear turret as the rest of the crew focused on the danger of flying into Nazi Europe. Then, masked head to foot, he took over the mid-upper turret. From then on, no one dared leave his battle station to venture back to the rear turret."

"Not when split seconds counted."

"When Ack-Ack spoke in his own voice from the mid-upper turret, those up front assumed he was back at the plane's tail. When he mimicked Jonesy from the same turret, he had five advantages. One, he used few words. Two, Jones's voice was new to the crew. Three, he had a Welsh accent. Four, the roar of engines muffled his voice. And five, all the crewmen expected some distortion because the moisture from their breath froze in their mikes."

"But why was Ack-Ack's identification found on Jones's skeleton in the rear turret?"

"My guess?" Wyatt said. "Jonesy was told he was part of a secret mission to win the war. That's why they were adding him to the *Ace of Clubs'* crew. If the plane was shot down in Germany, his role was to confuse the Gestapo by saying he was Ack-Ack. Then the real Ack-Ack—armed with false papers and able to speak fluent German—would be free to contact Judas."

"That's a dangerous ruse."

"I doubt Jonesy gave a damn. His wife had gone off to Australia with their child. Sweaty described him as quiet and withdrawn, eaten up inside. Now he was being offered the chance to make his life count."

"For king and country?"

Wyatt shrugged. "Actually, Jonesy was being set up to be stabbed. De Count was cracking from battle fatigue, so that gave Bomber Command the excuse to remove him from the plane. Jonesy came aboard ostensibly to replace De Count as mid-upper gunner, but he secretly assumed Ack-Ack's position in the rear turret and was killed there."

"Why not use De Count?"

"He was cracking and unpredictable. The crewmen knew his voice. And it's much easier to stick a knife into a stranger than it is to a friend."

"Why choose Jonesy?"

"He was expendable. His life was in the toilet, and he would hardly be missed. If Bomber Command was going to kill off one of their own, why not choose a miserable wretch?"

Rutger scowled. "Your theory holds up. With Ack-Ack gone from the rear turret, the Junkers 88 could fire at will. No danger of hitting the Judas goat. No worry about return fire.

When the attack began, Ack-Ack could raise the alarm, shooting the mid-upper guns *away* from the night fighter."

"As the *Ace* was going down, the pilot ordered the crew to bail out. Ack-Ack—wearing a gunner's Taylorsuit just like Jonesy's—scrambled to the front of the plane, shed the equipment masking his face, and jumped out through the forward hatch. In his pocket, he carried the handle of the knife."

"I like it," the German said. "The bomber crashed in this valley. If the Nazis had found it, the gunner sprawled dead in the rear turret would have had Ack-Ack's ID. If the conspiracy had somehow leaked at either end, they'd think the Judas agent was killed in the attack or the resulting crash."

"Meanwhile, if Ack-Ack met a crewman in a POW camp, he could claim he'd bailed out by the rear hatch. And if a mate had spied him in his forward escape, he could have said both gunners had switched positions so he could work on the interrupter gear."

"Ironically, the landslide buried the *Ace*, which prevented the Nazis from finding the plane," said Rutger.

"What happened to the Judas package, no one knows. The British disowned the mission for the sake of morale at Bomber Command. All that lived on was rumor—until now."

Rutger withdrew a hip flask from his pants. "Schnapps?" he asked, unscrewing the cap and handing the flask across.

Wyatt took a swig and passed it back.

"Well, we have a book, my friend," Rutger said. "We know the identity of the Judas goat."

"I think we know more than that."

"What?"

"We know who Judas was, too."

TIGHT SQUEEZE

✝

LONDON

"Heaven on Earth" was the theme of the paintings on the walls
of the Art Historian's London gallery and dealer's shop, a commercial satellite of his headquarters in New York. No prices
defiled the artworks. That would be gauche. If you have to ask,
you can't afford to buy it and you don't deserve to own it. Instead,
these glorious bits of heaven were sold by secret bid. People
would pay through the nose to escape from hell on earth by gazing at these uplifting visions in their extravagant homes.

In the realm of divine art, the depth of your pockets counts.
You can't have your own private Vatican on a shoestring budget.

So what does heaven look like?

To one side of the Art Historian hung *New Jerusalem*. The
heavenly city, the size of the moon, was made of see-through
gold and precious stones, as it was in Revelation 21. No need
for the sun when the glory of God shone through, casting off
a rainbow of dazzling colors. Its water crystal clear, the River
of Life flowed from the throne of Christ. The faithful at his
feet would spend eternity listening to the lessons he would
share. To augment the aura of this heavenly vision, the artist
had mixed the paint with prisms that flashed rainbows if the
light was right.

On the other side of the dying man hung *The Tree of Life*. Here, there was no death, crying, mourning, or pain. The eyes of the blind could see; the ears of the deaf could hear. The lame could leap, and the mute could shout for joy. Because all were pure creations, the rules of physics were gone. People could dance through locked doors and travel anywhere. With hate, grief, and trouble removed, love, joy, and peace reigned supreme. Eating was pleasure, not necessity, and in this new Garden of Eden there grew a tree of life that bore twelve kinds of fruit each month. Shame equaled sin, so the fig leaves were no more, and the artist had rendered each naked body in erotic detail.

This was the painting the Art Historian swiveled his chair to face.

You'd think that with that to look forward to—instead of this blood disease, with its symptoms of fatigue, weakness, weight loss, bone pain, enlarged organs, and anemia—the Art Historian would yearn for the rejuvenation of heaven. But he had too much money in the here and now, and his faith in the afterlife wasn't strong enough to chance everything on a single roll of the dice. That's why he wanted to find the Holy Grail, even if he had to sell his soul to grab it.

A bird in the hand . . .

Before flying to Germany for the resurrection of the *Ace*, Lenny Jones had emailed the surviving crewmen and the relatives of the dead to say that he was bringing his grandfather's archive with him. On the night Balsdon was gutted by the Judas chair, the Legionary had found that email among the navigator's papers. Balsdon's archive recorded his suspicion that Jones was the double agent. Not only was Jonesy new to the crew, but he was also one of the three who never came home.

Wrath.

Ack-Ack.

Jonesy.

Earlier on in the same day that Wyatt, Liz, and Sweaty arrived in Germany, the Legionary—pretending to be a reporter—had greeted the *real* Lenny Jones at the airport. Lenny told his soon-to-be killer that he was a stranger to the others. The Legionary clubbed him on the way to the hotel, then stored the body in the trunk to dump later. Because there was nothing in Trent Jones's archive to confirm Balsdon's suspicion that the mid-upper gunner was the Judas agent, the Legionary had assumed Lenny's identity and met the others the following day. When it turned out that none of them had brought archives of their own to Germany, the priest and the Art Historian abandoned the ploy. That's when Lenny's body was dumped in the river and left to float downstream, its face pulverized by hammer blows to hamper identification. Having left a secret note for Sweaty at his hotel, the Legionary and the Art Historian had trekked to London and waited for the old airman to join them.

"Did you tell the others?" was the first question the Legionary had asked.

"Against my better judgment, no," said Sweaty "What makes you think Jonesy was the Judas agent? And why the cloak-and-dagger routine to get me here?"

"I doubt you'd voice it in public—not with the others there—but I think you suspect that my granddad was the secret agent."

"Your note said you have proof."

The Legionary introduced him to the Art Historian.

"*I* have proof," said the older man. "A client offered to sell it to me at my gallery. It's a photograph of Trent Jones in a Nazi uniform. To check its authenticity, I traced Lenny to Germany and phoned him night before last."

"So that's why you left?" said Sweaty.

The Legionary nodded. "You're the last surviving member of the *Ace*'s crew. I was told the photograph is grainy and could be a fake. My mother was too young to remember her dad, so I need your confirmation if I'm to go public with my granddad's secret identity. If you can't say it's him, the puzzle remains."

"Show me the photo," said Sweaty.

"It's in my safe," said the dealer. "I don't know why Balsdon was killed, but I don't want to be next. I've kept this strictly need-to-know: Lenny and you."

"Where's the safe?"

"My gallery. Central London."

"Come on," the Legionary had said, picking up Sweaty's suitcase. "Let's have a look. Then I'll buy you lunch."

So now the Art Historian sat at his George III mahogany partner's desk, exhausted from his trip to the airport. People bustled to and fro on the street in front of the gallery. The sign on the door informed customers he was closed, but the dying man kept watch all the same.

The Art Historian listened.

But he couldn't hear shrieks from below.

The London under London was like a living organism. From Roman times, its arteries had borne the city's fluids, its lungs had enabled it to breathe, its bones had given support, its muscles had endowed strength, its nerves had transmitted signals, and its bowels had disposed of wastes. Those infrastructures were long-forgotten rivers, underground railways, tunnels and tubes, pipes and passages, neo-gothic sewers, crypts and cellars—like this vault—that twisted and turned, layer on layer, through the netherworld of Hades or hell.

There was a constant hum of noise. The gurgling of water from taps and flushed toilets. The whoosh of underground trains snaking from station to station. The *fzzzzz* of electrical pulses surging through billions of wires. During the Blitz of the early 1940s, frightened Londoners had huddled in this dank, murky bomb shelter beneath the gallery like slaves in the hold of a ship while Hitler's Luftwaffe rained firebombs down on their homes.

Now, all it harbored was a captive old man.

Another turn of the screw . . .

Another crack of bones . . .

Sweaty was transported from this purgatory of pain back to the Second World War. Once more, his head was sheathed in a leather helmet and oxygen mask, and he seemed to be strapped into his wireless operator's seat, except that his arms and legs were tied. Somehow, this chair had been jettisoned from the *Ace* and had landed in the tube, bringing Sweaty face to face with that obnoxious wartime creation of London Transport—smug, sanctimonious "Billy Brown of London Town."

This same poster had taunted Sweaty during the war, when he and Balls had railed it down to London on a break to binge in bars and chat up girls. Instead, an air raid had forced them to scramble into the underground with droves of weary Londoners, each person paying one and a half pence for a tube ticket to save his life. With suitcases to pillow their heads, hundreds of poor wretches stretched along the tracks, eating from shopping baskets or sipping from bottles of milk and ginger pop as they tried to ignore the stench of plugged latrines.

Subconsciously, these cave dwellers feared being buried alive, for all had heard of the bomb that exploded above Balham Station, bursting a water main that drowned sixty-odd people. In a pit, reduced to raw survival, what could be more intolerable than Billy Brown of London Town? In placards plastered every-where, that despicable cartoon character dogged these fearful people with exhortations delivered in insufferable verse.

Down below the station's bright,
But here outside it's black as night.
Billy Brown will wait a bit
And let his eyes grow used to it.
Then he'll scan the road and see,
Before he crosses, if it's free.
Remembering when lights are dim
That cars he sees might not see him.

Another turn of the screw . . .
More cracking of brittle bones . . .
The old man couldn't help it . . .
Sweaty let out a scream . . .
And the scream shot down the elephant-like trunk of the oxygen mask, where it was recorded before it burst out and echoed around the concrete confines of this bunker. Squeezing his skull was another device from the Inquisition, also stolen from the tourist-trap museum up in York.

Another turn of the screw . . .

"Talk!"

And another shriek . . .

Unlike Balls and Jonesy, the radioman had not gathered an archive during the war. His memories were all stored in his brain, so his torturer was using the Inquisition's headcrusher to squeeze them out. The device looked like a skullcap—the zucchetto that crowns popes, cardinals, and bishops—with a propeller on top. The propeller was a crank with thin threading, so it took a lot of twists to screw the skullcap down toward the metal bar under Sweaty's chin.

Twist . . .

His clenched teeth were grinding to dust in the mask, and he choked with every gasp.

Twist . . .

Sweaty's skull was cracking along its fault lines.

Twist . . .

His eyes bugged out of their sockets and the blood vessels popped one by one.

Whoever was turning the screw, it wasn't Lenny Jones. There was no doubt in Sweaty's compressed mind that he had fallen into the hands of the monster who had impaled Balls Balsdon on the Judas chair. He'd let his guard down because the Lenny Jones he'd met in Germany had seemed benign. He'd reminded Sweaty of those evangelicals who knock on your door because God has ordained them to save your soul. People like that had always given Sweaty the minor creeps, but he'd never expected to uncover a demon like this!

"Lenny" wasn't insane.

His curse went *deeper* than that.

The relentless squeeze of the headcrusher was focusing Sweaty's bugged eyes on the poster that had irked him so much during that London air raid . . .

He never jostles in a queue,
But waits his turn. Do you?

Sweaty had so hated Billy Brown of London Town that he'd used his pencil to scratch out his own pithy slogan . . .

You annoy so much, you really do.
I wish you dead. Do you?

Only in the moment before his head exploded did Sweaty come to realize that this little fucker with the pointed nose looked like Dennis the Menace's dad.

"You can talk through clenched teeth," the Inquisitor yelled in his helmet-covered ear.

Twist . . .

"Talk!"

Twist . . .

"Talk!"

Another turn of the screw . . .

Until . . .

Sartre wrote, "Hell is other people."

Sartre was wrong.

Hell was the last thing Sweaty saw before oblivion.

Hell was Billy Brown of London Town.

———•—•———

The Art Historian perked up when he heard footsteps climbing the stairs from the cellar.

"Well?" he asked of the shadow in the doorframe.

"Nothing."

That was disappointing.

Only when the shadow slipped into the glow of the gallery did the Art Historian gasp with shock, involuntarily crossing himself from brain to gut and shoulder to shoulder. One glance at the Legionary's face—all splattered with blood and brain matter, and pierced with shards of skull—and his doubts about his faith evaporated. Surely, he was face to face with Satan.

Now, more than ever, he had to find the Holy Grail and extend his existence on earth, since he knew for certain that when he died, he would be damned to hell for what he had set in motion by summoning the Secret Cardinal to New York.

"Who's next?" snarled the Legionary.

TOBRUK

As he did every day in this all-or-nothing struggle with the
Allied forces that had beached in Normandy on D-day, a month
and a half ago, Field Marshal Erwin "the Desert Fox" Rommel
visited the battlefront. His old adversary in North Africa,
Bernard "Monty" Montgomery, would soon try to smash his
way out of the frustrating bottleneck at Caen in a push toward
Paris, and that had to be stopped. After talking strategy with his
frontline commanders in the First SS Panzer Corps, Rommel
got into his car for the long drive back to his château. It was
after four in the afternoon on July 17. The air was hot and
heavy. So was enemy action along the highway.

Allied warplanes owned the air. The road was strewn with
burning trucks and other vehicles, some with dead drivers still
behind the wheel. The route was also cluttered with Frenchmen
fleeing in horse- or ox-drawn carts flapping white cloths they
hoped would spare them from the wrath of airborne cannons
and machine guns. As Rommel's car roared by, raising clouds
of dust, those who recognized him doffed their hats.

In the rear sat two officers and an air sentry looking out for
planes. The field marshal sat with the driver, a road map on his
knees. His faraway stare suggested he was planning the next

day's battles, but actually he was thinking back to his glorious triumph two years ago under a broiling African sun . . .

———•—

Fingerspitzengefühl, they called it.

Fingertip feel for the battle.

The sixth sense—"an intuition in the fingers"—that made Rommel a legend on both sides of the front line.

In the First World War, he had earned the Iron Cross and the Pour le Mérite, or the Blue Max, a Prussian military award that was also won by Manfred von Richthofen, better known as the Red Baron. In the Second World War, Rommel had added the Knight's Cross to his medals. Because the enemy never knew where his 7th Panzers would strike next, they earned the nickname "the ghost division."

"Where Rommel is, *there* is the front!" bragged his soldiers, for unlike lesser leaders, he directed his tanks from the thick of the battle. Oblivious to exploding shells and the threat of capture, Rommel flung himself into the fray with a gift for improvisation, tossing aside the musty manual of accepted military tactics.

Blitzkrieg!

Lightning war.

That was Rommel's genius.

He had exported those blitzkrieg tactics from the plains of Europe to the desert wasteland of Cyrenaica, the eastern half of Libya. There, around the Roman fort of Tobruk, the battle for control of the Mediterranean Sea, the Suez Canal, and the Arabian oil fields swung back and forth like a pendulum. Since biblical times, only camel caravans had ventured across this almost treeless landscape of sand and stone. Vipers, scorpions, and loathsome flies plagued anything that moved. Without warning, a sandstorm could blow in, whirling billions of tons of lashing red grit in fierce winds that infiltrated everything—tents, eyes, noses, engines, and even wristwatches.

Into this godforsaken hell burst the Afrika Korps. Panzer tanks had already spread the swastika from the gates of Russia to the Pyrenees of Spain, and now they'd brought it to the sands of the Sahara. The Panzer—a fire-spewing monster with a high-velocity cannon that could rumble across the desert in a nothing-can-stop-it drive—was the perfect weapon for this kind of war.

The men of the Afrika Korps were toughened by this terrain—hair tangled, skin blistered, eyes reddened, lips cracked, and bodies browned from the broiling sun. Tanks left in the open—and there was no shade—became like ovens set to 160 degrees Fahrenheit. Dehydration drove some men mad. The food was terrible. Gastric ailments were rampant. And the slightest scratch from a thorn bush festered for months, a permanent running sore on arm or leg.

But then there was Rommel.

Der Wüstenfuchs.

The Desert Fox.

Here was a man who liked nothing more than to trick his opponent into surrender. Time and again, this modern-day Hannibal had outmaneuvered his foe, snatching victory from the brink of defeat. A favorite trick was to drag bundles of brushwood behind his supply trucks. The billowing clouds of dust created the illusion of an oncoming full-scale assault. As the British withdrew to stage a defense, Rommel would circle around and attack from another direction.

The Desert Fox.

Prophetically, he had actually kept a fox as a pet on the Western Front in 1915.

In January 1942, the current onslaught had kicked off. The
Afrika Korps had seized Benghazi and pushed the British east,
all the way back to Tobruk. Rommel rode in the Mammut—
German for "mammoth"—an armored command vehicle that
he'd captured from the British. With black-and-white
Wehrmacht crosses painted over its bluish British camouflage,
the Mammut reflected the realities of war.

The victor and the vanquished.

Today—June 20, 1942—Rommel was up and ready for
action by 5:30 a.m. As always, he was dressed in full uniform.
His riding boots and breeches spread beneath his stocky
frame, and his tunic was open to display the crosses at his
throat. His cap was shoved back jauntily to his close-cropped,
receding hairline. Above the gold-braided peak sat an over-
sized pair of sun-and-sand goggles. These, too, were booty
from one of his conquests, and Rommel had turned them into
the trademark of his heroic image. Now, as the rising sun
glinted off the lenses, his blue eyes scanned the sky for the
gull-winged silhouettes of Stukas about to dive.

Boom . . .

Boom . . .

Boom . . .

Artillery pounded the perimeter of Tobruk as the planes
came into sight. One after another, 150 Stukas dropped their
noses and plunged down, wheel sirens screaming, on the minefield protecting the British fortress. Fountains of dust plumed
up from the bunkers as the dive-bombers, engines snarling,
swung away low over bloodied heads.

Infantry commanders stood up and blew their whistles, the
signal for engineers to rush into the chaos of choking dust and
smoke to stretch a steel bridge across the anti-tank ditch.

Around them, soldiers fought hand-to-hand with the Mahrattas and Gurkhas of the Indian Brigade. By eight o'clock, the anti-tank ditch was spanned and the way was open.

Panzers poured into the fortress.

Riding in a troop carrier with his combat squad, Rommel trundled through the gap in the wake of his tanks. Traffic jams clogged the breach as trucks blew up, hurling fragments of razor-sharp rock and shrapnel into the air. Panzers fanned out around the wrecks and rumbled toward the harbor, their engines growling as the drivers shifted gears.

The ancient outpost of Tobruk, seventy miles this side of the Egyptian border, was both the best harbor in North Africa and the final obstacle in Rommel's relentless drive to the Suez Canal and the precious oil fields beyond. It blocked a twenty-two-mile stretch of the coastal highway that ran like a strand of licorice along the former caravan route from the Holy Land to Gibraltar. With Tobruk in British hands, the supply lines for the Afrika Korps had to detour inland along a desert trail. British tanks could dash out of the fort and cut the Germans' supply lines at any time.

Today would end that threat.

The heart of Tobruk was its grungy port. The harbor wasn't big—two and a quarter miles long and a mile wide—but it was sheltering and deep. The far shore was protected by a lofty, tongue-shaped promontory, and that's where the Italians had built the town. Currently, ships weighing anchor in a desperate bid to escape the war by sea were flaming, exploding, and sinking in a graveyard already cluttered with the half-submerged funnels and masts of bombed wrecks.

The men in the tanks saw the battle through slits narrow enough to keep out bullets. If a track got blown off, the five soldiers within were trapped in a mechanized bomb with hundreds of gallons of gasoline, an arsenal of cannon shells, and almost four thousand machine-gun rounds, all primed to explode if the enemy scored a hit. Dozens of tanks were already knocked out of action, long tongues of flame curling out of every hole. Their hulls seemed to bulge and convulse from the havoc inside. Rivulets of molten aluminum seeped from the engines like tears, and black smoke roiled from burning rubber and oil. Around the gutted turrets sprawled headless, limbless corpses. From below one jammed hatch, shrieks punctuated the battle.

By afternoon, columns of British prisoners shuffled past Rommel, their heads bowed in defeat. The sun was setting as the Germans fought their way into town and turned their guns on the ships still moored in port. By nightfall, Tobruk was almost theirs.

Rommel ate a meal cooked from captured British goods. With his head against the window, he slumped asleep in the seat of his car. His staff lay wrapped in blankets on the hard ground outside. The stars were blotted out by a pall of smoke smudged red by fires.

At sunrise, Rommel drove into town.

So many times had Tobruk been besieged during the war that hardly a building remained that wasn't flattened or crumbling to rubble. Four miles out of town, the Desert Fox ran into General Hendrik Klopper, the commander of the garrison. There, the British surrendered at 9:40 a.m., and Rommel told the commander to follow him back to Tobruk.

"See to repairing the water supply," he told the short, wiry South African. "You and your officers will also be responsible for maintaining order among the prisoners."

"My officers demand to be segregated from the blacks," countered Klopper.

"No," said Rommel. "Blacks are South African soldiers, too. They fought side by side with whites. You'll share the same cage."

Meanwhile, the men of the Afrika Korps labored at gathering booty. In desert warfare, what counts is the capture or destruction of enemy hardware. From the rubble, Tobruk gave up two thousand vehicles and thirty usable tanks, four hundred guns, and enough fuel to fill the Germans' Panzers for a blitzkrieg into Egypt. There was even beer galore—with blue Löwenbräu labels!—bought by the British in Lisbon.

"General?"

"Yes?" said Rommel.

"What do you make of this?"

The soldier who'd waved him over was crouched beside the wall of an ancient building that had been hit by a tank round during yesterday's conquest of the town. The breached wall was actually two walls with sand packed in between. Sand flowing out of the open hole had bared a large pottery jar, also cracked by the Panzer's blast.

"I found these in that pot," the soldier informed Rommel. He held out two papyrus scrolls and a bundle of wrapped-up relics. "One of the scrolls is a map."

The general studied the artifacts. "I like maps," he said. "I'll see if an expert can figure out what the sketch depicts."

The soldier relinquished the bundle. "Your battle trophy," he said.

Miles away in Germany, Hitler was ecstatic. Trumpets interrupted radio broadcasts with the news that Rommel had taken Tobruk. A bridge was named for him. Movie theaters showed newsreels around the clock. In the Reich Chancellery, Hitler stood at the map table and rubbed his hands with glee.

A colonel unrolled charts of the Nazis' spreading domination. The British were in retreat from the Arctic to Cyrenaica, and the blitzkrieg in Russia was advancing on the Caucasus. The next day, the radio announced: "The Führer has promoted the commander of Panzer Army Afrika, Colonel General Rommel, to the rank of field marshal."

Field marshal!

The highest rank there was.

A rank for life, with a secretary, horse, car, and driver.

To be a field marshal was to be immortal.

By the time the news reached them, the Desert Fox and his men were on the move. "Mount up! Raise a lot of dust!" That was Rommel's order. With the road to Egypt open, the Afrika Korps charged toward the coastal railway stop where the Desert Rats were digging in to mount a last stand.

Rommel was heading for El Alamein.

He had the relics with him.

Now it was two years later and the war was all but lost. The Battle of El Alamein had proved to be the turning point. The Americans had rearmed the British Eighth Army with Sherman tanks; Churchill had sent a new commander, the bloody-minded Monty Montgomery; and Operation Torch had landed U.S. warriors with pistol-packing General George Patton in Algeria and Morocco. Loss after loss had reduced Hitler's Reich, until the only option was for Rommel to negotiate a treasonous surrender with Churchill behind Hitler's back.

To that end, the Judas package was on its way to Britain.

Had Rommel been able to foresee how well the D-day invasion would go, he could have passed the Judas package to the

Allies here in France. But plans were too far advanced by June for the conspirators to change the smuggling route. The package containing Hitler's atomic secrets and—for safekeeping and to show good faith—the biblical relics found in Tobruk was already aboard the *Black Devil*. A week from now, hopefully, this nightmare would be over, and Germany would be spared obliteration.

"Spitfires!" barked the air sentry in back of Rommel's car.

Wrenched from reliving his glory days at Tobruk, the field marshal craned around in the front seat. The sight of eight enemy planes around Livarot had them using evasion tactics wherever possible. For miles, they'd followed a treed lane that ran parallel to the highway. The car was back on the main road when the lookout spied two marauding Spitfires thundering in behind them at treetop height.

"Speed up! Pull off!" Rommel shouted.

The driver hit the gas.

The car raced toward a narrow side road three hundred yards ahead, but before it could reach it, the lead Spitfire opened up with its machine guns and wing cannons. Rommel saw the flashes and shell explosions stitching a line of potholes at the car. Then the barrage of bullets tore up the left side, shattering the driver's shoulder and arm and peppering the field marshal's face with fragments of hot metal and glass. Careening down a long hill, the car crashed into a tree, spilling out its occupants before it overturned in a ditch.

His skull caved in, Rommel was thrown clear. Blackness engulfed him as the other Spitfire swooped down to strafe the car and pick off survivors.

DEVIL'S ADVOCATE

GERMANY, NOW

They stood on the rim of the pit, gazing down at the *Ace of Clubs* as the clouds overhead slid sunlight and shadow along its fuselage.

"Do you believe in God?" Wyatt asked.

"Yes," Rutger replied. "I'm a practicing Catholic."

"Oh?"

"You sound surprised. 'God is dead. God remains dead. And we have killed him. How shall we comfort ourselves, the murderers of all murderers?' Is that what you expect from me?"

"Nietzsche *was* German. And God-is-dead thinking *is* the mainstream for modern historians."

"I'd rather allow for light beyond the darkness, wouldn't you? That shaft of hope that sneaks through the chinks in our armor can exorcise despair."

"I wish I could believe," Wyatt said. "As Sir Thomas Browne put it, 'There's another man within me that's angry with me.'"

Rutger shrugged. "We're all Jekyll and Hyde. I'm in a constant battle with faith and skepticism. I'm a doubting Thomas in an age of doubt. That's how I grapple with faith and disillusionment. But human nature isn't black and white. It's black and gray. I doubt myself. I doubt others. And sometimes, I doubt God. But it's my ultimate *doubt about doubt* that keeps me clinging to faith."

"The Crusades, the Inquisition, the witch hunts, colonialism, the wars ignited by religious hatred—all this fuels my skepticism. Our religious impulse is like our sex drive— primal, powerful, and potentially explosive. What turns me off religion is its insatiable appetite for violence."

"Are you an atheist? Do you reject Christ?"

"I accept Jesus—factual or fictional—as one of the pathfinders to faith," Wyatt said. "My big 'if' surrounds the existence of God. As long as that remains an 'if,' I'll compromise and call myself agnostic."

"The death of God means the death of a meaningful cosmos. Ethical chaos—nihilism—lurks at the end of that dark road," Rutger warned. "So what brought on this discussion of metaphysics?"

"I can't get the horrifying image of Mick Balsdon spiked on the Judas chair out of my mind. And now we have Lenny Jones with his face pulverized. The motive for both murders has to be related to the contents of the Judas package. It can't be decades-old atomic secrets. So it must be the biblical relics that Judas is supposed to have included in the package."

"I agree," said Rutger.

"Let's make use of your Catholic training. Are you up for a game of Devil's Advocate?"

The devil's advocate was a canon lawyer appointed to argue *against* a person's candidacy for sainthood. His job was to take a skeptical view of the candidate's character, look for holes in the evidence, and argue that miracles attributed to the proposed saint were fraudulent. Wyatt's Devil's Advocate was a game for solving history's whodunits.

"What's the question?" asked Rutger.

"Who was Hitler's Judas?"

Wyatt fetched a coin from his pocket.

"Heads or tails?"

"Tails," chose the German.

The American flipped the coin.

"Heads it is. Me first. You're the devil's advocate."

He switched the coin for a notebook and tore out two pages, handing one to Rutger. Each man then wrote down the name of the traitor he thought was Judas.

Rutger folded his sheet of paper, and Wyatt held his out.

"Rommel," it read.

"Chivalry," said Wyatt. "That's the key. Rommel called the war in North Africa what?"

"*Krieg ohne Hass*," answered Rutger. "War without hate."

Wyatt flipped to a page of jottings in his notebook and read aloud, "'We have a very daring and skillful opponent against us, and, may I say across the havoc of war, a great general.' That was Churchill's opinion of Rommel in 1942. After Rommel's death in 1944, Churchill said, 'He also deserves our respect, because, although a loyal German soldier, he came to hate Hitler and all his works, and took part in the conspiracy to rescue Germany by displacing the maniac and tyrant. For this, he paid the forfeit of his life. In the sombre wars of modern democracy, there is little place for chivalry.'

"Of all Hitler's generals, Rommel was the *only* adversary admired by those he fought. He wasn't a Nazi. He was nonpolitical. He ordered his soldiers to fight clean, and he treated prisoners well, reducing the rations of his own men so POWs could eat. He ignored several of Hitler's orders: to execute captives of the Jewish Brigade, to execute all commandos, and to stand fast at El Alamein and sacrifice his men in the process. Faced with certain defeat, Rommel ordered a retreat. General Paulus, on the other hand, followed the order at Stalingrad, and tore the guts out of the German army.

"The phrase 'doing a Rommel' became the British soldiers' slang for having success at something. A British commander actually found it necessary to issue a memo saying, 'It would be most unfavorable for our soldiers to attribute supernatural powers to him.' Montgomery hung a framed portrait of the Desert Fox in his trailer. Even the hardest of hard-asses, General George 'Old Blood and Guts' Patton allegedly declared Rommel to be a 'magnificent bastard.'

"So to my mind, the only German leader with the stature to negotiate an armistice with Churchill behind Hitler's back was Rommel," concluded Wyatt. "Over to you."

This was the point where Rutger, the devil's advocate, was supposed to rush in swinging and knock the stuffing out of Wyatt's theory.

Instead, he opened his paper and held it out.

It read, "Rommel."

"Why?" asked Wyatt.

"Rommel returned from Africa disillusioned. He'd been fighting a gentlemen's war, but then he learned of the death camps, slave labor, the extermination of the Jews, and other atrocities. He asked Hitler to disband the Gestapo, redistribute members of the SS among the regular forces, and stop enlisting young boys. Hitler refused. That's when Rommel became convinced that Hitler's intransigence would result in the Fatherland's utter devastation.

"By 1944, there were *two* plans to topple Hitler. A group in Berlin—the *Berlinerlösung*—was willing to use any means, including assassination, to get rid of Hitler. There's no credible evidence that Rommel fell in with the July Plotters, however. He feared that killing Hitler would turn him into a martyr.

"The other group—the *Westlösung*—focused on the force preparing to meet Eisenhower's imminent invasion of France. Their aim—like you said—was to negotiate an armistice with Britain and America so that Germany could hurl everything it had at the dreaded Russians. To do that, they needed Rommel. They sent Dr. Karl Strölin, a soldier who had served with him in the First World War, to recruit him at his home in Herrlingen toward the end of February 1944."

"A month before the *Ace* went down," said Wyatt.

"The timeline works," said Rutger. "Rommel was perfectly placed for the western conspiracy. At his home, Rommel talked to Strölin for several hours about the fact that Germany couldn't win the war, even with the secret weapons mentioned in propaganda reports. At some point, Rommel acknowledged that it might be his 'duty' to come to the rescue of Germany."

"Why do you think he did?"

"The atomic bomb," said Rutger. "By 1944, Rommel's overwhelming fear was that Hitler would issue the same insane order for a suicidal last stand at the end of the war that he had at both El Alamein and Stalingrad. If he did, that might induce the Allies to use the atomic bomb on Germany."

"So he launched a *third* plot against Hitler."

"The Judas conspiracy."

"A plot so secret we still don't know for sure who Judas was."

"To the Nazis, Hitler was the savior of Germany. So whoever tried to betray him to Churchill in 1944 was equivalent to Judas. The Bible tells us that Judas was possessed by Satan, so the traitor who tried to negotiate an armistice with Churchill was . . ."

"The devil's advocate," Wyatt said.

Both players grinned.

"From February on, Rommel was in a more extraordinary position than any general in history. On the one hand, he was the chosen defender of France against invasion. On the other hand, he was advancing a secret peace agreement with Churchill. Churchill respected him for the reasons you mention, and he was more pragmatic than America when it came to unconditional surrender. We know from his 'Iron Curtain' speech that he believed the Russians were a postwar threat. Here was a way to have the Germans hold the Soviets back. Hitler would be overthrown in favor of Rommel, who was a hero on *both* sides of the conflict and was supported by the anti-Nazi *Westlösung*."

Wyatt jumped in for the kill.

"So Churchill sent Ack-Ack DuBoulay in the *Ace of Clubs* to hook up with Rommel. To show good faith, Rommel packaged up Heisenberg's file on Hitler's atomic bomb and prepared to smuggle it to Britain in a U-boat. That gamble wasn't as perilous as it seems, for America was way ahead in the bomb race. But actions have always spoken louder than words in my country, and it would have given Churchill the card he required to bring Washington on board. America's great Satan has *always* been godless Communism."

"The sub must have been on its way to Churchill when the twist of fate occurred. By chance, a marauding fighter spied Rommel's car on the road, so down swooped David to strafe it with machine-gun and cannon fire."

Wyatt perked up.

The game's afoot, he thought.

This friendship was not without its one-upmanship. The game of Devil's Advocate had elements of rivalry. The fun was trying to trap the other guy with the scope of your knowledge, and like most Europeans, Rutger felt those on his side of the pond had a broader view of history than the somewhat isolationist cowboys on the other side.

Cowboys like me, thought Wyatt, who always loved a pissing contest.

"David?" he prodded.

"The myth-busters," Rutger teased. "They're not big enough for a swagger in their stride, so they pride themselves on being Davids to our Goliaths. A David got Rommel."

"Wasn't the plane a P-47 Thunderbolt?"

"So you Americans claimed. But every witness on the ground said it was a Spitfire. Finally, in 2004, David was officially credited with the strafing of Rommel. He joined the company of his countryman who shot down the Red Baron."

"I thought that was Snoopy."

"No, that was Roy Brown. But now the evidence seems to indicate that the Red Baron was shot from the ground."

"Scratch one David, huh?"

Think, Wyatt, think. The clue is "Not big enough for a swagger in their stride."

"That leaves Charley Fox," offered the German.

"Who got Rommel, right?"

"Time's up," Rutger said. "Fox and Brown were . . ."

Work the odds, Wyatt. Who trained the most war pilots? Who put Sweaty in the air before we joined the war?

"Canadians," he snapped.

"You lucky devil," Rutger conceded.

"Double or nothing," Wyatt said. "Let's go for the Blue Max. The big question is, What happened to the sub?"

SEA WOLVES

✝

SCOTLAND, 1944

"*Los!*" barked the skipper.

Fire!

The bow of the sub shot up with the sudden loss of torpedo weight. The *Black Devil* had the first practical "swim out" torpedo tubes. Contra-rotating propellers drove the "eel" forward at nine knots, and the bubble-free ejection left no surface wake. Since this was a test trip with tight rules of engagement, the torpedo was set to shoot straight and sink if it missed its target.

"*Scheisse!*"

Shit! swore the skipper. "Not even close!"

No detonation jarred the U-boat or lit up the viewfinder of the periscope. The Old Man—his entire body arched forward with tension—grappled with the massive shaft as if it were a dancing bear. Having spotted the intruder in the Firth of Forth, a British destroyer was coming to attack. This wasn't how the delivery of the Judas package was supposed to occur, but necessity is the mother of invention. If only Stürmer could have a look through the periscope at the Scottish waterway, or at least get a running commentary from the skipper.

"The second tube," the Old Man snapped. "This time, get it right. Miss with our last eel and we won't jump off the devil's shovel."

Translation: we're dead.

"Skipper," yelled the radioman from below. "Another one coming portside!"

Destroyers specialized in hunting and killing subs. Armed to the teeth with radar, sonar, guns, torpedoes, depth charges, and spigot mortars, these "tin cans" could zigzag in crazy doglegs and fill the depths with enough TNT to crumple Davy Jones's locker. In this game, a sub had two options: kill or dive out of the way.

Two destroyers and one torpedo.

Calculate the odds.

The *Black Devil* was fitted with the best mechanical director angle computer. With his eyes glued to the periscope shaft, the skipper called out estimates of target range, target speed, target angle to the bow, and torpedo speed for Stürmer, the first watch officer, to feed into the computer. It calculated the firing angle and trajectory needed to hit the destroyer, and transmitted that information to the gyroscope aiming the torpedo. Everything having to do with firing the sub's torpedoes was controlled from the conning tower, and the computer kept adjusting the steering mechanism right up to the moment of ejection from the tube.

Stürmer heard the computer purr as it performed.

"Here's something to chew on," the captain growled at whatever he saw through the periscope. "Tube two . . ."

A measured pause . . .

"Fire!"

Again, the *Black Devil* bucked from loss of weight. Down below, the chief engineer reacted, flooding the ballast tanks the moment the eel ejected to make sure the sudden buoyancy didn't force the boat to surface and turn it into a sitting duck.

"Crash dive!" the Old Man ordered.

The eel had an impact—not a magnetic influence—fuse. To detonate, the firing pin and whiskers required at least a glancing blow. But even if the torpedo scored a hit and took out one destroyer, there was no defense against the other sub killer, except to dive as fast as could be down, down, down to the depths of the sea.

"Into the cellar," the skipper said as the periscope retracted. Rung by rung, they scrambled down from the conning tower, one man's boots chasing the other's grasp on the ladder.

A jarring percussion rocked the boat.

"A hit!" the men below rejoiced in unison.

But the triumph was short lived.

The *Black Devil* was in a steep plunge. The bilge water rushed forward beneath the floor plates. The sausages dangling overhead swung like pendulums. "All hands forward!" the Old Man ordered those standing by, and they charged toward the bow to add body weight.

"Depth charges coming," warned the radioman.

The hydrophones were picking up sonar pings. The noise was like a hammer hitting a tuning fork. The ship stalking them was pulsing out high frequencies and catching anything that bounced back from submerged objects like this submarine.

Ping . . .

Ping . . .

Ping . . .

Blechkoller was the term. "Tin-can neurosis." The numbing dread that seized submariners under depth-charge attack.

Ping . . .

Ping . . .

Booooom!

Sound is five times louder in water than it is in the air. The force of the first charge slammed the sub like a sledgehammer. The boat vibrated violently from bow to stern. Crewmen not holding on to something were knocked off their feet. The first casualty of the shock wave was the Old Man. A metal surface caught the skipper under his chin, jerking back his head so sharply that his neck snapped.

Booooom!

The second blast snuffed the lights.

Every sound was amplified in this dark kettledrum. Their sole protection from the sea was a sheet of steel, and the thud-thuds knocking them about were testing its stress resistance. Crockery smashed to pieces, and the floor plates jumped and clattered. Light bulbs popped from their sockets, and instruments shattered. Wood splintered while food cans flew like caged canaries. How much more jolting could the *Black Devil* take before it split at the seams? Before one of the hull welds cracked and the green sea poured in?

With the skipper dead, Stürmer took command. Surrender the sub in the Firth of Forth and he could finish delivering the Judas package.

The destroyer was racing up and down under full steam, a poacher fishing with bombs.

The tension was nerve-shredding.

Stürmer held his breath.

White cones from flashlights cast circles on the dark. Oil-smeared faces twitched in the pools of light. One seaman chewed his lip. Another scrunched his eyes. Two, like turtles, hunched their heads down between their shoulders.

Emergency lights came on and bathed the sub in electric blue. Drops of perspiration splashed into the bilge. The crew feared the next depth charge would nail the lid down forever.

Every sailor's deepest fear is the cruel sea. Water strangles slowly in a drowning submarine. A trip to the bottom takes time. Will the water pressure compress the sub to a lump? Do corpses rot in the lower depths, or do fish gnaw flesh from the bones?

A drum roll of explosions boomed on all sides. A double whammy beneath their feet punched the sub in the gut.

"Leakage!" someone yelled.

Jets of water spurted, drenching the sailors and filling the sub with dense blue clouds.

"Blow the ballast tanks," Stürmer commanded. "All hands prepare to surface." .

Down here, men were wholly dependent on equipment. Batteries, in any sub, posed two perils: damaged cells could cause the loss of underwater power, and battery casings cracked by depth-charge jolts could spill their electrolytes into the bilge. Electrolysis of the sodium chloride in the brine would then produce—

"Gas!"

There was no mistaking this pepper-and-pineapple smell. Chlorine gas—the chemical weapon used in the Second Battle of Ypres during the First World War—billowed up through the floor plates from the storage trough below. As the *Black Devil* struggled to claw toward the surface, the greenish-yellow poisonous haze overpowered the crew.

The metallic taste of the gas stung Stürmer's throat and lungs. One by one, the men around him crumpled to their knees, suffocating in agony. Their rudimentary oxygen masks were of little use to those stumbling to strap them on, for just then, a depth charge exploded beside the sub, hurling the men still standing against metal edges.

Every bone in Stürmer's face smashed to splinters.

The sub broke the surface.

But no one escaped.

By the time the Royal Navy pried open the hatches, fourteen corpses manned the sub.

The date was July 19, 1944.

Two days after Rommel was wounded by the Spitfire attack in France, and one day before the July Plot bombers would fail to assassinate Hitler.

TICK-TOCK

GERMANY, NOW
The next day

From the window of a tower, Wyatt looks down at a bonfire blazing on an island in a pond. Through the flames, he glimpses Joan of Arc, lashed to a stake, cross in hand, as she's burned alive. Masked by hoods, Catholic Inquisitors ring the heretic. Only when she screams his name does Wyatt identify the doomed witch as Liz Hannah. The upside-down crucifix she holds comes from the beam above the Judas chair in Balsdon's cottage. Recoiling in horror, Wyatt sees iron bars on the window.

"Wyatt!

"Wyatt!

"Wyyyatt!"

Vertigo assaults him as he whirls about in this cell high up in the turret of a castle. He rushes to the only door in the circular wall, gives it a frantic rattle, and learns he's imprisoned in a locked room. Dropping to his knees, he peers through the Judas window in the door. His jailors are playing chess. Detective Inspector Ramsey, who suspects Wyatt of killing Mick Balsdon, and Detective Inspector Stritzel, who has him in the frame for the murder of Lenny Jones, make the same move.

Both castle their rooks . . .

Wyatt jerked awake to find himself in bed. The clock on the nightstand said it was 4:13.

Tick-tock . . .

He tried to go back to sleep, but sleep eluded him. So Wyatt rolled onto his back, locked his fingers behind his neck, and plumbed the anxiety that had stalked him out of dreamland.

Whoever had skewered Balsdon on the Judas chair wasn't hunting for decades-old atomic secrets. The killer had to be after the biblical relics rumored to be in the missing Judas package. The only clue to the location of the relics hid in the recollections of the crewmen of the *Ace of Clubs*. Had Balsdon believed Trent Jones was the agent? Having extracted that from the old man by torture and reading his pilfered archive, had the killer flown to Germany to steal Trent Jones's papers from his grandson, Lenny?

But if Jones wasn't the Judas agent—and Wyatt had proved he wasn't by solving the locked-turret puzzle—then the killer had yet to find what he was looking for. That meant he was *still* on the hunt. Would he go after Sweaty and Liz next?

Tick-tock . . .

Unless the religious signature left at the Balsdon murder was a red herring to blindside the police, the killer exhibited symptoms of paranoid psychosis fueled by Catholicism. The crucifix and the Inquisition instrument found in the cottage indicated that the killer was a religious nut.

There's *nothing* more dangerous, Wyatt thought as he threw back the covers, sat up in bed, and glanced at the clock.

Tick-tock . . .

Better safe than sorry.

Though it was ultra early, Wyatt phoned Liz's London flat. Her machine answered.

"Hi. It's Wyatt. Call me on my cell."

He left his number.

For a moment, Wyatt pondered going to the German federal police with his concern about Sweaty's and Liz's safety. He could ask them to contact the British police. But both forces viewed *him* as their prime suspect. Before the cops turned their attention to phantom killers, would they not wish to eliminate the only person who had appeared mysteriously at *both* murder scenes? Particularly if that suspect tried to elbow into the investigations like Raskolnikov did in *Crime and Punishment*?

You bet your booty they would, Wyatt concluded.

He decided that the German half of the Judas puzzle was best left to Rutger, who'd now returned to Berlin. There was nothing to keep Wyatt here, so he packed his bags, checked out of the hotel, drove to the airport, turned in the car, and caught the first available flight to London. From Gatwick, he hopped a train to the Achilles heel.

Tick-tock . . .

Trundling along in this train carriage brought Alfred Hitchcock to Wyatt's mind. Hitch made a number of train movies: *The 39 Steps*, *The Lady Vanishes*, *Strangers on a Train*, *North by Northwest*. And in explaining the "MacGuffin"—the generic, non-specific engine that sets a film in motion—Hitch had two men traveling on a train from London to Scotland. On the luggage rack above their heads jiggled an oddly shaped package.

"What's in the package?" asked one of the men.

"That's a MacGuffin," replied his companion.

"What's a MacGuffin?"

"It's a device for trapping lions in the Scottish Highlands."

"But there aren't any lions in the Scottish Highlands!"

"Well, then, I guess that's no MacGuffin."

For Hitchcock, the MacGuffin could be anything from a strip of microfilm (*North by Northwest*) to a coded message in a piece of music (*The Lady Vanishes*). All that mattered was that it seemed to be of vital importance to the characters in the film.

Well, that's what Wyatt had here. A MacGuffin that was valuable enough to someone that he was willing to slaughter Balsdon and Lenny Jones to get it.

Of course, Wyatt had no inkling what the MacGuffin was. But he sensed he was closing in on the secret by concluding that Judas was Erwin Rommel. Rommel's battles in North Africa, Wyatt knew, took him to the border of the Holy Land, where he might have chanced across some biblical relics.

Tick-tock . . .

As the train slinked southeast toward the Achilles heel of England, Wyatt passed the time by leafing through Rutger's files on U-boats sent to Britain between the night the *Ace* was shot down and the day the July Plot to assassinate Hitler failed. Each file included a group photograph of the crew snapped before the sea wolves went hunting.

For a man whose life centered on books, Wyatt wondered why he never had a bookmark at hand. As always, he had to dig out his business cards and slot them into places that he would revisit later. As he looked over the men in each picture—their young faces frozen in time—he wondered which one was Ack-Ack DuBoulay.

———•—•———

Wyatt checked his bags at the station and walked into town. He was here to accomplish several tasks. The relatives of the *Ace*'s crew had kept in touch, and two of them—the son of the flight engineer, Hugh "Ox" Oxley, and the daughter of the bomb-aimer, Russ "Nelson" Trafalgar—were married to each other and lived by the sea. Wyatt figured they'd have phone numbers for Liz's mother and grandmother, and he could call them to see if she was with them. He'd also be able to get a look at any archives kept by Ox and Nelson during the war. And he could borrow a photo of Ack-Ack DuBoulay to compare with the faces of the sea wolves in the U-boat files.

Tick-tock . . .

The Achilles heel of England was the weak spot where the invaders stormed in. Six centuries before the Romans landed, Celts from northern Europe had opened the gateway to pre-Christian Britain. Julius Caesar came, saw, and didn't conquer in 55 B.C. But the legions returned to stay a decade later, and refused to leave for four hundred years. When the Romans withdrew to defend Rome against pillaging heathens, the Angles and the Saxons—and later the Vikings and the Normans—sought out gaps in the coastline as their entry points. Each group of invaders threw up fortifications to bulwark themselves from the next, and today the shores bristle with forts, castles, moats, cannons, drawbridges, and portcullises resembling fangs about to chomp. In 1940, the bluebirds over the white cliffs of Dover were chewed by Nazi planes attacking during the Battle of Britain. Now, foreign conquerors came in by ferries and Chunnel trains, then fanned out to overrun England's teashops.

The cannons were for Catholics and Napoleon.

Catholics in case they tried to invade on behalf of the pope.

As for Old Bony, he failed to show.

Tick-tock . . .

Far from the madding and the maddening crowd, the clifftop path was all but deserted. Armed with a hand-drawn map, Wyatt snaked along the undulating cliff edge as the hungry tide below undercut the terra firma beneath his shoes.

The Sussex shore had been a haunt for smugglers. Towered over by the humps of the Seven Sisters and the knob of Beachy Head, pirates of old had hauled their contraband in through gaps in the cliff. The tales of these buccaneers provided J. M. Barrie with the inspiration for Captain Hook, and they also underpinned "Little Bo Peep." The "sheep" in that nursery rhyme were in fact Sussex smugglers, and their wagging "tails" were casks of French brandy being dragged in from the sea.

Lore like that cluttered Wyatt's mind as he closed on the lonely cottage ahead. This small home had once stood inland, but a sudden crumbling of the chalk had moved the seaside drop to its front yard. The yard was marked by stone walls that left just enough open space along the new edge for amblers to pass. Unaware that the clock was ticking toward devilry, Wyatt paused at the precipice to experience an epiphany.

Tick-tock . . .

The smell of the sea was in the crisp air. The offshore breeze was bracing. The sky was noisy with the cries of migrant birds landing to rest and feed on shrub berries. There had been a land bridge from here to Europe, until the English Channel relentlessly ate it away. Gazing down at the high tide eighty feet below, Wyatt wondered how deep the water was.

His epiphany was to recall John Donne, whose poem took on deeper meaning here at the rim:

No man is an island,
Entire of itself;
Every man is a piece of the continent,
A part of the main.

If a clod be washed away by the sea,
Europe is the less.
As well as if a promontory were.
As well as if a manner of thine own
Or of thine friend's were.
Each man's death diminishes me,
For I am involved in mankind.
Therefore, send not to know
For whom the bell tolls,
It tolls for thee.

Tick-tock . . .

Turning his back on the sea, Wyatt fished one of his calling cards from his wallet as he walked across the yard toward the front door. The cottage was what the locals called a tile-hung house. Rows of scallop-edged tiles hung like armor over the wood and plaster to protect it against the weather. Set in the door was an eye-level Judas window, like a spyhole into a cell. Wyatt wondered why it was called a Judas window. Because it betrayed what went on within?

Tick-tock . . .

He reached the door and peeked inside.

Tick . . .

"Bloody hell!"

HACELDAMA

Shortly before noon on October 14, Erwin Rommel went to his room in his villa at Herrlingen and changed from the brown jacket he usually wore over his riding breeches into his favorite uniform, his open-collared Afrika Korps tunic. He put on his Blue Max medal, its enamel chipped from the car crash that had nearly killed him four months earlier, and examined the scars left by the crushing of his skull.

At twelve o'clock precisely, a dark green car with a Berlin number plate stopped at the gate to the house. The driver wore the black uniform of the SS. The jackboots of his passengers crunched on the gravel driveway that led to the door. One was General Wilhelm Burgdorf, a big, red-faced man who came with orders from Hitler. The other was General Ernst Maisel, who was short and skinny, with a long, pointed nose and suspicious eyes.

On July 20, three days after Rommel's car crash, Colonel Graf Schenk von Stauffenberg had planted a briefcase bomb under the conference table at Hitler's Rastenburg headquarters. Luckily for the Führer, someone had inadvertently kicked the case behind a stout oak table leg that shielded him from the blast. Since then, Burgdorf and Maisel had been stalking officers suspected of taking part in the July Plot. Thousands had died in the purge.

The generals rang the bell and entered the house. In the hall, they exchanged salutes with Rommel.

"Will you stay for lunch?" asked the field marshal's wife.

"No," replied Burgdorf. "This is official business. May we talk in private, Herr Feldmarschall?"

Rommel ushered the men into his ground-floor study. As soon as the door closed, Burgdorf stated the purpose of their visit: "You have been accused of complicity in the plot on the Führer's life." Then he read out a number of damning statements made by army assassins under Gestapo arrest. "The Führer offers you a choice between trial for treason and the officer's way out. If you choose public humiliation, you will die at the end of a rope, and your family and staff will suffer. If you choose suicide, your death will be called natural, you'll be given a state funeral and burial at home, and your family will receive a pension. I have the poison with me. It works in three seconds."

Rommel was shaken. So it had come to this. Yes, he had planned to negotiate peace with Churchill to save the Fatherland. But he was not involved in the failed assassination. That, however, meant nothing now. Both acts were considered treason.

Tired and still unsteady from his injuries, he slowly climbed the stairs to his wife's bedroom. "In fifteen minutes, I will be dead," he said calmly, then explained the ultimatum.

Lucie looked faint, but she held back her tears. The former teenage sweethearts embraced for the last time, then Rommel heard her sobbing as he went to inform their son.

Downstairs, a servant helped him into his topcoat and handed him his cap and field marshal's baton. Months ago, back in France, he'd been given a dachshund puppy, and now the dog jumped at him with a bark of joy.

"Shut him in the study," Rommel told his son.

The Desert Fox stepped out into a fine afternoon of autumn colors. The generals were waiting by the garden gate, and as he approached, they snapped their right arms in the Nazi salute.

"*Heil* Hitler!" they said.

The SS driver swung open the rear door and stood at attention. Rommel shook hands with his son, then climbed into the back of the Opel. Burgdorf and Maisel joined him, and the doors slammed shut. The driver engaged the clutch and drove up the hill and around the bend toward the next village.

Rommel didn't look back. His eyes stared forward. To occupy his mind, he recalled the stormy night seven months ago when he'd knocked on the door of a house in Munich and solved the Tobruk puzzle . . .

The son of a schoolmaster who taught "modern side" subjects instead of classics, Rommel took no interest in books. He was drawn to the army—he enlisted at eighteen—and after serving in the First World War, he wrote *Infantry Attacks*, a manual on military tactics. When he read, it was always a book on soldierly subjects. While in North Africa, however, he took some interest in local history, and was mildly curious about the Greek and Roman ruins of Cyrenaica. A photograph was snapped of him gazing at bits of Roman pottery dug up by war correspondents. Nazi propagandists spun that into a story that he'd kept up his classics and was a keen archeologist who spent his leisure moments digging for ancient relics. In reality, he'd asked the reporters, "What the hell do you want with all that junk?"

But even if Rommel had been a classical history buff, he wouldn't have known what to make of the relics found in Tobruk. He realized that only an expert versed in the languages of biblical times could unravel the puzzle hidden in the papyrus scrolls he'd brought home with him. That's why he took advantage of this trip to Munich and ventured out on a stormy night to seek the opinion of the Art Historian to the Vatican.

His knock on the door of a well-maintained old Bavarian mansion was answered by a fretting man with a well-groomed Vandyke beard. It was evident from the puffy bags weighing down his bloodshot eyes that he had gone with too little sleep for too many days. Listlessly, the wretch welcomed the visitor into his house, leading him to a magnificent library burnished by its hearth.

"Thank you for seeing me, Herr Professor."

"The honor is mine, Herr Feldmarschall. Excuse my appearance, but I have a dying son. You must have passed the doctor on the road. I'm told my boy will not survive the night."

"I'm sorry."

"You have a son, I believe?"

"Manfred. He's fifteen. If you prefer to be alone, I'll return later this week."

"I'd rather keep occupied. There'll be time enough to worry once you leave."

A flash of lightning electrified the room. Thunder rattled the windows and shook the art in the nooks between the floor-to-ceiling bookshelves. As near as Rommel could tell, the miniature galleries advanced through time from prehistoric carvings to paintings by Dali. The gramophone murmured chamber music by Mozart.

"You have something to show me, Herr Feldmarschall?"

The waterproof case was basically a flattish rectangle hanging from a handle. Opening it, Rommel extracted a page in a glass frame.

"Our bombing of Tobruk cracked apart an ancient wall. Inside was a pottery jar surrounded by sand. The jar contained a papyrus map in a script unknown to me. I brought it to Germany and would like to know what it says."

The art historian donned a pince-nez. He set the papyrus down on a table and turned on a gooseneck lamp. When he looked up, amazement creased his face.

"The script is Aramaic, the colloquial language of Jews in the time of Jesus. The city is Jerusalem in the Second Temple Period."

"What's the purpose of the map?"

"That's intriguing. This document," the art historian said, "appears to be a treasure map."

A blackboard on an easel sloped beside the table. With a piece of chalk, the art historian sketched a rough version of the city drawn on the papyrus:

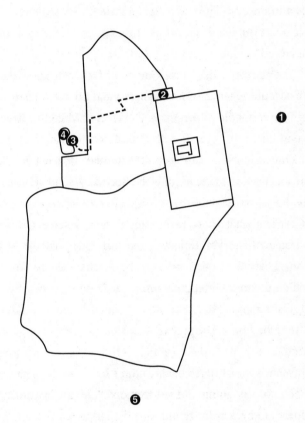

"Jerusalem sits in the Hills of Judea, where the Hinnom Valley and the Kidron Valley meet. The city was raised on the crest of the ridge that forms the watershed between those hills and the Judean Desert to the east. The site made Jerusalem easy to defend.

Rommel nodded. He was an expert at selecting a battle-ground.

"The number 1 marks the Garden of Gethsemane, at the foot of the Mount of Olives. That's where Judas betrayed Jesus with a kiss. The rectangle to the left is the Temple Mount as it was on the day Christ was crucified. The map says the Roman governor condemned him to death at the Praetorium, which I've marked with a 2. The arc to the north is the Second Wall of Jerusalem. It turns south to join the First Wall after it jogs around points 3 and 4. Though it's not on your papyrus, I've dotted in the present-day route of the Via Dolorosa, the path that we believe Jesus followed to his execution on Golgotha, outside the city walls.

"I've marked Golgotha as number 3, and the nearby tomb of Jesus is number 4."

"Are they on the papyrus?"

"Both are described in the script. The quarry outside Jerusalem's walls dates back to the First Temple. The hill on the edge of the gouge in the ground was ideal for executions, and burial caves were bored into the slopes of the pit. Those tombs were sealed with stones rolled across their mouths."

"Is that the focus of the map? The spots where Jesus was betrayed, crucified, and buried?"

"No, the map centers on what I've marked as number 5. That place is Haceldama, the site where both the Bible and this papyrus say Judas Iscariot died."

The art expert fetched a leather-bound Bible from his book-shelves and flipped through its pages.

"We have two versions of how Judas Iscariot died. The Gospel of Matthew says:

And when morning was come, all the chief priests and ancients of the people took counsel against Jesus, that they might put him to death.

And they brought him bound and delivered him to Pontius Pilate the governor.

Then Judas, who betrayed him, seeing that he was condemned, repenting himself, brought back the thirty pieces of silver to the chief priests and ancients,

Saying: I have sinned in betraying innocent blood. But they said: What is that to us? Look thou to it.

And casting down the pieces of silver in the temple, he departed and went and hanged himself with a halter.

But the chief priests having taken the pieces of silver, said: It is not lawful to put them into the corbona—the place in the temple for gifts and offerings—because it is the price of blood.

And after they had consulted together, they bought with them the potter's field, to be a burying place for strangers.

For this cause that field was called Haceldama, *that is, the field of blood, even to this day.*

Skipping to later pages, the expert said, "The alternate version, Acts of the Apostles—the second book of Luke—says:

Concerning Judas, who was the leader of them that apprehended Jesus:

Who was numbered with us, and had obtained part of this ministry.

And he indeed hath possessed a field of the reward of iniquity, and being hanged, burst asunder in the midst: and all his bowels gushed out.

*And it became known to all the inhabitants of Jerusalem: so
that the same field was called in their tongue,* Haceldama, *that
is to say, The field of blood.*

Closing the Bible, the expert returned to his drawing of
Jerusalem on the blackboard and tapped the number 5.

"Haceldama—called the potter's field because a potter had
once owned it—sits on a terrace south of Jerusalem, on the
south face of the Hinnom Valley, just before it joins the Kidron
Valley. Hinnom runs the length of the city's south wall, and
Kidron runs down the east wall between the Temple Mount and
the Mount of Olives."

"That's where Judas hanged himself and was buried?"

"According to both the Bible and the script on your
papyrus map."

"Is Haceldama still there?"

"Very much so. During the Crusades, it was the burial
ground for European knights."

The art historian ushered Rommel to a corner of the library
dedicated to the Holy Land. Maps of Jerusalem in different
periods—the First Temple, the Second Temple, the time of
Jesus, Aelia Capitolina, the Byzantine, the Early Arab, the
Crusader, the Ayyubid, the Mamluk, the Ottoman, the British
Mandate—were framed on the wall. Down one side of this
map collage ran a chronology.

"Do you like solving puzzles, Herr Feldmarschall?"

"Military ones."

"Then permit me to pose a biblical puzzle with war the key
to solving it. The puzzle is, What makes your papyrus map
from Tobruk a biblical earthshaker?"

JUDAS WINDOW

The Legionary was lashed to Satan by a black umbilical cord. His belly heaved as the beast within writhed through his gut and gnawed at his soul. Poison polluted his veins, rotting his body and sickening his mind. The clifftop cottage stank of sulfur and decaying flesh. Thrashing back and forth like a windshield wiper, the priest in him had tried to shake off the Devil's yoke, but Satan had all but conquered any good left in him. Instead of visions of God, the Virgin, and Jesus Christ, his head was stuffed with horrific images of the Inquisition to guide him through what he was doing now.

With every turn of the screw, the woman shrieked louder.

Her screams, however, were muffled by the gag.

Tears ran streaks of makeup down her gin-blotched cheeks.

"For the love of God!" beseeched the man tied to the plank. "You have it *all*!"

His begging resulted in another twist of the crank.

Since God made man in His image, He alone knows how to break him. That's why God inspired the tools of the Inquisition, and taught His Vatican inquisitors how to use them to exorcise Satan's secrets from his disciples.

Crank.

The danger wasn't the witch's tit. That was just the sign of women who consorted with the Devil. No, the peril to the souls of mankind was the witch's womb, which would produce the Devil's spawn, the Antichrist!

Crank.

To combat that, the Inquisition had created the Pear. The Pear was a bulbous metal invader shaped like the fruit. Having tied the daughter of the *Ace*'s bomb-aimer to the corners of her four-poster bed, the Legionary had inserted the witch-hunting device into her vagina and was now twisting the crank to spread the bulb like a blooming flower.

Crank.

The expanding Pear ripped her womb apart.

"Moses," the Devil inside him sneered, "try holding back *this* red sea."

Turning to focus on the man, the Legionary caught his reflection in a mirror. His skin was stretched across the bones of his diabolic face. As toxic fumes roiled from his lips, Satan's guttural growl rumbled deep within his chest. The priest gagged like a vomiting monster, and his fingers crooked into claws. The eyes that fell on the pleading man were intense and piercing.

"You next," Satan snarled.

To render the son of the *Ace*'s flight engineer almost unable to speak, the Legionary had wedged a Heretic's Fork under his chin. Held in position by a loose iron collar around his neck, the double-ended fork jabbed his upper chest and the flesh beneath his chin. The husband lay stretched along a bench that rocked on the fulcrum of a kitchen stool. His head was outside the bedroom door, so he could see his wife from the corner of his eye and hear what was done to her. He was the one who had given up their fathers' wartime archives, answering every question the home invader put against the background of his wife's mewling.

Hell, the fool had even offered up his soul.

Gotcha!

To lever up the man, the Legionary wedged the foot end of the bench under a heavy armchair. He used a clothespin to plug the man's nose, then the priest yanked his jaw down on the prongs of the Heretic's Fork just enough to be able to jam a funnel between his teeth. It took quart after quart of water poured down the funnel's spout to bloat the husband's stomach to maximum distention. A kick from the Legionary's foot shoved away the chair so the head end of the bench slammed down. Water spewed from the open mouth as the full weight of the stomach pressed against the inverted heart and lungs. The unbearable pain was etched into the man's eyes, as was the fear of suffocation.

Whap!

Whap!

Whap!

Using a wooden mallet, the Legionary hit the man's bloated belly with harder and harder blows, until he burst open like Judas at Haceldama.

What a mess!

All that remained was to leave Satan's signature. As the possessed priest walked the floor of the cottage to smear the number 666 across the walls in the woman's blood and suspend an upside-down crucifix from a ceiling beam, his footsteps sounded like the clomping of cloven hoofs.

Having cleaned up at the sink and with the archives clutched under one arm, he turned to exit by the door that opened on the yard fronting the cliff-edge path, and that's when he saw the bewildered face of Wyatt Rook peering in through the Judas window.

His hand went for the gun.

JUDAS PUZZLE

✝

"What makes your papyrus map from Tobruk a biblical earthshaker, Herr Feldmarschall?"

Moving to the chronology beside his map collage, the art historian touched the uppermost date.

"Clue one," he said, "is background to the puzzle."

Rommel read:

1000 B.C.: King David captures Jerusalem and makes it the capital of the Israelite kingdom. David's son, King Solomon, erects the First Temple in Jerusalem, on Mount Moriah, at the site of the Foundation Stone, where Abraham almost sacrificed his son, Isaac, to God.

"From then on," said the historian, "Jerusalem was of religious significance to Jews."

His finger dropped.

"Clues two and three," he said.

586 B.C.: Babylon's King Nebuchadnezzar conquers Jerusalem, destroys the First Temple, and exiles the Jews to Babylon, about fifty miles south of what is now Baghdad, Iraq.

538 B.C.: King Cyrus of Persia, now Iran, conquers Babylon. He allows the Jews to return to Jerusalem and resurrect their temple from the ruins of the first one. The Second Temple is dedicated twenty-two years later.

"The Second Temple is on the papyrus map," said Rommel. His host nodded. "Clue four," he continued.

63 B.C.: The Roman general Pompey, a third of the triumvirate that includes Julius Caesar, conquers Jerusalem. Accountable to Rome, King Herod ascends to the Judean throne in 37 B.C. He constructs a manmade Temple Mount on Mount Moriah, surmounted by a refurbished Second Temple. He also adds the Second Wall of Jerusalem, to expand the city to the north.

"That Second Temple and that Second Wall are the ones sketched on the papyrus map," said the historian. "That's how Jerusalem appeared when Christ died."

His finger touched a wall map titled "The Time of Jesus."

"Clue five," he said.

33 A.D.: Tensions rise in Jerusalem because Jews resent the Roman occupiers. Jesus enters the city, confronts the high priests in the Second Temple on the Temple Mount, and by order of Pontius Pilate, the Roman governor, is crucified on Golgotha.

"So," said the historian, "from then on, Jerusalem was of religious significance to Christians." He pointed to the same crucifixion sites on "The Time of Jesus" map that he had chalked on the blackboard across the room.

Gethsemane.

Golgotha.

Haceldama.

"Clue six," he said, returning to the timeline.

70 A.D.: The Third Wall of Jerusalem—to the north of the Second Wall—is built between 41 and 44 A.D. and later strengthened by the Zealots fighting Rome in the Jewish War. That wall brings Golgotha inside the city. In 70 A.D., the Romans sack Jerusalem, demolish its walls, and raze the Second Temple. All that's left is the Temple Mount's western retaining wall (which becomes the Wailing Wall, the holiest site for Jews). All Jews are expelled from Jerusalem.

"The Third Wall's not on the papyrus map," noted Rommel. "Clue seven."

65 to 100 A.D.: The Gospels of Matthew, Mark, Luke, and John—the core of the Bible's New Testament and the Four Pillars of the Church—are written. The probable dates are:
Mark—around 70 A.D.
Matthew—after 70 A.D., since it refers to the destruction of Jerusalem.
Luke—after 70 A.D., since it also refers to the destruction of Jerusalem.
John—after 70 A.D., most likely in the 90s.
Conservative theologians suggest earlier dates, pushing Mark back to the early 50s.

"And finally," concluded the historian, "clue eight."

135 A.D.: Hadrian crushes the Bar Kokhba Rebellion and expels all Jews from Palestine. Left without a homeland, the Jews are dispersed around the Mediterranean. Jerusalem is renamed Aelia Capitolina, and Hadrian raises a temple to the Roman god Jupiter on the ruins of the Second Temple. He fills in the quarry with the tomb of Jesus to construct a Temple of Aphrodite on the summit of Golgotha.

"Herr Feldmarschall, those are the clues to solving the puzzle. Do you now understand what makes your papyrus map a biblical earthshaker?"

Rommel knew the answer.

As a battlefield commander, he could read a map.

But before the Desert Fox could speak, the art historian asked a follow-up question.

"The Aramaic script on the map refers to a confession and 'the means of the crime.' The map was drawn to show where these things were buried at Haceldama. Did you also recover those relics from the pot that was cracked open in Tobruk?"

———•◦•———

From his waterproof carrying case, Rommel removed a second papyrus sheet he'd pressed under glass. As the art historian translated the document aloud, his brow furrowed more deeply with every line. Another sizzle of lightning invaded the besieged room, and in that flash, the antiquarian seemed to transmogrify into Mephistopheles. Rommel could be Faust, here to sell his soul.

"If the relics were removed from Judas's grave at Haceldama, how did they get from the outskirts of Jerusalem to Tobruk?" asked the field marshal.

"Neither document says, but I'll hazard a guess. You fought in the easternmost province of Libya, next to the Egyptian border. The name of that region is Cyrenaica, the same name it had in biblical times. Colonized by the Greeks roughly six hundred years before Christ, it was usurped by Alexander the Great in 331 B.C. Later, about 100 B.C., Cyrenaica became a province of the Roman Empire."

He produced a map of the Mediterranean Sea.

"If you traveled west from the Holy Land along the Mediterranean coast of North Africa in biblical times, you would pass through Alexandria, at the mouth of the Nile, then Tobruk, a Roman fortress guarding the empire's frontier, before reaching Cyrene, the capital of Cyrenaica, on the bulge that juts north toward Greece. To escape from persecution in Jerusalem, Christians and Jews fled west along the coastal caravan route."

"To Tobruk?"

"The best port. They carried with them anything of value to their religion, or someone else's religion, if it would bring money. Perhaps that's what happened with your Judas relics. They would have been of value to both Christians and Jews."

"How'd they end up in the wall?"

"The wall probably served as a safe. Perhaps the grave robber hid the relics there and then was killed, his secret dying with him. The influx of exiled Jews certainly fueled anti-Semitism in Cyrenaica. In 115 A.D., those Jews rebelled under a leader named Lukuas, a self-proclaimed messiah. Tens of thousands of people died when Trajan suppressed the uprising with brutal force."

"Including the grave robber?"

"Is that not historically convincing?"

"It works," said Rommel.

"And then the relics stayed hidden in the wall until you bombed it," concluded the art historian. "Do you have them?"

Rommel watched the man's face as he pulled the Judas relics out of his case. There was no need for discussion. The artifacts spoke for themselves. The antiquarian shivered as he took them in his outstretched hands.

"Are you aware that what you have here is the Holy Grail?" he asked. "As one father to another, may I ask a favor? My sick child is dying. The doctors offer no hope. May I take the Holy Grail upstairs and touch my son with it?"

Rommel agreed, and followed the desperate man up to the room where his doomed boy sat lashed to an armchair. The feverish lad mumbled a childish mantra as if the words were all that kept him clinging to life.

"Itchy and a burny and a sting!"

The room reeked of vomit.

The boy's skin was bleeding where his fingernails had once clawed deep into his flesh.

"Christ, cure my son," his father prayed, then he touched the boy with the Holy Grail.

Once back downstairs, the art historian offered Rommel a drink. From a sideboard, he poured them glasses of kirsch. The schnapps burned on its way down.

"The Judas puzzle," Rommel said. "You asked if I could solve it. The question you posed was: What makes the papyrus map from Tobruk a biblical earthshaker? The answer lies in what is drawn on the map. A treasure map is of no use unless it contains the *contemporary* features of the landscape.

So whoever sketched the map of the city of Jerusalem did so *before* the Romans destroyed both the Second Temple and the Second Wall during the Jewish War in 70 A.D. The map, however, doesn't show the Third Wall, which was built between 41 and 44 A.D., so the sketch *predates* that decade. That means the map was drawn sometime between the crucifixion of Christ, in 33 A.D., and the raising of the Third Wall, about ten years later. Since the script on the map refers *specifically* to the confession and the relics found with it, those artifacts must date from that time, too. The most conservative theologians say the gospels of the New Testament were written no earlier than 50 A.D., so the Judas relics *precede* the Bible by a decade or more. The earlier the record, the closer it is to the truth. So this confession of Judas is the best explanation we have of *why* Christ was crucified. What's more, since Haceldama is named by both Matthew and Luke as the place where Judas was buried, that *independently* proves this is the Holy Grail."

The historian raised his glass.

"Well put," he replied. "But if I were you, I'd keep the pedigree of the Holy Grail to myself. These are dangerous times. With the German army occupying Rome and the Allies storming in fast, now is not the time to mention these relics to the pope. But soon the war will be over, Christians will thank God, and I will convince the Vatican to make you a very rich man in exchange for a gift of the Holy Grail."

"Stop," ordered General Burgdorf.

The SS driver brought the car to a halt. They'd traveled no more than a few hundred yards from Rommel's Herrlingen home, just up the hill and around the bend from sight. The stopped car jerked the field marshal out of his memory and back into the here and now. Burgdorf motioned for General Maisel and the driver to get out and stroll up the road. The car was parked in an open space on the edge of a wood. Rommel caught sight of a few Gestapo men from Berlin, no doubt with orders to shoot him dead and storm the house if he bolted.

So this was it.

Burgdorf offered him the poison.

"Three seconds," he said, "and it will be over."

Rommel took the vial. He held his own death in his hand. For a moment, he envisioned Christ hanging on the cross, the crown of thorns on his head. The U-boat bearing the Judas relics had vanished somewhere between Hamburg and Scotland's Firth of Forth. No doubt, the relics were now at the bottom of the sea, lost wherever the sub had come to rest.

In the massive purge that followed the failed plot to kill Hitler, all those who knew that the Judas relics were on their way to Britain in the *Black Devil* died at the end of wire nooses in the torture cells under Gestapo headquarters. To thwart spies and prevent leaks, Rommel had decided that not even Churchill would be made privy to the smuggling route. He'd said nothing about the botched plan for fear the Gestapo would exact revenge on his family.

Negotiating peace was dead.

Let sleeping dogs lie.

So now he crushed the vial between his teeth to release the poison, knowing that with him would die the secret of the Judas relics, and that he was one of a handful of people in all of history to have held the Holy Grail.

Seconds later, Hitler's Judas was dead.

NO PARACHUTE

✝

"Bloody hell!"

Terror assaulted his mind as Wyatt peered through the Judas window in the door of the clifftop cottage. There was no entrance hall, just a big open space with rooms off it. Beyond the threshold to the bedroom, a woman lay spread-eagled on a four-poster bed. A pool of blood spread fingers across the floor toward the door. This side of the threshold, a man had spilled his guts on the hardwood, in a pile that looked like a nest of purple snakes. Against the grisly backdrop, Wyatt spied a gore-spattered ghost approaching the Judas window.

"Lenny?" he gasped.

The dead man's head was no longer caved in by a hammer, nor was his body bloated from the German river. Instead, the phantom was alive and well, and aiming a silencer-equipped gun between Wyatt's wide-eyed pupils.

On instinct, the target ducked and flung his hands up to protect his face from flying glass. The Judas window shattered as Wyatt's fingers splayed, flipping his calling card away from his grasp.

There was no time to retrieve it.

Wyatt turned and ran.

Never had he been so thankful for his incarceration at that boarding school. "A sound mind in a sound body," the Nose used to say as he ordered the boys to drop to their knees on the soccer field and bow—under threat of the Paddle—in the direction of his outstretched arm.

"Do you know what you're bowing to, boys?"

"To Mecca?" Wyatt answered.

"No. To *my* house. And don't you forget it."

That was back in feudal times, before the school did away with corporal punishment. At the start of the year, the Nose laid down the punishment for any infraction of his "No Talking without Permission" rule: four of the best on the backside of every lad in class—the first on entering the gym, the second on going into the showers, the third on coming out with bums wet, and the final one as they exited for the next class.

After one transgression, yakking ceased, and there was no need for the Nose to re-enforce the rule.

"Rook?"

"Yes, sir."

"What will your sport be?"

"Track, sir."

"You'd better run like the wind. And don't you forget it."

So run he had. Faster, and faster, and *faster*! Good at long distances for the runner's high. And the best in school at the hundred-yard dash for the adrenaline rush.

"Rook?"

"Yes, sir."

"It's time for hurdling. I want those long legs limbered up for next week's track ribbon. Give me ten straddles off the springboard and over the wooden horse."

That hurt. It was like doing the splits.

"Rook?"

"Yes, sir."

"This time, knees to chin. I want those long legs tight for the track ribbon. Give me ten through the hoops of your arms, off the board, palms on the horse."

"Sir?"

"What?"

"My legs are too long for that."

"Nonsense."

"Show him, sir." Jack came to the rescue.

"Yes, sir," the rest of the class piped in. "We all need to see how it's done."

The Nose was not a man to walk away from a challenge. Not if his Latin machismo was on the line.

"Lead from the front, sir," Jack encouraged.

The Nose was sporting his usual gym attire: sneakers; gray slacks with knife-sharp creases; tight, white T-shirt flaunting his buff pecs; the ever-present whistle around his neck.

He hit the board, planted his palms, tucked up his knees, and caught his toes on the underside of the wooden horse. In a flail of arms and legs, with change flying out of his pockets, he took the upper half of the horse with him as he crashed to the mat on the other side.

"Not a word!" he shouted before crawling from the wreckage.

"Stay in line!" he ordered as he slammed the halves of the wooden horse back together.

Then he took a running start and hit the springboard as hard as he could, launching himself so high in the air that his palms missed the horse by a mile, and an ambulance had to be called to cart him away with a broken leg.

Well, thank God for the Nose, for the moment the adrenaline hit Wyatt's heart, he bolted from the cottage door just as he had been trained to do under threat of the Paddle.

The stone walls along both sides of the yard rose too high for him to hurdle. The stretch beyond was springy turf just waiting to twist an ankle. The odds favored a jerky side-to-side run down the shooting gallery. But at the end, he'd have to choose to go right or left along the cliff path, and that would make him an easy target for miles in either direction.

Or . . .

Wyatt didn't hear the shot, but he saw the effect. A mist of blood spewed forth from his arm.

No man is an island . . .

And he couldn't afford to be on this one.

If a clod be washed away by the sea . . .

That was his only chance.

Each man's death diminishes me . . .

Especially if it's your own.

Send not to know for whom the bell tolls . . .

A leg shot would cripple him.

It tolls for thee.

So that made up his mind.

Run, Wyatt. *Run!*

He made a mad dash for the beckoning edge of the crumbling cliff, then swapped dry land for thin air and an eighty-foot drop to the carnivorous sea.

"Rook?"

"Yes, sir."

"What will your sport be?"

As he took this leap of empty faith, he wished he'd said, "Diving."

On the way down, he thought of Sweaty's story of the rear gunner who fell eighteen thousand feet without a parachute into the cushioned arms of some fir trees.

Agnostic though he was, he prayed for deep water.

TRUE CROSS

✝

So what became of the True Cross?

That's the question that plagued the mind of the Secret Cardinal as he stood in the portico of St. Peter's Basilica and contemplated Bernini's sculpture of Constantine awed by the vision of the cross in the sky. According to the legends of the Roman Catholic Church, Empress Helena, Constantine's mother, made a pilgrimage to Jerusalem in 326 A.D., and there, in a cistern near the hill where Christ was crucified, she uncovered the *actual* cross on which he'd hung.

The holiest relic in Christendom was the True Cross. The empress had it broken up, and a piece was left in the care of the bishop of Jerusalem. Periodically, pilgrims saw the venerated cruciform. But Jerusalem fell to Muslim invaders in 638 A.D. They erected the Dome of the Rock on the Temple Mount, for Islamic tradition says that's where Muhammad ascended to heaven. In the centuries that followed, their empire grew, eventually stretching from India to the kingdom of France.

By the eleventh century, Christendom was ready to strike back. Christian knights from the fiefdoms of Europe answered Pope Urban II's call for holy war. With crosses stitched on the tunics they wore over their armor, they went off by the thousands to Jerusalem. On July 15, 1099, they stormed the walls with siege machines and took back the city.

The Secret Cardinal imagined the crusaders rampaging through the streets. The ferocious summer sun radiated off their helmets, chain mail, and double-edged swords. They hacked down anyone in their path as they chased the defilers of Jerusalem up the Temple Mount. Mounds of infidel heads, hands, and feet piled up in the streets and squares, until the crusaders were literally up to their ankles in blood. Loot belonged to whichever knight seized it first, so men laid claim to gold and silver, mosques and houses, horses and mules. Rumor was the Saracens had gulped down coins before the battle, so squires and footmen slit open their bellies to retrieve them.

The Muslims fell back to the Dome of the Rock, but the crusaders flushed them out. As knights pillaged that sanctuary, the infidels sought refuge in the nearby al-Aqsa Mosque. The crusaders forced their way in and put them all to the sword. Then they surrounded the Jews hiding in their synagogue and torched the building in retribution for their crucifixion of Christ.

The Jews burned alive.

This was no regular conquest by an invading army. This was a ritual slaughter, a cleansing of the temple. The bodies of the infidels, every pound of flesh, got piled outside the city walls and burned in pyres that Christians would later describe as flaming pyramids.

The Secret Cardinal saw the First Crusade as an exorcism.

Expelling the Devil from Eden.

Cleansing original sin.

So to offer thanks to God, the crusaders gathered in the Church of the Holy Sepulcher, built by Constantine on the crest of Golgotha and over the tomb of Jesus. "Oh day so ardently desired!" they prayed. "Oh time of times the most memorable! Oh deed before all other deeds! Let this sacred city, so long contaminated by the superstitions of pagans, be cleansed from their contagion!"

It was in the Church of the Holy Sepulcher that Arnulf Malecorne of Chocques, chaplain of the crusader army led by Robert of Normandy, William the Conqueror's son, rediscovered the True Cross. Hidden by Christians, it had gone missing in 1009. The discovery was a blessing from God, for an Egyptian army was coming to expel the crusaders. Arnulf carried the True Cross at the vanguard of Christ's army when it met and defeated the infidels at the Battle of Ascalon.

Onward, Christian soldiers, marching as to war,
With the cross of Jesus going on before—

The phone vibrating in his cassock summoned the Secret Cardinal back to the twenty-first century.

He hoped it would be the Legionary, but it was the Art Historian.

Only those two had this number.

"Eminence?"

"Yes," the cardinal whispered.

"Have you heard from him?"

"No."

"Something's wrong. He should have called me by now."

"Have you called him?"

"Yes. No answer. He said he'd phone to confirm as soon as he got the archives."

"When was that?"

"Early this morning. From Sussex."

"Have you reason for concern?" asked the cardinal.

"I fear he's unstable. I don't think he's psychologically fit for this crusade."

"How so?"

"I fear he's *too* true a believer."

———•◦•———

The crusaders held Jerusalem for eighty-eight years. The True Cross led them into battle twenty times. Dead crusaders were buried at Haceldama, just as Judas Iscariot was. A massive sepulcher was raised over natural grottos. Lowered through holes in the roof, bodies were left to rot there until the bones piled up fifteen feet.

The warrior who united the Muslims for revenge was Saladin, the sultan of Egypt, Syria, Arabia, and Mesopotamia. A Kurd from Tikrit, in what is now northern Iraq, he was almost fifty years old when, in March 1187, he called for *jihad* against the crusaders. "When the forbidden months are past," he read in the Koran, "then fight and slay the infidels wherever ye find them and seize them, beleaguer them, and lie in wait for them in every stratagem of war."

Saladin did just that.

With the Saracens massing on the border of Christendom, the king of Jerusalem, Guy of Lusignan, summoned twelve hundred knights and twenty thousand footmen to the citadel of La Safouri, site of the largest reservoir in the Holy Land. He also had the True Cross sent from the Church of the Holy Sepulcher so his soldiers could march to war behind the sacred relic.

Saladin, however, prayed to the same God. To bait his trap, the sultan besieged the castle of Count Raymond of Tripoli. Chivalry demanded the rescue of the count's wife, so the crusaders departed from their plan, trudging fifteen miles along a dry valley and over a saddle-shaped desert hump called the Horns of Hattin to save their damsel in distress.

Waiting for them along that route were thirty thousand Muslims flying the apricot banners of Saladin. His archers used charge-and-retreat tactics to harass the crusaders. Like irritating flies that wouldn't be shooed away, they returned again and again. Then, as the hammer of the sun beat down on its anvil, thousands of horsemen swung around behind the Christians to block their retreat.

The crusaders suffered a sleepless night beside a dry well. Archers picked off their horses in the dark, and foot soldiers choked their camp with brush fires to increase their thirst. Musicians kept them awake with drums, horns, and cymbals, while scorpions and tarantulas crawled into their armor.

Come morning, they plodded on toward the sight of Saladin's men pouring water on the sand to taunt them. The Muslim camp had water tanks replenished by camels circling to Lake Tiberias and back. With the enemy between him and the answer to his thirst, the king pitched his red tent on the crest of the Horns as a rally point. Only when the sun was in the crusaders' eyes and the heat and wind were up did the sultan attack.

The thundering hoofs of horses threw up a cloud of grit. Lances, maces, and crescent blades flashed in the haze. Boxed in on the heights, weary knights grew more dehydrated with every swing of their swords. Men on foot crumpled under a rain of arrows. Whittled down, the Christians crowded around the True Cross. Saladin's son cried, "We have beaten them!" "Be silent," his father replied. "We shall not defeat them until the red tent of the king falls." A second later, the tent collapsed. The king of Jerusalem was captured, along with two hundred knights. The True Cross vanished in the dust.

Three months later, Jerusalem fell. When he heard the news, Pope Urban III died of shock.

Saladin became the hero of the Muslim world. Allah, Mohammed, Saladin. God, prophet, liberator.

Muslims view the crucifixion as a sacrilege, a story unworthy of a proud religion. Jesus was human, not divine. Jesus was a prophet, not the son of God. To flaunt their contempt for that ignoble demise, the victors marched the knights' Golgotha relic to Damascus stuck upside down on a spear.

The last time anyone saw it—according to legend—the True Cross was being dragged through the streets of Damascus tied to the tail of Saladin's horse.

It was a long way from the dusty Golgotha of Cutud to the magnificence of the Vatican. From the portico, the Secret Cardinal crept into St. Peter's and marveled at its treasures. Lifting his eyes toward the soaring dome, he imagined fragments cracking off and falling to earth. He was gripped by a sickening vision of the Church crashing down around him.

Help me, Lord, he prayed.

Damascus was not the end for the True Cross. The legend is that during the Fourth Crusade, in 1204, knights sacked the city of Constantinople—now Istanbul—and seized one of the pieces brought from Jerusalem by Constantine's mother, Empress Helena. That piece was broken up and distributed among the crusaders, and so many bits of the relic were bequeathed to the Catholic churches and monasteries of Europe that the Protestant John Calvin later joked, "Collected together, they would make a big shipload. Yet the gospel testifies that a single man was able to carry it."

This modern-day crusade, however, was far more crucial.

If the Judas relics were what they were purported to be, they would be the most earthshaking find in the two-thousand-year history of Christendom.

Even more sacred than the True Cross.

If he succeeded in his crusade, the Secret Cardinal would undoubtedly qualify for sainthood.

Divine inspiration.

But if the relics were as false as all those pieces of the True Cross from Constantinople, they would bring the Holy See crumbling down.

Again, the phone in his cassock vibrated.

"Yes?" he whispered.

Nothing.

Only ragged breathing.

Then . . .

Barely audible . . .

"Father . . . Help . . . I need an exorcist . . ."

BRONZE MICE BOWL

✝

Daniel Defoe took his inspiration for *Robinson Crusoe* from the coastline of southeast England. But lucky Crusoe was cast ashore on the sands of the warm Caribbean, not here in the chilly English Channel with shingle as a beach.

Thank God for high tide and a dip in the seabed created by the cliff's tumbling. Wyatt struck the bottom feet first, but not hard enough to fracture his legs and spine. He was able to claw his way to the surface and cling to the chalk until the tide ebbed, exposing the shore at the foot of the cliff. His arm hurt like hell from his weight, but the bullet hole was a flesh wound, not something serious. Salt in the wound made it worse, and he hoped that, in the age of pollution, it was still true that sea water was good for a cut.

Ha!

In his bag stored at the station, Wyatt had antibiotics. He'd learned from past travels never fly to a Third World country without a medical kit, so he had a vial of unused drugs from last summer's trip to Botswana.

He was freezing. Survive this and he'd probably catch his death of cold.

Ah yes, the smell of sea air.

A day at the beach.

Waiting for the tide gave Wyatt time to assess his situation. The moment the cops got their claws into him, he knew he'd be tossed in the clink. He was up to his neck in circumstantial evidence before this, and now he'd left his calling card at two more murders.

The hand that had aimed the gun was wearing gloves, he recalled.

That meant there'd be no prints from the killer in the cottage. Just his calling card on the mat, dropped when he stopped by to butcher two more descendants of the *Ace*'s crew.

Wait a sec.

The hand, he thought.

What was that mark on the hand?

Not the gloved hand of the Lenny aiming the gun at him through the Judas window, but the bare hand that shook his when he met Lenny in Germany. Wyatt recalled seeing a scar on the back of that palm.

And later, while swilling beer to the oompah band, he'd noticed a similar scar on Lenny's inside palm.

Only now did Wyatt connect the dots. The scar on the inside palm was on the *left* hand, but Lenny had shaken hands with his *right*.

That seemed to indicate that something the size of nails had passed through *both* palms.

Another recollection.

From the cottage crowning this cliff.

When Wyatt peered in through the Judas window, didn't he see a crucifix strung upside down from the ceiling?

The *same* way a crucifix was hung from the beam in Balsdon's Yorkshire home.

"Jesus Christ!" he swore. The cops would find his calling card at this murder scene and trace the inquiries he made to find the clifftop cottage. Meanwhile, Lenny would surely be on his way to York, to find Liz and Sweaty at Balsdon's funeral. If Wyatt went to the cops, they'd be busy giving him the third degree while he tried to convince them that the ghost of one of his alleged victims was on the hunt.

No matter how, he *had* to get to York.

———————

Liz Hannah was screaming.

So hysterically was she struggling against the ropes that bound her wrists and ankles to the posts of the bed that she was tearing off her underlying flesh. Turned upside down on her naked abdomen was a bronze bowl. A small fire built in the hollow of the bowl's bottom was heating the metal and turning it into a miniature oven. Inside, mice clawed at the metal in a frantic attempt to escape. When they found themselves unable to break out through the dome of their bronze prison, the panicked mice began digging tunnels into Liz instead. One burrowed through her intestines and ate its way out above her navel. Another gnawed into her chest cavity and chewed at her lungs and heart.

No sooner had the Legionary ended his plea for an exorcist than Satan snuck that premonition of what would happen to Liz into his mind.

"Do it!" Satan commanded.

So now the Devil's disciple was on the road from Sussex to York, heading north to the funeral, where he would seize Liz and act out the vision.

On the seat beside him sat the Bronze Mice Bowl he'd stolen from the Inquisition.

In the cage next to it scurried five mice.

LAMENTATION

Sunset stained the horizon beyond the window of the plane. Drops drained from the sky to redden the North Sea as the aircraft flew to Leeds, the nearest airport to York. Wind heralding a storm crumbled the scattered clouds like wafers disintegrating in the hands of a frightened priest.

An omen? the exorcist wondered.

Stored in the bag at his feet were the sacred implements of his calling.

One way or another, this trip would bring to a climax the crusade launched by the Secret Cardinal in New York's Metropolitan Museum of Art.

"There are three threats to the Church, actually," the Art Historian had said then, reiterating what he was once told by his father, who held the same position at the Vatican during the Second World War.

"First, there's the threat that the map Rommel brought home from Tobruk came from Haceldama. Because the map predates the destruction of Jerusalem and the construction of the Third Wall, it also predates the New Testament Gospels of Matthew, Mark, Luke, and John. If the map is genuine, so must be the confession of Judas and the relics wrapped in it. The Judas relics are referred to in the confession.

"The New Testament gospels agree on three facts about Judas. One, he was one of the twelve disciples. Two, he condemned Jesus to death by singling him out in the Garden of Gethsemane with what we now call the Judas kiss. And three, the motive for that betrayal was money: the thirty pieces of silver.

"Judas's betrayal is crucial for the Passion of Christ, for if Judas didn't cause the crucifixion, *who did*? We know from the Bible that Jewish priests feared an uproar on Passover if they took public, heavy-handed action against Jesus, so they postponed his arrest until *after* the holy day. It's only because Judas helped them arrest Jesus overnight that he was crucified *before* Passover."

"Not on the festival day, lest there should be a tumult among the people," the Secret Cardinal quoted.

The Art Historian nodded. "That's set in biblical stone. So without Judas's betrayal, the Passion doesn't work. His betrayal is crucial if we're to believe that Jesus suffered unjustly on the cross.

"Threat number two is Judas's confession, found with the relics. According to my father, it's written in Aramaic, the language of Judas and Jesus, and dates from the time *between* the crucifixion and the resurrection. It discusses the former but not the latter. In effect, the confession is a suicide note.

"Instead of the sinister traitor, the chief villain of the crucifixion, Judas says he was the main confidant of Jesus, and got to hear things kept from the other disciples. According to the confession, Jesus asked Judas to betray him to his foes, and out of love for Jesus, Judas did what he asked. They were *collaborators*. Judas sold Jesus out to those who hated him because he thought the Messiah would use his God-given powers to survive being nailed to the cross. And that, he believed, would ignite a Jewish revolt against Rome."

"What you are going to do, do quickly," the cardinal quoted.

"But then Jesus died like an ordinary man. And the other disciples accused Judas of causing his death. After the descent from the cross, the traitor was given the relics as a damnable symbol of his betrayal. Overcome with guilt, Judas dictated his confession during Passover, then hanged himself. Somehow both it and the relics got buried with Judas at Haceldama. The confession survived as rumor, until it was recorded by the Gnostics as the Gospel of Judas."

The Art Historian approached *The Lamentation*.

"Do you see the threat? If Jesus set himself up to be sacrificed, what is there to lament about? And did he also set up his resurrection, to advance his ministry after death? If Jesus colluded with Judas, did he also conspire with those who claimed to have witnessed his resurrection?" he asked. "Of course, all of that is heresy without substantiation, as long as the Gospel of Judas remains a heretical text. But if the confession of Judas *predates* the Gospels of Matthew, Mark, Luke, and John, it becomes a *biblical* text."

There was no need for the Art Historian to elaborate. The problem with the Bible is that it was compiled by men, and the New Testament is the product of the Church. In the earliest centuries of Christianity, eighty gospels at least were written, and one of them was the Gospel of Judas, recorded by the Gnostics in the second century. The priest who deemed it heresy was Irenaeus, the bishop of Lyon. He announced in 180 A.D. that only the Gospels of Matthew, Mark, Luke, and John had divine inspiration. Those four gospels come from the *first* century, while the writings of the Gnostics come from the *second* century. Insisting that the Gospel of Judas says anything factual about Jesus is like saying a document written two centuries after Julius Caesar died tells us the inside truth about his conquest of Gaul. The *later* each gospel was written, the less likely it was to bear witness to the truth.

The Bible didn't come chipped in stone like the Ten Commandments. It was commissioned by Constantine the Great, after he legalized Christianity. The Church wanted a Bible that confirmed Jesus was the son of God, and it rejected as heresy any gospels that didn't support that viewpoint. In 397, the Council of Carthage produced the official Christian canon of scripture for the Old and New testaments. And ever since, *that* Bible has been called the Word of God.

The Gospel of Judas didn't make the cut. Irenaeus called it heresy, and heresy it remains. The discovery of the Coptic Scrolls at Nag Hammadi in 1945 and the Dead Sea Scrolls in the Judean desert in the 1950s didn't change that; nor did the surfacing of the Gospel of Judas in 2006.

But the confession of Judas!

That would shake the Bible to its spine.

For here would be an account written by one of the participants in the Passion of Christ that not only tied Jesus to a sacrilegious conspiracy, but also leapfrogged the Gospel of Judas to the *front* of the biblical timeline. The original manuscripts of the accepted gospels no longer exist, so they must be taken on faith, but here would be the *actual* parchment of the *real* first gospel.

That would be so contrary to Catholic catechism in the eyes of those who say the Vatican hides the truth about Jesus that the Confession of Judas might as well have been locked in a popes' safe for two thousand years!

And then there was threat number three.

The Judas relics themselves.

Was it any wonder that since the Art Historian's father had first warned the pope about Rommel's discovery, the Vatican had appointed a succession of Secret Cardinals to respond to the threat if the relics surfaced?

And now there was threat number four.

Satan was a-hoof!

———•◦•———

The Art Historian was so sickly that he would have looked more at home at death's door than the airport arrivals gate.

"It's on the news," he whispered. "Two more bodies. The son and daughter of *Ace* crew members. The police are looking for a man to help them with their inquiries."

"Who?"

"They won't say."

"If it's the Legionary, we're all in danger."

"That's for sure."

"I pray he shows," said the exorcist.

"He's on his way to York."

"You spoke to him?"

"No."

"Then how do you know?"

EXORCIST

The moon was high, and its colorless beams transformed the graveyard into a chessboard of black and white. The Legionary lurked among the headstones, watching the Secret Cardinal pass back and forth between the light within the church and the stained-glass window. The ancient abbey's stone had been shaped by ax and chisel, its wood by saw and adze. The wind of the oncoming storm howled under the eaves and drove the tattered clouds before it like whipped slaves.

White, then black . . .

Black, then white . . .

White, then black again . . .

The moon and its shadows fought for control of the boneyard. The Benedictine abbey dated back to the time of the Black Monks, centuries before King Henry VIII seized it in the 1530s, when he broke ties with Rome over the pope's refusal to divorce him from one of his six wives. Now, the church was back in the fold of the Vatican, and it had recently been reconsecrated as a holy place.

Black, then white . . .

White, then black . . .

Black . . . black . . .

This was the hour for the legion of darkness to sack the besieged church, so as black rain began to pock the Yorkshire soil, the Legionary skulked from the crooked headstones. As he closed on the church door, he could hear the wailing of lost souls buried in unsanctified graves after King Henry replaced the Roman Catholic Church with the Church of England.

Satan laughed within the possessed priest.

More work for the undertaker.

———•—•———

Devil detox.

That was the Vatican exorcist's calling.

Jesus performed exorcisms in Matthew 12, Mark 5, and Luke 11. His disciples became exorcists, too, and the God-given power was vested in the Vatican through St. Peter. The Rite of Exorcism—the ceremony for driving Satan and his demons out of a possessed wretch—derives from the Roman Ritual of 1614. Pope John Paul II revised the ritual in 1999, conducting at least three exorcisms himself.

The Secret Cardinal knew only too well the danger of satanic possession. Through scourging and crucifixion, he'd beaten back the Evil One in the Philippines. But as proved by the number of Catholic priests under investigation by the Holy Office for sexual abuses, the smoke of Satan was everywhere. And now the Devil had his filthy claws in the beautiful boy the priest had loved from afar in the South Pacific.

The cardinal *had* to save him.

So let this battle begin.

———•—•———

The Beasts of Satan had shocked Italians, but not the Legionary. For in that locked room of the Holy Office, he'd been exposed to centuries of dark deals with the Devil.

The Beasts of Satan was a heavy metal band. In the winter of 1998, under a full moon, the group held a satanic rite in the woods north of Milan. The ritual began with a night of drinking at a rock club called Midnight, then the devil worshippers drove to the woods, where a deep pit waited. Though her room was decorated with black candles and a goat's skull, their vestal of Satan was believed to have links to the Virgin Mary. In a sacrifice to the Evil One, the leader of the Beasts stabbed her in the heart with a knife. When the band's sixteen-year-old singer struggled to save her, he was clubbed with a hammer. The bodies were dumped in the pit and urinated on. In lieu of flowers, they got scattered with cigarette butts. After filling in the grave, a Beast danced on it, chanting, "Zombies! Now you are only zombies!"

The leader of the Beasts returned the next day to splash ammonia about to repel dogs. No one talked. The sacrifice remained secret until, six years later, in 2004, the ex-girlfriend of the head Beast threatened to inform the police. He lured her out to a remote chalet and shot her in the mouth, then called a friend to help bury her alive. His buddy finished her off with a shovel. An accident occurred while the leader was getting rid of her car, and the resulting police inquiry brought all three killings to light.

Eight devil worshippers were tried and jailed.

The leader of the Beasts kept a diary on how to conduct satanic rites in a bag filled with human hair and teeth. "Blood and death, blood raining down, blood bathing all my body, blood thirsty for blood," he recorded. "Pitiless, we will eliminate and cleanse, donating the ash of our enemies to he who sits on the throne."

For too long, the Holy See had been willfully blind to Satan. The Bible isn't logical. It comes from faith, not reason. Evil spirits are universally feared. There's never been a time or a culture free of them. But only the Bible reveals *why* they plague us. They dwell in a realm that we can't see, touch, or hear. Once, they were angels created by God. But Satan rebelled against God and was cast out of heaven. Banished to hell, he was joined there by the other bad angels, and they became demons. That legion of malign entities lacks physical form. So to unleash hatred in the world, they must take possession of a human body. Unless that wretch's soul is saved by the intervention of the Catholic Church, it too will be thrown down to hell.

To be blind to Satan *is* to reject the Bible.

A blind eye has always been the Devil's best weapon.

The Evil One fell out of fashion with the Enlightenment. The possessed were no longer possessed. They were now mentally ill. That was the explanation given in 1972, when a man leapt from the crowd viewing Michelangelo's *Pietà* in St. Peter's Basilica and—while shouting, "I'm Jesus Christ!"— took a hammer to the statue, smashing the Virgin Mary's face and one arm.

For two hundred years, exorcism languished in the shade, away from the light of God.

But no longer!

At Via degli Aldobrandeschi 190, on the outskirts of Rome, you'll find a new Vatican-affiliated university run by the Legionaries of Christ: the Athenaeum Pontificium Regina Apostolorum. In 2005, during the trial of the Beasts of Satan, a hundred clean-cut, fresh-faced priests in black cassocks filed through the iron gates and made their way to the lecture hall for the inaugural session of a course unlike any other. Over the next two months, they were taught how to determine satanic possession and drive out demons. Since then, the campus has turned out several hundred exorcists to confront the rising obsession with witchcraft and the occult.

The Evil One, however, had bigger fish to fry. He wasn't after the Harry Potterites and Da Vinci conspirators. He was after God, Jesus, the popes, and the one true Church. To that end, he now had complete possession of the Legionary, and he was tracking the Judas relics that could pull the Bible down.

Only one obstacle stood in his way.

The Secret Cardinal.

The exorcist summoned by the last vestige of goodness in the damned priest.

Knock, knock …

The Legionary knocked on heaven's door.

Numerous candles flickered inside the hollow cross, for the church was a cruciform. Wind howled around its central stone tower, which had been designed as refuge from Viking raids. Rain hammered the window at the end of the chancel reserved for the main altar. The alignment dated from the days of pagan worship, when the altar had to be lit by the morning sun. Forsaken now by the light of God, the window was black. The Doom was painted above the chancel arch, so the perils of the Last Judgment confronted the worshippers in their pews. Glow from the candles picked out details. In the upper center, Christ raised his hands in judgment. To the left, St. Peter held the keys to the gates of heaven, while angels welcomed the saved to eternal happiness with God. The mouth of hell yawned to the right, with the damned whipped in by demons to endless torture and pain.

Except for the Secret Cardinal, the church was empty.

The exorcist was governed by the Roman Ritual. One rule held that the rite should be performed in a church. Another called for images of the crucifixion and the Virgin Mary, Satan's sacred nemesis, to be displayed. Life-size statues of both flanked the altar. The exorcist wore the proper vestments: a black cassock and a white surplice, with a purple stole. Around his neck hung a silver cross on a chain, signifying the defeat of Satan, the architect of original sin, through the crucifixion of Christ at Jerusalem.

The Secret Cardinal looked commanding with his salt-and-pepper hair.

As the wind whined, the rain rattled, and the storm grew ugly, the exorcist opened the case he'd stored at his feet on the plane. One by one, he withdrew his tools for the rite. A silver crucifix, big enough to hold by hand. A silver aspergillum, to sprinkle holy water from Lourdes. A small canister of holy oil. And a thin red book of prayers approved for exorcism. Had he had the Judas relics in hand, there could have been no better test of their divine power.

Knock, knock …

The Devil was at the door.

Clutching the bigger crucifix in his right hand, the Secret Cardinal crossed himself three times.

On the forehead.

On the lips.

On the left side of his chest.

The exorcist strode to the door and yanked it open. Unprepared for what he faced, he gasped from shock. His beautiful boy had transformed into a monster. His hair plastered to his forehead by the pouring rain, his sunken eyes encircled by dark rings, this demon on the doorstep was hell incarnate. As the exorcist froze on the threshold, the shell of the Legionary vomited forth a guttural wail from his gangrenous soul.

"Dio onnipotente!"

God almighty!

"Immondissime spiritus," the exorcist said, *"in nomine dei patris, et filii, et spiritus sancti."*

On instinct, he had launched into the discernment, for the first step in exorcism is to recognize the Devil. What distinguishes possession from worldly mental illness is visceral aversion to Christian symbols. As the exorcist raised the crucifix in one hand and signed the cross over the possessed priest with his other, the Evil One let out a blasphemous snarl that curdled the cardinal's blood.

There would be no sprinkling of holy water or anointing with holy oil. No time. The fight was on.

The exorcist draped the tips of his satin stole across the Legionary's shoulders, tying Satan and his demons to him with a purple chain. When he placed his hand on the drenched head, the Devil reacted violently. The skull rocked back and forth, and convulsions wracked the bones. As the face twisted into a mask of fury and the sunken eyes rolled in disgust, the raspy throat spewed gibberish in a growl as deep as a werewolf's.

"N'gai, n'gha'ghaa, bugg-shoggog, y'hah: Yog-Sothoth . . ."

Was he speaking in tongues, the sure sign of possession? Or was he echoing blasphemies he'd read in the files of the Inquisition?

"State your name!" the Secret Cardinal commanded. Interrogation was crucial for this ritual, as banishment came from hurling the Evil One out in the name of a greater power.

The name wasn't sound and smoke.

The name was word and fire.

With the name, he would *know* the demon he was facing.

"My name is *Legion*!" snarled the Legionary.

"Do you believe in God?"

"*Fuck* God!"

"Do you believe in Jesus Christ?"

"*Fuck* him too!"

Incensed by such sacrilege, the exorcist pressed the cross against the demon's forehead.

"I command you, Satan! Leave this servant of God!"

The demoniac brushed the cross aside with a backhand swipe.

The exorcist faced icy eyes.

"Fuck *you*, asshole," the Devil within cursed. "You're busting my balls!"

The Secret Cardinal yelped when an underhand scoop seized hold of his testicles and twisted them around like the head of the girl in that film.

"Use them or lose them, secret sodomite!"

The exorcist squealed as the grip tightened and the silver cross fell from his hand.

"Turn a blind eye on me, will you? Here! Turn *two*!"

With his other hand, the Legionary clawed the exorcist's face. Sinking crooked fingers into both eye sockets as if they were the holes in a bowling ball, he dragged the Secret Cardinal out of the church, then swung him around like the hammer thrown in those Highland games.

Beseeching God, the exorcist was hurled into the darkness. Doomed to hell on his hands and knees, the blind man groped among the headstones, dragging the stole behind him.

Suddenly, the crucifix around his neck struck him under the chin. It cut off his scream as the links of the chain bit tightly into the flesh of his throat.

The last thing he heard before lack of oxygen shut down his brain was the snarl of Satan behind his ear.

"Die, Priest!

"Die, Priest!

"Die . . ."

SNEAKY

On a clear day, you could see the towers of York Minster miles away, but this morning, through the teeming rain, you could barely see to the edge of the churchyard. The church—Holy Cross—was grubby gray from the soot of centuries. Yorkshire was church country, with a history of Christianity dating back to the *Lindisfarne Gospels* and the Venerable Bede's *Ecclesiastical History of the English People*. That was the time before clocks, so a Dark Ages sundial—useless today—sat over the door as mourners in black exited Mick Balsdon's funeral.

"Ms. Hannah?"

"Yes?"

The broken-nosed man who stopped Liz outside the church looked like a battered boxer knocked over the ropes of the ring.

"Detective Inspector Ramsey."

The Yorkshire CID cop flashed his identification as Liz popped her umbrella against the rain.

"We're blocking the door," she said. "Let's move across to the headstones."

The rural church was besieged on all sides by graves. This section was so old that a thousand years of rain had erased whatever had once been carved in the stone.

"I'll get to the point, Ms. Hannah. We're looking for Wyatt Rook. When did you last see him?"

"Days ago. In Germany."

"Have you talked to him since?"

"No. I've not been home. My grandmother is sick. I borrowed her car to drive here."

"Cellphone?"

"I don't carry one, except for work. And I'm on leave."

"When will you next see Rook?"

"We were to meet at this funeral. But neither he nor Sergeant Earl Swetman attended."

"You might be in danger."

"Why?"

"Someone is after crewmen and relatives of those who flew in the final mission of the *Ace of Clubs*. That person's after any information they might have."

"And you think Rook's the killer?"

"He's our prime suspect."

"Then I'm the *last* person in danger from him. Rook already knows everything I do. That's why I hired him. So I could know more."

The cop's eyes narrowed.

"Look, Sergeant Balsdon raised questions about the *Ace of Clubs*. The plane was missing, and so was my granddad. Then the plane was found, and I wanted answers. I hired the person I thought was the best digger for the job. Rook located my grandfather's grave, so I flew back to Britain. I had what I wanted. End of story."

Ramsey passed her his card.

"If Rook contacts you, you'll call me, right? We don't want to see someone else get killed, and you involved. Life is too short to waste it in prison."

"I'll call."

"Promise?" His was a cold smile.

"Cross my heart."

———•—•———

Liz watched the detective wend his way to his car through the dispersing mourners. Many were elderly veterans from the Second World War, and some had wounds they'd carried most of their lives. After Ramsey drove away, Liz returned to the walkway that led from the church to its parking lot. She sloshed to her grandmother's Rover. A taxi was idling in the space next to her driver's door, and as she inserted her key in the lock, a voice called out.

"Pardon, lassie."

Liz turned.

"Is the funeral over?"

The vet in the rear of the cab had facial scars so horrific that Liz almost glanced away. Not only had he lost one eye, but the skin on that side of his head was a patchwork of grafts made to repair third-degree burns. Liz wondered if he had bailed out of a blazing bomber.

"Yes," she said. "It's over. Did you know Sergeant Balsdon in the war?"

"No. I know Sweaty."

Liz approached the rolled-down window. "Sergeant Swetman said he'd be here."

"It's me," Wyatt whispered from the mouth of the scarred veteran. "There's a pub a mile to the north. Make sure you're not followed. Meet me round back."

———•—•———

The empty taxi passed her on the rural road a minute before Liz pulled into the carriage loop behind the Black Bess Pub, named for highwayman Dick Turpin's horse.

Wyatt and his bags were waiting by the door. The sign beside him read, "We do bed-and-breakfast." His bags went into the back seat, then he strapped into the front.

"The police want you," Liz said.

"I know. Let's park somewhere and talk."

They found a lovers' lane and got lost among the dripping trees. They looked like a couple having a quickie instead of lunch. Soon, the windows fogged as if they were.

Wyatt filled her in on the double murder in Sussex.

"Lenny tried to kill you?"

"The fellow we knew as Lenny in Germany wasn't the real Lenny. He killed the real Lenny before we arrived and dumped his corpse in the river. The German police fished him out after you left. The guy we knew as Lenny—the gunman who took a shot at me—was an imposter. He must have learned from the real Lenny that none of us had met him."

"And infiltrated our group to learn what we know?"

"Has to be."

"And your disguise?"

"I found Balsdon's body. The Yorkshire cops suspect me. I was in Germany when the real Lenny was found. The German cops suspect me. Then I found two more bodies, conveniently leaving my calling card at the door. The Sussex cops will suspect me. I'm a lawyer. That circumstantial evidence is so strong that I'd consider prosecuting me. I went to Sussex to get your number, to warn you that the killer might be stalking you and Sweaty. That failed, so I had to slip through a tightening dragnet to get here. That's when I remembered a sign I saw in a shop near where we first met."

"At the bookstore?"

"A costume shop down the street had makeup artists in to do monsters for Halloween. I got my bags from the Sussex station, changed into dry clothes, and hopped a train to London before the police could react. The makeup artist who worked on me was reading a graphic novel. I asked if he knew Two-Face—"

"The *Batman* villain?"

"Uh-huh. And he asked if I knew the *Dick Tracy* villain who was inspired by Two-Face."

"Did you?"

"Sure. Haf-and-Haf. That got us yakking about the Phantom of the Opera and Jekyll-and-Hydes who show *both* personalities on their faces. I asked him to make me up like a geriatric half and half so I could baffle everyone at my Halloween party."

"Sneaky."

"When you first saw me, how did you almost react?"

"I wanted to avert my eyes."

"We all do. It's gauche to stare. I trained it from London to York, with everyone trying *not* to stare at me. Ramsey walked by and didn't twig."

"You do a good old man."

"I used to act in school." Wyatt spread his arms for the footlights, as far as the confines of the car would allow. "It's great to be back on Broadway!" he said in his best Barrymore.

"A man of many talents. *King Lear* at age fifteen?"

"I was the Fourth Wise Man in the Christmas pageant."

"Never heard of him."

"That's because on his way to that manger in Bethlehem, he came across Roman soldiers about to kill a mother and child. So he offered his gift of the magi to buy their freedom, and never got to give it to the baby under the star."

"Is that what you artistes call 'dramatic irony'?"

"My wise man shuffled, and when I first stepped onstage, I managed to kick the fire, knocking off the red cellophane. The audience had to watch a biblical play with a bare light bulb onstage. When it ended, no one clapped. I thought I'd bombed. Only later did I read the notice in the program: 'Due to the content of this production, we ask you refrain from applause.'"

"Some people take their religion *way* too seriously."

"As we're finding out."

"When did you get to the funeral?" asked Liz.

"After it started."

"How did you know my car?"

"The bag in the back seat is the one you had in Germany."

"Any idea who our Lenny is?"

"Someone hyper-religious. Did you notice the Christ-like scars on his hands?"

"Stigmata?"

"More like nail holes."

"He was *crucified*?"

"Wouldn't that fit? An ultraconservative Christian wants the Judas package."

"For what?"

"The package will tell us. Before I turn myself in to the cops, there's one more clue to follow. I need a photograph of Ack-Ack DuBoulay. He was the secret agent aboard the *Ace of Clubs*."

"That's easy," said Liz. "My grandfather's photo album was at my grandmother's house. So, in case it might be of use when we met up here—"

"You brought it with you?"

TIN CAN

"Eureka!" Wyatt exclaimed. "I've seen this face."

He touched the picture of the crewmen of the *Ace of Clubs* standing under the bomb bay doors of an RAF Halifax and zeroed in on the warrior next to a young Sweaty.

"Where?" Liz asked, excited.

"In one of the U-boat files I got from Rutger."

The rain was drumming down so hard they had to yell to be heard in the tin can that was Liz's car, and the weak light forced Wyatt to pull off his eyepatch to see. On the train ride down to Sussex before his dip in the Channel, he'd moved the group photo of each U-boat crew to the front of its file. With the photo of Ack-Ack resting on the console between their seats, Wyatt and Liz compared his face with each submariner's.

"Found him," said Wyatt, waving a photo. "The Judas agent flown in by the *Ace* shipped out to Scotland in a U-boat called the *Black Devil*."

Papers passed back and forth as they analyzed the file. Booting up his laptop, Wyatt researched the *Elektro* boat, then read and reread the British military report—a copy of which was in Rutger's file—on a submarine captured in the Firth of Forth in July 1944.

The deeper the historian delved, the deeper the frown that creased his brow.

"What are the odds?" he muttered.

"Of what?" Liz asked.

"Us having to solve *another* locked-room puzzle. First, a bomber in the air. Now, a sub under the sea. Am I being haunted by the ghost of John Dickson Carr?"

"Lay it out," said Liz.

"Look at the back of the photo. It lists the crew in order. Ack-Ack was the first watch officer. The 1WO. That means he was second-in-command, and he would have been in the conning tower. Just him and the skipper. The rest of the crew was stationed down below.

"The Type XXIII *Elektro* boat didn't enter service until late in the war. The *Black Devil* was sent on a secret run to the Firth of Forth to test its revolutionary, silent-running, electric-propulsion system. It was to make the trip *entirely* underwater. And not to engage the enemy unless attacked.

"So say I'm Ack-Ack. What would I do? I'd stay in my role as second-in-command until we entered the Firth of Forth. I'd have the Judas package stashed aboard with me. I'd put the skipper out of commission—maybe with poison—and take command of the sub. Then I'd find a way to surrender to the British."

"Package delivered," said Liz.

"But the scheme went wrong. The *Black Devil* was spotted in the Firth of Forth—perhaps radar picked up the periscope—and suddenly, the sub was under attack. It fired its torpedoes. One missed, but the other hit a destroyer. A depth-charge barrage forced the U-boat to surface, and also caused chlorine gas to kill the crew. The British had to pry open the sealed sub. Inside, they found a crewman with a smashed-in face, the result of being hurled about by the blasts. Unrecognizable, Ack-Ack was never identified."

"What happened to the package?"

"That's the puzzle. All the Germans knew was that they'd lost another sub. The casualty rate for U-boats was seventy-five percent. Their average life expectancy was three cruises."

Liz whistled.

"Do you know the story of Enigma?" Wyatt asked.

"The cipher machine captured from a U-boat during the war?"

"Decoding it made it possible to intercept wolf packs on the hunt and blast them before they struck. That helped the Allies win the Battle of the Atlantic. By capturing the *Black Devil*, the Royal Navy had the most sophisticated submarine in the world in hand. They would have searched it with a fine-toothed comb."

Liz tapped the copy of the declassified report in the file. "But there's no mention of the Judas package."

"So where did it go?"

"Perhaps they kept it from the report."

"But surely the relics would have come to light by now. Or there'd be rumors of their existence."

"We have quite a puzzle," said Liz. "Ack-Ack had the package on the sub. It wasn't found in a thorough search. So how did he make it vanish from the submerged boat?"

"Exactly."

"Through the torpedo tubes?"

"In this type of U-boat, the torpedoes were loaded from outside. So that means nothing could have been ejected from inside the hull through the torpedo tubes. The crew couldn't reload."

"Through the snorkel?"

"The snorkel was connected to the diesel engine and used to expel fumes while charging the batteries. No way."

"Through the periscope?"

"It, too, was sealed."

"Through the toilet in the head?"

Wyatt laughed. "It was hard enough to get waste out that way. Whatever was in the package, it was too big."

"Maybe the sub surfaced?"

"It didn't. The Brits captured the log. The whole idea of the test was to stay submerged."

"I'm out of ideas."

"So am I."

"Assuming the package was aboard, it's baffling."

"It's your classic locked-room puzzle. How do you sneak a sardine out of a tin can that's sealed and remains sealed after the sardine is gone?"

"Ramsey thinks you're dangerous. He threatened to send me to jail if I help you."

"You'd better play it safe and drop me somewhere."

Liz slipped into her Texas drawl and sang the first few bars of "Do Not Forsake Me: The Ballad of High Noon."

"Tex Ritter, you're not."

"I like a man who knows his movies. I'll not have my cowpoke go it alone against the Miller gang."

"*Your* cowpoke?"

"So where do we go from here?"

"First, let's get out of Dodge. We'll drive north from Yorkshire until Sheriff Ramsey is eating our dust. Then we'll find a room for the night and puzzle this out."

"Don't take off the makeup."

"I won't."

"As little girls, we're raised for a night like this."

"I don't get it."

"*Beauty and the Beast?*"

"Liz Hannah," Wyatt said, raising an eyebrow. "Inspector Ramsey got it wrong. *You're* the dangerous one."

———•─•──

A listening bug affixed to the rear window of the car transmitted everything they said to the Legionary. He knew where Liz would be from their discussions in Germany, and he'd used the time while Liz was at Balsdon's funeral service to plant the bug and a GPS tracking device. When Wyatt arrived later, it made this a double header.

Good, thought Satan.

They'll go to hell together.

SCAVENGER HUNT

✝

THE NEXT DAY

He awoke with a start.

Gotta be, Wyatt thought. How else could Ack-Ack have made the Judas package vanish from the sub?

"Wake up, Liz." He shook her.

"Uh?" she groaned.

"The Beast wants Beauty to hit the road."

"What time is it?"

"Too early."

"Where are we going?"

"Guess."

"Why are we going there?"

"Meet me in the shower and I'll scrub your back."

Allied destroyers tracking deep-running U-boats were often puzzled by the sound of a huge underwater explosion, followed by silence. It was assumed that when a sub sank in bottomless seas, the hull gradually collapsed. After the war, however, the Royal Navy did tests with surplus subs and found they suffered a sudden catastrophic implosion instead. That's what caused those mysterious "explosions" when no depth charges were being dropped.

While reading in bed last night, after he and Liz were carnally reacquainted, Wyatt had wondered which would be worse: to be trapped in a sub plunging to the bottom of the sea, praying the implosion came before rivets started popping and tearing through bodies like bullets, or sinking to the seabed with the air supply dwindling, as your gasping buddies suffocated to death around you?

That in mind, Wyatt had turned out the light.

His night was plagued by dreams of U-boat escapes as harrowing as the one Nick Alkemade had made by freefalling out of a Lanc. In October 1943, a plane sank U-533 in the Gulf of Oman. Three crewmen stayed calm enough to unclip a hatch cover and let the sub sink until the pressure inside blew them clear. One survived by drifting for thirty hours before reaching land. In August 1944, U-413 fell ninety feet to the bottom of the English Channel. An engineer rushed forward to assess the damage, and an air bubble blew him out of the sub and to the surface. The other men perished. In January 1945, U-1199 sank in 240 feet of water. A petty officer opened the tower hatch and used his Dräger apparatus—a facemask attached to an oxygen canister—to swim to the surface. That remains the deepest-known operational escape.

Swim out, Wyatt's sleeping mind had thought, and that jerked him awake.

Where had he read those words?

That had to be how Ack-Ack made the Judas package vanish from the sealed sub.

He didn't break the seal!

Yesterday, during Liz and Wyatt's escape north from Yorkshire after the funeral, she had pointed east to the coast as they neared the border with County Durham.

"Yonder lies the port of Whitby, where a ship crashed into the pier under East Cliff. A big dog jumped down onto the sand

and disappeared into the darkness. Pray tell, Mr. Walking Encyclopedia, who had just arrived in England?"

"Dracula."

"Ahead lies Croft-on-Tees. The River Tees is the border between Yorkshire and Durham. Lewis Carroll's father was the rector of a church by a bridge over the water. In *Alice in Wonderland*, Carroll created the Mad Hatter. Hatters really did go mad. Why?"

"Mercury poisoning. Mercury was used in curing felt. Exposure to the vapors caused confusion, hallucinations, and severe tremors called 'hatter's shakes.'"

"You're a sponge," Liz marveled.

"You're asking the right questions. There's an interesting juxtaposition in those two examples. Horror from without, and horror from within. '*Dracul*' is Romanian for 'devil.' Our Lenny with the holes through his hands? Is he possessed? Or a mad hatter?"

"Vlad the Impaler?"

"Good pun. You're my kinda girl."

"Remember the White Rabbit that Alice follows down the hole?"

"'I'm late, I'm late for a very important date.'"

"Men rushing across the bridge from Durham to Yorkshire used to shout something like that as they passed the church run by Carroll's father. Why?"

"You've got me," Wyatt conceded.

"Because the pubs stayed open longer on the Yorkshire side."

Today, after a healthy English breakfast of kippers, bacon, sausages, eggs, beans, tomatoes, toast, and a yummy fried slice, they forsook rainy England for soggy Scotland. They angled east to the coast at Lindisfarne, for centuries a hub of early Christianity, and followed vast stretches of tawny sand up to the border. Gray, gray, gray was the color of the day, with towering gray cliffs sheltering small gray fishing ports battered by a gray sea beneath a gray sky. This coast was rife with monuments to men who had lost the eternal battle of the brine. Seabirds by the hundreds wheeled and dived offshore.

"Gloomy," Wyatt said.

"How's your wound today?"

"It still aches. But you're a soothing nurse."

They passed Dunbar to round the bulge of East Lothian, the gateway to the Firth of Forth. This stretch of Scotland was known for its golf. Too many pubs had names like the Golf Bag and the 19th Hole. Links ran for miles along the water. Muirfield was the headquarters of the Honourable Company of Edinburgh Golfers, founded in 1744. Wyatt's mind, however, probed the dark nooks. East Lothian was the birthplace of Sawney Bean, head of a mythic cannibal clan. Back in the 1500s, *The Newgate Calendar* says, his incestuous kids waylaid travelers and butchered them for meat. Limbs hung from hooks in their sea-side cave, and leftovers were pickled in barrels. Captured, the Beans were hauled in chains to Edinburgh's Tolbooth jail, then executed without trial. Hands and feet were cut off the twenty-seven men, and the twenty-one women had to watch them slowly bleed to death. Then they were burned like witches.

Wyatt cleared his throat.

"Ahem. Testing, testing, one, two, three. 'The Ballad of Sawney Bean.' Or, 'Local Boy Makes Good,'" he said:

Go ye not by Gallowa'
Come bide a while, my frein
I'll tell ye o' the dangers there;
Beware o' Sawney Bean.
There's naebody kens that he bides there

For his face is seldom seen
But tae meet his eye is tae meet your fate
At the hands o' Sawney Bean.
For Sawney he has ta'en a wife
And he's hungry bairns tae wean
And he's raised them up on the flesh o' men
In the cave o' Sawney Bean.
And Sawney has been well endowed
Wi daughters young and lean
And they a' hae ta'en their faither's seed
In the cave o' Sawney Bean.
An Sawney's sons are young an strong
And their blades are sharp and keen
Tae spill the blood o' travelers
Wha meet wi Sawney Bean.
So if you ride frae there tae here
Be ye wary in between
Lest they catch your horse and spill your blood
In the cave o' Sawney Bean.
They'll hing ye ap an cut yer throat
An they'll pick yer carcass clean
An they'll yase yer banes tae quiet the weans
In the cave o' Sawney Bean.
But fear ye not, oor Captain rides
On an errand o' the Queen
And he carries the writ of fire and sword
For the head o' Sawney Bean.
They've hung them high in Edinburgh toon
An likewise a' their kin
An the wind blaws cauld on a' their banes
An tae hell they a' hae gaen.

"Heavens above!" said Liz. "I'm chauffeur to Robbie Burns. What brought that on?"

"As a young bairn, I learned that a well-placed poem helps seduce the lassies."

"And *that's* the poem you think will work on *me*?"

"Stop here," Wyatt interrupted.

"North Berwick? Why?"

"Out there hides the answer to our sealed-sub puzzle. That's where the Royal Navy seized the *Black Devil*."

They parked the car, got out, and strolled along a shore battered by salt-spraying waves. In calmer weather, you could see across the Firth of Forth to Fife; but today, the inland waterway was eerie with Scotch mist, a clammy combination of fog and drizzle. North Berwick was a dignified, though shabby, Victorian seaside resort, twenty-three miles east of Edinburgh. Behind its harbor loomed the volcanic cone of North Berwick Law, visible for many miles in all directions. It was topped by the ruins of a watchtower built for the Napoleonic Wars and a lookout used in the Second World War. Flanked by sandy bays, the rocky harbor was home to the town's yacht club, the Scottish Seabird Centre, and Auld Kirk Green.

To the mournful bellows of ships passing in the Firth, Wyatt and Liz, huddling together on the harbor wall, peered into the haze to glimpse the islands offshore. When Robert Louis Stevenson lived in North Berwick, his imagination turned Fidra into Skeleton Island, in *Treasure Island*. To the east, Bass Rock loomed where the Firth of Forth joined the North Sea. Legend says it dropped there off Satan's cudgel when he waded home from doing evil. It used to be a prison—"Scotland's Bastille"— but now cameras transmitted live images of its colony of gannets to the seabird center for the entertainment of tourists. Lost in the fog, closer to Fife, was the Isle of May. There, French Masons say, the Knights Templar stashed their treasure before being burned at the stake for heresy on Friday, October 13, 1307.

The origin of paraskavedekatriaphobia?

Fear of Friday the thirteenth?

There, too, less than an hour before the official end of the Second World War, the *Avondale Park* became the last merchant ship sunk by a U-boat. As fireworks signaled the peace onshore, a convoy of five ships and three armed escorts sailed from port on Fife. Cut off from its headquarters and arguably unaware of the order to surrender, U-2336 lurked in the Firth. As the convoy sailed by the Isle of May, the sub's first torpedo hit the Norwegian freighter *Sneland 1*. It exploded in flames. The second—and last—torpedo struck the *Avondale Park*. It sank in two minutes. Though a destroyer pursued it firing depth charges, the U-boat—a Type XXIII *Elektro* boat like the *Black Devil*—escaped.

And that tale contained the final clue Wyatt had used to solve the locked-room puzzle.

"Don't tell me you're going to recite *The Rime of the Ancient Mariner*," Liz teased.

"By my calculation, the *Black Devil* was there," Wyatt said, pointing. "The destroyer coming at it was nearer to Fife. The sub fired both torpedoes toward the ship. One torpedo missed, but the other one hit. We know both torpedoes were launched because there's no record in the skipper's log of an earlier firing, and both were gone when the sub surfaced."

"Got it!" said Liz, snapping her fingers. "Carr's sixth explanation—it's a murder committed by a killer *outside* the room, although it seems as if the killer must have been *inside*."

"How do you sneak a sardine out of a tin can that's sealed, and remains sealed after the sardine is gone?"

"You can't, unless the sardine is hidden *outside* the seal."

"Unlike other U-boats, the Type XXIII was stocked with ammunition from outside. The sub's stern would be tipped down in dock and the torpedoes dropped in like shot into muzzleloaders. The torpedoes were a new 'swim out' kind. In effect, a torpedo fired at a target was a gyro-controlled mini submarine."

"Risky operation."

"Audacious. The best kind of plan. By 1944, subs were taking any crewmen they could get. The Judas conspirators smuggled Ack-Ack into the *Black Devil* as a technical specialist tasked with testing its new torpedo computer. The Judas package was hidden in a dummy torpedo dropped into one of the tubes in Germany. The trip to Scotland was a test run, not an attack mission. Not only was Ack-Ack in control of launching the torpedoes, but he also punched in the coordinates that determined where they went. The computer, of course, wasn't electronic like nowadays. It used gears and mechanical linkages to calculate the trajectory needed to hit the target, and to adjust the gyroscope aiming the torpedo. A torpedo that missed its target was designed to sink at a preset distance. So once the *Black Devil* entered the Firth of Forth, Ack-Ack could launch the torpedo containing the Judas package and program it to sink where British frogmen could retrieve it."

"And if the torpedo got lost?"

"Then Judas would lose the nebulous Christian relics, but not the atomic secrets. He'd have copies of those and could try again."

"Got it!" said Liz with another snap. "The torpedo that missed the destroyer!"

"Bingo!" Wyatt beamed. "At the end of the war, another sub sank two ships in the Firth of Forth. *Both* torpedoes hit. Here, just one found its mark. Maybe everything that could go wrong didn't. The destroyer attacked the *Black Devil* before the dummy torpedo got launched, so Ack-Ack ignored the coordinates he got from the skipper and instead set the torpedo to miss. Off went the Judas package to sink safely in the Firth near Fife, then—for self-preservation—Ack-Ack fired the live torpedo at the destroyer and hit. Those involved in the plot were killed or never talked. Because Churchill never knew that the sub had the Judas package, there was no hunt for the dummy torpedo."

"It's still out there!"

"Maybe. Maybe not. But we've got everything to gain and nothing to lose from a scavenger hunt."

WITCHCRAZE

"Vatican Exorcist Strangled."

The headline stopped Wyatt in his tracks. He'd gone off in search of two cups of takeaway tea, while Liz was out talking with researchers at her TV network on a public phone, to prevent the police from tracing a call made from Wyatt's cell. She was asking her office to hunt down any references to U-boat torpedoes salvaged from the Firth of Forth near Fife. Wyatt bought every newspaper with an article on the killing of the priest and read them after delivering a tea to Liz at the phone box. The death raised intriguing questions.

"I've loosed the hounds," Liz said, joining him. "Hopefully, we'll have an answer today."

"Here. Read the papers."

"An *exorcist* from the Vatican?" Liz said on finishing. "What does that mean?"

"It means someone with lofty church connections thinks the Devil is at large in Yorkshire. The priest was found in the graveyard of an old Benedictine abbey yesterday, but he'd been killed the night before. Luckily, I have several witnesses to verify I was in London that night. The police suspect me of the murders of Mick Balsdon and the Sussex couple, but if their killer also killed the exorcist, it had to be someone other than me."

"Lenny," said Liz. "Whoever he is."

"Come on. I've got to think this out, and I know just the place. As I recall, North Berwick is the site of possibly the most infamous satanic mass in history."

"Auld Kirk," said Liz. "My network did a documentary on it a few years back."

Auld Kirk Green and its medieval church used to dominate an island just offshore. Over the centuries, the island was linked to the mainland by a series of bridges, and now it's connected by a stone causeway that shelters the harbor of North Berwick. Violent storms had crumbled the main church to ruins, leaving only its porch still standing, and waves crashing in from the Firth of Forth had eaten away the graveyard, exposing coffins and bones.

From his car parked along the beach, the possessed priest watched Wyatt and Liz walk between a towering Celtic cross and the seabird center to Auld Kirk. Through a National Lottery grant, Auld Kirk had been restored as a tourist attraction by 2005, with information boards illustrating its history from the seventh century on. Along with Roman coins, a Viking comb, and the skeleton of an old murder victim, archeologists had uncovered signs of a pagan temple beneath the church.

Lacking the bug he'd left on their car, Satan couldn't eavesdrop on what the two were saying.

He could, however, relive the night when two hundred warlocks and witches had conjured him up in Auld Kirk.

Halloween, 1590 . . .

St. Andrew's Auld Kirk.

The tale began, as you'd expect, with the namesake of this church. Andrew—like his brother, Peter—was a fisherman on the Sea of Galilee when he met Jesus and became his first disciple. Known as the Protocletus, or the First Called, Andrew urged Jesus to summon Peter as a disciple as well. After Christ was crucified, Andrew preached the gospel in Greece. He infuriated the Roman governor by converting his wife and his brother to Christianity. Andrew was crucified upside down so he could gaze at heaven, where he would meet his Lord.

Legend says a monk named St. Rule was told by an angel to carry St. Andrew's remains to the "ends of the earth" for safekeeping. In those days, Scotland was about as far away as you could go, so the monk took a tooth, an arm bone, a kneecap, and some fingers from the saint's grave and sailed west. Shipwrecked off the coast of Fife, St. Rule brought his precious cargo ashore just north of the Firth of Forth, and then he built a church where the town of St. Andrews is today as a shrine for the relics.

In time, St. Andrew was embraced as the patron saint of Scotland. The X-shaped cross—or saltire—on which he was crucified became Scotland's flag. Christian pilgrims from Lindisfarne and communities to the south flocked north to worship St. Andrew's relics, but they were blocked by the Firth of Forth. So in the Middle Ages, a ferry began running from North Berwick to Fife, and in 1177, this Auld Kirk was dedicated so pilgrims could pray for a crossing safe from the storms of the North Sea.

"Ten thousand pilgrims a year," Wyatt read from the information board. "That's quite the tourist trade."

"Multiply that by the more than five hundred years of the ferry run, from the twelfth century to the seventeenth," added Liz, "and wouldn't I love to have a monopoly on these things." She showed him a picture of clay molds used for making pilgrims' badges in the shape of St. Andrew crucified on his cross.

Wyatt pointed north across the waterway. "The relics of St. Andrew were over there. The Judas relics aboard the sub vanished here." His finger dropped to the waves of the Firth. "Whatever the Judas relics are, they have meaning for *both* groups that held masses in Auld Kirk: Christians and satanists. Upside-down crosses at the murder scenes—that's satanism. Upside-down *crucifixes* indicate a satanist with a Catholic fixation. The appearance of an exorcist from the Vatican means deep church connections. Crucifixion scars suggest a person living out Christ's Passion. Put those pieces together and what do you get?"

"A priest who believes he's possessed," said Liz.

"Whatever the Judas relics are, he thinks they're worth killing possible clue holders and even the exorcist sent to drive out his demons."

"What's worth that?"

"Relics so holy that Rommel believed they'd have the earth-shaking impact of an atomic blast."

"They must be from Jesus," said Liz.

———————

A cow produced no milk. That was the Devil's doing. A woman couldn't bear children. An old crone used her evil eye. Witchcraft was rife in Scotland when Francis Stewart, the Earl of Bothwell and pretender to the throne, summoned the witches of East Lothian to Auld Kirk to meet the Devil. By foot and by boat, they swarmed to North Berwick, and there, under the orange moon of Halloween, they conjured up . . .

Me, thought the Legionary.

As the wind groaned and the surf crashed and chaos claimed their souls, the women writhed wildly among the headstones of the graveyard, plucking bones from coffins that had resurfaced. They wrapped themselves in winding sheets stolen from the corpses and carried the ingredients for their "magical cookery" into the church.

Inside, the witches' Sabbath was bubbling full boil. King James VI was sailing home from Denmark with his new wife, and the earl howled for this gathering to demolish his rival with a spell. Ringed by black candles, the Devil's disciples handed a black cat back and forth across the blazing hearth. As the witches molded images of the king out of wax, Agnes Sampson tied hand and foot joints from the corpses to the paws of the cat.

Satan bared his backside on the Auld Kirk pulpit, and his disciples took part in a black Mass by kissing it in turn. Then they carried the black cat to the edge of the Firth of Forth and hurled it into the sea to brew up a drowning storm.

It almost worked.

The king's boat nearly capsized.

The coven came to light when one witch's master tortured her to see if she had dark healing powers. Crushing her fingers with thumbscrews and tightening a cord around her skull, he searched her body for the witch's tit and found it on her neck. She confessed to having attended the gathering on Auld Kirk Green, then told him of the spell brewed up against the king. Agnes Sampson, she revealed, was "the eldest witch of all."

Satan reveled in that.

Sampson was tortured by the king himself at Holyroodhouse, his palace. She was fastened to the wall of her cell with a witch's bridle, and a sharpened crucifix was forced into her mouth.

The prongs pressed against her tongue and the inside flesh of her cheeks. Through that mouth, Satan boasted of flying in to watch the king deflower his bride on their wedding night.

The North Berwick witch trials ran for several years. Satan smiled as hysteria spread like the Black Death. As the witch hunt swept through Britain, Agnes Sampson was half strangled and burned alive, and the king wrote a book on the threat, *Daemonolgie*.

Satan could hear the fifteen hundred Scottish witches shrieking in the flames, but it angered him not that his disciples perished this way.

Their souls weren't trophies in his collection.

They were Protestants.

———•◦•———

"Sindrie of the witches confessed they had sindrie times companie with the devill at the kirk of Northberwick, where he appeared to them in the likeness of a man with a redde cappe, and a rumpe at his taill," the two read on Auld Kirk Green.

"'Double, double toil and trouble, / Fire burn, and caldron bubble.'"

"Oh no," Liz said, shoulders slumping. "He's going to recite all of Shakespeare next."

"Do you think the Three Witches in *Macbeth* were inspired by the North Berwick witch trials? Shakespeare's play was first staged shortly after the Auld Kirk mass."

"It must have been quite a getup that allowed the Earl of Bothwell to pass as Satan and bare his rump to the witches from the pulpit."

"Talk about kissing ass."

"'An tae hell they a' hae gaen,'" echoed Liz.

"Speaking of disguises, let's get a room in Edinburgh so I can shed mine."

As he followed the car to Edinburgh, the Legionary overheard his prey discussing the torpedo.

On the seat beside him, a witch's bridle rattled against the Bronze Mice Bowl.

As for Wyatt Rook, he'd die like St. Erasmus.

HOLYROODHOUSE

"To none but those who have themselves suffered the thing in the body," wrote Robert Louis Stevenson, "can the gloom and depression of our Edinburgh winter be brought home." It wasn't winter yet, but Wyatt absorbed the dark mood of a city weighed down by ominous clouds that threatened to flush it away. From the window of their hotel on Princes Street, he gazed across the sunken gardens dividing New Town from Old Town, with its Royal Mile. Of all the cities in the world, Edinburgh held the tightest grip on his imagination. Above the craggy, soot-blackened mound of Castle Rock, the lit-up walls and battlements of Edinburgh Castle hovered over his view. The oldest part of the fortress was little St. Margaret's Chapel, honoring the queen who brought the Roman Catholic faith to Scotland in 1069. There, also, was the room where Mary, Queen of Scots gave birth to the king who later produced the King James version of the Bible and burned the Auld Kirk witches on the castle's esplanade. Today, that spot is marked by the Witches' Well, a cast-iron fountain embossed with a serpent that represents the evil spawned by the Devil.

Connections?

Beyond the castle, Wyatt knew, was the Devil's work. The gallows were fed flesh in the Grassmarket, near West Port, the hunting grounds of Burke and Hare. Those Edinburgh body snatchers had dispatched seventeen victims—most killed by smothering, spawning the verb "to burke"—to supply Dr. Robert Knox, a teacher of anatomy, with cadavers for dissection. After reading Stevenson's "The Body Snatcher" when he was a boy, Wyatt imagined the "resurrectionists" stalking him through foggy Auld Reekie—Old Smoky—a nickname for Old Town. The ghouls of Edinburgh added yet another verse to his ever-expanding collection of memorized ditties:

Up the close and down the stair,
In the house with Burke and Hare.
Burke's the butcher, Hare's the thief,
Knox, the boy who buys the beef.

Back there, too, was Darwin, learning anatomy so he could rock the faith to its soul with his theory of evolution. Just off the Royal Mile, which ran from the castle down to the Palace of Holyroodhouse, was Brodie's Close, the workshop of the infamous Deacon William Brodie, respected man of business by day, thief and burglar by night. The cabinetmaker gambled, kept mistresses, and fed five illegitimate kids on his ill-gotten gains, until he was hanged on a gallows he had designed.

A Brodie cabinet furnished Stevenson's home. Intoxicated by ergotine, a hallucinogenic drug he took to control bleeding in his lungs from tuberculosis, the writer explored the dichotomy between Brodie's respectable façade and his inner Darwinian nature in *The Strange Case of Dr. Jekyll and Mr. Hyde*. In the story, the duality of man's nature leads to regressive animality. When *Jekyll and Hyde* played the London stage through Jack the Ripper's autumn of terror, uptight Christians fainted in the theater.

Jekyll is possessed, and Hyde wins.

Connections?

Outbreaks of ergotism most likely triggered the Salem witch trials of 1692.

Holyroodhouse, backed by the brooding bluffs of Arthur's Seat, was a murder scene. Legend says King David I went hunting on a holy day and was attacked by a stag. Grabbing hold of the antlers to keep from getting gored, the king made the beast vanish. Left in his hand was a holy rood—a holy cross. Holyrood Abbey, built on the spot where that miracle occurred, was for centuries the burial site of Scottish kings. In the palace beside it, Holyroodhouse, a gang of nobles led by Lord Darnley, the husband of Mary, Queen of Scots, set upon David Rizzio, the secretary to the queen, and stabbed him fifty-six times. Mary was six months pregnant with James, and Darnley believed the pregnancy was the result of a love affair with Rizzio. The queen was forced to watch the murder by the Earl of Ruthven, who warned he'd hack her "into collops" if she shied away.

Connections?

Having discarded his disguise and showered himself clean, Wyatt stood drying his hair at the window in a hotel bathrobe. Darkness fell by the minute. Though he loved New York, this city ignited the historian in him: layer on layer of life lived by a hundred generations. A bored boy at boarding school, Wyatt had *become* Sherlock Holmes, attacking the plots and puzzles with pen and paper at hand, jotting down his guesses to out-think the great detective. Here he was where it all began, for Edinburgh was the birthplace of Sir Arthur Conan Doyle, and the university beyond the Royal Mile had introduced the author to Dr. Joseph Bell, the model for Holmes.

In "The Crooked Man," Holmes tells Watson, "It is one of those instances where the reasoner can produce an effect which seems remarkable to his neighbor, because the latter has missed the one little point which is the basis of the deduction."

Click.

Wyatt's thoughts were broken by the unlocking of the door behind him.

He didn't know it yet, but his mental walk through Old Town had given him the clues he needed to solve the motive behind the vicious murders of those connected to the *Ace of Clubs.*

"Wow," said Liz. "The Beast turned into Prince Charming, thanks to a kiss from me."

"If that's what you call kissing."

"Get dressed, Sawney. The game is afoot. I called my researchers while you were singing in the shower to see what they found. Here's a map." She held it up. "And here are the directions to the place we're going."

"Fife?" guessed Wyatt.

"A salvage yard over there has the torpedo."

SALVAGE YARD

Where do old ships go to die? Where do ghost ships give up the ghost? It used to be that they would slip away to Inverkeithing, a bay that bit into a point on the north shore of the Firth of Forth. A few miles north of Inverkeithing is Dunfermline, Scotland's former capital. Robert the Bruce, Scotland's greatest hero because of his triumph over the loathed English at Bannockburn, is buried there. The breastbone of his skeleton is sundered, for the Bruce asked on his deathbed that his heart be cut out of his chest and carried by crusaders to the Holy Land.

Dunfermline is the heart o' Scotland.

And Wyatt's heart . . .

Thum-thum . . .

Thum-thum . . .

. . . was in his throat, for he knew he could be closing on the solution to a biblical puzzle that had taken several innocent lives.

Thum-thum . . .

Thum-thum . . .

He was excited . . .

This was what he was about.

Inverkeithing is one of Scotland's oldest royal burghs, but nothing can stand in the way of progress. Once James Watt invented the steam engine, the Industrial Revolution was under

way, transforming the hamlets of this shoreline into something
hellish. Farmland was overlaid with looming shale heaps.
The collieries sent a cloud of coal grime drifting across the
countryside. When oil replaced coal, a thousand chimneys
spouting steam and flare-stacks blowing ribbons of flame
usurped the mudflats. Vast power stations rose to feed them
juice, and Rosyth—a graveyard that once contained a vault for
storing corpses to save them from the ghouls supplying the
anatomists of Edinburgh—became one of the Royal Navy's
predominant warship docks.

Thus Inverkeithing, the heart of heartless shipbreaking.

HMS *Dreadnought* in 1923.

The *Olympic*, the *Titanic*'s sister ship, in 1937.

The *Mauritania* in 1965.

Those—along with a doomed armada of rusty aircraft car-
riers, battleships, destroyers, freighters, tankers, and fish
processors—reached the end of the line in the dissection yards
of Inverkeithing. There, magnetic cranes tore the guts out of
hulls, and boat anatomists sliced them up like loaves of bread
to the crash of metal shears on steel and the rasp of cutting
torches. This is known in the trade as "making razor blades."

"How'd you find the torpedo?" Wyatt asked in the car. They
were driving north from Edinburgh, past the airport and over
the soaring span of the Forth Road Bridge.

"Wartime bombs, shells, and torpedoes must be reported so
they can be defused. Back in the 1950s, a weekend diver
exploring the seabed discovered it off Fife. My researchers dug
up the demolition record, then followed the paper trail."

"Do we know it's the right torpedo?" Wyatt asked.

"It was pulled from the sea exactly where we thought it
would be—at the end of a straight trajectory from the *Black*

Devil past the oncoming destroyer. Explosives experts determined that the pistol—the device that blows the warhead—was a dud, and the TNT had been swapped for canisters of junk."

Wyatt grinned. "Yep, it's the torpedo."

"Evidently, the Germans had lots of problems with the weapon. It was common for guidance systems, pistols, and depth-keeping gauges to be defective. Plus, there was factory sabotage. Once it was declared safe, the torpedo was released to the scavenger."

"Why was it never sold for scrap?"

"The diver who found it was the son of the salvage yard owner. The owner's brother died in the Battle of the Atlantic when a U-boat sank his vessel with a torpedo. The owner saved the torpedo from scrap as a memorial to his dead brother."

"Thank you, Jesus," Wyatt said, clasping his hands.

At the end of the bridge, the road pressed on between Rosyth and Inverkeithing. Time and tide wait for no man, the proverb warns, and like the highway branching east along the coast of Fife, time and tide were passing Inverkeithing by. The town made no tourist's list of "must-sees," and these days, most big boats are broken up in Asia, where labor is cheap and environmental safeguards lax. At Alang, India, ships crawl in at high tide and beach when the tide ebbs out. A horde of hungry workers sludge through the mud and break the vessels apart with hammers and pry bars.

How does Inverkeithing compete with that?

The salvage yard was off the docks of a run-down harbor besieged by warehouses, storage tanks, and housing estates. In daylight, it would be the color of rust, but tonight, the foggy pen was haunted by big, black machines. As they drove in through the open gate, Wyatt could make out the silhouettes of

fragmentizers for breaking vehicles down to their basic components, mobile shears and baling presses for offsite destruction,
and a separation plant to channel scrap to monstrous heaps of
copper and brass, zinc, aluminum, stainless steel, and plastic-
coated wires. The breakers' yard was surrounded by derrick
cranes. A ship was half dissected, like the good old days, but it
was a minnow, not a whale.

The man advancing to meet them could have swung a clay-
more at the Battle of Culloden. With his greasy hair, barrel
chest, and forearms as thick as Popeye's, he would look
awesome decked out in full Highland tartan. If only he weren't
clad in grubby overalls.

"Thanks for staying open after hours," Liz said, shaking his
massive paw.

"Aye, but you mentioned *rrrr*iches," said he, rolling the
r through a Scottish burr.

"Wyatt Rook," Wyatt said, offering his hand. It came back
feeling like the victim of a baling press.

The salvage man led them across a minefield of puddles,
dog shit, and junk fumbled by forklifts to the beckoning door
of a Nissen hut. Wyatt wished he'd worn gumboots.

Though he never got to sail on Captain Cook's *Endeavour*,
Wyatt was reminded of the poop deck of that vessel—whatever
a poop deck was—as he gazed around the inside of the hut. The
floor was planking from a windjammer, and the artifacts clutter-
ing it had circled the globe in the days when the sun never set
on the British Empire. The sleek torpedo from the *Black Devil*
seemed out of place in this world of crow's nests atop main-
masts; tide clocks, sextants, and signal flags; steering wheels,
portholes, buoys, and binnacles; octants and figureheads of
bare-breasted mermaids.

"Whatever treasure you seek, it's long gone," said the Scot. "I did some digging, as you see."

The torpedo stretched along the floor for a length of twenty feet. It wasn't mounted. Not at more than three thousand pounds. The scavenger had removed the nose to get at the components. Basically, a torpedo has six parts: warhead, pistol, depth-control device, propulsion and guidance systems, and outside shell. U-boat submariners used to joke they were in the scrap-metal business, and in this case, the joke was on them. The warhead had been replaced with canisters of scrap, one of which lay open on a workbench.

"Nothing but nuts and bolts. Same with the other cans. They were X-rayed by bomb men back when I found the torpedo off Fife. Tonight, I used a portable scanner to check again. The rest of the parts follow this Nazi blueprint exactly."

The Scot ruffled a sheet on the bench.

"Nuts and bolts, and *nothing* else?" Wyatt pressed.

"Well, there are spikes in that one, if you want to get picky."

"Spikes? You mean nails?"

"Aye."

"Open it up!" Wyatt said.

———•—•———

The canister was soldered shut to make it watertight. The scavenger used a blowtorch to melt the seal, then cracked the container open as gingerly as he could. Spikes by the hundreds clattered onto the bench, along with a pouch stuffed with documents wrapped around three more nails.

"The Judas package!" said Liz.

Most of the papers were Werner Heisenberg's notes for Hitler's atomic bomb. But some of the sheets appeared to be a letter from Rommel, with a map that detailed the wall of a building in Tobruk. Wrapped inside those documents were several parchments and a map of a city that must have ceased to exist as drawn a long time ago.

Jerusalem?

That would explain the three nails.

No wonder some religious fanatic with scars through his palms was willing to kill anyone to get hold of these. Of all Christian relics, what could be more significant than the nails actually used to crucify Christ?

Thumthumthumthumthumthum ...

Wyatt's heart surged from the adrenaline, but that was nothing compared to the jackhammer beat that overtook it as he examined one of the nails.

"Can it be?" he wondered.

A sudden thump to his side broke his train of thought, for the Scot had crumpled to the floor as if having a heart attack. Only as Wyatt bent over him did he spot the dart in his neck.

Then . . .

"What the hell?"

. . . he felt a sharp jab, too.

The light went dark and the floor came up to meet him.

I AM LEGION

Clang . . . clang . . . clang . . .

Wyatt emerged from his blackout to the sound of metal clanging on metal and the sight of bars caging his eyes. He couldn't move his head. It was bolted to the wall. And his mouth had been invaded by some sort of bridle with four wicked prongs gouging his cheeks and tongue. From the taste of it, blood dribbled down his jaw.

His wrists and ankles were also fastened to the wall, cuffed by U-shaped clamps that kept his feet together and stretched his hands as wide as Christ's on the cross. He was lucky. That's as close as he came to crucifixion.

Clang . . . clang . . . clang . . .

The Scot, on the other hand, was being nailed to the floor.

The salvage man was also clamped in a Christ-like pose, but he had a ball stuck in his mouth, instead of a witch's bridle. The demon who had ambushed them with a dart gun was kneeling beside the supine man with a hammer raised in his hand. Down came a blow hard enough to drive the nail flat against the palm.

Clang . . .

Surely the Scot was screaming, yet not a peep escaped his mouth.

Clang . . . clang . . . clang . . .

The tortured man thrashed and writhed.

All Wyatt could do was watch.

And wait his turn.

How many paintings of hell had he seen? Every rendition of the Last Judgment showed monsters, demons, and tortures awaiting sinners who didn't embrace Jesus. As an agnostic, Wyatt doubted that he would encounter such a fate after death. So it was ironic that he seemed doomed to suffer it here instead.

Death was one thing.

An ugly death was another.

And no death was uglier than this.

Stiff upper lip be damned!

Wyatt was terrified.

So he did what any intelligent agnostic would do in his place.

He hedged his bets.

He prayed.

A trickle of blood from the Scot's wounds ran across the planks to Liz, spread-eagled beside him. Her wrists and ankles weren't cuffed with U-clamps like the men's. Instead, Liz was tied to the clamps with ropes, so her limbs were loose enough to allow triangular wooden blocks to be wedged beneath her joints.

Wedged beneath her elbows, and wedged beneath her knees.

Wyatt winced.

He knew what the blocks were for.

When he was finished nailing the Scot to the floor, the demoniac followed the trail of blood from the outstretched hand to Liz. Except for a silver crucifix hanging upside down from his neck, the killer Wyatt knew as Lenny was dressed in bible black. Crouching, he pulled a knife and slit open Liz's blouse, then he began searching every inch of her bare skin.

Like the Scot, Liz was gagged with a ball. That meant she could speak only through her eyes, and the silent shriek Wyatt saw in them deafened him.

Dissatisfied, the demoniac flicked the blade at Liz's bra, then used the tip to flip the released cups from her heaving breasts. When he failed to find what he sought, the inquisitor slashed her pant legs from her ankles to her groin. He gave up once Liz was naked except for a swath around her waist. Even now, the fallen Christian couldn't shed his prudery. His fig leaf out of Eden.

"No witch's tit," he declared. "Virgin flesh. I heard you say in the car that you're agnostic. Before I'm through with you, you *will* believe in me. I am *Legion!*"

The Inquisition wheel had spokes and a heavy iron rim. It would be rolled across the blocked-up lengths between a victim's wrist and elbow, elbow and shoulder, ankle and knee, knee and hip, splintering the bones into sharp shards that pierced the skin. The salvage museum didn't offer a big, rolling wheel, but it did have a heavy gun carriage from the battery deck of a man-o'-war. If that rumbling wagon was pulled across Liz's wedged limbs, her bones would be pulverized to dust.

Near her sat a bronze bowl and a cage of mice.

What were they for?

A diabolic *coup de grâce?*

Rumble, rumble . . .

The gun cart was on the move.

Wyatt couldn't bear the thought of witnessing this, so he jerked at his shackles as violently as he could, hoping a miracle would tear the bolts from the metal walls. His mouth worked so hard to shout at the killer—anything to distract him—that the spikes of the witch's bridle jabbed through his cheeks.

The gun carriage stopped rumbling.

The demoniac turned.

"You want to go first?" he asked.

From inside the cage around his head, Wyatt watched the priest drag an old steering wheel assembly from a sailing ship over to him. Using his knife, the demoniac slashed Wyatt's clothes to bare his belly, breastbone to groin.

"Does your agnosticism extend to ignorance about the death of St. Erasmus?"

It didn't.

Wyatt had seen Poussin's painting *The Martyrdom of St. Erasmus* in the Vatican Museums. The bishop had been killed for preaching the gospel during Emperor Diocletian's persecution of the Christians in 303 A.D. Roman executioners slowly wound his bowels out of his belly using a sailor's windlass. Wyatt knew he was minutes away from such a disemboweling, and he quivered as the killer's fingers probed his abdomen to find where to insert the knife. The demoniac would slit a small hole in his gut, just large enough to extract a coil of bowel, then hook one end of his entrails to this steering wheel and turn, turn, turn, winding his ropey viscera around the wheel's axle like a fireman does to reel in his fire hose.

To *feel* your belly emptying!

Slither, slither, slither . . .

To be hanged, drawn, or quartered.

Which was the worst?

Wyatt braced himself for the stab of the knife.

The man he knew as Lenny moved in close to stare directly into his eyes.

"*I . . . am . . . Legion!*"

Then both eyes bugged out of his head.

And the side of his face away from the door blew out in a blast of blood and bone.

───·•·───

Pfft! Pfft! Pfft!

The silencer-equipped gun whispered as the Art Historian to the Vatican pulled off three shots. At least one of the bullets struck the Legionary in the side of his head. Knife clattering to the floor, he dropped like a stone between the old steering wheel and Wyatt Rook.

The anemic ghost at the door shuffled toward the treasure on the workbench. His co-conspirators had been motivated by their need to save the Catholic Church, but he was trying to save *his* earthly life. With that at stake, he couldn't chance betrayal by the priests. For all he knew, the Secret Cardinal would give the Holy Grail to the pope with no thought of curing his leukemia first. Or worse yet, the Legionary—if he was indeed possessed by Satan—would hurl it into the Firth of Forth to destroy any proof that Jesus Christ *is* the son of God.

Thirty pieces of silver.

That's all it took to entice Judas to nail Christ to the cross.

Imagine the value of the nails in the secular marketplace.

How much is your life worth to you?

No, he couldn't risk letting anyone betray him for a motive either sacred or profane.

Not with *his* life depending on it.

So the Art Historian had supplied the Legionary with the tools he needed for the British leg of his crusade: tracking devices, the pistol he fired at Rook in Sussex, and the dart gun that subdued the three captives in this Nissen hut. But to keep track of the Vatican's attack dog, the dying man also had his *own* receiver monitoring the bug on Liz Hannah's car, as well as a GPS tracker hidden in the receiver used by the Legionary. That's how the Art Historian could assure the Secret Cardinal that the possessed priest was on his way to York. And how, tonight, he had tracked Liz, Wyatt, and the demoniac to Inverkeithing.

Struggling against weakness to reach the workbench, the doomed man closed his hand around the nails that had cured his meningitis as a boy.

"Cure me, Christ," he prayed, raising the relics toward heaven as a shudder shook him to his diseased soul.

Ironically, his tire had been punctured by a nail on the road approaching the yard. Too weak to change it, the Art Historian now required a substitute means of escape, for he had no intention of spending his soon-to-be-recovered life in prison. He wondered if the salvage yard had a motorboat. With the fog thickening by the minute, he might be safer by sea than chancing a road accident in a car stolen from what would soon be a murder victim.

Retrieving the knife the Legionary had dropped, the Art Historian cut the tape around the Scot's mouth, yanked out the ball, and aimed the gun between the man's eyes.

"Do you have a boat?"

The pent-up pain from the spikes piercing his flesh must have been too much, for the Scot cried out in what the Art Historian assumed was Scottish Gaelic.

It was.

"Mharaigh!"

Translation: "Kill!"

Wyatt saw the shadow before he saw the fur and fangs. It came from the open door moments after the Scot's command and was in the air before the gunman whirled toward it in fright. The jaws of the shadow tore into the fleshy throat, and the beast took the sickly man down with its pouncing weight.

Wyatt recalled the minefield of puddles, litter, and shit on the path from the car to the Nissen hut.

Every salvage man keeps a junkyard dog.

EUCHARIST

✝

LONDON
Three days later

If the Holy Grail equals holy blood, what could be closer to the blood of Christ than the nails that *actually* crucified him? Not some cup that supposedly collected his blood *after* death, and not some putative offspring of Mary Magdalene.

So Holy Grail equals holy nails.

What makes more sense than that?

The Empress Helena, legend holds, found both the True Cross and the crucifixion nails. Returning to Constantinople, she had one nail added to the helmet of her son, Constantine, to protect his head from the weapons of Rome's enemies. A second nail formed the bridle for his horse, to shield the steed from injury.

Today, more than thirty "holy nails" are venerated in Europe, but like the fragments of the True Cross brought back from Constantinople, they are medieval frauds.

No wonder archconservatives in the Roman Catholic Church were willing to kill to get their hands on the Judas relics. The holy nails! Now that Wyatt had acquired translations of the Aramaic parchments and Rommel's letter, he knew how strong their pedigree was.

Earthshaking.

The Judas relics had traces of what was believed to be Christ's blood, as well as a chip of bone that was probably caught when the nails were yanked out.

DNA lasts at least two thousand years.

That's what got Wyatt thinking when he first examined the nails.

And that's why Wyatt was here in this DNA lab, where the human genome had been broken into all its constituent genes so scientists could map the Darwinian blueprint of life all the way back to the primordial ooze.

Christ's DNA.

What could be more threatening to the Vatican than that?

"The Church draws her life from the Eucharist," Pope John Paul II maintained. "For this very reason the Eucharist ... stands at the center of the Church's life. . . . The Eucharist is too great for anyone to feel free to treat it lightly and with disregard for its sacredness and universality."

That's because the Eucharist isn't simply a representation of Christ. Through Transubstantiation at Mass, the Host becomes *the actual body of Christ.*

In 2007, Pope Benedict XVI reasserted the primacy of the Roman Catholic Church. Other Christian denominations are not true churches, he declared, because they don't have the "means of salvation" provided by Mass and the Eucharist. "Christ established here on earth only one Church," he said. Other Christian gatherings "cannot be called churches in the proper sense," because they don't have apostolic succession— that is, the ability to trace their priests back to Christ's original apostles.

Back to St. Peter and his keys to heaven.

Back to Christ himself.

Back to the son of God, the product of Immaculate Conception.

So a lot was riding on this DNA test.

If the DNA recovered from the holy nails showed *two* parents, a male and a female, the thinking man could only conclude that Jesus Christ wasn't the son of God, and that his resurrection was a hoax. This would particularly be so if that male parent—like all humans alive today—shared 99 percent of his genes with a chimpanzee.

But if the DNA showed just one parent, then the only rational explanation would be that Jesus was created by Immaculate Conception by an unseen God.

Therefore, Jesus *was* the son of God.

"I like a man with dimples," said Liz as they waited for the computer to print the results of the test.

"Very funny."

"Really. I saw how you struggled when I was about to get crushed by the gun carriage. How heroic that you would mar your handsomeness for me."

Liz kissed the scabs on his cheeks.

"The salvage man has a better story to tell his grandkids," said Wyatt. "His scars are through his palms and feet. Lucky for him—and for us—that his wife had a roast in the oven and went looking for him when he stayed too long at work. He could have bled to death."

The lab tech gave them a sign the printout was imminent.

Wyatt phoned Rutger in Germany.

"Well?" Rutger answered.

"It's coming. Liz wants a word with you."

Wyatt passed her the cell.

"How gracious of you to cut me in for a third of the Judas book," Liz said.

"Fair's fair," Rutger replied. "Wyatt and I are friends because we both know the other is fair."

Liz passed back the phone.

Wyatt's heart was pounding with excitement. Not every historian gets to be a hinge of history. The Old Testament survived for millennia until Darwin hammered the nail of evolution into the coffin of fundamentalism.

So long, original sin.

Now, the Judas relics could be the final nail in the coffin of the New Testament.

If Jesus was betrayed by his own DNA, that would be the ultimate Judas kiss.

So long, salvation through Christ.

"Here it comes," Wyatt said.

The geneticist reached for the DNA profile as it emerged from the printer.

"Well?" asked the rational historian.

"My God," said the scientist.

AUTHOR'S NOTE

This is a work of fiction. The plot and characters are products of the author's imagination. Where real persons, places, incidents, institutions, and such have been incorporated to create the illusion of authenticity, they are used fictitiously. Inspiration was drawn from the following non-fiction sources:

Ainsworth, Maryan W. *Petrus Christus: Renaissance Master of Bruges.* New York: The Metropolitan Museum of Art, 1994.

Bahat, Dan, with Chaim T. Rubinstein. *The Illustrated Atlas of Jerusalem.* Trans. Shlomo Ketko. New York: Simon and Schuster, 1990.

Botting, Douglas. *The U-Boats.* Alexandria, VA: Time-Life, 1979.

Bowyer, Chaz. *Guns in the Sky: The Air Gunners of World War Two.* New York: Scribner's, 1979.

Brickhill, Paul. *The Great Escape.* London: Faber, 1951.

Brownrigg, Ronald. *The Twelve Apostles.* New York: Macmillan, 1974.

Buchheim, Lothar-Günther. *U-Boat War.* Trans. Gudie Lawaetz. New York: Knopf, 1978.

Burman, Edward. *The Inquisition: The Hammer of Heresy.* Stroud, UK: Sutton, 2004.

Carver, Michael. *Tobruk.* London: Batsford, 1964.

Clutton-Brock, Oliver. *Footprints on the Sands of Time: RAF Bomber Command Prisoners-of-War in Germany 1939–1945.* London: Grub Street, 2003.

Cornwell, John. *Hitler's Pope: The Secret History of Pius XII.* New York: Viking, 1999.

Currie, Jack. *Lancaster Target*. London: New English Library, 1977.

Dalin, David G. *The Myth of Hitler's Pope: How Pope Pius XII Rescued Jews from the Nazis*. Washington: Regnery, 2005.

De Campos, Redig, ed. *Art Treasures of the Vatican*. Englewood Cliffs, NJ: Prentice-Hall, 1975.

Debray, Régis. *The New Testament through 100 Masterpieces of Art*. Trans. Benjamin Lifson. London: Merrell, 2004.

Editors of Time-Life Books. *Wolf Packs*. Alexandria, VA: Time-Life, 1989.

Edwards, William D., Wesley J. Gabel, and Floyd E. Hosmer. "The Physical Death of Jesus Christ." *Journal of the American Medical Association* 256 (March 21, 1986).

Fraser, David. *Knight's Cross: A Life of Field Marshal Erwin Rommel*. London: HarperCollins, 1993.

Friedländer, Max J. *Early Netherlandish Painting: The Van Eycks— Petrus Christus*. Brussels: Sijthoff, 1967.

Gill, Anton. *The Great Escape*. London: Review, 2002.

Grubb, Nancy. *The Life of Christ in Art*. New York: Artabras, 1996.

Harvey, J. Douglas. *Boys, Bombs and Brussels Spouts*. Toronto: McClelland and Stewart, 1981.

Hastings, Max. *Bomber Command*. London: Wade, 1979.

Irving, David. *The Trail of the Fox: The Search for the True Field Marshal Rommel*. New York: Dutton, 1977.

Jones, Terry, and Alan Ereira. *Crusades*. New York: Facts on File, 1995.

Kaplan, Philip. *Bombers*. London: Aurum Press, 2000.

Lane, Barbara G. *The Altar and the Altarpiece: Sacrificial Themes in Early Netherlandish Painting*. New York: Harper and Row, 1984.

Lewy, Guenter. *The Catholic Church and Nazi Germany*. New York: Da Capo Press, 2000.

Liddell Hart, B. H., ed. *The Rommel Papers*. London: Collins, 1953.

McDowell, Bart. *Inside the Vatican*. Washington: National Geographic, 1991.

McKee, Alexander. *Dresden, 1945: The Devil's Tinderbox*. London: Souvenir Press, 1982.

Martin, Malachi. *Hostage to the Devil: The Possession and Exorcism of Five Living Americans*. San Francisco: HarperSanFrancisco, 1992.

Metzler, Jost. *The Laughing Cow: A U-Boat Captain's Story*. London: Kimber, 1955.

Meyers, David John. *The Illustrated Life of Jesus through the Gospels, Arranged Chronologically*. New York: Hylas, 2005.

Middlebrook, Martin, and Chris Everitt. *The Bomber Command War Diaries: An Operation Reference Book, 1939–1945*. London: Penguin, 1985.

Millard, Alan. *Discoveries from the Time of Jesus*. Oxford: Lion, 1990.

Miller, David. *U-Boats: History, Development, and Equipment, 1914–1945*. London: Conway Maritime Press, 2000.

Möller, Eberhard, and Werner Brack. *The Encyclopedia of U-boats: From 1904 to the Present Day*. Trans. Andrea Battson and Roger Chesneau. London: Greenhill, 2004.

Nesbit, Roy Conyers. *RAF in Action 1939–1945*. London: Public Record Office, 2000.

Nijboer, Donald. *Gunner: An Illustrated History of World War II Aircraft Turrets and Gun Positions*. Erin, ON: Boston Mills Press, 2001.

Oesterreich, Traugott K. *Possession and Exorcism among Primitive Races, in Antiquity, the Middle Ages, and Modern Times*. Trans. D. Ibberson. New York: Causeway Books, 1974.

Overy, Richard. *Bomber Command 1939–1945*. London: HarperCollins, 1997.

Pearce, Joseph. "Graham Greene: Doubter Par Excellence." http://www.catholicauthors.com/greene.html.

Peden, Murray. *A Thousand Shall Fall*. Toronto: Stoddart, 1988.

Pelikan, Jaroslav. *The Illustrated Jesus though the Centuries*. New Haven, CN: Yale University Press, 1997.

Peters, Edward. *Inquisition*. New York: Free Press, 1988.

Pritchard, James B., ed. *The Harper Atlas of the Bible*. New York: Harper and Row, 1987.

Reston, James, Jr. *Warriors of God: Richard the Lionheart and Saladin in the Third Crusade*. New York: Doubleday, 2001.

Rhymer, Joseph. *The Illustrated Life of Jesus Christ*. New York: Viking, 1991.

Riley-Smith, Jonathan. *The Crusades: A Short History*. New Haven, CN: Yale University Press, 1987.

Riley-Smith, Jonathan, ed. *The Atlas of the Crusades*. New York: Facts on File, 1991.

Silver, L. Ray. *Last of the Gladiators: A World War II Bomber Navigator's Story*. Shrewsbury, UK: Airlife, 1995.

Taylor, Frederick. *Dresden: February 13, 1945*. New York: HarperCollins, 2004.

Trench, Richard, and Ellis Hillman. *London under London.* London: Murray, 1985.

Wilkinson, Tracy. *The Vatican's Exorcists: Driving Out the Devil in the 21st Century.* New York: Warner, 2007.

Wilson, Patrick. *The War behind the Wire: Experiences in Captivity during the Second World War.* Barnsley, UK: Pen and Sword, 2000.

Wray, T. J., and Gregory Mobley. *The Birth of Satan: Tracing the Devil's Biblical Roots.* New York: Palgrave Macmillan, 2005.

Young, Desmond. *Rommel: The Desert Fox.* New York: Harper, 1950.

Zuccotti, Susan. *Under His Very Windows: The Vatican and the Holocaust in Italy.* New Haven, CN: Yale University Press, 2002.

MG
2/10

ML   3/09